THE CHAINS OF ALBION

Edwin Thomas

BANTAM BOOKS

LONDON • TORONTO • SYDNEY • AUCKLAND • JOHANNESBURG

THE CHAINS OF ALBION
A BANTAM BOOK: 0 553 81515 6

Originally published in Great Britain by Bantam Press,
a division of Transworld Publishers

PRINTING HISTORY
Bantam Press edition published 2004
Bantam edition published 2005

1 3 5 7 9 10 8 6 4 2

Set in 11/13pt Caslon by
Falcon Oast Graphic Art Ltd.

Bantam Books are published by Transworld Publishers,
61–63 Uxbridge Road, London W5 5SA,
a division of The Random House Group Ltd,
in Australia by Random House Australia (Pty) Ltd,
20 Alfred Street, Milsons Point, Sydney, NSW 2061, Australia,
in New Zealand by Random House New Zealand Ltd,
18 Poland Road, Glenfield, Auckland 10, New Zealand
and in South Africa by Random House (Pty) Ltd,
Endulini, 5a Jubilee Road, Parktown 2193, South Africa.

Printed and bound in Great Britain by
Cox & Wyman Ltd, Reading, Berkshire.

Papers used by Transworld Publishers are natural, recyclable
products made from wood grown in sustainable forests. The
manufacturing processes conform to the environmental
regulations of the country of origin.

for Helen and George
for being so generous with hospitality,
encouragement, criticism
and their daughter

and for Panos

who didn't like the navy either

Tu veux, mon cher ami, que raniment ma verve
Je te peigne sans fard, sans crainte, et sans réserve,
Le Tableau des tourmens et de l'affliction
Sous lesquels sont plongés les captifs d'Albion.

So, my friend, shall I gird up my soul,
And fearless, careless, plainly paint the whole
Scene of torments and travails
That drowned us deep in Albion's jails.

> Sergeant-Major Beaudrouin,
> French prisoner-of-war

1

❧❧❧

I was twenty-six when they gave me my first command:
two years older than St Vincent, six behind the precocious
Nelson, and – as my uncle vigorously reminded me – far in
advance of my merits. But while those great stalwarts of the
sea began at the nub end of the navy, prancing about in
cutters and gun-brigs, I walked straight into the great cabin
of a two-decker, a mighty ship-of-the-line fit for an admiral,
with eight hundred souls under my sway and bulwarks
wrought to withstand the heaviest French iron. Not, of
course, that I expected to meet any, for while Nelson
relished every opportunity to sail his floating snuffboxes
under the guns of his enemies, my ship – the *Prometheus* –
would never again leave the cosseting waters of the
Medway. Her spars and sails had been confiscated, and her
masts sawn down to stumps: the only cloth that now hung
from them was laundry. A host of shabby excrescences had
sprouted from her sides: ramshackle huts and gantries,
ladders, galleries and chimneys, destroying the handsome
lines of her original design. Four anchors chained her to the
oozy mud beneath her keel, and the only voyage which
remained to her was up the river to the breakers' yard – if
her crumbling hull did not send her to the riverbed first.
She was a prison hulk, a floating gaol for our captive

enemies, and I was content that as long as her walls kept the Frenchmen in, they would keep me well protected from the dreadful hazards of war.

With hindsight, I should perhaps have paid more attention to the state of her rotting timbers before I built my hopes on them. But on a hot afternoon in late July I was happy enough to luxuriate in my captain's perquisites, chief among them the right to entertain whom I pleased, and the privacy of a suite of rooms in which to do so. Certainly the particular delights of that moment would not have been the same behind the canvas screen of a lieutenant's hutch, but in the privacy of the dining cabin, the windows fastened shut to keep in the noise, I could give lusty voice to my enthusiasm. The stout support of the dining table precluded the worry that a swinging cot would spill us both onto the floor, and I was able to devote all my attentions to admiring the lithe body which wriggled and giggled athwart me. She was entirely naked, her clothes discarded in the great cabin aft – tupping like a lady, she called it, though there was little ladylike in her present exertions. Her dark hair, curled into ringlets, was plastered around her face, while in the close summer heat sweat glistened on her throat, and down the shallow dip between her breasts. Her name was Isobel, and I had found her in my bed one night during my time in Dover. With little effort on my part, she had kept returning, and after she had rendered me some exceptional assistance I had had no choice – or desire – but to bring her with me. For propriety's sake she stayed in a boarding house in Chatham, styled herself an indeterminate cousin of mine, and visited me with exceptional cousinly devotion. Had I known that such would be the rewards of rank, I might have exerted myself a great deal earlier in my career.

A noise from the outer door reminded me of another benefit: a marine sentry to guard against untimely visitors. I tried to put the sound from my mind, to concentrate my energies on my fast-advancing pleasure, but to my irritation the voices persisted, rose, and culminated in a crisp knock on the door.

I paused, lifting my hands to hold Isobel still. She did not look happy at the interruption.

'Captain Jerrold, sir.' The sentry's voice was muffled by the door. 'The master's asked to see you urgent.'

The sound of my new title was an ongoing delight to me, but not at that moment. 'I am enjoying a private dinner with my cousin,' I shouted. 'Inform Mr Mallow he may wait until I am finished.'

That should have been the end of it, but it seemed the privileges of my rank did not extend to having my orders obeyed. This time the master spoke directly.

'Beggin' your pardon, Captain, but it's urgent. I found a Froggy cuttin' through the hull in the privy.'

'Christ.' I looked up at Isobel, seeing her nose wrinkle with displeasure. 'I'd better see the wretch before Mallow has him keel-hauled.'

Isobel arched her back and trailed a hand across my chest, reminding me all too sharply what I would forgo. 'You'd better make sure to come back quick. You'll leave your cousin hungry, running away from dinner like that.'

'Captain Jerrold, sir?' It was the sentry again, and the plaintive note in his voice suggested he was struggling to withstand Mallow. It would hardly do for the master to catch his captain indelicately entangled with his cousin. With a groan I extricated myself from beneath Isobel and strode out to the main cabin.

'I shall be with you directly,' I yelled. 'I am just, ah . . . finishing my wine.' That at least was a credible excuse. I hopped about as I pulled my stockings over my feet, hoping that the men on the *Bristol*, our companion ship anchored astern, were too far away to see through the broad windows. Her commander already thought me enough of a buffoon for my lax ways with the prisoners.

11

Thankful that none could pass judgement on a captain's disarrayed dress, I crossed to the door. I was cautious lest anyone see Isobel's clothes strewn over the floor, but as I glanced back they seemed to have disappeared. Perhaps she had gathered them up. Still, I would not risk Mallow's scavenging eyes in the cabin: straightening the lapels on my coat, I edged open the door.

Immediately, the master's face filled the crack. Despite the heat, he wore his jacket fully buttoned, and his pockmarked skin gleamed with sweat.

'Thank you for waiting. I was just finishing my dinner.'

Too late, I saw my servant hovering in the background. 'Shall I collect the plates, sir?'

'No. Absolutely not. I may return to pick over the bones once I have seen to this matter.' I turned to look at the scrawny figure cowering beside Mallow, his yellow suit frayed and ragged. 'Is this the man?'

'I found him tryin' to worm his way through the hull behind the necessary.' There was triumph in Mallow's rattish face. 'I'll drop him in the black hole, shall I?'

Perhaps in other circumstances I would have said yes, and possibly thereby spared myself much that followed, but I had been finding Mallow's cruelty and disrespect grating ever more on my temper, and I took childish delight in toying with his request.

'Not so hasty, Mr Mallow,' I said loftily. 'I shall have to inspect the alleged damage myself before reaching any conclusions. It will afford me the opportunity of examining the prisoners' condition.'

'I *have* inspected the damage, sir, and there's nothin' for it but to lock up the scum on his own to learn him his lesson.'

I looked at the prisoner in question, noticing the white welts where the skin bulged under Mallow's fingers. 'Does he offer any explanation?'

There was a movement from further back in the passage,

and Dumont, my interpreter, stepped forward. He was a diminutive fellow, almost feminine under his swab of dark curls, and the fruits of his position had kept his delicate features from the worst ravages of disease and hunger. Mallow must have interrupted him at his toilet, for his shirt was untucked from his trousers and soap froth still clung to his half-whiskered face. That morning he had asked to borrow my razor, I remembered.

He murmured a few words in the prisoner's ear, to little obvious effect.

'He has no excuse,' he announced.

'Then let us proceed to the gun deck and examine his misdeed.'

I squinted as the door admitted me to the unbroken glare of the sun outside. Off each quarter, the green banks of the Medway rose from the yellow reeds to wooded hillsides beyond, while before us the river widened into the broken channels of her estuary. A dozen of my crew stood on the poop deck, chewing tobacco and keeping untroubled watch over our charges, while on the larboard side a gang of prisoners hauled huge butts of water from a lighter. Three of our veteran soldiers leaned on their muskets looking bored, while under their decrepit eyes two hundred prisoners sat waiting for the war to end. Some plaited straw hats or baskets, others inked elaborate designs into wood or ivory, while up on the fo'c's'le a carpenter was hammering together a broken mess table. He was making an extraordinary job of it, I noticed, rolling and spinning it so that the legs flew about like the arms of a semaphore tower.

'I tell you, sir, there's treason in that work.' Mallow interrupted my contemplation of their industry with his own opinion. 'How's good Englishmen to earn a livin' when these bastards can undercut 'em 'cos of they're bein' fed, dressed an' sheltered by the navy?'

I sighed, for this was not a new dispute. 'I doubt there

are many free-born Englishmen who'd swap their lot with these wretches. The more they occupy themselves with trades, the less they occupy themselves plotting to murder us in our beds or break out through the hull.'

'Not this bugger.' We had reached the ladder, and Mallow shoved the prisoner so harshly he almost tumbled to the open deck below. 'That's the trouble with the Frenchies – make themselves look all 'spectable, so you never sees the knife comin'.'

It was an impolitic remark, for we were now in the well of the main deck. I did not like to be down here among the sad and bitter faces, to become the object of so much hate and hope, as if *I* had the power to free them from their ordeal. I could no more end their captivity than end the war, indeed could barely ensure that their rations were adequate. And these men on the main deck were the best of the convicts, those who used their talents to keep themselves passably well fed and clothed. Not all were so industrious – or rather, they were industrious only in ruinous pursuits.

I was about to descend the ladder to the gun deck when a gesture from Dumont, the interpreter, paused me.

'If you do not have more to say to the prisoner, Captain, I can go back to my cabin?' He wiped away a little of the soap that was dribbling down his chin. 'I am not finished.'

'Certainly.' I waved him away. 'Come and find me after-wards so I can inform the prisoner of his punishment.' It would be better than having Mallow make it understood.

I rarely had cause to go down to the lower deck, save for a weekly inspection of the prison, but each time I did I felt that I entered some twilight world of horrors, depravity lurking in every shadow. Despite the gunports being open the brightness of the day hardly penetrated at all, but the heat was undeterred and turned the tight space into an oven of sweat and grime. In the darkness, the enveloping sounds had an almost solid feel to them: the click of makeshift billiard balls, the slap of cards on tables, the creak of hammocks and, most of all, the hubbub of voices – excited, angry, morose or plaintive – unceasing from dawn to dusk. I could quite see how some of the prisoners lost all grasp of their senses here.

Endeavouring to ignore the sordid surroundings, I followed Mallow to where a shredded sheet of sailcloth gave a scrap of privacy for the prisoners' necessary. I had hung it only a fortnight earlier, yet already it was reduced to the merest ribbons, doubtless carved into stakes for a hand of cards.

'This is the place.' Mallow pushed the bucket aside with the toe of his boot and pointed to the wall behind, where a scuttle allowed just enough light to show a thin, uneven crease in the adjacent planking. He squatted down, working the tip of his knife into the crack and pushing down on the handle. The blade flexed, and I feared it would snap into his face, but suddenly it disappeared into the wood as a square panel came free of the hull. It was barely more than eighteen inches wide, but behind its façade the damp, black timbers had been scraped away to a considerable depth.

I took a deep breath, and swiftly wished I had refrained. 'Well. Does the prisoner offer any explanation?'

I hoped he did not, for my tolerance of that foetid atmosphere was almost exhausted, but I saw immediately that there would be further delay, for the interpreter was gone. 'Mr Mallow, fetch Mr Dumont if you please.'

Mallow did not have time to move, for at that moment there was a commotion by the ladder, and a flushed corporal came running out of the gloom.

'Beggin' your pardon, Captain, but the *Bristol*'s just signalled.'

I looked at him as severely as I could manage with my eyes watering from the stink. 'A signal?'

'Mutiny!'

15

I would have needed little prompting to leave that awful place, but the threat of mutiny had me up the ladders and on the quarterdeck in seconds. Our entire complement of guards had lined the gangway, muskets at their shoulders, while the seamen tried to shepherd the remaining prisoners down to the gun deck. By the davits, the rest of the crew were already lowering the jollyboat into the water.

'Make fast the hatches and put ten men on each deck, bow and stern. We'll not have any contagion here.' I seized a spyglass from the rack and trained it on the *Bristol*, moored less than half a cable off our transom. Through my lens I could see the colours of her desperate signal hanging limp from her truncated mast, and some sort of struggle happening on her fo'c's'le.

'What in the devil's name . . . ? Now they're signalling a quarantine.' Even as I watched, the signal flags tumbled to the deck and a faded yellow cloth jerked up into its place.

'That's not a quarantine flag.' A brief gust of wind had caught the fabric and stretched it out, so that even Mallow, without a glass, could see that it was in fact a yellow waist-coat stamped with the initials of the Transport Office, the sort we issued to prisoners. 'An' look there, amidships. She's smoking.'

I swung my telescope back along the *Bristol*'s deck to her waist, where a plume of grey smoke was rising out of her well. 'Musket smoke?'

'Too thick for that. An' I didn't hear no bangs. Prisoners must have set her ablaze.'

That was an unthinkable danger, for if they cut her loose she could drift down upon *Prometheus* and burn us to the waterline. 'Mr Mallow, take the starboard watch in the jollyboat and render the *Bristol* whatever assistance she requires.'

'Not the best idea, sir, if you don't mind me sayin'. Looks as though her captain's lost control of the ship –

16

might even be dead. You'll want more'n a master to get them lot settled.'

I would want more than a jumped-up lieutenant inclined to foul himself in the face of danger. Nor did I care to leave my own ship in the hands of the devious Mr Mallow, even for a few minutes, but there was enough sense in his suggestion that I could not argue. As I looked down into the well I saw the last prisoners being prodded through the hatch; I doubted the mutiny could now spread to *Prometheus*.

'Very well. Mr Mallow – take command. I shall repair to my quarters to arm myself and return forthwith.'

I ran aft, past the sentry who still stood guard, and into the great cabin. Isobel was there, unaccountably dressed in one of my shirts and a pair of my breeches.

'Are you trying to set a new fashion?' I asked, rummaging through a chest for my pistols.

'My dress wasn't here.' Having been abandoned naked on the dining table, Isobel did not seem pleased that I was now preoccupied with the hunt for my guns.

'Perhaps the servant tidied it away.'

'Perhaps.' She did not sound convinced. 'Why's there so much noise and fuss outside?'

'*Bristol* has signalled a mutiny.' I found my pistols and thrust them in my belt – I could load them in the boat. 'It might be best if you went ashore. You never know what mischief the French may concoct.'

Isobel looked even less happy at this suggestion, but she could hardly stay aboard a ship with eight hundred restless convicts while her guardian was otherwise engaged. We hurried back outside, where a dozen men already awaited me in the jollyboat.

'Midshipman Davis,' I called. 'Lower the gig and have Miss Dawson rowed ashore.'

The young midshipman, interrupted from gazing at the commotion aboard the *Bristol*, frowned. 'But she's already gone, sir. In the carpenter's boat.' His voice faltered away as Isobel appeared over my shoulder.

'Clearly she has not,' I snapped. 'You are mistaken. Now please execute my order before the prisoners have time to rig a topmast and sail the *Bristol* back to Calais.'

The men at the oars pulled us quickly over the brief distance that separated *Prometheus* from the *Bristol*: in our perpetual mooring, boatwork was the one art of seamanship they had not lost. How would their fighting skills be, I wondered, if they came to be called upon?

My misgivings deepened as we came under the *Bristol*, for there was an unsettling silence about her now wholly at odds with the earlier action. The yellow jacket was gone from her masthead but no pennant had replaced it, and no guards patrolled the gallery around her hull. I tensed as our prow bumped against her, and looked up at the distended walls that loomed over us.

'Ahoy?' I hailed. '*Bristol* ahoy!'

There was no answer.

'You'd best climb aboard and see what they done,' one of the seamen suggested unhelpfully.

I shot him a disgruntled look, and raised my pistol above my head as I peered up the slimy stair that rose to the quarterdeck.

'*Prometheus* boat ahoy.'

So surprised was I by the sudden call from above that I almost discharged my gun into the face which had spoken, the blue-coated figure I belatedly recognized as the *Bristol*'s commander.

'Captain Harris,' I shouted. 'We came in response to your signal. We saw the struggle on your fo'c's'le, and feared your ship had caught fire.'

'Your aid is prompt, but tardy nonetheless. Damn French took us unawares with a charge to the foremast. Once we had the guards mustered they folded quietly enough. Not much stomach for a fight, the French.'

'Indeed.' I lowered my pistol, feeling a little foolish. 'Then I suppose we had best—'

I broke off, for it suddenly occurred to me that perhaps this was a ruse, that they might well have a knife at the captain's back. It was a thought I would quite happily have ignored, but I could see that if I was wrong a court martial would take a dim view of an officer who had been so easily duped.

'Do you need any further assistance, Captain Harris?'

'None at all, Captain Jerrold.'

'Then, ah, shall I . . . Which is to say, may I come aboard and use your necessary?'

I could not tell whether Captain Harris scowled or smirked; certainly there were a few undisguised sniggers from the men in my boat.

'If you feel it absolutely *necessary*, Captain Jerrold.'

By the time I had scrambled to the top of those stairs the weakness in my bowels made it very much necessary. The treacherous steps demanded my utmost attention, preventing me from guarding against danger, while I felt Captain Harris's condescending eyes follow me all the way up. As I neared the rail it was all I could do to leave the pistol tucked into my breeches, and when my head cleared the side I almost flinched at the anticipation of a musket ball coming to tear me apart.

I gained the deck and looked around. There were no convicts to be seen, and only a few fresh welts gouged out of the foremast to suggest that any kind of battle had taken place. Down on the main deck a pile of black ashes was still smoking, charred scraps of rope and canvas just discernible among the cinders. The fire did not seem to have done great damage, and a crew of seamen were carefully shovelling the ashes into buckets to be thrown overboard.

'What happened?' I asked.

'Bastard French suffered a moment of madness, tried to

19

cause as much mischief as they could for five minutes and then gave up. Could have burned the ship to her keel though – have to make them pay for that.'

If the *Bristol*'s timbers were half so waterlogged as *Prometheus*' it would take more than a desultory campfire to get them burning, but I did not say so. It seemed strange that the French should risk whatever punishment Harris would devise for a few minutes' devilment, but I did not voice that thought either. Who knew to what insanity their confinement might drive them?

Harris's caustic voice forestalled further thought, though I did not hear his words.

'The quarter gallery,' he repeated. Then, reading the blank look on my face: 'The necessary.'

It was some time before all was calmed aboard *Prometheus*, for the prisoners were incensed that I would not allow them on deck again before their curfew. I often surrendered to their demands when I could think of no good reason to deny them – to the inevitable disgust of Mallow, who saw frustrating the prisoners as the essence of our task – but this time I held firm: there had been too many strange happenings that day for me to risk further trouble. Still, the light was almost gone by the time I retired to my cabin.

My servant had laid out a cold supper for me, and without Isobel there to share it I reached for my logbook. It was a handsome volume, bound in calfskin and printed with columns for every detail the dutiful officer might wish to record. Isobel had given it to me as a gift when I took command of *Prometheus*, and though I fear it was designed for a more active career than my own, I kept it as diligently as I could. Certainly more diligently than when I'd been aboard the *Temeraire*, and paid a midshipman to copy the fourth lieutenant's log into my own.

I turned to a new page, headed 'A Journal of Occurrences Aboard H.M. Ship *Prometheus*', and wrote in the date.

Latitude – ditto. Longitude – ditto. Heading – nil. Wind . . . With not a single yard of canvas, this seemed an irrelevance, but I dutifully noted it, together with brief observations on the weather and the stores we had taken aboard that day. *General Remarks – Answered a signal to attend Captain Harris aboard H.M.S.* Bristol. *Discovered prisoner trying to cut through hull in the necessary.*

At that my pen paused in mid air, dripping ink over the pristine pages. In all the confusion, I had forgotten to assign the man his punishment. I rose, crossed to the door and summoned the sentry.

'Be so kind as to fetch the prisoner caught trying to escape today,' I told him. 'And the interpreter.'

The sentry nodded and ambled off, leaving me to return to the book. I tried desperately to think of more to write, to fill in those broad pages whose emptiness, I fancied, served as a rebuke to my long, untroubled days.

'Nonsense,' I muttered. This was a worthy command and a valuable task – doubly valuable for keeping me well away from the bloodthirsty attentions of our enemies. Here I never had to worry about wind or tide or reef or storm. I commanded two dozen men, most of whom the master dealt with, and oversaw a gaggle of soldiers whom His Majesty deemed unfit for service anywhere that battle might actually threaten. Otherwise I was charged only with ensuring that none of the prisoners succeeded in chiselling his way through the hull, and that nothing interrupted their gambling. For which I was paid fully twenty-four pounds a year more than those who risked their lives at sea, plus an allowance for my servants, and the opportunity to indulge in all the luxuries of the shore – Isobel chief among them. Any doubts as to the merit of my service must be merely the insidious workings of an uncharacteristic conscience.

Taking my pen with renewed purpose, I wrote down my concluding observation. *Number of prisoners: 793.*

An agitated knock at the door reminded me there

was one further piece of business to attend to. 'Come in.'

To my irritation, the sentry had returned alone. 'I couldn't find 'im, sir. 'E's not 'ere.'

'What? You do not mean to say that a prisoner caught attempting an escape this afternoon has now been allowed to achieve his purpose?' To my superiors that would indeed seem a poor piece of gaoling, even by my meagre standards.

The sentry breathed hard and leaned over his musket. 'Not that prisoner, sir. Mr Dumont, the interpreter.'

'Mr Dumont? Are you sure?'

'Searched everywhere, sir. 'E's gone. Clear off the ship.'

For a moment I could think of nothing to say, but gaped at the sentry in incomprehension. At last, recollecting myself, I lifted my pen and inscribed a resigned row of x's through the last figure in the log.

792.

2

My first thought, I confess, was disbelief; chased swiftly on by distress that I had failed in my duty, and fear for the consequences when my superiors discovered it. But a sense of proportion soon reasserted itself. The French navy would not rise from the ashes of Trafalgar because of one seaman more or less, and the rogue would anyway probably be caught within a day. Losing one prisoner was not a disgrace: it was an expected part of the job, natural wastage. No captain would lose his commission for that. Only a month earlier, three prisoners aboard the *Bristol* had stolen a water lighter and made their way as far as Sheerness before being apprehended, yet Captain Harris still enjoyed his command. Perhaps I could even turn this to my advantage, for it might prove to my superiors that my regime was not so benevolent that none wished to leave it – as some, I knew, suspected. Dumont had done me a good turn, and if I felt a pang of betrayal that a man to whom I had shown preferment had used his position as a platform for escape, then that was a price I could afford.

Clearly, though, I would have to make some effort to catch him. Outside the stern windows the river was dark, save for three small beacons where the *Bristol* had hoisted lanterns, and even if Dumont were still on the water he would be invisible.

'Send for Mr Mallow,' I told the sentry, 'and rouse the soldiers. Tell your lieutenant to double the patrols on the gallery, and to fire a rocket to alert the shore guard. Mr Dumont may be beyond our reach, but we do not want others following his example.'

The sentry saluted and ran off. He might have had the initiative of a bollard, I reflected, but he was the sort of man I enjoyed commanding. Unlike Mr Mallow.

'I knew it,' he hissed, crashing a bony fist into his palm. 'Knew we was bein' too soft on 'em. An' it's the softest of 'em all, the one what got his own cabin, what's run off.'

'Nonsense. And be that as it may, our immediate concern is seeing that none follow him. I want you to make an inspection of the ship and determine how he escaped. Are any of the boats missing?'

'None.'

'Then he must have swum.' I did not envy the man trying to find his bearings in the black water, still less trying to clamber out of the river across the oozing mudbanks that could swallow a man to his neck. 'Even *our* guards would have reacted if they'd heard a splash, so I take it there must be a hole in our hull near the waterline.' I leaned forward. 'I rely on you to find it, Mr Mallow.'

Mallow looked as though he would have liked to argue, but the opportunity of turning several hundred Frenchmen out of their hammocks was clearly too dear to pass up. I heard him bellowing for extra hands as he stamped out onto the deck. When I was sure he was gone, I picked up the lamp which my servant had lit, stepped outside, and descended the ladder to the main deck. The guards by the companionway, belatedly alert, stiffened as I approached, but I ignored them and made my way back towards the stern of the ship. By the fierce ructions coming from

24

the deck below, I guessed Mallow had already started his search.

Every man aboard *Prometheus* lived above his station – save the prisoners, naturally – and what had once been the wardroom for her lieutenants was now the accommodation for her petty officers. Mallow had the first lieutenant's cabin, while the others were shared between the boatswain, purser, surgeon and midshipmen. And one spare for the interpreter, an incentive to the honest performance of his duty.

A light showed under the door of the purser's cabin and I could hear muffled voices talking within, but otherwise all was dark. Raising my flickering lamp a little higher, I turned the handle of Dumont's door and slowly pushed it in. Though I well knew he was far from the ship by now, there remained something illegitimate about sneaking into his room that hushed my movements and made me crave silence. Trying to still even my breathing, I hung my lamp on a hook in the ceiling and looked curiously about the room where Dumont had planned his treachery.

There was little enough to see, for the room was barely eight feet square, and not so different from the quarters I had inhabited in my inglorious few months aboard the *Temeraire* – though as *Prometheus* would never again be cleared for action, the canvas partitions she had carried in active service were now replaced with solid walls. There was a cot, slung from the beams and invariably too short for a man of my height; a small desk against the facing wall, and a washstand in between. A basin sat atop it, the lamp-light casting a sheen over the milky surface of the water. Looking closer, I could see a scum of soap and black hairs around the bowl: clearly the fastidious Mr Dumont had finished shaving before making his escape. Shaving with *my* razor, I remembered, for the prisoners were forbidden the possession of sharp blades, and Dumont had asked to borrow mine. Ever the willing idiot, I had agreed – thank

God he had not used it to effect some violence. It was nowhere to be seen now; it must still be in his possession.

Trying to stifle my growing unease, I turned to the desk. As interpreter, Dumont had had the use of a writing box, a small dictionary and as much paper as he needed to copy out my orders. All were there, together with a couple of books he must have bought with the pittance I paid him. I picked up the topmost of them and leafed through it. It seemed to be a French translation of some classical author, Lucian, not a man who had figured in my education. As my French was even worse than my Greek, it meant little to me.

Nonplussed, I put the book down and shuffled through the papers loose on the desk. There was a copy of my standing orders, an unfinished petition to me on the subject of salt herring, and – in a hand different to his own – a collection of letters. I doubted they contained anything relevant, for they would all have been examined by the agent's staff before being forwarded to *Prometheus*.

A quick glance established that whatever their contents, they were in French. I set them aside. Of course there would be no obvious clue, no diagram or schedule of his intentions, but I could manage without them. Mallow would not rest until he had found the secret of Dumont's exit, and once the Frenchman reached the shore he would be the dragoons' concern. Really, the greatest inconvenience I faced was an unshaven chin.

With that thought, I stooped to peer more closely into the shadows around the edge of the room, wondering whether he might have dropped the razor in his haste to be away. There was no sign of it, but a dark lump on the floor under his cot drew my attention, and I reached to drag it into the light.

'He'll not be inconspicuous for long without these,' I murmured. It was his suit: the yellow coat, waistcoat and short trousers issued by the Transport Office. I held the coat up to the light. It was in better repair than most prisoners', clean of obvious stains and only a little frayed. There was an untidy tangle of loose threads along the lapel, but those could easily be sewn together, and I would be able to reissue the suit to another prisoner. I bundled it up, thinking to leave it with the purser.

But as I did so a sound halted me – something was rustling inside. Could it be paper? My hopes surged implausibly: perhaps he had actually left some revealing document. I unrolled the coat and plunged my hands into the pockets.

Hope receded as swiftly as it had come, for the pockets were empty. But as I held the coat by its lapel, I felt something under the wool which was firmer, harder-edged than the fabric. I looked again at the hem, peering more closely at the threads hanging off it. They were not just the legacy of wear; they seemed to have been cut open. And where they no longer held the cloth together, they left an opening about the width of a man's hand.

I reached in, and felt a rare thrill of success as my fingers closed around a folded square of paper. What could he have had to hide but the particulars of his escape? If I was lucky, he might even have jotted down the route he planned to take back to France, in which case I could arrange his recapture and turn an embarrassing lapse into a triumph. Breathing faster, I pulled out the paper and unfolded it beneath the lantern.

'*Mon cher fils* . . .' Inevitably, I could not read the French. Nor, of course, could I summon the interpreter. I tossed the letter onto the desk and bundled up the suit. The sight of the open lapel piqued my thoughts again – it was strange that he should have taken the trouble of unpicking the seam but left the hidden paper within – but I was tired of this charade, and eager for bed. Let the dragoons catch him if they could: clearly there was little I could add.

I turned to leave, and started as I saw Mallow standing in

27

the door. Though he had all the grace of a twenty-four-pound cannon, he could move with remarkable silence when he chose. I stiffened, almost crowning myself on the ceiling.

'Did you find the hole?'

'Nothin'.' Mallow's eyes were thin with fury. 'Searched every corner of the ship and not a bloody thing.'

'What of the hole in the privy?'

'First place we looked, wasn't it. Bos'n nailed it up soon as we'd found it, and it's not been touched since. All the bars is snug over the scuttles, an' there ain't no holes on the outside neither.' He leaned forward, dropping his face into shadow. 'What's that you got there?'

'Mr Dumont's suit. It seems he discarded it before he escaped.'

'Prob'ly to rub himself up with fat from the ration,' said Mallow moodily. 'I seen it done before. Keeps 'em warm in the water.'

'Not that we know how he got into the water.' I stepped forward to leave, but Mallow did not move and I was brought up short.

'One o' the Frenchies got to know how he done it. You could muster 'em all on the main deck an' not let 'em back to bed until someone talks.'

'I could, but I will not. I suspect they will be more amenable after a good night's sleep.' Certainly, I would be. 'We will muster them tomorrow morning, and see then what answers they can provide.' I dropped the yellow suit at his feet. 'I would be obliged if you returned these to the purser.' I stepped around him, and just managed to squeeze through to the door. 'Goodnight.'

For all my bravado with Mallow, I slept uneasily. However much I reassured myself that the loss of a single prisoner was a trifle, it was a constant effort to quell my lingering doubts, and I turned uncomfortably in my cot all night. I

28

was more than a little dishevelled when Samuel brought my breakfast, and my appearance suffered further from the continuing absence of the razor. I ate little, preferring the sustenance of brandy that my nerves required. Outside, I could hear the shouting and trudging of the prisoners being mustered, and I prayed with zealous fervour that I had lost no more.

Donning my dress coat and hat despite the July sun, I joined Mallow on the quarterdeck. 'How many?' I asked tentatively.

'Seven hundred an' ninety-two.'

'You're certain?'

'Counted 'em twice.' Mallow rubbed a sleeve across his moist forehead. For a thin man, I had noticed, he seemed unduly affected by the heat. 'We'll see how many's left once we've got the bastard's secret out of 'em.'

'They're prisoners of war, not convicts,' I reminded him. 'You can't flog them as you can our own tars. I shall appeal to their better natures.'

I lifted a speaking trumpet to my mouth, recoiling slightly at the way it shivered my lips and distorted my voice. 'Prisoners of His Majesty. One of your number has performed a most wicked and despicable act – he has escaped from his gentle captivity here aboard *Prometheus* and spirited himself away. Doubtless he will be apprehended soon, but in the meanwhile I am offering each prisoner the chance to improve his lot. If any of you can reveal the manner by which Dumont effected his exit, or provide information which results in his capture, I urge you to declare it. A reward of one golden guinea awaits the first man whose intelligence proves satisfactory.'

I lowered the speaking trumpet and looked down at the men ranked before me. Seven hundred and ninety-two faces stared back in silence.

Mallow chuckled unpleasantly, his narrow throat

29

thrusting out like a rooster's. 'Beggin' your pardon, sir, but it might work nicer if you spoke it in Frog.'

I hissed with exasperation, and felt my face grow hot. 'Does any of you speak English?' I shouted through the trumpet.

None volunteered that they did. The only answer was Mallow's continued mirth.

'I shall be in Mr Dumont's cabin under the quarterdeck.' I fumbled in my pocket, and pulled out the guinea I had brought to concentrate their thoughts. 'This coin will await you there.'

I thrust the trumpet into Mallow's arms and marched down the ladder. If there was one thing I hated about command, other than the master's endless gibes, it was the great scope it gave me to make an idiot of myself.

In Dumont's cabin all was as I had left it, though there was a nasty tidemark around the inside of the basin. I ran a finger over the stubble sprouting from my cheek, and cursed the rogue for leaving me helpless on so many fronts. And for casting me into such irrational despondency. A new razor would be easy to find in Chatham, and I did not doubt that of the seven hundred and ninety-two prisoners at least one would speak passable English and find the lure of his own cabin too beguiling to resist.

Almost as if I had willed it, there was a tap on the door, and a midshipman's voice calling, 'Two prisoners to see you, Captain Jerrold.'

'Send them in.'

Though ragged in every way, the prisoners who entered were more salubrious than many of their number: either they did not indulge in the gambling that ruined so many, or else they had better luck than most. Both seemed less substantial than they might once have been – there was a slackness to their flesh and their clothes hung loose over their frames. The taller of the two, whose unrestrained hair was coming to resemble the sort of wig my grandfather might have worn, was unknown to me, but there was something familiar about his companion's crooked jaw and wide nose. With all that had happened since, it was a moment before I realized he was the man Mallow had caught cutting his way out of the necessary the day before.

The taller of the two shuffled forward. 'Monsieur Capitaine,' he said tentatively. 'I am Croyette. I translate for you.'

'Marvellous.' I gestured about the room. 'You may live here, and take a shilling a week for your work. Who is your companion?'

'He is Meunier. He wants your gold.'

'Can he earn it?'

Croyette nodded. 'The escaped man, Dumont, he told Meunier to not try his escape. He did not want the guards to be alert.'

'*More* alert,' I corrected him.

'Meunier, he thinks Dumont betrayed him to you. Now Meunier tells you Dumont's secret. For gold.'

'He'll get the gold if he deserves it.'

'And no punishment for what he has done?'

'I can suspend punishment if I believe the offender has repented.' I folded my arms, aware that I sounded uncomfortably like a papist. 'What does he have to say?'

The diminutive Mr Meunier bit his lip, and began speaking in quick, uneven sentences. I waited until he had finished, unsure whether to look to him or his companion, then gave Croyette a quizzical look. 'By which he means . . . ?'

'He says Dumont shaved off his beard and put on a dress he stole. When you came down, he went to the deck and pretended he was your whore. Then the men in the carpenter's boat took him to land.'

'He pretended to be my *whore*?' Too slow to be outraged, I at last took his meaning. 'He pretended to be Isobel?

31

Using the dress he stole from my cabin while I was . . . otherwise occupied?'

'*Oui.*'

'Christ almighty!' I did not care for this Frenchman's tale at all; I wondered, indeed, if it was a pack of lies concocted by the prisoners to antagonize me. But there was too much in it that rang true – far too much for my own comfort.

I saw the midshipman still hovering in the passage behind the prisoners. 'Midshipman Davis,' I snapped. 'Yesterday afternoon, when the *Bristol* made her signal and I ordered you to send Isobel ashore – you thought she had already left?'

The midshipman bobbed his head nervously, eager to please but uncertain what was expected. 'I did, sir. In the carpenter's boat. I was certain she'd gone, sir, until I saw she was still aboard of course.'

'And then you took her ashore in the gig?'

He must have surmised from my tone that I did not like his answers, and faltered a little before speaking again. 'Yes, sir.'

'And did you notice anything curious about her?'

'Which one, sir?' I feared the fragile midshipman was about to burst into tears. 'The first time she left – that I thought she left – she was very quick about it. Bustled past with not even a smile like she usually gives me, begging your pardon, Captain. I thought it was queer, but the sun was in my eyes and it was all so bothered with *Bristol*'s signal and all, sir.'

I cut his babble short. 'Indeed. So it would appear that Dumont disguised himself as Isobel and made good his escape in the confusion of the *Bristol* mutiny.' I swung back to Croyette. 'Was that planned too? Were there accomplices?'

There was a short burst of renewed chatter, and Croyette spoke again. 'There was a woman. Not your whore,' he added, seeing the anger flare in my eyes. 'An older woman.

32

She visited Dumont often. Always after she came, he was in happy moods.' A gesture which needed no translation suggested the origins of this happiness. 'She made him *un peu fou*, I think. One time after she came, he said an English lord will save him.' He paused as his companion interjected something, waving his arms with typical Gallic frenzy. 'This was after she gave him the papers.'

'What papers?'

Croyette consulted with the little man Meunier. 'Secret papers. Dumont has kept them hidden always, but he boasts about them. He says they are the key that will unlock this ship, so he can do his duty to France. Never he lets anyone see this paper: he keeps it in the coat.'

I looked down at the desk and rummaged with controlled panic for the paper I had extracted from Dumont's jacket, alive with hope for what it might hold.

I found the paper and thrust it before Croyette. 'Is this it?'

Croyette shrugged, impervious to my excitement, and opened the letter. '*Mon cher fils . . .*' he read aloud, lapsing into silence as his eyes darted over the page. I could have torn it from his hands had I only understood French, but ignorance kept me penned in impotence until the Frenchman looked up.

Disconcertingly, he chuckled. 'Where have you found this?'

'What's that to you? Sewn inside the lining of his coat.'

Croyette's face stretched into a wide smile, revitalizing the tired folds of his face. Ignorant of the joke, but with deepening suspicion that it would be at my expense, I snatched the paper from his grasp.

'Well? What does it say?'

Croyette whispered something in French to his companion, stretching my patience almost to breaking, then looked at me with merry glee. 'It is a letter from his mother.'

It was not what I expected, but I recovered quickly. 'Or purports to be. Such vital correspondence would naturally hide its true origins. Now read it for me, if you please – and do not try to hide anything, for I shall have the agent's translator examine it later.'

Croyette blew air through his nose, and with an un-apologetic '*S'il vous plaît*' took the letter back from me.

'*My dear son,*' he read. '*I think every day of the misery you suffer in that terrible prison of the English, whose inhumanity is legendary.*' He gave a significant stare over the top of the paper, which I tried to ignore. '*Truly the English are a nation without pity or humanity. Their barbarism is well known, and I tremble to think that you suffer at what they call their mercy. Imagine, my dear son, how much greater is my concern when you do not answer my letters. Do the perfidious English withhold them from you? I have written down the dates of all the letters I have sent you, so that you will see if the evil capturers forbid you even this small pleasure. Twenty-first February 1806; twenty-second August 1805; thirteenth March 1805; eleventh January 1806.*' Croyette raised an eyebrow at me. 'There are many dates here, Captain. Do you want that I read them all?'

'That will not be necessary.' It was tedious enough hearing him recount the slurs against my regime with such evident relish. 'But what else? Surely there must be more.'

'*I kiss you, my dear son, and pray for your safely return. Your loving mother.*'

'Is that all?' I did not like having to trust this Frenchman's account of what the letter held, but I liked its innocuous contents far less. Why would Dumont have gone to such lengths to hide this piece of maternal drivel?

Croyette's gaze was still flitting over the page. 'There is something more,' he announced importantly. 'Here, on the back. But it is written by another hand.'

I took the letter back and turned it over. As he had said, there was indeed more on the reverse, just a few words scrawled in what was manifestly a different, sharper hand.

I scanned the impenetrable words and felt a shiver of vindication – their very shape seemed to me invested with mystery and significance.

'Tell me what they say,' I ordered, relinquishing the paper.

Croyette stared at it, and his face seemed to crease with amazement. He swallowed, and looked about to say something, but my stern look of command returned him to his purpose.

'*Of generous many kissed worry cities rivers seas. One had woman were carried loving. Many come carried come.*'

There followed an astonished silence, Croyette looking as taken aback as I. But where his surprise was tinged with wry amusement, mine was licked with anger. 'You're lying,' I said forthrightly. 'Or so incompetent that you've no business being my translator.'

That, at least, tempered his humour. 'Monsieur, I could not invent this if I tried. In any language, it is words of madness. Ask who you want, they will tell you the same.'

His robust defence, on top of the gibberish he had just spoken, left me unsteady, and I leaned against the table to right myself. Perhaps Dumont had been mad. He had talked of powerful lords and secret papers; had hidden letters from his mother in the greatest secrecy and then left them behind aboard *Prometheus*. Yet his escape had been so methodical.

I tried to consider the facts before me. The message was unintelligible – and important enough to have been hidden in a most secret place where it would never leave Dumont's person. If he was not a lunatic, then . . .

'It must be a cipher.' I spoke with the wonder of revelation, and looked at the two Frenchmen before me. 'Do either of you know any secret French codes?'

The moment I spoke the words I realized their naivety, and the half-pitying head-shakes I received in answer were more generous than I deserved. I was about to ask Croyette

35

to repeat what he had read, to see if I might squeeze any hidden meaning from it, but before I could speak I heard the sound of footsteps in the passage, and Mallow's wheedling voice – unusually deferential – announcing, 'He'll be in here, I reckon, sirs.'

I crossed to the door, for if Mallow was toadying to visitors they must be significant. I looked into the corridor and there was Captain Hutchinson, his hat crooked under his arm and his head bowed beneath the beams, following the obedient Mallow. He was the agent for prisoners at Chatham, my immediate superior, and despite his corpulent joviality I trembled each time he came aboard. Never more so than now.

'Captain Hutchinson,' I said, more weakly than I would have liked. 'What an unexpected honour. I did not hear your boat arrive or I would naturally have welcomed you on deck.'

Hutchinson waved a fleshy hand. 'No need, Jerrold, no need. Your enterprising master here saw me safely aboard.' Mallow simpered with satisfaction. 'A hulk's command is a busy life, what?'

'Of course, sir.'

'Especially when one of the rascals flies the coop, I'll be bound.'

'Especially then,' I agreed. 'It is that which brings you here, I take it?'

Hutchinson snorted. 'Good God no, Lieutenant. What's one of these rascals more or less, that's what I say. Richer pickings to be had if you lose a few of 'em now and again. You'll send his particulars to my clerk in due course, though – get some handbills printed up. Doesn't do for the locals' nerves if there's a prisoner on the run too long.'

My heart relented its pace a little. 'So if the fugitive is not your concern, sir, may I enquire what occasions this honour?'

'This fellow here.' Hutchinson stepped aside, revealing

a man in a crisp blue Guards uniform standing behind him. The shadowy passage and Hutchinson's bulk had entirely hidden him from me, and I was glad of it, for I do not think the sight would have soothed my humour. He was undeniably handsome, but there was something a little too pronounced in the jaw that protruded over his scarlet collar, a little too narrow in the cheeks, and a little too cold in the eyes, which combined to produce an unsettlingly lupine quality.

'Major Lebrett has just arrived from London,' Hutchinson was explaining. 'Wants to interview one of your prisoners. Urgent, apparently.'

Though it was an innocuous request, innocently made, I still felt a ghastly premonition building within me, the sense of an unshakeable doom approaching. I thought back to Trafalgar, to those moments waking in the darkness just before the first cannon fired, aware that something was dreadfully wrong yet unable to name it.

'A prisoner?' I repeated. 'Well, we have seven hundred and ninety-two to choose from. Is there an individual you seek, or will one chosen at random suffice? You must take care, Major – some of them have lost all semblance of civilization.' Aware that I was chattering uselessly, I fell silent.

Major Lebrett bared his teeth. 'Only one interests me. His name is . . .' He made a great show of pulling a piece of paper from his coat and examining it, though I did not think he needed the prompt.

'His name is Dumont.'

3

There are moments in one's life when only a deft word or quick thought can avert certain disaster, and sadly it has ever been a facility I lacked entirely. The shock of the major's request, perhaps abetted by his predatory leer, was like a cork in my mouth, and I could only gape mutely in response.

Mr Mallow, by contrast, had no such delicacy. 'Dumont, he's the one what escaped.' He sounded almost proud of the fact.

In an instant, Hutchinson's ebullient face went dark, and his great bulk seemed to loom over me. 'Escaped?' he echoed. 'Mr Dumont escaped? Is this true, Jerrold?'

In a voice that sounded almost as far away as I wished to be, I confirmed that he had.

'Well.' Hutchinson's mouth flapped open like a carp's. 'This is most unfortunate.'

'More than unfortunate,' corrected the major. 'My business with Monsieur Dumont was of the greatest significance. If you cannot keep him safe in a floating prison in the middle of a river, Hutchinson, you may struggle to answer the questions my superiors in London will ask when they hear of it.'

'Questions?' Hutchinson's chin wobbled. 'Major

Lebrett, it was not *I* who was charged with keeping this prisoner caged, dear me no. It was Lieutenant Jerrold. It is he to whom your superiors should address their questions.'

I'd been in enough similar situations to see that coming and have my defences prepared. 'No-one informed me that Dumont had any significance. Naturally, if they had, I should have taken the greatest precautions.'

'Instead of makin' him your translator, and givin' him coin and a cabin and all the softness he asked for.' Mallow folded his arms over his chest, and nodded soberly. 'I seen he was up to no good.'

Hutchinson's eyes swivelled round. 'Is that so, Jerrold? The man was your interpreter? You gave him run of the ship?'

'But how was I to know that he was . . . whatever the major thinks him to have been? Surely I am blameless in his escape.'

'That rather depends on how he managed it,' said Lebrett.

The cold silence which followed offered no respite. 'He dressed as a woman,' I confessed, looking at my shoes. 'He persuaded the carpenter to take him ashore.'

'A *woman*? What on earth possessed him to try that? Surely the presence of a *woman* aboard your ship would have been remarked upon.'

'That's not so, sir,' piped up Mallow, crashing another shot below the waterline of my foundering innocence. 'Miss Dawson was here so often they said we should muster her into the crew.' He smiled charmingly. 'That's the captain's lady,' he added, anticipating Hutchinson's inevitable question.

'Lady? I did not know you kept a wife.'

I twisted the button of my coat between my fingers. 'Miss Dawson was – is – my cousin, sir. She attended often to pay pastoral visits.'

'Pastoral visits?' There was a lethal calm in Lebrett's

39

voice. 'Do you think Mr Jerrold apprehends the difference between a prison ship and an orphanage, Captain Hutchinson?'

'What's that? No, no – apparently not.'

'He'll have them eating off the best china next,' Mallow suggested.

Even now, and even by his trying standards, this seemed intolerably insolent, and I looked to Hutchinson to rebuke him for the presumption. But despite a brief look of discomfort, he said nothing, while the major allowed himself to chuckle openly.

At that my hopes collapsed in ruin. I did not know who Major Lebrett was, or why he had poisoned Hutchinson against me; I certainly did not know why a single French seaman should occasion all this trouble, but it was clear now that they would show me no mercy. Part of my mind rebelled at the injustice of it, for my past disgraces had at least been plain to me, but mostly I clenched my body and awaited my fate.

Major Lebrett, whose role had rapidly become that of an executioner, handed Hutchinson the metaphorical axe.

'Surely, Captain, you cannot allow one of your hulks to be commanded by a man so negligent of his duty.'

In my mind's eye Hutchinson took the axe and raised it over my head, though in truth he did little more than harrumph into his collar.

'Certainly not, Major Lebrett.' He turned to the master. 'Mr Mallow, you seem an officer of exactitude. You will take acting command of this ship until I find a more permanent replacement.' He looked back at me, and though I searched his eyes for the least sign of confusion or hesitation, I saw none. 'Lieutenant Jerrold, you are relieved of your command.'

The axe struck home, and my comfortable life on the Medway was severed from me.

* * *

'Have your servant pack your trunk, and make ready to go ashore.' Hutchinson gave the order with as much feeling as if he were ordering a sailor to coil a line. 'You may send for your furniture in due course, perhaps once Mr Mallow has made arrangements for his own. You would not, I am sure, wish him to sleep on the floor.'

I certainly would not; I would much prefer to see him sleeping in the hold, half drowned in bilgewater and nibbled on by rats. I did not say so.

'Where shall I go?'

Hutchinson glanced uncertainly at Lebrett. 'Naturally, Lieutenant Jerrold, under the circumstances . . .' His words faded as we both noticed he had not considered the consequences of his swift decision. 'Perhaps you should seek lodgings in Chatham until your position is more certain. I will write to the Admiralty and request . . . clarification.'

I could well guess on whose desk his letter would land. I flinched even to think of it.

But it seemed Major Lebrett, who still lingered in the passage, was not yet satisfied with the carnage he had wreaked on my career. 'A word, Captain Hutchinson, if I may,' he said. 'Perhaps while Lieutenant Jerrold attends to his baggage.'

Whatever Lebrett had to say, I doubted it would be to my benefit. In other circumstances I might have purposely stood my ground to spite him, but my spirit was bruised by my astonishing fall and I lacked the strength. Nor, if some greater calamity were to befall me, did I want my possessions to pass into Mallow's hands. Without a word, I pushed past them towards the ladder, suddenly desperate to gain the sanctuary of my cabin. Before it became Mallow's cabin.

I felt a wave of relief as I passed the sentry and came into the peace of my own room. Samuel, my servant, was sitting under the stern windows studying the nautical almanac. The coffee pot and breakfast plate were still on the dining table.

'Pack my clothes and everything valuable,' I told him. 'I am no longer the captain aboard this ship.'

Samuel's book thudded against his knee, and he stared at me with wide eyes. 'Not the captain, sir? But what . . . ?' He sniffed loudly, and swallowed. 'What'll I do?'

'I hardly know what I shall do, so I cannot imagine what will become of you.' I sank into a chair and reached for the decanter which I kept conveniently close. 'Mr Mallow will be in command – you can offer to serve him, if you wish.'

'Will he keep me on the books, though, sir?'

Somehow, through no encouragement of mine, and despite being barely fourteen, Samuel had taken it into his mind that he would be the next Lord Nelson. When he agreed to serve me, part of our bargain had been that I would enrol him in the muster book, so that he could begin to accumulate the years of service necessary to become midshipman. Now his dreams too were brought down by my fall. Had I had any pity to spare from my own misfortunes, I might have felt some for him.

'If I were you, I would not stay,' I told him. 'The new king rarely favours the old courtiers. Come ashore with me, and we'll see how we stand.' Though as I considered my plummeting career, I feared I would have to sink to the bottom of the hole before I found my feet.

Samuel rubbed an eye with his sleeve. 'And where're you going, sir?'

'To stay with Isobel, in her boarding house.'

At that, Samuel looked more hopeful. He had once served the same diabolical master as she, and she had become to him something of a surrogate mother. 'Miss Isobel, sir? That'll be all right. She'll know what to do.'

'*I*'ll know what to do,' I corrected him, aggrieved he showed so little faith in me. 'But she will keep a roof over our heads until I have found a way.' The only alternative was returning home to my parents in Hampshire, and I had been there recently enough – with Isobel – to know the folly in that.

I left Samuel throwing my belongings into the chests he had dragged out from their stowage, and stepped outside onto the gallery which ran across *Prometheus*' transom. I enjoyed this luxury – *had* enjoyed it, I reminded myself – and regretted that the fashion for ship design had swung away from it in more recent times. I looked out across the river, beyond the black hulk of the *Bristol* behind us to the low land that rose from the water's edge. The town of Chatham was some way distant, but in the clear sunshine I could see the walls of her castle and the spires of her churches breaking the line of the shore. Soon I would be there – but then what?

'I suppose you are wondering what will become of you?'

It was as well the rail I leaned on was more solid than the rest of the ship, or I might have plunged through it, so powerfully did I start at the sound of the voice. Major Lebrett had appeared, as if from the air itself, and was watching me with chill amusement. Even my private gallery was no longer my own.

'I am wondering what you will inflict on me next.' I had a sudden, barely resistible urge to tip him over the rail. If I was to be hanged for a sheep, I might as well be hanged for mutton.

'You inflict it on yourself,' said Lebrett. 'Your lax over-sight enabled the prisoner to escape.'

'The prisoner would have escaped whatever my methods. Men escape from even the cruellest hulks – more, in fact, than from gentle restraint.'

'Dumont had a cabin, an income and a position of eminence aboard the ship. The most cosseted prisoner aboard, and still he ran. What does that tell you?'

'It tells me that he would have run from the luxury of his cabin or the solitary confines of the black hole irrespective.

Doubtless you may test such a theory once the dragoons have caught him.'

Lebrett rested his elbows on the rail and leaned out over the water. '*If* the dragoons catch him. He is an ingenious man in a desperate predicament – and he has a night's start on us. I would not gamble too much on the dragoons.'

'I don't much care.'

To my satisfaction, the words seemed to provoke him. To my concern, he jerked around and advanced down the gallery towards me.

'Yes, you do, Jerrold – indeed you do. The master's appointment aboard this ship is not permanent. There are still avenues open to you by which you might exculpate yourself, and so restore yourself to the position you lost.'

'I did not lose it. You took it from me. For reasons which are still opaque to me.'

'Reasons which are no concern of yours. Suffice it to know that if you ever hope to set foot on a quarterdeck again, you had best *find* Dumont before he achieves his purpose and escapes entirely.'

No man who knew me, not even one with sharp teeth and an overweening glare, should have wasted a second believing that the prospects of my career in the navy could motivate me. I would tell him so, I decided, and be rid of the whole sorry business. Then I could resurrect my life and start anew, in a less hazardous profession to which I would clearly be more suited.

To my irritation, the words never emerged. Perhaps I caught sight of Samuel through the glass, packing away the remnants of my existence, and remembered his thwarted dreams of glory; perhaps I thought of Isobel, an ill-used girl who I feared looked to me – though she never said so – to elevate her into respectability. Deluded they might be, but I could not deny their hopes. Perhaps I thought of the joy on my mother's face when she had received the unique letter from my uncle stating that I had not, contrary to all expectation and precedent, disgraced myself in Dover. Perhaps, as I found the words of acquiescence drifting out of my mouth, I simply wanted to discover Lebrett's secret so I could taunt him with it. I do not know.

Whatever the reason, I was sure of one thing. I would almost certainly regret it.

4

Even thus prepared, I was surprised by how soon the regrets came. Before I had left the stern gallery, my chests were locked and loaded into the jollyboat, and there was little for me to do but gather my hat and proceed to the stairs. Lebrett's company did not encourage dalliance, and I did not care to linger: although I ached at the loss of my command, there was much unhappiness aboard the *Prometheus* that I would be glad to be free of.

On deck, the prisoners were amusing themselves in the well, but they paused in their crafts and stared as I passed above them. More with curiosity than interest, I guessed, for I knew by my own experiences of captivity that gaolers are little more than adverse natural phenomena to their prisoners. Their sullen faces observed my transit as they would a star or comet, emotionless and detached.

It was more than Mr Mallow, who did not even acknowledge my departure despite having contributed so effectively to its occurrence. He was busy on the poop deck examining the binnacle, too preoccupied to notice my passing. My hatred for him flared just a little brighter: I would have preferred it, I think, if he had jeered me away from the ship in triumph, for at least then I would know that I had signified something to him. To be ignored in my despair seemed a particularly lonely fate.

Though of course I was not alone. As I seated myself in the jollyboat's stern, flinching at the hot wood under my legs, I still had company. Samuel was perched in the prow of the boat, looking anxiously forward to the horizon, while Major Lebrett had taken the bench opposite me and was tapping a rhythm on the thwart. He was as tall and broad as was to be expected of a Guards officer, with the hard bearing brought on by years in the saddle. His hair was black and polished as his boots, and I guessed him to be only a few years my senior, yet there was a chill in his blue eyes that seemed ageless. It was with evident unease that Hutchinson sat beside him as the jollyboat pulled away from the *Prometheus'* dank hull, past the great pair of chains which stretched taut from her hawse holes.

Lebrett leaned back against the side. 'It is my guess that Dumont will have pursued one of two courses. Either he will have made east for the coast to find a willing smuggler, or he will have gone west to London.'

'And how many escaped prisoners have you reeled in to bring you to that conclusion?' There was much unexplained about Major Lebrett and the effortless destruction he wreaked, and I was in no mood to play his hound.

'More than you, I'll warrant. Your credit on that account is currently owing.'

'But why would he go to London if he's so keen to escape? Surely the coast is his only hope.'

Lebrett tipped his head back and looked up at the sun. 'He might well go to London purely to confound anyone simple enough to believe that the coast was his only hope. Or he might go there to lose himself – it is easy to chase a man into London, but far harder to bring him out. Or maybe he has a favourite *cousin* he wishes to visit.'

I ignored the slight against Isobel, and directed my attention to the approaching shoreline. We had come upstream now, and the long dockyard waterfront stretched across the river bank ahead. It was an impressive sight, a vast foundry of naval power whose slips were filled with half-built vessels raking up from the river. Some were little more than skeletons, as if the carcasses of ships had been washed ashore and rotted away to their ribs, while others shone with fresh tar and paint and copper in the dry docks, and seemed to want only a full tide to launch themselves into the oceans. Further out, in the waters we were now navigating, half a dozen more ships lay at their moorings in various stages of fitting out. To my right I could see the tall arms of the crane on the sheer hulk swaying a frigate's mast into place, while next to her a group of riggers was mounting stays on a sleek new brig. The ships seemed to glow with the purpose of youth, fresh at the dawn of their lives. It was a morbid contrast with *Prometheus*.

The jollyboat grazed against the stairs at the foot of the wharf. A seaman leaped out and held her steady, while I clambered onto the brick landing.

'Where now?' I asked.

'Wait here with your boy,' said Lebrett. 'I must rouse some dragoons if we are to have any chance of catching Dumont before he reaches Paris. He already has half a day's start.'

Hutchinson sniffed loudly. 'I believe you will find, Major, that the dragoons have been out for some hours now. From the moment we received Lieutenant Jerrold's signal last night, in fact. They rarely fail to turn up the rascals eventually.'

'*Eventually* is not satisfactory, Captain. Indeed immediately is hardly soon enough. I will need at least twice as many men – and men who have been made to understand the enormity of this situation. As Lieutenant Jerrold has.'

Leaving behind a spluttering captain and a morose lieutenant, he strode away through the bustling dockyard.

As soon as he had vanished into the crowd of labourers and shipwrights, Hutchinson followed.

I sat down on a trunk which the seamen had hauled ashore. A glum Samuel seated himself on the box next to me, and – chins in our hands – we looked out over the river. *Prometheus'* jollyboat was already lost in the crowded waters, but there was no shortage of other small craft buzzing about to distract my eyes and thoughts. Hoys loaded with provisions were pulling around the sharp bend upstream, where the victualling yard lay hidden behind a thin promontory. The river was not wide here, and I had to marvel at the fleet handling of their masters, who steered a fine line between all the hulks, tenders and ships-in-ordinary that clogged the waterway. It was typical of the navy, I thought, to site their pre-eminent dockyard in so inconvenient a position. Even now, a timber barge was gliding downstream, her long deck piled high with fresh tree trunks, and I wondered that with the weight of her cargo and her unwieldy shape she did not run aground or career into the side of another vessel.

The sight of the hewn logs on the boat stirred a thought within me, and I stood abruptly. If Dumont had made his escape in the carpenter's boat, then it seemed reasonable to enquire whether he had let anything of his plan slip, or at the very least where he had disembarked. I glanced over my shoulder, noticing Samuel watching me with some concern. Lebrett was nowhere to be seen and, having ruined me, probably no longer cared much for my plight. Yet if I was to rehabilitate myself, then any fragment of Dumont's trail I could unearth might prove critical.

'I am going to find the carpenter and ask some questions,' I told Samuel. 'Wait here with the baggage in case Major Lebrett returns.'

'He might not be so happy if he finds you've gone.' Samuel sucked on his knuckle anxiously.

'I shan't be long,' I assured him. 'And if I find something

of value, he will have nothing to complain of.' I was fed up with playing the gull, kicked and shoved at the whim of my superiors; it was important, I felt, to assert myself.

Though the moment I turned my back on the river, I saw how laborious that might be. Everywhere in the vast panorama before me were pieces of wood – the ribs of unfinished ships reaching for the sky like pollarded elms; lattices of unsawn tree trunks piled atop each other; planks being pulled from the ovens in gouts of steam; rough timbers lying across the sawpits, with the sawyers standing atop them like acrobats. There must be more wood now than when all the land was forest, and everywhere men were working it in their hundreds. I could spend a week seeking out the man who had attended aboard *Prometheus* and not find him.

Evidently I did not have a week. Indeed, I doubted I had more than half an hour before Lebrett returned. If I was to prove my resourcefulness before then, I would have to work quickly, and with scant regard for rank. Leaving a forlorn Samuel sitting on the quayside, I hurried across to a passing caulker, who informed me that the master carpenter might be anywhere in the yard where there was wood, but would most likely be inspecting the work on the new seventy-four in number three slip, the *Impregnable*. Whence I hurried immediately, all the while keeping one nervous eye wary for Lebrett.

I found the slip easily enough, though in her current state the *Impregnable* little resembled the optimism of her name. I have never understood the navy's habit of naming ships with grandiose adjectives, for it has ever struck me as a reckless way to invite the contradiction of fate. Perhaps it is intended to inspire the crew with a sense of the desired quality, but having served turns variously aboard *Indomitable*, *Glorious* and *Temeraire*, I can vouch that in all my time aboard I never felt their benefit. As for the

Impregnable before me, at present she looked decidedly flimsy, little more than a keel sprouting a set of ribs. An incomplete set at that, I noticed, for the last starboard rib seemed to lack a larboard pair.

A wiry man in brown trousers and an open shirt was directing proceedings, and from the adze in his hand I guessed him to be some sort of shipwright or carpenter. 'Is this how you make your vessels?' I hailed him, pointing to the missing timber. 'Snapping a rib off one to make another?'

He gave me a queer look. 'Ribs ain't done yet,' he said slowly. 'Shipwright's cutting it up to kelter.'

'I see.' I felt a twinge of irritation that my joke had gone unappreciated, but tried to maintain a cheerful countenance. Labourers in my experience needed little encouragement to surliness. 'Anyway, I am seeking the master carpenter. Do you know if he is to be found here?'

'I am.'

'Ah – you are he?'

'I am.'

'Then I wonder whether you would know of a man who carried out repairs aboard the *Prometheus* hulk yesterday?'

Unexpectedly, his face cracked into a broad smile and he chuckled. 'Snap the ribs off,' he said. 'Like in the story of Adam.'

'Er, yes.' I was glad he had finally seen the humour of my jest, but by now my attention was firmly on finding the carpenter. 'Do you know . . .'

'Of course it ain't that easy for us,' said the master carpenter cheerfully. 'An' it takes us a fair sight more'n six days to make the blessed thing.'

'Indeed.' I forced a small laugh. 'But do you know the man I seek?'

'Collins.' The carpenter's face lapsed into impassivity again. 'Over there, fitting the deadwood.'

He did not point, but his glance gave enough direction

for me to find the man he meant, sitting athwart the keel in the shadow of one of the ribs. He was working a plane back and forth over the wood in a desultory fashion, mopping frequently at his brow with an untied neckerchief. His dark hair was slick against his head, and there was a sour look on his face.

'Mr Collins,' I shouted from the edge of the slip, looking down through the wooden frame. 'Is that you?'

Apparently it was, for he laid down his tool and peered up at me. 'Sir?' he answered lazily.

'Mr Collins, were you working aboard the *Prometheus* hulk yesterday afternoon?'

'I were. Fitting a fresh arm to the davits.'

'And when you departed, Mr Collins, did you take anyone ashore with you?'

Collins swung a leg over the keel so as to face me. 'A molly. Mairt took quite a shine to 'er.'

'Mairt?' I queried, struggling to follow his idiosyncratic vocabulary.

'The boy. Me apprentice.'

Under other circumstances, I might have chuckled at the poor youth's unfortunate judgement, falling in love with a dressed-up Frenchman, but my time was too urgent. 'And where did you leave the woman?'

'Quayside, near to the dry docks.'

'Did you see where she went afterwards?' Every sensible instinct told me that Dumont would be far gone from here, but a small voice suggested that he might have chosen to hide himself somewhere in the sprawling dockyard until the hunt had moved on. If that were so, then I might yet find him without Lebrett's assistance.

The carpenter gave little weight to that hope. 'Saw 'em heading for the gate.' He huffed, and pumped his finger up and down in a hole bored in the wood, though I could not tell if he was searching for splinters or mimicking something crude. 'En't come back since.'

'I beg your pardon?'

'Mairt. En't come back since 'e 'scorted the missy to the gate.'

'Your apprentice walked the woman to the gate and has not returned?'

'Dozy fobble couldn't keep 'is eyes from 'er. Not that 'er bubbies was much to see. I likes 'em plumper,' he explained. 'But that mairt, 'e'd poke 'is rod up a musket if it was warm enough.' He rubbed a callused hand over the wood he was planing. 'An' 'is lazin' means I's to do the work o' two. 'E'll get a good bannickin' when 'e slouches back, that an' no mistake.'

With that threat, he looked back at his timber, reminding me that I would not be thanked for keeping him from his work. I dredged my mind for any last question I might ask, but the combination of his impenetrable dialect and angry mood hobbled my thoughts.

'Mr Collins,' I began, by way of farewell. 'My thanks—'

A scuffling commotion interrupted my words as another labourer, mallet in hand, came running to the edge of the pit.

'Collins!' he shouted. 'They found ye mairt.'

The carpenter swung himself down from the keel and squeezed through the ribs which caged him. 'Did they, by God?' he muttered, mounting the ladder out of the slip. 'With the molly, was 'e?'

The other man shook his head impatiently. 'In the sawpit.'

I would have wanted to speak with the carpenter's mate in any case, but there was a wild urgency in the man's voice that seemed to bespeak something calamitous. Nor was I alone in thinking so, for right across the dockyard I could see scores of workers dropping their tools and moving together in a great throng. The carpenter broke into a run towards them, sprinting over the dusty ground, and I followed as quick as I could. As we drew nearer our progress slowed, for there was a tremendous crush of bodies to thread our way through. Several times an impatient jab of my elbow drew a brusque response in like kind, for all were jostling for a better view of the sight that had drawn them. But Collins the carpenter was unyielding in his determination to find his errant apprentice, and bored a path which I, for the most part, could follow.

The path ended abruptly on the lip of a pit – so abruptly that in my haste to keep pace with him, and with the crowd surging into the gap behind me, I almost dropped headlong in. It was a large hole, perhaps ten feet square and six deep; overlaid with parallel logs across which lay a thick trunk of timber. A long saw was stuck upright through it, protruding from either side and wobbling in the air. Looking down, I could see a gaunt man in a floppy hat who seemed to be sobbing, and slumped in the shadows against the earth wall another figure, motionless.

The carpenter by my side acted first: he sat himself on the edge of the pit, slid down through the wooden bars and stood over the prone figure.

'Hem me,' he murmured, his voice barely audible over the surrounding uproar. 'That's the lad. What happened?'

The man in the battered hat tilted his head up a little, addressing the crowd as much as the carpenter. He had a hooked nose and a crooked chin, and from the sawdust plastered to his sweating face I guessed he must be the sawyer.

' 'E was buried in the shavins,' he wailed. 'I didn't know nothin' 'til I felt somethin' 'ard under me foot. I thought it were a log fallen in, but then I seen it got a boot on. That's afore I saw the rest of 'im. 'Orrible, it were, 'orrible, 'orrible.'

Every man around that pit craned his head forward, hoping for a closer view of the promised horror, but our ghoulish eagerness thwarted our hope, for the shadow we cast only deepened the gloom below.

54

Terrified of what I would find, and of losing the anonymity of the crowd, yet compelled to know more by a fear that it somehow touched on my errand, I positioned myself between the slatted logs and dropped into the pit. I heard a murmur of interest from above at this new turn, and was suddenly overwhelmed by the sickening sense of caged bestiality. The tight space, the thick sawdust under my feet, the spectators leering through the bars and the bared teeth of the saw dangling by my face, all made me feel like some cock or bear primed for baiting. That, and of course the stink of blood.

I stepped over to the earthen wall and looked down on the unfortunate apprentice. Whatever bargain he had struck with Dumont, he had been cruelly deceived. His trousers were pulled down about his knees, leaving him not the least shred of modesty in his death, and the staring eyes were fixed in eternal surprise. Wood shavings clung to his shirt where the blood had soaked through it, and flies buzzed at the ugly gash under his chin. A gash, I noticed, as the bile rose in my throat, which looked distressingly like the work of a gentleman's razor.

5

To the mercy of my dignity, I did not vomit before the assembled labourers. As the sawyer gabbled out his story again, I helped the carpenter lift his dead apprentice off the ground and pass the corpse up to the reluctant hands that reached for him. It afforded me the chance to examine the body more closely – more closely indeed than I would have chosen, for it was a foul thing, and the only observations I could make did not repay more intimate examination. The blood was dried and hardened, despite the great profusion in which it had left him, and his arm, when I gingerly lifted it, was cool to the touch. He must have been dead many hours, and I guessed his killer would not have loitered about the dockyard waiting for the alarm to be raised.

If Dumont had escaped, it must still have been as a woman, for he had left the apprentice his clothes. And yet from the half-removed trousers, now pulled up to the waist in a belated attempt at decency, it seemed he had tried to take the man's garments. Whatever the apprentice's understanding, whether he had been in league with Dumont or an innocent promised carnal favours, the Frenchman must have lured him to the pit and killed him for his clothes. Had he then been interrupted before he could take them?

I turned to the gangly sawyer, standing silent in the corner. 'Who was working here yesterday?'

The sawyer scratched his cheek, his nail carving a thin line through the caked dirt. 'Yesterday, sir? There was none workin' 'ere yesterday as I saw. None until we come down today, not above an hour back.'

No wonder Dumont had fixed upon the pit for his wicked purpose. The vast stacks of uncut timber that surrounded it would have shaded him from casual view, and once in the hole even a scream would probably not have been heard. And yet someone must have happened upon them. I looked to the carpenter, who would have the strongest motive for catching the killer.

'I believe your apprentice was killed by a Frenchman who escaped from my ship,' I told him. 'Can you ask about the dockyard whether any of the men saw anything?'

To my surprise, and then concern, the carpenter did not take kindly to this suggestion. 'If it's one o' your hem Frogs as squeaked the mairt, then this'll all be your fault.' He looked past me to the bloodstained sawdust where the boy had lain. 'Four years I was tryin' to get 'im bangin' a straight nail, an' you've sundered 'im.'

'I have done no such thing,' I protested, all too aware that the looming faces above were turning to spite. 'It was your boat he escaped in, after all.'

It was an unfortunate truth to mention, and immediately I saw that it had enraged the carpenter. He growled with anger and squared himself towards me, emboldened no doubt by the approving growl that rose from above the pit. My legs began to weaken as I pressed myself back against the earthen wall, feeling all too much the dire isolation of this hole. Nor did I think any help would come from above, for the labourers had lost one of their own in terrible fashion and they would harbour few scruples.

The carpenter was not a large man, but his trade had imbued his thin frame with an undeniable strength, and I trembled to see his bony fingers curling themselves into a fist. This was madness, I told myself. Even struck with grief for his lost apprentice, surely he would not risk his livelihood in an act of mutiny that would avail him nothing. But the bitter look in his eye, and the reckless encouragement of his fellows, gave little reason to hope. I dug my fingers into the crumbling earth at my back, as if unconsciously trying to tunnel my way out.

Between the logs, the saw and the cowering sawyer, there was little space to hide in that pit, and unless reason prevailed the carpenter would be upon me in a second. I heard a commotion from above as he closed on me, noticed the press of faces thinning, and assumed that the wiser among the audience were absenting themselves to avoid any suggestion of complicity. Their prudence must have affected the carpenter, for he checked his advance and looked up uncertainly. Perhaps, I thought wildly, I could escape this place without violence.

A long shadow fell over my face, but it was not the crowd of labourers, who had now almost entirely vanished. It was a man on horseback, silhouetted against the sky and fragmented by the logs that barred my view. I could see little of his features, but there was something in the way he held himself which identified him even before I heard his rich, condescending voice.

'What the devil are you doing in that hole? I ordered you to stay with your baggage on the waterfront.'

The carpenter had retreated in the face of this new arrival, but I saw a flash of satisfaction cross his face at my humiliation. I would not give him or Lebrett the gratification of accepting it humbly.

'I do not wait on your command, Lebrett. As you seemed otherwise occupied, I took the liberty of making enquiries into the manner of Dumont's escape.'

'Did you find anything?'

I disliked the underlying sneer in Lebrett's tone, the

58

more so since I had in fact made considerable progress. 'I found the body of a man he killed. Down in this pit. From the condition of the corpse, I deduce that the crime must have occurred soon after his escape, and I infer that Dumont will likely have fled afterwards, as I believe he was disturbed in his crime. I was just investigating who might have witnessed it when you interrupted me.' This last was a trifle ungrateful, in view of the mauling from which he had saved me, but there was little in his manner to inspire gratitude. For further effect, I added, 'And what have you achieved?'

Lebrett leaned forward past the neck of his mount. 'I have discovered, from the marine sentry on the gate, that Dumont left the dockyard at six o'clock yesterday evening, in the guise of your woman. So much for your inferences and deductions. As for the witness you expected to find, has it not struck you that any man who saw his fellow being killed might have reported it unprompted? If no-one has come forward with intelligence by now, then *I* infer that no-one saw anything.'

'But he was interrupted in trying to remove the man's clothes,' I protested.

'Perhaps it was his conscience.' Lebrett kicked his horse, circling it around the mouth of the hole. 'Now if you have satisfied yourself with your idle suppositions, perchance you will climb out of your hole and accompany the marines in their hunt for the villain.'

Knowing that a single question at the gatehouse could have answered all my enquiries was embarrassment enough; having a triumphant Lebrett thrust it in my face was infinitely worse. Squinting to keep tears of shame from my cheek, I hauled myself undecorously out of the pit and trotted after the major's horse.

The gate was a squat, square structure at the top of a rise behind the storehouses, its stern aspect designed as much to keep dockyard materials in as spies and saboteurs out. A company of marines was arrayed in two lines before the guardhouse, sweating under the weight of their wool coats in the noonday heat. Their captain paced impatiently before them, the sun radiating off the burnished gorget about his throat, and he snapped the lid of his watch shut as Lebrett and I appeared.

'Captain Gifford, Lieutenant Jerrold.' Lebrett did not bother to dismount, forcing the captain to shield his eyes with his hand as he looked up.

'I trust he will repay the time we have lost waiting for him.' There was nothing friendly in Gifford's clipped voice. 'There's little value offering a thousand pounds' reward if we're to be kept on parade all morning.'

This was the first I had heard of a reward – and far more than was conceivable merely for an escaped prisoner. Events had moved too quickly that day for Lebrett's dire warnings to carry much force, but if he would offer that bounty he must truly be desperate. Suddenly, my motivations for finding Dumont became rather more active, and I could quite see why the marine captain was eager to be away.

'Lieutenant Jerrold is one of the few men likely to recognize the prisoner,' Lebrett announced. I felt a pathetic flash of pride at being deemed useful. 'Having, as he has, extended the intimacy which allowed the escape.'

I did not bother trying to defend myself, but listened mutely as Lebrett gave us our orders. Once again I was struck by the effortless authority he seemed to exercise over every dominion – the navy, the marines, to say nothing of his rightful place in the army. I could not decide which was the more remarkable: his complete presumption, or our meek submission.

'Take your company east, down the Canterbury road,' Lebrett was saying. 'I want your bayonets prying in every ditch and hedgerow, and men knocking at every house you pass.'

'But he's been gone the best part of a day,' I protested. 'He could be in Dover by now. Why prod around here when he's probably long gone?'

'You will prod around here because I tell you to do so.' Lebrett picked a strand of cotton off the white gloves he wore. 'There is no accounting for the logic of a desperado, and we will leave nothing to chance. Mounted dragoons are already patrolling the further limits of where the rogue may have gone; they will work inwards, and you out, and somewhere between us we will hope to crush him.' I noticed his fingers tighten at the thought. 'Now if you have nothing more with which to waste my time, gentlemen, I must go and meet the cavalry.'

'What shall we do when we catch him?' Captain Gifford asked – bravely, in my view, for Lebrett clearly detested delay.

'Bind him in as many chains as he can carry, and bring him back here.' Lebrett stretched out his leg, so that the cut-throat spurs on his boots hung before Gifford's face. 'Should you achieve anything, you can be sure I will hear of it.' And before we could pester him any further, he touched his rowels to the horse's flank and cantered out of the gate in a swirl of dust.

Gifford slapped the dirt off his blue lapels and sucked his lips tight together. 'I hope you can march, Lieutenant.'

6

❦

I marched, though without the prospect of the reward and the threat of Lebrett's fury I doubt I would have gone more than ten paces. As it was, I found myself trudging along after Gifford, with the rest of the column behind. The marine sergeants carried long pikes instead of muskets, and I could not escape the fear that if I dallied too much I would find one of those gleaming points up my backside.

We filed out of the dockyard under the thick arch, past a few of the meanly built houses in Chatham, and then turned towards Canterbury. The road took us away from the river, in the shadow of wooded hills on our left and open fields on our right. On the slope above us I could see four windmills, their sails still in the hot summer's day. Insects hummed about us, and the hedges were alive with all manner of wildlife hidden in their dappled shadows, but we took no pleasure from nature, for every rustle in the undergrowth meant a halt and a pike or musket poked into the branches. Each time we passed a cart or drover the air was thick with dust, clogging my nose and leaving a dry taste on my tongue, and the effort of marching in the close heat soon had my shirt soaked through with sweat.

'This is ludicrous,' I complained, voicing a thought I had

been considering for some time. 'He could be anywhere, and if we look in every copse and foxhole we'll be here until the war's ended.'

Gifford did not look back, though I saw his jaw tighten. 'For a thousand pounds, Lieutenant, we can afford a great deal of trouble.'

Perhaps we could, though I suspected Gifford was driven at least as much by a fear of Lebrett's unspoken power.

'Why such a vast reward?' I wondered. 'Did Lebrett divulge to you the man's significance?'

The back of Gifford's head seemed to stiffen under his cocked hat. 'He confided that it would mean a great deal to my career if the man were caught, and a great deal otherwise if he was not.' He paused, stepping carefully over some dung in the road. Then, reluctantly: 'Did he reveal any more to you?'

'Nothing – only the misfortunes that would befall me if the man escaped. Tell me, Captain, do you know anything of Major Lebrett?'

Gifford shook his head. 'I met him half an hour before I met you, when he roused us from the barracks to catch this Dumont. He made an immediate impression,' he added drily.

He pulled his sword from its scabbard and scythed it through the golden grass which grew by the roadside. I wondered if he too was imagining the fragile stems as Lebrett's neck.

'Go and investigate that spinney, Corporal,' he shouted, pointing across the fields to a small cluster of trees.

Half a dozen men broke off from the column and pushed their way through the thickly knit hedge on our right. I watched them trampling a path through the wheat, and wondered how many farmers would be threatening us with their dogs before the day was out.

'Hold up,' I said suddenly. 'What's that?' From around a bend in the road I could hear shouts, and the braying of horses. It sounded too angry for a drover – could it be the dragoons tussling with Dumont?

Gifford must have had the same thought. 'If that's the cavalry earning their reward, we'll curse ourselves for standing here. Come on!'

The excitement did not last long. Even before I had rounded the corner, I saw from the way the marines slowed their pace and lowered their muskets that we would not be claiming any reward. More relieved than disappointed, I carried on under the boughs of an ancient elm to see what had troubled us. It was a coach, a finely crafted chaise whose elegant cabin sat on four leather springs to minimize discomfort. Doubtless it was a feature its passengers particularly appreciated at that moment, for it might partially have compensated for the fact that two of the wheels were lodged in a ditch, and the entire contraption hung precariously on the edge of the road. Two ill-tempered footmen were tugging on the horses' bridles, trying to coax them forward, while the coachman sat on his box and lashed them with whip and words alike. They did not seem to have made any progress with extracting the carriage; indeed, as I watched, it seemed to roll further back into the ditch in defiance of the driver's imprecations.

'Look lively,' Gifford shouted. 'Sergeant, let us have six men put their shoulders against her and see if that does not make the difference.'

If his men resented this new labour, they did not complain – perhaps they preferred a task which offered some prospect of success. Under the brisk direction of the sergeant they scrambled down into the ditch, laid down their muskets and leaned in underneath the carriage, heaving it up the slope like a boulder.

'They'd better not scratch the gilding,' I murmured, though I was more concerned that a sudden loss of momentum would roll the coach back on top of them. The wheels slipped on the embankment, grinding up the grass and spraying earth onto the doughty marines, but it did not collapse on them. With a final effort they pushed it over the lip of the slope, and the coachman had to drop his whip and grab the reins to prevent it from careering straight across into the facing ditch. Eventually, and with much cursing, he brought the carriage to rest.

'That was a nasty bump,' said Gifford, who had been watching his troop labour. 'You might have snapped the axle.'

The marines were milling about in the obvious hope of recompense, but the driver ignored them and scowled at the captain. 'A phaeton damn near run us off the road,' he complained. 'Wasn't my doing.'

'You still might show the man some gratitude.' A new voice spoke, and I looked around in confusion for a second before realizing it had come from within the swaying carriage. It was a woman's voice; she must have been inside all the time we were trying to shift it.

Gifford lifted his hat. 'You might have spared the horses some effort, madam, if you had lightened their load.' He was unimpressed by her indolence, and did not try to hide it.

Her coachman, though, was all indignation. 'My lady dismounts when she pleases,' he announced grandly. 'It's not for her to be standing at the side of the highway.'

He was probably correct, and most gentle ladies might well have done the same rather than risk sullying their petticoats, but my mind was on edge and alert to anything suspicious. 'Why?' I challenged the driver. 'What does she have to hide?'

'Her dignity.'

But Captain Gifford must have grasped my point, for now he weighed in. 'A prisoner has escaped from the hulks, and we are indisposed to treat kindly with any who hinder us – or harbour him.'

The driver snorted, and seemed about to answer with derision when the opening of the carriage door interrupted him. The dim interior was all the darker against the brightness outside and I could see little of its occupant, but I glimpsed a veiled face peering out at us with concern.

'A prisoner?' she asked, her voice delicate. 'Is he dangerous?'

'He's already cut one man's throat.'

'My God.' Her feminine sensibilities were clearly shocked profoundly, for she spoke almost in a whisper. 'And you think he may be near?'

'I shouldn't worry, madam,' Gifford reassured her. 'He'll be keeping himself as quiet as possible – he would not dream of attempting violence on your carriage.'

I saw the flash of white teeth in the gloom; possibly she was biting her lip. 'Nonetheless, this is most alarming. Can you describe him, lest we see him on our journey?'

'He's of middling height, with dark and curly hair. His complexion is pale and very fine, almost girlish. Indeed, he may have tried to disguise himself as a woman, in a blue dress and bonnet. Or not,' I concluded vaguely, remembering how he had tried to take the boy's clothes. Was there another corpse, I wondered, lying naked in a ditch nearby? It was a horrible thought, with the image of the dead apprentice still vivid in my mind.

'You seem singularly ignorant of him,' she reproved me. 'Do you even know which way he has gone?'

I tried to prevaricate, but could find no satisfactory words. 'No. But we suspect – very strongly – that he will have made for Dover.'

'Then I shall keep a keen watch for him.' She fumbled about with something in her carriage, and extended a bare arm towards me. I marvelled at the lustrous perfection of her pale skin, and almost dropped

66

the few coins which tumbled into my hand.

'For your men,' she said. 'With my thanks for their aid.'

'No less than their duty,' I said gallantly, ignoring the fact that they were not my men, and that I had done no more than spectate. 'It is an honour to be of service, Mrs . . . ?'

She hesitated a second, as if wary of this intimacy. 'Mrs Weld. But we must be on our way, and you about your task. Hoyle! Bates!'

The two dusty footmen, who had been murmuring behind the carriage, took up their positions on its rear.

'Farewell, sirs,' she said. 'My thanks. And if we should encounter each other again, do bring me news of this dangerous Frenchman. I would sleep much easier knowing he was secured.'

I started, and peered into the darkness of the carriage, though she must have sat back for I could see nothing of her. 'Frenchman, you say? How do you come to know his country?'

'Why you yourself told me,' she said brightly. 'Of middling height and with pale complexion. I recollect it very clearly.'

'Oh.' I struggled to think back on what I had said. 'Ah yes, I recall.' I did not, but I must have, for how else would she have known it? Yet the suspicion she had raised reminded me of other duties. Although her voice and manner, so clearly of the first rank, had seemed to place her beyond reproof, I could ill afford to be so trusting.

'Before you go, milady, you will not object if we examine your carriage.'

She affected to laugh, though her tone was cross. 'Do you really believe that I am in the fashion of helping despicable Frenchmen escape captivity?'

'Certainly not. But the French can be crafty. He may have hidden himself without your knowledge.'

She sighed. 'Very well, sir. Do as you must.'

I waved one of the marines to examine the driver's box, while I swung myself inside. It rocked a little on its suspension, and I almost pitched headlong into the lady's lap before I could right myself.

'I beg your indulgence,' I said, aware that in the close space I was rather nearer her than propriety allowed. Even without the sun glaring in my eyes I could still see little, for she had all the curtains drawn over the windows, but the light from the door revealed a round chin and bright eyes watching me warily from behind her veil. Her skirts rustled as she recomposed herself, and the warm air was rich with the scent of rosewater.

'You see, sir,' she said, 'I am alone. The wicked Frenchman did not clamber in unnoticed.'

The absurdity of that idea was quite apparent, for a mouse could scarcely have crept in unobserved, but I did not quite relent my hopes. 'Are there any other compartments in here?' I asked. 'Under the bench, for example?'

In answer, she raised herself off the seat and gestured me to examine it. My optimism fading, I tugged at its top; only the cushion came away.

'As you know,' I said lamely, 'we must take all precautions.'

We watched Mrs Weld's carriage roll away down the road, though not before I had given both of her footmen a sharp look, and returned to the tedious business of scouring fields and thickets. The sun was hotter than ever, with not the least cloud to shade us, and as the afternoon wore on we all of us stripped off our coats and hats. Nor was there any semblance of order in our progress, for the company was now spread out across nearly half a mile of countryside, bunched together in small knots or strung out in thin lines as the ground allowed. Captain Gifford and I stayed on the road, where at least our progress was not broken by streams or brambles, but it meant that we were constantly halting carts and wagons, inspecting them for any sign of the prisoner. Inevitably, we drew nothing save abuse for our pains.

We must have spent two hours or more in that thankless work, when one of the marines who had gone ahead of us came running back down the road. I groaned, for he had been ordered to look for Lebrett's rendezvous, but the news that came tumbling out with a slack salute was rather more heartening.

'At the inn,' he gasped, swigging water from his flask. It trickled over his chin and down the neck of his shirt. 'There's a farrier I passed said he seen a foreigner at the next inn.'

'Did you see for yourself?' demanded Gifford. 'What did he look like?'

'Beg pardon, sir, but I didn't think to look. I come to get you straight off. I didn't want you thinkin' I'd be going after the reward on my own,' the marine added slyly.

'Charitable fellow.' Gifford peered keenly down the road ahead. 'Well done, Private. How far to the inn?'

'Not above half a mile, the farrier said.'

'Then let us hurry.'

The captain and I and the half-dozen of his men who were to hand broke into a run, each doubtless impelled by the thought of the gold. With neither sword nor musket nor crossbelts to impede me, and glad to stretch my limbs after the hours of faltering progress, I easily outstripped the others, and was at the inn before they had even come into sight of it. 'The Duck', the sign said, though there was nothing in the small pond opposite save two boys trying to drown each other.

The yard was ripe with dung and hay and horseflesh. I passed the lounging ostlers with barely a glance, and ducked under the lintel into the taproom. It was broad and low, and though the day was cooler and dimmer in here, the lazy stillness of the summer afternoon had still penetrated. There was a pervading smell like dry paper, while by the windows motes of dust danced in the beams of sunlight. Only three men were in the room, and all seemed under the spell of the enveloping hush.

A small bell rested on the counter; I lifted it delicately between forefinger and thumb, and shook a few chimes from it. Three faces turned slowly to watch me, though none said a word, and I waited self-consciously for almost a minute until a gawky youth, his face scarred by some unhappy pox, ambled out of the shadows.

I put a shilling on the counter top and leaned over it. 'I hear there is a foreigner here,' I murmured. 'Can you find him for me?'

The boy pulled the shilling from under my finger and ran a nail over its milled edge. 'Over there,' he said, unhelpfully loud. 'In the window.'

No sooner had I looked than my hopes were confounded. The man he had indicated – and there was no mistaking him, for he sat alone at a round table in the alcove under the window – was not Dumont. He must have been twenty years older at least, in his forties or thereabouts; his loose brown hair was edged with grey and his worn features were riven by experience. Not all of it benign, for on his left cheek a deep-cut scar was carved across the natural etchings of time.

Nor had he failed to notice my interest. 'Do you ask for me?' he enquired. His voice carried clearly around the room, its confidence manifest in the slow, unaffected drawl. I cursed silently, and mourned the waste of a good shilling. Not only was he the wrong man, but the wrong species of foreigner entirely. His accent was that of an American.

And being an American, and thus perhaps more susceptible to raw distrust of his mother country, he would not let me escape with a mumbled apology for my mistake.

'Is this another example of English liberty?' he

demanded, rising to his feet. Though he was not large to look at, his frame seemed to fill more than its share of the window. 'Can armed soldiers burst into a public house and drag a man away from his meal merely because he is a foreigner? That, sir, is why we threw off the yoke of your oppression. To show the world how to live free from the chains of tyranny.'

Though I had done little, I believed, to provoke him, there was a weight in his words which seemed pregnant with danger. But at that moment the military state which the American so deplored came to my rescue. The door behind me crashed open, and Captain Gifford and his men charged in bristling with bayonets and gleaming blades.

'Is he here?' Gifford asked, his sword outstretched. He caught sight of the American standing before me and raised his guard. 'Is he the foreigner?'

'He is,' I said, observing him carefully. Though clearly taken unawares by the invasion, he had not been panicked, but gave instead the air of a man appraising odds. 'But he is not the foreigner we want.'

'Blast!' Gifford stabbed his sword down in frustration, watching it quiver in the floorboards. He turned to the American. 'My apologies, sir, if we alarmed you. We are hunting an escaped Frenchman, and every report of a stranger must be investigated.'

'It's as well you realized your mistake when you did.' The heat of anger had cooled to an icy calm in the American's face, but his words still sounded more dangerous than magnanimous. Without further comment he sat back down at his table, smoothed his green coat under him and began chewing on his pork.

'Where now, Captain?' asked a sergeant, trying to keep his pike from scraping the rafters. 'Back to the road?'

'Back to the road,' I agreed, forgetting that I no longer merited even a titular 'captain'. I spoke without enthusiasm, for neither the thousand pounds nor the prospect of rank

71

regained were proving enough to sustain my impetus. Even the rough glass of wine which I drained before we left was little use.

I emerged onto the road in front of The Duck, shielding my eyes from the late-afternoon sun, and scanned the road in each direction. Honour, gold and drink might fail to inspire me, but the fear of Lebrett was overwhelming. Though he held no authority in the navy, I had no doubt he could make my life still more excruciating if he chose.

A bird was chirruping in a leafy oak to my left, while before me the two boys sat on the edge of the pond and skipped pebbles across it, aiming for a hole in the opposite bank. A haycart must have passed recently, for the ground was scattered with loose spikes of straw, and I wondered idly if I should chase after it. Gifford was still reorganizing his men in the stable yard behind me, and to my right a lone man was walking slowly up the road.

As I waited for Gifford, I let my eyes settle on the approaching figure. I could see little of his face, for he wore a wide-brimmed hat that drooped over his shoulders; it seemed more rustic than the rest of his attire, which was perfectly correct if a little outmoded. He was a full-sized man, with something almost military in his shoulders, yet he walked with a tall stick, and could not move three paces, it seemed, without checking his stride and darting his head about. Perhaps he had fallen on hard times, I decided, and was wary of being robbed on the road even in broad daylight.

Behind me I could hear shouted commands and the stamp of boots, the marines marching out, and I began to turn my gaze back to them. But as Gifford and his sergeants came into the road, I saw the figure in the distance jerk to a standstill; then, with studied poise, he turned his back to us and began walking away. His legs seemed to swing more freely now, the stick barely touching the ground, and in a few moments he would vanish around the corner.

'Stop!' I shouted. There were all sorts of reasons, legitimate or otherwise, why a man might shy away from a company of marines, and none of them would concern me. But on that road, that day, I was disinclined to trust anyone.

Nor had the man done anything to soothe my doubts. He did not even turn his head to my challenge, but hastened on with an ever-faster, loping stride. I shouted again, this time drawing the surprised attention of the marines, and again he ignored me utterly.

This was too much for Captain Gifford, who perhaps imagined that a thousand pounds was disappearing around the bend. He grabbed a musket from the arms of a startled marine, lifted it to his shoulder and fired it in an explosion of noise and white smoke. Birds rose indignantly out of the trees, while the two boys by the pond gazed at us in awe, but still the figure carried on, now in open flight. I could hardly blame him, for though the musket ball would barely have reached him, and though I had seen Gifford aim deliberately wide, an unprovoked shot seemed unlikely to rein in anyone.

'After him!' Gifford shouted, not even looking at me for confirmation of the man's identity. He had pulled a pistol from his belt and thrown it to an ensign, who fumbled anxiously with the ramrod, but without waiting for his weapon he charged after the fleeing figure. What could I do but follow, with thirty marines hard behind me.

I reached the next bend to find Gifford halted. He was looking about, kicking at the roadside weeds with his boot. Of the mysterious fugitive there was no sign.

'Was it Dumont?' he demanded.

'I could not tell,' I admitted. 'The hat shaded his face.'

'Then what the devil were you shouting for?'

'He ran away when I hailed him. It seemed suspicious.'

'Well, the bastard's vanished now. Thank you.' Gifford took his pistol from the ensign, who had belatedly caught up with his superior. 'I tell you, Lieutenant, I don't care for suspicious happenings under these circumstances. Could you describe the man?'

I was about to detail what little I had noticed, but one of the sergeants broke in before me. 'Wearin' a brown coat an' trousers, was 'e? An' an 'at like a cowherd?'

It was a passable description. But the questioning tone in the sergeant's voice puzzled me, until I saw that he had his long pike outstretched towards the adjoining field. It took me a second, for the wheat was high and his clothes well matched to the landscape, but then a rise in the ground lifted him above the background and I saw him.

'That's him.' Excitement and confusion mingled in my voice, but there was no delay in Gifford's orders.

'Skirmish line,' he bellowed. 'And get some men in that next field too. We'll close up around him. Watch yourselves,' he added. 'We don't know yet if he's armed.'

That checked me, for I knew all too well the state of my own defences and they were not reassuring. But already the marines were scrambling through the fence and fanning out across the fields, a crimson cordon ploughing great furrows through the ripening wheat, and I had no choice but to follow. With more thought for my own safety than the farmer's crops, I made sure to stay tight in the tracks of a man before me.

The flat report of a musket to my left brought the whole line slewing to a standstill, weapons raised and shoulders taut. I looked over, baffled that the fugitive could have moved so swiftly across our line, but the shamefaced marine who held the smoking gun inspired little elation. He bent down, almost vanishing in the tall wheat, and re-emerged a second later holding a bloody, feathery bundle. It looked like a grouse, or some other gamebird, though a musket ball and point-blank range had precluded any appearance on the dinner table. A few of the men laughed, but Gifford had no patience for it.

'Dammit,' he roared, 'this is no time to be thinking of your belly.'

The blushing private mumbled an apology and let the bird drop to the ground. Gifford's attention had already swung back to the low ridge before us.

'There he is, blast him.'

Several of the marines took the obscenity literally, and musket shots rippled down the line as I watched a flash of brown move over the brow of the hill. In his rustic garb, half obscured by grass, he looked as much like a fawn or buck as a man. And not yet brought to bay.

Spurred on by the sight of him vanishing across the hill-top, the line was surging forward again, but as the ground rose under us I changed direction, veering across towards Gifford. Now I was no longer in a well-trampled path, and it took greater exertion to wade through the waist-high wheat that snapped and rustled around me. My footing was almost invisible, and at several points I almost turned my ankle on sudden stones or hollows in my path, but with much sweat and desperate breathing I finally came within reach of Gifford at the top of the slope.

'What are you doing?' I demanded, clutching my stomach where a cramp had seized it. 'Are you trying to kill him?'

Gifford pulled off his hat and wiped his damp forehead with a cloth. 'Dammit, Mr Jerrold, of course I would not choose to shoot a fleeing man in the back. But you cannot expect my men to have such scruples when a thousand pounds are at stake. And Major Lebrett's orders were that we should bring Dumont back – he did not specify the condition.'

From what I had seen of Lebrett, I did not doubt he would far rather greet Dumont's corpse: for all his over-weening bullying, he gave the air of a man desperate to see the affair concluded in a manner that brooked no further enquiry. For that reason alone, to discover what Lebrett feared and whether I could use it against him, I wanted the Frenchman brought in alive. But as I looked out over the land before us, it seemed Dumont – if indeed he it was out there – had no need of my good offices to keep from harm. An open field dropped down to a low stone wall, beyond which, at the bottom of the incline, a copse of trees clustered around a thin stream. The ground rose again on the far bank to another crest, beyond which I could see the sparkling veins of the estuary, and the marshes which bounded it. The light turned the ribbons of water to copper, and looking over my shoulder I could see that the sun was now rubbing against the horizon. Already the little dell before us was falling into shadow, and soon even the higher ground would be dark.

I turned to Gifford. 'Do your men carry lanterns?'

He shook his head. 'If we find some branches among those trees, we can improvise torches, perhaps. We cannot let the blackguard escape us now.' The force of his words could not disguise his faltering hopes.

'He may be making for the coast,' I warned. 'Perhaps there's some fisherman or smuggler waiting in the Swale for him.'

Gifford swore again, then shouted to one of his subordinates. 'Lieutenant Jerrold believes the Frenchy may be aiming to escape out to sea. Send a drummer to inform the agent at Chatham that we will need a guardboat in the channel.'

The sergeant saluted, and I saw one of the men who had been trailing after us hurry back down towards the road. It was a pointless errand, for it would be well past sundown before he reached Chatham, and it would be a bold master to take his vessel over the shifting mudbanks of the Medway after nightfall. Almost as foolhardy, I feared, as splashing through those marshes that now glinted so bewitchingly in the distance. In their reaches, in the dark, we would be lucky to find our own feet.

Now the line was on the move again, advancing down the slope towards the stream and the coppice. I heard a sergeant shouting to his captain that he had seen the Frenchman, but Gifford made no reply. He must have been as apprehensive as I about pursuing this quest in the dark, but despite the murk I guessed the thousand pounds of gold still gleamed brightly enough in his mind's eye. Before he could move, I tugged at his sleeve.

'It will be far better if we catch Dumont alive,' I told him.

His grey eyes showed little sympathy, but he did shout at his sergeants to keep the men from firing if they could help it, and I heard the order repeated down the line in desultory fashion.

Darkness was coming fast, particularly in the hollows, and by the time we reached the bottom of the slope I could see barely ten yards before me. From the curses and shouts to my left and right, it seemed the line was losing its order – hardly surprising, given the terrain and light. If Gifford's men did not hold their fire we would probably end up blasting each other. I let my pace flag so that I did not get on the wrong end of a musket barrel.

Yet still no-one called a halt to the lunacy. We splashed through the stream in the crook of the valley and stumbled up the far escarpment, tripping and stubbing ourselves all the way. As we reached the next ridge I saw the moon beginning to rise on my right, but there was still light enough in the sky to reflect in the distant water, the East Swale and Herne Bay beyond, with the dark mass of Sheppey a shadow in the background.

'Madness,' I murmured to myself, but there was no-one to hear me, for the marines were already hastening on down towards the sea and the marshes. They were little more than dark silhouettes in the blue half-light, and in the evening silence I could hear their pouches and powder horns slapping against their sides as they navigated the broken shadows of the landscape.

At length the slope we were descending began to level out, but it brought no respite: the ground grew ever stickier, more slippery, and soon every step brought cold water bubbling up around my feet. The grass was taller here, and spiky, bristling out of the mud in thick, sharp clusters. Now I had no time to keep an eye on the rest of the line, let alone watch out for Dumont, for the treacherous going demanded all my attention. On my left I could see a black finger of water, a creek or inlet, and I realized the land I stood on had become a labyrinth of causeways and peninsulas through the salty swamp. I tried to remember which direction the tide was heading, and prayed I would not be marooned on a sinking island.

And still we pressed on. Our line had become little more than a scattering of straggled soldiers, each as nearly lost as the next; every so often I would see one caught in the moonlight, at greater or lesser distances. There did not seem to be much direction to their movements – they were probably stumbling about as best the faltering ground allowed – and they held their muskets over their heads to keep their powder dry. Most, though, had already fixed their bayonets, for in those conditions they were unlikely to see Dumont until they were almost over him. If then.

'Christ!'

Too late, I found that a single moment of faltered concentration had undone me: my foot rolled over a half-rotted branch embedded in the mud, and before I could even throw out my arms I had been pitched forward on my face. Had I had the time to think, I would have hoped for a soft hummock to break my fall, but there was nothing so gentle; instead, a chill slap and a desperate choking as I plunged into a hidden channel. Salt water filled my mouth and nose, searing my throat, and I flailed to find my footing and get my head clear. It was not deep, but there was no strength in the bottom, and even as I let my weight settle on one foot I felt it sinking deeper in the mire.

A fresh wave of panic burst over me, and I kicked out with my free leg while scrabbling desperately for a hold on the coarse grass in the bank. I had visions of being dragged beneath the water, entombed alive in the mud for the crabs and worms to feast on, and I heaved like the devil to pull my foot from the sucking mud. It wrenched free, though the feel of water between my toes told me the boot was lost. No matter: of more concern was that my other leg was now bearing all my weight, and likewise being dragged down through the ooze. I cried out in desperation, tasting mud in the back of my mouth, though I knew that in that swamp help would come with terrible delay. If at all.

As I struggled to stay afloat, to keep free of the bottom's clutches, my hands closed about a wiry tussock sprouting from the islet before me. It was a parlous lifeline, but with little else to trust I could only pray that the salt-hardened fibres would hold, and the grasping mud would keep its roots held firm.

It was strong enough. Hand over hand I dragged myself over the slimy lip of the land before me. My stomach pressed into the mud, and I felt like some ancient sea-serpent slithering forth from the depths, but that was no bar to the relief which swept through me as I felt firm ground under my exhausted body. I lay there motionless, glad I had not relied on the help of marines who had still not appeared, and thanked all creation for my escape. Thanks which froze stillborn in my thoughts as I noticed the gleam of the gun-barrel.

Though I could not see his face behind the shadow of the reeds, he must have been watching me for some time, must have seen me foundering in the marsh and shouting for help, yet he had never moved. I felt a prick of pique that he should have offered no aid, after I had begged Gifford to show restraint with his muskets, but that affront was drowned by the pulsing terror of what he would do with the pistol. Why had he not used it already? He could hardly have failed to notice me. Perhaps he did not want to draw the attention, for a gunshot in these surrounds would bring even the worst lost of the marines running. Perhaps he hoped, even now, that I would not spy him, that I would trudge on and leave the way clear for his escape. Certainly the rest of the line must be well past him by now – was I the only obstacle remaining? That was not an agreeable thought.

Whatever his reasoning, he had seen me stare too long in his direction. The gun rose, and I saw the muzzle aim squarely for my temples. In a desperate haze I pressed my raw hands against the ground, trying to lift myself out of his path, but the sticky mud seemed only to grasp me tighter. At such close distance, I would never have moved fast enough anyway. His finger tightened around the trigger, and the hammer slammed forward.

And nothing else happened. For a second I had been frozen by fear; now I was stricken with shock, unable to believe that my blood was not already seeping into the surrounding mire. *The water*, I thought wildly: it had almost drowned me, but now it was my salvation, for it must have soaked through the charge in his gun and stifled its power. I felt my arms shaking, convulsing with the sheer improbability of survival.

Survival which was not yet assured, for as my opponent realized his misfortune he launched himself out of the reeds in a furious bound. I tried to roll aside but again the mud ensnared me, and his lunging fist caught me on the shoulder. I howled with pain and clawed out a hand, wrapping it into the cloth of his shirt and pulling him into a violent embrace to cramp his attack. He hissed a curse, words I recognized from frequent use aboard the *Prometheus*, but before I could truly register that he had spoken in French a hard punch crashed into my cheekbone. I felt something metal – perhaps a knife, perhaps a ring on his finger – gouge a welt out of my skin and I screamed again, loosening my feeble grip on him. *Where in hell was Gifford?* my mind demanded, even as blood dribbled over my face and into my mouth. This man was strong, and I did not think I could long resist him in a test of might.

Free of my grasp, he leaped back into a poised crouch, rocking forward a little on the balls of his feet. With faltering hopes, I saw that a knife had appeared in his hand.

He sprang forward, and it was all I could do to swing my bootless leg into his path. It was a feeble defence, but it caught him mid-bound and deflected his attack, so that he landed awkwardly away to my right. It was a brief respite, for in seconds he was on his feet again and advancing, looming over me like some angel of death. Fright and fatigue and the sucking mud kept me rooted in place, and I did not doubt that he would easily dodge whatever meek defiance I could muster.

A curious stillness came over me. With almost innocent curiosity I looked up at his face, seeing the vicious snarl of battle frozen in moonlight. It was not Dumont, I thought dully: he was too large and too old to be the slender young Frenchman. His eyes were black in the cavities of his grizzled face, and his grey lips breathed triumph. He was not Dumont, but he spoke French and he would kill me. It did not seem fair.

And yet suddenly a change came over him. His body tensed, even as his legs sagged from his waist, and I saw his shoulder jerk back, throwing him off balance. A dark cloud burst from his collarbone, and his hands clutched his throat as if he choked. In the distance I could hear shouts and bangs, but my enemy reacted to none of them. He swayed on his feet as blood flowed through his fingers, then – struck by an invisible blow – toppled back into the reeds. I heard the trickle of water rising around his corpse.

As shocked to be alive as to see him dead, I pulled myself to my knees. I dared not stand for fear of meeting the same end as the Frenchman, but gasped out pleas for help until a pair of luminous crossbelts splashed through the water and emerged beside me.

'Don't shoot,' I mumbled. 'You have got the man we were after.' The fear that had frozen my soul was thawing, and I convulsed with the torrent of emotion which it unleashed.

The marine, whom I did not recognize, poked at the body with his bayonet. 'Got 'im,' he repeated in wonder. 'A thousand pounds.' He jerked his head back to me. 'Now don't you go sayin' you got 'im, sir – it was my shot what done it.'

I would never argue with a bayonet in the hands of avarice. I stayed there, sunk on my knees, while shouts of elation echoed across the marshes. It was not long before Gifford arrived.

'Jerrold,' he exclaimed, looking with disapproval at my mud-soaked uniform, my scarred face and my single boot. 'What the devil are you doing?'

'I fell into the bog, and then straight into the arms of our quarry.' I waved a weary arm at the body. 'His pistol was damp, but he was about to kill me with his knife when your men opened fire.' I remembered my earlier insistence on taking the man alive, and felt a fresh kick of foolishness. 'Thank God.'

'And is it the prisoner?' There was a cold hunger in Gifford's voice which the moonlight served only to harden. The rest of his men leaned closer, equally intent, and I wondered whether my answer might not provoke more violence.

'He is French, or at least he swore at me in French. But he's not Dumont.'

'Not Dumont?' Gifford's gaze snapped away from the corpse to stare into my face. 'But how can that be? How can there be two Frenchmen skulking about the countryside here? How can we have chased him through all this filth and ooze and failed? How ... What in Christ's name is *that*?'

I thought his last question was aimed at the body, but his eyes had swung up and were now staring back towards the land. I could hear more commotion, and though my eyes were barely higher than the grass and reeds, I could see the flickering glow of fire advancing towards us.

A shadow fell over me as the moon was eclipsed, and I raised my eyes to see an enormous horse and rider towering into the night. The horse was dark, almost black, with a white star blazed on its forehead, while the rider was dressed in the red-faced coat of the Horse Guards and a short riding cape. An aide held a burning lantern on a pole beside him, casting a macabre orange veil over the scene, but I needed no light to recognize the voice.

'Lieutenant Jerrold. You appear to have killed the wrong man. Can your superiors *never* trust you out of their sight?' The lethal bite in the words was unmistakable, and so sharp that I could not even find strength to stand, let alone meet his mocking eye. Absently, I wondered how he knew already that the body was not Dumont's.

Never even looking at the corpse, Lebrett shifted his attention to Gifford.

'Lieutenant Jerrold has led you on a fool's errand, Captain, but your men are no longer required. You may form them up and return to your barracks.'

'No longer needed?' Gifford spoke the question that I was too cowed to voice. 'Is the prisoner apprehended, then?'

Lebrett made a rasping, hissing noise in his throat. 'He is not. But we found ... *this*.'

Something splashed into a puddle in the ground before me; I glanced down, seeing silver catch the moonlight, and felt about in the murky water. It was a razor, the square blade unclasped, and I needed neither moon nor lamp to know that inscribed on the handle, in letters which my mother had commissioned, were the initials M J.

'That's . . . that's mine.' Thankfully, he must have washed it since murdering the carpenter, for it was tolerably clean, though there was a dark spot in the crook of the hinge which I tried to ignore. 'Where did you find it?'

'The ploughman on a nearby farm had it. A man much resembling Dumont had sold it to him, he said.'

'When was this?' Gifford asked.

'A little before noon.'

'Then what does it signify?' I gave full force to the frustration that had built at Lebrett's constant, inconclusive sneering. 'If he was nearby five hours ago, then he could be twenty miles away by now.'

Lebrett's horse tossed its head, and he ran his knuckles over its flank. 'For a start, it signifies that he probably murdered the carpenter with your razor. That should weigh something on your conscience, Jerrold, that you allowed him to make off with a dangerous weapon.' He paused, his eyes drilling into me. 'Unless, that is, you gave it to him?'

'Of course not.' There were enough black marks beside my name that I would not readily admit to having supplied the murderer with his blade.

For the moment, Lebrett accepted my assurance. 'As for the second fact which it signifies, that is rather more germane. As soon as the ploughman had made the exchange, he witnessed Dumont climb aboard a stage-coach. Bound for London.'

Ever prone to optimism in the face of severe odds, I spoke hastily. 'Capital. Then you can send word to the Horse Guards to keep watch in the city, Major, while Captain Gifford and I return to our duties at Chatham.'

Lebrett's long nose twitched as his eyes fixed on mine. 'Captain Gifford will return to Chatham. He is of no more use to me. You, on the other hand, will accompany me. Your part in this disaster still has some distance to run – which is as well, for you will need every scrap of time you can scavenge to amend your errors.'

Resignation settled over me, and as I lifted myself out of the mud I could only accept that the nightmare of this errand would continue unabated. In London.

7

I awoke to the feel of crisp white light on my face, and crisp white sheets about my body. I must have slept like the dead, for they were scarcely creased, while my pillow bore only a single crater where my head had struck it the night before.

I propped myself up on one arm, surveying the room. It was not my cabin aboard the *Prometheus* – so much was obvious – and though it swayed a little, I suspected it was the waves of dizziness in my head that rocked it, rather than any motion of the sea.

My gaze dropped to the floor. Some foul beast seemed to have slithered through the room, leaving a wanton trail of muddy debris across the floorboards and interspersing it with a few mud-crusted articles of clothing. I could see a blue coat, its tails steeped in grime, and a shirt with a ruddy stain on the collar. A pair of tolerably white breeches lay turned inside out, and balled by the foot of the bed were some mouldering rags that might have been stockings. A lone boot, sitting in the middle of the room in a puddle of ooze, completed the scattered ensemble.

I fell back into the forgiving pillow as gobbets of memory rose in my mind. I remembered the horrific chase through the swamp, the Frenchman who'd almost killed me, and

Lebrett lowering over me on his horse like some portent of the apocalypse. I remembered a saddle chafing through my sodden clothes as I clung on to a borrowed horse in the moonlight, and the long journey in the commandeered coach, with only Lebrett's hostile, unspeaking company. That was a memory I would rather forget – by the time we reached Deptford, I had almost wished for a highwayman to abduct me, if only to free me from the relentless bore of Lebrett's eyes. At last, I recalled, we had crossed a bridge over the Stygian expanse of the Thames and rattled through the empty streets of sleeping London. Too tired and cowed to question anything, I had sat still until the carriage halted and Lebrett forced me out to the door of a boarding house. Though it was well past midnight, he had had little difficulty in persuading the landlady to accept my custom; to my inestimable relief, he had not taken a room himself but driven on into the night. Whence, I fervently hoped, some footpad or cut-throat might make certain he would never return.

A timid tap at the door knocked my thoughts back to the present. My clothes, or what remained of them, were all accounted for on the floor, and I pulled the sheet closer around me. The prim woman who had shown me to my room the night before had had the usual way of landladies, and after the indecent hour of my arrival I did not wish to assault her sensibilities yet further.

'Come in,' I called, though I could see the handle turning even before I spoke. It was not the landlady who peered curiously around the door, but a girl, scarcely older than Isobel, with bright ginger hair spraying out from under her cap and a face mottled with freckles. At some point in her young life she must have fallen victim to a brawl or a dentist, for when she smiled there was a large gap between her foremost teeth.

'Mrs McCaird said to ask if you wanted breakfast,' she said, edging further around the door. There was a coy lilt to her voice which, in my nakedness, seemed particularly prominent.

'Breakfast would be a godsend.' I had not eaten since the previous morning, and was ravenous.

'Will you take it in the parlour?'

'In my room, if you please. With a bath.'

'I'll get the boy to bring that up.' The girl inclined her head and leaned forward, so that the loose neck of her smock dropped away. I had neither strength nor inclination to avert my gaze from the full figure she displayed. 'For a little extra, I'll give you some 'elp with the scrubbing.'

Well, that was not the sort of service I had expected would be offered here. What sort of boarding house had Lebrett put me in? But the blue walls and white sheets were too well ordered to admit to any ill repute; it seemed more likely that the girl was acting on her own behalf, supplementing her wages or feeding her appetites. No matter how professional her offer, there was no denying that a warm body and quick pleasure would be a welcome restorative after my ordeals. My flesh was already showing willing, and I had to pull up my knees to prevent the sheet from betraying my eagerness too soon, for my mind was in uproar. Could I afford to dally with the maid while my career foundered? Did I want to risk greeting Lebrett with my upraised buttocks, if he should come to fetch me? And what would Isobel think – or do – if she knew of it?

This last thought, compounded perhaps by hunger and weariness, decided me. Looking up, I saw that the girl had advanced into the room with alarming confidence, and I raised the sheet before me to ward off her design.

'I will manage by myself,' I told her stiffly. 'But if you want for employment, you can give those clothes by your feet a scrubbing.' I would rather have thrown them on the fire, but I feared I would need the use of them until I could find a tailor and a cobbler to remedy the deficit.

The girl put a finger to her lip, then slowly stroked it

over the top of her plumped-up breasts. Again, decency deserted me as she stared with a mixture of invitation and contempt, but I withstood her gaze until at last she bent over – affording another alluring view – and gathered together the mud-stained garments on the floor.

'Don't forget the breakfast,' I called, as she closed the door.

She did not, though it was a rude meal that she eventually brought, all salty bread and wet jam. Her collar seemed to have slipped a little further, but she made no effort to engage me in conversation and swiftly left me alone. Though I would admit to a little regret at the opportunity I had spurned, my addled thoughts were taxing enough company.

As I chewed on my meal, my mind, which for so long had been fixed on the immediate horrors of successive predicaments, began to expand its scope. I could not remember what Lebrett had said in parting, for I had been too eager to be free of him, but I feared he would return for me sooner rather than later. Clearly I would need a new suit by then, for I could hardly traipse around the city as his bedraggled, half-shod companion.

What about my belongings? Suddenly I remembered Samuel, sitting on the quay at Chatham, and wondered whether the obedient idiot was still waiting there with my chests. If not, where would he have gone? To Isobel? What would she think, to hear that I had been relieved of my command, then wandered off to make a few enquiries and never returned? Would she fear for my life, poor creature; would she sicken with worry that I had been knifed in the back by a desperate Frenchman? And what should she do? If I was to stay in London until Dumont was found, I might be ten years in my quest, like some latter-day Odysseus adrift in the world. Would she be my faithful Penelope? More pertinently, could I resist the charms of every passing red-headed Circe?

Another knock on the door gave the question fresh immediacy. To the mercy of my virtue, it was not the maid but her mistress, the landlady. One sniff of her rigorous rectitude banished all notion of wickedness from my heart.

'A visitor has called for you,' she said, glaring at the dirt I had dragged across her floor, and my abandoned déshabillé. 'Shall I admit him?'

My cowed spirits recoiled still further. 'A visitor? A Guards officer, the man who brought me here last night?'

'A clerk.'

I allowed myself a deep sigh of relief. 'Does he say what he requires?'

'He wishes you to accompany him to the Admiralty.'

My relief had been premature. I slumped down in the bed and let the sheet slip unheeded from my neck. Mrs McCaird pulled her shawl more tightly about her shoulders at the sight of my uncovered chest, but that would be the least injury to her sensibilities if I could not get my clothes back.

'I will need my uniform,' I said, willing myself to focus on the practicalities of the moment. 'I gave it to your girl to wash.'

Mrs McCaird raked me with a look which, I fancied, spoke all her suspicions of what the girl and I might have contrived under her roof.

'It was only a short time ago,' I continued, as though that were any defence, 'but as you will have seen last night, I have nothing else with me. My journey here was … unanticipated.'

If Mrs McCaird pitied my plight, she concealed it well, but she did disappear down the stairs, to return some minutes later with a basket of sodden clothes. The worst of the mud had been scrubbed out of them, but there were still broad stains, while their abrupt recall from the laundry had left them soaked through and laden with soap. It was a terrible effort to get the breeches tugged over my legs and fastened about my waist – they had been growing ever more snug since I took up my sedentary commission aboard the *Prometheus* – and once on they chafed my tender skin no end. Nor could I feel less than completely ridiculous with only a single boot to stand on. But all those humiliations would be as nothing against the onslaught awaiting me at the Admiralty. My uncle was rarely backward in upbraiding my shortcomings; with Lebrett to spur him on, I imagined he would be furious.

Descending the stairs, I saw the messenger waiting in the neat hallway. He wore a brown suit and a sour face, and I guessed he did not relish the errand even before he saw its disreputable object.

'Did your landlady inform you that you are to come to the Admiralty?' he asked, staring at my attire.

'I came here at regrettably short notice. Doubtless their lordships will understand.'

The clerk raised his eyebrows in the time-honoured manner of subordinate officials, and said nothing.

'Will you be wanting these?' The landlady pushed past me, brandishing a folded paper and a silver razor. 'I found them in the laundry. The maid said she took them from your coat when she washed it.'

Though I had two days' stubble obscuring my cheeks, I doubted I would ever use that particular razor again, but perhaps I could get a guinea for it at the two-for-one shop. I took it gingerly from the landlady and dropped it in my pocket, together with the paper. It reminded me of another duty I had best perform quickly.

'I wonder, Mrs McCaird, whether I might have the use of a pen and paper, and some ink?'

The clerk scowled, and began to complain at the delay, but I cut him short and followed Mrs McCaird into her parlour. I did not bother to sit down, but scrawled a few brief lines, smudging the ink so horribly that it seemed the words must have been dredged from a river. I folded it in three, wrote a brief address, and handed it to the watchful landlady.

'I should be grateful if you could see that this reaches the Post Office.'

She took it carefully, doubtless wondering what disgraceful tattle I might be writing. As there was no sealing wax to hand, I suspected she would find out as soon as I was gone, but for the moment she merely examined the address.

'That will be sixpence.'

'You shall have it when I settle my account,' I promised, careless of where I might find the resources on that day of reckoning. Then, with the clerk's patience clearly exhausted, I stepped out into the street.

It was some months since I had last been in London, and if they had dulled the memory of the extraordinary swarm of humanity that coursed through it, I needed little more than to step off Mrs McCaird's doorstep to feel its full, vital force. Apart from a sense that my night's sleep had been too short by several hours, I had little idea of the time, but that did not matter for the crowd would remain undimmed from dawn until sundown. I felt myself tensing at the onslaught of sensation: the clamour of the hawkers and costermongers and duffers and dustmen; the reek of soot and sweat, dung and straw; the sight of a thousand faces swarming about like flies on a carcass. It was as though I had stumbled into some primitive ritual dance, of whose steps I was utterly ignorant, and if I made but the least deviation from its complex pattern a barrage of elbows and shoulders bombarded me back into the prescribed place. My unprotected foot suffered untold agonies, yet I could not stop or even look about, but must fix my eyes on the clerk and plunge after him, relegating the magnificence of the metropolis to an unheeded blur at the edge of my vision. Live eels writhing on forks vied for my attention with ladies whose beds, clearly, were not intended for repose, but I ignored them all and the myriad other delights to be had. The prospect of a meeting with my uncle did not admit to much joy.

Near the navy office at Somerset House, we turned right into the Strand. Here the crowds were even greater, and the refined arcades of shops did nothing to dissuade the coarser elements of commerce from competing. Seeing a cobbler, I forced the clerk to wait while I reshod myself, and though he complained about the cost of the delay it was nothing against the usurious price of the shoes. Worse, most of the money seemed to be for a pair of garish silver buckles that felt like shackles on my feet, and made me look more like a Pall Mall dandy than a sober officer of His Majesty. The shoes were a strange complement to my ragged *tout ensemble*, and if the smirk they elicited from the surly clerk was any guide, hardly flattering.

Nonetheless, for all their frivolity they had the practical effect of speeding our progress, even against the hardening flow of human traffic, and it was not long before we had swung around the crusted spire of Charing Cross and through an arch under the stone eyes of two winged horses. I felt giddy to be suddenly in the relative space and quiet of the courtyard, but there was no time to catch my breath for we pressed on relentlessly up the steep stairs. Thick, archaic columns towered over us, while in the centre of the high pediment above was carved the wound anchor of the Admiralty. It was as if we entered some ancient temple, supplicants to the deities who ruled our lives, and I could not shake the fear that it would take more than prayers to placate these gods.

I was not made to wait; instead, the clerk swept imperiously past the doorman and led me up a curving staircase to a broad landing. Here there was more activity, men bustling to and from their offices, and the black and brown coats of the clerks mingled with the blue cloth of uniforms, mostly cloyed with gold. I ignored them, and followed the clerk down a corridor to my left. It was not where I remembered calling on my uncle previously, but then visits to him seldom occasioned memories to dwell on.

Indeed, the very thought of those visits slowed my pace. The haste of the errand, and the difficult push through the bustle of London, had demanded all my attention, but now that I was here in the sombre hush of the Admiralty I could forget it no longer. Chill beads of sweat emerged on my forehead, and the damp collar of my shirt was suddenly very close about my throat. I tried to breathe deeply, but it seemed that scarcely a tenth of the breath I drew reached my lungs. What fresh disasters awaited me in this sepulchral building? While Lebrett's punishment had been miserable, I had borne it in the knowledge that it had to be temporary, that though he could knock my life askew he had no sanction over its longer course. Now that the Admiralty were involved, whether by Lebrett's doing or through my uncle's keen nose for self-preservation, that comfort was gone, and with it my last hopes for swift relief.

The clerk paused before a broad door and knocked, his ear cocked for any reply. It must have come immediately, for even before I caught up with him the door was swinging open; I had barely time to register the words BOARD ROOM blazed in gold on the panelling before I was stumbling into the brightness of a tall, airy room. A wide table stood in its centre surrounded by eight crimson chairs; on the wall behind it two Attic bookshelves flanked a globe imprisoned in a glass cabinet. Above, a brass dial the size of a ship's wheel indicated that the wind was from the south, though the three high windows to my left admitted nothing but sunlight. Yellowed maps hung rolled up on the facing wall, their edges torn and tattered, while high above me I could see plaster swirls and lozenges in the bevelled ceiling. It was a sumptuous room, though it could have used some of that south wind to blow away the musty smell which infused it: if it was my uncle's, then his fortunes must have advanced as precipitately as mine had collapsed.

But it was not his office. The sign on the door had declared it the board room, and though my heart stuttered to see my uncle's overbearing frame hunched forward in one of the chairs, he was not alone. Another man sat on his left, at the head of the table, and while my uncle wore all the pomp and frippery of his rank, his companion was dressed as a gentleman. Standing hesitantly before them, I wondered what new calamities this presaged.

'Lieutenant Jerrold.' To my surprise and relief it was not my uncle who spoke but the other man, and he did not couch his words in the clipped fury I had expected. His tone was relaxed, almost indolent, and well in harmony with the way he lounged back in his chair, as comfortable as my uncle was stiff. He was younger than my uncle, perhaps close to forty, and though his brown hair was in retreat from his forehead he had the well-maintained features of a man I suspected was as fascinating to himself as to women. He seemed neither hostile nor friendly, but his eyes wandered over various invisible points in the air as though he could not believe that I merited precise attention. Given my circumstances, he was probably right.

'Lieutenant Jerrold,' he repeated, his gaze settling on me with mild surprise. 'Have you managed to find your own private thunder-shower on this fine summer's day?'

For a moment I did not see his meaning, until I looked down at my dank imitation of a uniform. I tried a feeble laugh, and mumbled something about the laundry.

'Please, sit down.' He waved me to the empty row of chairs on his left and I sat apprehensively, choosing a seat at a small remove so that I was neither immediately beside him nor directly opposite my uncle.

'Would you care for some tea, Lieutenant?'

This was all remarkably civilized from a man I had expected to cashier me in short order – rather too civilized, my terrorized mind worried. But I accepted his offer of the tea, though I would have preferred brandy, and watched him pull the black cord which hung from the high ceiling. I assumed that thereafter it would be straight to business, but he seemed reluctant to start without refreshment and fiddled with a large pocket-watch while we waited in silence.

The delay afforded me time for reflection. Through all this genteel ceremony, my uncle had remained silent in his chair, watching our host with a caution that verged on deference. For a man who rarely contained his opinions for more than a moment in my company, it was restraint of the highest order. And there was an alarming look on his face, the fat lips stretched tight between two bulging cheeks, which suggested that either he had suffered a violent seizure or else he was trying to be ingratiating. No wonder I had not recognized the mood. I had rarely, if ever, seen my uncle with his superiors, for they were few in number, but if he could be driven to silence and sycophancy by the mere presence of this colleague, then the man must be so illustrious as to be almost beyond conception, at the very least a fellow Lord of the Admiralty.

The arrival of a steward with a silver tray broke the uncomfortable silence, and I was glad of the distraction of watching him set out the slender teacups, the chiming of the pot as it jostled their rims and the bubble of the tea as it poured out. The lord, whoever he was, took his cup immediately, eagerly, and bent low over it as if paying homage, inhaling the steam in deep draughts. Once satisfied with the aroma, he sipped a little, then tipped back his head and slid down in his chair.

'Much better. How do you find it, Lieutenant?'

My hands still flinched to touch the side of the cup, but at his question I grabbed it and snatched a brief sip. In my haste, I scalded my tongue, and added a fresh stain to my beleaguered breeches, but I suppressed my instinctive yelp and managed to mumble a few appreciative words.

'I esteem it greatly,' he informed me. 'I have it blended to my own recipe by Mr Twining on the Strand. But I fear we cannot pass this day in the delights of Epicurus. Doubtless you will want to know why we have summoned you.'

I feared I knew the reason all too well, but allowed him to continue uninterrupted. Though it would have been satisfying to embarrass my uncle by antagonizing his superior, it would probably have been unwise.

'A French prisoner escaped from your ship,' the lord was saying, as if this might be new intelligence to me. 'A Mr . . .'

'Dumont.' My uncle supplied the name.

'Dumont.' The lord took another appreciative measure of his tea. 'Now to you, Lieutenant, he may have been merely another prisoner among hundreds—'

It seemed an eternity since that had been the case, though in fact it was little more than a day.

'. . . but we have reports that his designs may be rather more sinister than merely creeping home to see his family.'

'How sinister?' It was hardly a thoughtful question, but I had grown impatient of unknown men talking vaguely of dire threats.

'Extremely sinister.' He deposited his cup on the table. 'More so than you would dare contemplate.'

I had not expected to draw his anger, and lowered my eyes in unwitting shame. Support, though, now came from the most unlikely quarter.

'I believe what my – what Lieutenant Jerrold – purposed to say was that it might help find the villain if we knew his intentions.' My uncle studied his fingertips as he spoke, avoiding both my astonished gaze and his colleague's undisguised irritation.

'I apprehended the lieutenant's meaning with perfect

clarity, thank you. But I cannot – which is to say, I am not at liberty to – divulge such portentous secrets.'

For the first time in our acquaintance, my uncle looked almost contrite, and had I not had long years' practice in loathing him I might have felt pity. But I could not ponder that conundrum, for the eminence was still handing down his lecture.

'It is of signal importance for our ministry that you find this Dumont, Lieutenant.' There was something ominously possessive in the way he referred to 'our' ministry, and for a ludicrous second I wondered if he could even be the King in disguise. That nonsense subsided almost immediately, but there remained the definite impression that he held a personal stake – or role – in the government. He was not Fox, for him I would have recognized, and he did not match what I had read of Lord Grenville. Reason therefore suggested he could only be the First Lord of the Admiralty.

The cup rattled on its saucer as I took another swig of his beloved tea, trying to steady my cankered nerves. Confronting my uncle had been a gruesome enough prospect; sitting here being lectured by the First Lord of the Admiralty, subject only to God and the King in the naval cosmology, was almost like martyrdom. I wished I could roll myself up like the maps on the wall and hide, but instead I sat there, rooted to my chair, and listened to his conversation.

'The agent at Chatham, Captain Hutchinson, has telegraphed to say that he has suspended you from your command. A trifle harsh, perhaps, but at least it affords you the time and the freedom to pursue this Dumont.'

I stared in astonishment. 'But did you not send Major Lebrett . . . ?'

'Who?' Though he delivered his thoughts in an easy, almost casual fashion, he did not take kindly to interruption. But confusion outweighed caution, and I carried on heedless.

'Major Lebrett, from the Horse Guards. It was he who brought news of Dumont's importance to us in Chatham. And he also who convinced Captain Hutchinson to remove my command.'

The First Lord and my uncle were united in their looks of displeasure. 'From the Horse Guards, you say? How could an army officer hold any sanction over a navy commission?' The First Lord, I saw, had become only the latest, if most illustrious, of those superiors who believed me to be a credulous simpleton. 'We in the cabinet heard of Dumont's importance only last night – I cannot believe that this *major* was privy to news of such significance before we were told.'

Though it showed a naive faith that intelligence could flow only downwards through government, it was a fair question, and one I had not considered: why had Lebrett been looking for Dumont almost before the man escaped?

I could consider that later, for I saw that I was losing the First Lord's patience. For the time being, I battened my mouth and prepared to hear his instructions. Having a command of my own, I realized, had disaccustomed me from accepting nonsense from superiors. By way of clawing back favour I took an ostentatious sip of his beloved tea and made appreciative faces, though it was in truth a feeble brew which he did not even sweeten with sugar.

'I will not presume to tell you how to accomplish your vital task, for I have great confidence that your ingenuity will carry the day.'

Few people had ever expressed such confidence in me; fewer still had been vindicated by it.

'As you are temporarily under Admiralty orders, you will make report of your progress here at Whitehall. My clerk will take the particulars.' He leaned forward, his face pursing with the effort. 'You cannot fail, Lieutenant. Too much depends upon your mission for that to be allowed. Be assured that you will answer for it if you do.' His eyes flickered across to my uncle. 'You, and your superiors.'

He did not stand, but I sensed the interview was concluded and rose from my chair. The plush carpet deadened my footfall as I walked the long length of the room, and the only sound I could hear was the creak of the wind gauge changing course, and the delicate ring of the First Lord's teacup. Doubtless it was a genteel noise which would echo in every respectable drawing room that day, but to me it sounded more like the bells of St Sepulchre, tolling for my soul.

8

There was no-one to escort me out, and I pushed through the hurrying officials in an isolated daze, wondering what new calamity might befall me next. There are some sounds, however, that will call any man from his thoughts, and my uncle's voice was one: he did not need to speak more than once to seize my attention.

I turned on the stairs. Even in my bleak mood, I was astonished by how quickly fresh disaster had manifested itself, but my uncle, uncharacteristically, did not radiate displeasure. Instead, he advanced slowly down the stairs, seeming almost furtive, though the voice that he used like a cannon did not lend itself to subtlety.

'Jerrold,' he barked. 'Come with me.'

It seemed the First Lord's threats had acted as a spur to his ill humour rather than a bridle, but I had little choice: I let him sweep ahead of me, out past the doorman and across the courtyard into the thriving street beyond. Nothing so vulgar as mere humanity could brake my uncle, and I toiled to keep close behind him as he drove a path through the crowd. We were retracing our steps, I saw, turning right at Charing Cross into the Strand, and then left up a narrow side-street where the crowds were thinner. So fanciful had my thoughts become that I almost feared he might be leading me into a hidden alley, where he could remove my blighted name from the family escutcheon once and for all.

Less dramatically, and more hospitably, he brought me into a coffee shop. It was a humble place, with bare wooden floors and splintering chairs, but it seemed he was well known there, and despite the crowded custom a table was found for us in a dim corner. Without prompting, a thin man in an apron fetched two steaming cups of coffee and set them before us.

My uncle stirred his drink, then looked up at me. I felt a fresh draught of panic, to be seated so close opposite him with no ready means of escape; I bit my lip and squirmed in my seat, and waited for his judgement.

'Jerrold.' He said the name as Sisyphus might have spoken of boulders. Normally a few reflections on my character would have followed, but he seemed too weary to indulge such habits. He puffed up his scarlet cheeks, and pressed the air out through his lips. 'I doubt you ever expected you would be charged with an errand by the First Lord himself.'

I doubt my uncle had ever expected it either.

'So it was the First Lord?' I asked.

My uncle nodded lugubriously, his chins working like bellows. 'Indeed. How did you find him?'

Apart from truly mortal hazards, there are few things more dangerous in the navy than being drawn for an opinion of your superior. 'He seemed . . . fond of his tea,' I said carefully.

'Hah! Fond of his milksop concoction indeed. No stomach for anything stronger.' My uncle took a firm gulp of his coffee, as if in demonstration of his own, superior digestion. 'Man came in with his Foxite friends and hasn't stopped making mischief since. Won't stop until he's ruined the navy – and the army and the country too, the worm.'

'Does he . . . ?'

My uncle's spleen needed no prompt. 'Wants to pack the fleet with papists and Irishmen. The poltroon doesn't even believe in war with France – claims it's a waste of money, if you can imagine such a thing. And if he has his way further, he'll hand over the country to the rabble, give every rustic with half a farthing a say in Parliament – women and dogs too, I shouldn't wonder.' He pressed his elbows on the table and rose forward, like a hawk launching itself into flight. 'Why spend a lifetime trying to unseat that Corsican ogre Buonaparte, if men like the First Lord would have us live like Frenchmen? And,' he concluded, his face turning a dangerous shade of crimson, 'not content with seeing Romish cut-throats taking the King's commission, he wants to pack the Admiralty with his party lickspittles and toadies.'

Had I not had two very large, very angry eyes drilling into me, I might have laughed. Though I well believed my uncle's indignation was unfeigned on the subject of Catholics, Irishmen, Foxites, republicans, Jacobins, democrats and other vermin, I could see what must truly have sparked his fury. If the new First Lord wanted to load the Admiralty with his own followers, at the expense of those who had adhered to the old ministry, then I was not the only man whose career hung by a thread. And if there was one danger certain to bring out the full, almighty force of my uncle's wrath, it was a threat to his lofty position.

'Of course,' I said thoughtfully, 'the First Lord does have his supporters. He has, after all, just increased my pay by a full shilling a day.'

A fat finger stabbed out at me, almost breaking the bridge of my nose. 'That is precisely the gratuitous excess for which he and his friends are famed. They buy popularity among the credulous and venal, so that none will stand on principle to defy their disastrous schemes. I dare say I should have known better than to think you might see beyond such shameless inducements. Though having taken the First Lord's bounty, the least you might have done is spend it on a respectable suit of clothes, rather than those ridiculous shoes.'

I had feared he would find occasion to comment on my attire, which was now beginning to emit small curls of steam – whether from the heat of the close room or my uncle's scorching words, I could not tell. But it would afford neither of us any benefit denouncing patronage, for we were each as bound to it as the other. I tried to return our conversation to more fertile grounds.

'How do we proceed?'

My uncle set his cup on the table, with such force I was surprised the handle did not snap off. 'How do *you* proceed? You will find this villain Frenchman, you will load him with enough irons to sink a first rate, and you will bring him to me. In confidence.' His broad hand slapped against the arm of his chair to punctuate each step of this optimistic plan. 'Then we will see how much the good Mr Grey and his party value it. With luck, it may cause him to choke on his precious tea.'

I did not bother to enquire how my uncle expected me to find Dumont in a city of a million souls, for I saw that he, like his superiors, would delegate such details to me. But it seemed I would shorten the odds a great deal if I understood why, in little more than a day, Dumont's escape had resonated from Chatham to Whitehall.

'How is it, do you suppose, Uncle, that a single French sailor can have our government in such disorder? And what do they know of him, or his intentions, that so alarms them?'

My uncle shrugged his shoulders dismissively. Clearly this too could be considered my domain, if it did not immediately threaten his office. 'How they discovered this egregious toad's significance I do not know – doubtless through the usual secret channels.' That drew a thought in my mind, though I put it aside for later consideration. 'As for what the rogue intends, it hardly signifies: what could a single sailor achieve while in hiding in a foreign country? Doubtless some excitable spy has fed them a tale of *agents-provocateurs*, or assassins, or the usual nonsense, and the poltroons at Westminster are petrified that it will reflect ill on them if it is known he has escaped their captivity. In between packing the navy with papists and dismissing half our army, they cannot be shown to have utterly failed in the restraint of the thousands of enemy prisoners we keep on our shores. Consider the capital their opponents would make of that.'

It was an assessment typical of my uncle: unimaginative, and steeped in politics. 'But if that's true,' I objected, 'then why should you want Dumont found? I should have thought you would be happy to see Fox and his friends gone from government.'

My uncle hissed a sigh. 'In the unlikely and frankly unfortunate event that you should ever reach a position of rank, Jerrold, you will perhaps learn a simple truth. Governments come and go as the King decides: we who serve must endure regardless. If this government falls, you may be certain that they will take me over the precipice with them. Most especially if they have your incompetence and failure to prod me with.'

I could see his predicament, bound to a government he roundly despised yet clinging to his office throughout. But he was wrong on one point – it would need no great string of promotions for me to see the prime importance of endurance, for I had had my fingernails dug into the crumbling wall of survival since first I was rated midshipman. What surprised me, and in sobering fashion, was that even at his exalted station my uncle still suffered the same anxiety. I had assumed that at some distant stage I might advance beyond it.

Whatever the truth of the matter, I would not advance further than a court martial if I could not find the errant

Frenchman at the root of this disaster, impossible though that task might be. The same thought must have struck my uncle, for he abruptly pushed back his chair and stood, spilling my untouched coffee across the table.

'I had best return to my office, before I find some Foxite leech has his name on it. I trust that with the stakes so high, you will manage more than your habitual catastrophes.'

He did not sound as though he held much hope.

9

It was an astounding thought that my uncle's career rested in my hands – for how many long years had the reverse been true? – but I could not savour the moment, for I was as much in the mire as he. Though I valued my employment infinitely less than he did, I could ill afford to incur the wrath of the most powerful men in the country, let alone my uncle's fury. And I did not doubt that at some moment, doubtless inopportune, Lebrett would make an inimical reappearance.

Yet I was little inclined to fight their cause if it was all merely the factional manoeuvring that my uncle inferred. It seemed an unlikely idea, but I could think of no other reason why a single Frenchman might be deemed such a hazard, and I trusted my uncle to read the pulse of the body politic with fair accuracy. Yet there seemed too many questions outstanding for that to be the complete explanation, and I had little conception of how even to begin to answer them.

I did, however, have one card to play. My uncle's cursory reference to secret channels had reminded me of someone: a man who, in my brief experience of him, kept remarkably well abreast of others' private business. What he would divulge I could not tell, for he was niggardly with his intelligence unless it suited his purposes, but with him I began with one inestimable advantage: at least I knew where to seek him.

A few enquiries of the other patrons at the coffee shop set my course, and though it seemed that a single road would bring me straight to my destination, it took the better part of an hour to manage the two miles' distance. Nor did I want for diversion en route, for on that one street was housed every flavour of the nation's affairs: the flash shops of the Strand and the monumental edifice of the Bank of England; the churches and cathedrals dedicated variously to the Saints Clement, Mary, Dunstan and Paul; the fragrant Inns of Court and the stinking Fleet Prison. To which august list I could append, in an imposing building on Lombard Street, the Post Office.

I was glad to arrive there, for my shoes were no more practical than tasteful. Even so, it was no easy matter to push my way through the rows of waiting coaches, their horses pawing urgently at the ground, and the throng of postmen in their royal livery. Inside was even greater pandemonium: porters heaved great sacks of correspondence on their shoulders and upturned them onto broad tables, where nimble-fingered clerks dealt them out like the sharpest of card-smiths. Before them, sitting on a stool behind a high desk, a white-haired secretary kept a jealous eye on every coming and going. I doubted I would progress far without his leave, and as I needed direction, I approached his perch like an advocate to the bar.

'Good morning,' I greeted him, hoping that the bulk of his desk would blind him to my ragged attire.

I got no further, for immediately he had lifted a silver watch into the air before him and snapped open its case. He peered at the dial between his ink-stained fingers, with the air of one who did not lightly give credence to any man.

'Good afternoon,' he said crisply. 'It is half-past the hour. If you have letters, you may deposit them as directed.

London, Country, Colonial and Irish posts are to your left. Scottish, Bye and Cross posts to your right. Foreign post you may leave with me.'

He detailed the instructions with almost mechanical precision, as if measuring each word against the beat of his watch.

'Actually, sir, I have no correspondence. I am looking for a man.'

'A man?' His tone implied I might as well seek a mermaid.

'A man who works here. His name is Nevell.'

The secretary raised his head in exalted thought, so that I could see little more than his nostrils twitching above me. He licked a finger, and began turning the pages of a thick ledger.

'We employ no Mr Nevell,' he informed me, removing his spectacles. 'Nairn, Naughton, Niddle. No Nevell.'

'Oh.' I could not dare suggest that his list might be incomplete, especially as I had not spoken with Nevell in months. He might have left the Post Office long since. And yet, if he were still in the same business as before, I supposed it entirely possible that his name might have escaped the orthodoxy of official lists.

'Mr Nevell worked – works – in rather sensitive affairs,' I tried. 'He might . . .'

I heard the neat slap of a book being closed. 'Sensitive affairs? You mean to say: *secrets*.' There was a guarded poise in the secretary's manner now.

'Secrets, exactly. Would you know . . . ?'

'He may well work for the Secret Office.'

That sounded very much the sort of place where Nevell would work. 'Where might I find this secret office?' I looked about the bustling hall: dozens of doors led away in every direction, but though some bore the names of officials or departments, none proclaimed itself to be secret.

Behind the glass of his spectacles, the secretary's eyes narrowed. 'The location of the Secret Office is, perforce, secret.'

'I understand that. But I must speak to—'

'The identities of its staff – if indeed such there are – are equally secret.'

'Yes, but—'

'It would of course be superfluous to mention the reasons for this secrecy.'

'Of course.'

'So you see I could not direct you to your Mr Greville—'

'Nevell.'

'Even if I so desired.'

The din of my surrounds seemed to hammer on my ears. Nevell had been my one vague hope for finding Dumont, and this obstinate secretary was strangling that chance with officious protocol.

'Can you at least tell me if Nevell is here today?' I implored him, trying to find a gap in his punctilious armour.

'If Nevell is where?'

'Here. Or at the Secret Office? Or . . .' I surrendered to the fixity of the secretary's stare. 'May I at least leave a note for him?'

'You may write him a letter,' said the secretary brightly. 'You will find an inkstand under that window.'

'And paper?'

'There is a stationer's across the road which will supply the necessaries.'

A quarter of an hour later, and a few pennies poorer, I returned to the desk. The secretary looked disdainfully at the folded paper I handed him, and did not take it from my hands.

'You have not paid the postage,' he informed me. Though he was a peculiarly joyless specimen of humanity,

110

I fancied he had begun to take a personal interest in my travails. Not, I feared, a benign interest.

'How much will it cost?' The little purse that I had carried with me from the *Prometheus* was almost empty, and I would have felt not the least surprise had it transpired that the stamps for my letter demanded a farthing more than my means.

'Fourpence.'

I fumbled for the coins, but the secretary had elevated his gaze and refused even to see my money.

'You will pay the clerk over there.' A black finger extended across the room to another desk, where a thin queue of men and women clutched their letters. I turned to join them.

'One last thing,' I said, looking back to the secretary. 'If you should see Mr Nevell before my letter reaches him – ' if indeed a letter addressed to *Mr Nevell, The Secret Office*, ever reached its target – 'tell him that Martin Jerrold asked after him. He may find me at Mrs McCaird's boarding house, on Burleigh Street.'

If the secretary intended to treat this information more sympathetically than any other of my pleas, he kept it well hidden.

Having waited my turn, paid my postage and deposited the letter in the correct box, I emerged into Lombard Street. The bells of the adjoining church were chiming the half-hour – half-past one, I realized – and though it was early for dinner, my many exertions and dismal breakfast left me much in need of nourishment. A stallholder across the road was bellowing the merits of his meat pies, and I had just enough coins in my purse to procure one. I stepped forward, but was immediately checked as a steady hand grasped my collar from behind.

It needed only the briefest touch of those fingers on my neck to spin me around in terror, for I knew all too well the ugly tales of robberies and worse which pervaded London. I had only a few pennies and an unwanted razor to steal, but that did not lessen my fear of falling victim to such vagabonds. Would my meagre belongings satisfy them, these desperadoes who could strike on a public thoroughfare in daylight, or would I find my razor's blade sliding across my throat like the poor carpenter's apprentice?

The hand slipped from my shoulder as I turned around, and I looked into a pair of amused blue eyes. His coat was the colour of claret, and his breeches a spotless white despite the grime of the city. His brown hair had been cut shorter since I last saw him, but the quizzical smile, and the watchful confidence, were as evident as ever in his young face.

'Nevell,' I said, as calm as I could manage. Frustration at the hour I had wasted with the clerk, and the lingering pangs of my fear of assault, stifled my warmth a little. 'It seems the Post Office have outdone themselves in delivering my letter. I don't suppose it's a coincidence you've found me here?'

Nevell's smile broadened. 'The door clerk sent word that you had enquired after me.'

I scowled. 'He claimed never to have known you.'

'Come, Jerrold.' Nevell touched my arm lightly, though I saw in his face that he would not pursue this exchange. 'The doormen guard us jealously – and with reason. In fact, you would not have been treated nearly so courteously had I not warned them to look out for you.'

I struggled to decide whether he spoke in earnest or deep sarcasm. 'You told them to look out for me? But how did you know . . . ?'

'How did I know you would come?' Nevell gave me a look that would have addled a sphinx. 'Come inside, and I shall explain.'

That I very much disbelieved, but I followed him around the corner, away from the main gate, and down a narrow lane. Most of it was hemmed in by the high wall of the Post Office, but a handful of small houses had managed to intrude into the gaps. It was one of these that Nevell approached, a whitewashed building which looked more like Mrs McCaird's lodging house than a secret office. Curtains were drawn across the windows, and the bright blue door seemed to have neither knocker, handle nor keyhole, yet it swung in silently before Nevell had touched it. We stepped through into a dim corridor, which despite the unaided opening of the door was entirely empty, and mounted a steep staircase at its end.

'It may be a secret office,' I observed to Nevell, 'but hardly safe. What if I had simply walked in here from the street?'

Nevell looked back, a pained expression on his face. 'That would have been unwise.'

Another door met us at the top of the stairs, this one with a brass lock set in it, but Nevell already had a key out and was turning it. I had to step back as the door opened towards us, for it brought with it a gush of foul vapour as if something was being singed, smoked and boiled in vinegar all at once. I wrinkled my nose and breathed through my mouth, and followed Nevell into the Secret Office.

I do not know what exactly my expectations had been, but the reality certainly disappointed them. It seemed more like a curiosity shop than a hive of deceit and skulduggery, all permeated with the thick, acrid air I had smelled from the door. In a succession of three small rooms, half a dozen men sat or stood at tables laden with all manner of apparatus. A beetroot-coloured liquid simmered in a kettle atop a coal stove, while on the bench beside it were arrayed scores of bottles and vials, each labelled in scrawny letters. 'Phosphatic Acid', read one; 'Gum Fabaceae', another. One man sat before a tray full of seals and waxes, peering at them through a thick monocle; another was dripping liquid onto a sheet of copper which sizzled and hissed and steamed with the impact. In the centre of one room was an enormous iron machine, the bastard offspring of a mangle and a pumping engine, and elsewhere an entire wall was given over to every shade of ink imaginable in tightly corked jars. Yet another room was lined with books: lexicons and grammars of all the principal languages and well-thumbed works of poetry and literature – Shakespeare alone seemed worthy of seven editions. Three men sat at a desk in this room with pens and ink, apparently making duplicates of letters that lay before them, and to my inexact eye they seemed to approach their task with the studied concentration of the artist rather than the bored routine of the copy-clerk.

Ignoring all these mysteries, and doubtless many more which escaped me, Nevell brought us at last into a small room, where a single desk sat under a broad skylight. A few prints hung on the walls – mostly savage cartoons, which I was surprised his masters tolerated – and there was a low bookshelf in one corner, but otherwise it was uncluttered. A wooden trolley sagged under a pile of folios, ledgers and sheaves of paper beside the desk, while behind it was a simple, wing-backed chair. Nevell eased himself into it, and waved me to sit opposite.

'Welcome to the Secret Office,' he said crisply, rummaging inside one of his drawers and emerging with two tumblers and a decanter. 'Few men know of its existence. Fewer still are ever admitted.'

Doubtless I should have felt gratitude for the confidence, but I was more interested by my drink. I sniffed it carefully, remembering the jars of sinister liquid in the outer rooms, but it smelled no more dangerous than brandy.

Nevell must have observed my equivocation, uncharacteristic in the face of liquors. 'It's perfectly safe,' he assured me with a smile. 'French. A souvenir of our adventure in Dover, in fact.'

That prompted more memories than I cared to recall,

though not so many that I refused his offer of a second measure when the first was gone.

'I take it,' I began, 'that you did not bring me here to reminisce the downfall of Mr Drake.'

'No.'

'Yet you said you had told the secretary to expect me. I myself did not know I would be coming here until barely two hours ago. How could you possibly . . . ?'

Nevell, who had been shuffling through some of the documents by his desk, looked up. 'I told the secretary to keep watch for you. I did not expect you, exactly; rather, I suspected you would turn up eventually.'

'But why? How? How did you even know I was in London?'

Nevell passed a single sheet of paper across to me. 'This arrived here this morning. I suspected you would soon follow.'

Private and Most Secret, I read.

Nevell lifted his hands in permission.

A French prisoner of war, M. Dumont, has escaped from aboard the Prometheus *hulk near Chatham, Martin Jerrold, Captain, and is believed to have made for London. This Dumont representing a grave and dangerous threat to our nation, you are hereby directed to use all the powers of your Office to apprehend him, and render his person into His Majesty's confinement. Any such discoveries as you may make are to be reported, promptly and in person, to the Secretary of State.*

The signature was illegible, but I did not doubt it was authentic. I put the paper down and looked at Nevell, who was watching me carefully from across the desk.

'This came this morning, you say?' I scratched my temple. 'Lebrett must have gone straight to his superiors last night.'

'Who?' Nevell was, as ever, quick to pounce on any scrap of fact.

'Major Lebrett. A Guards officer. He arrived in Chatham yesterday morning looking for Dumont.' I did not care to think about Lebrett; I glanced back down at the letter. '*A grave and dangerous threat.* But this does not explain what that threat might be, why Dumont commands so much panic in our halls of government. What does he signify?'

Nevell let his head loll against the wing of his chair. 'I had rather hoped, Jerrold, that you would answer that yourself. All the intelligence I have been given is written on that paper. Naturally, I am not completely blindfolded – there are various channels that I may choose to pursue.' He poured me another brandy, almost draining the decanter. 'But perhaps it would be best if you told me what you know thus far.'

I gripped my glass tighter, and began to recount the extraordinary misery of the past two days. In view of how little I knew, it took a surprising time to tell. I told of Dumont's escape, omitting only the precise manner in which he had obtained Isobel's clothes; how Lebrett had appeared like a vengeful demon the next morning demanding to see Dumont, and how he had forced Captain Hutchinson to suspend my command when the prisoner was found missing.

'Major Lebrett arrived seeking Dumont before it was known he had escaped?' Nevell interrupted.

'Yes.' It was a curiosity that had played in the back of my thoughts for some time, though I had not yet managed to make anything of it.

'So Dumont had significance to someone – or some persons – even in captivity.' Nevell was now sitting upright on his chair, his head snapping about like a pennant in a squall. 'Who are Major Lebrett's superiors?'

I shrugged. 'He serves in the Horse Guards.'

'So someone in the army knew that Dumont was a

danger and was likely to escape. Or else, that the danger existed even in your prison ship.'

I thought back to the rotting *Prometheus*, her nail-studded bulwarks, her barred scuttles, her melancholy occupants, and wondered what Dumont could possibly have achieved there. 'I suppose he could have cut my throat,' I ventured. I doubted the Secretary of State would have appreciated that to be a grave and dangerous threat.

Nevell graciously forbore from comment, and waved me to continue my story. I explained how I had found the carpenter's apprentice dead in a pit, how we had patrolled the road in vain, and the final lunacy of our chase through the moonlit marshes. By the time I had finished the brandy was gone, though I did not remember drinking it.

Once again, Nevell's interest had been pricked. 'He spoke in French, you say, this man you hunted through the swamp?'

'As best I could tell. I did not sit there with a dictionary and a copyist.'

'And the fact that a lone Frenchman was at large in Kent did not strike you as odd?'

I threw up my hands in frustration. 'The circumstances did not admit to much contemplation. All I cared was that it was not Dumont, and an hour later I was locked in a coach with Lebrett and being kidnapped away to London. Of course it was odd – but no more so than anything else which happened that day.'

Nevell had the grace to affect humility. 'Of course, Jerrold, my apologies. But it does imply, do you not think, that Dumont may have had accomplices? Unless there were other prisoners aboard?'

'None from my ship.'

'So if we assume that the Frenchman you killed in the marsh was there to assist Dumont, then we can infer that whatever his purpose, it has significance for Buonaparte and his government.' Nevell had hopped out of his chair and was pacing about. 'Something more complicated than a sailor trying to escape home across the Channel.'

I remembered my uncle's cursory opinion that the government merely wished to avoid embarrassment while trying to impose its reforms on the military. It had seemed improbable to me then, and if the Frenchman in the mud had been Dumont's accomplice, then there must certainly be deeper currents at work. Which left the outstanding question: 'What is it that he intends?'

Nevell sat down again, rubbing a quill pen between two fingers. 'We return whence we began.' I saw him hesitate a moment, his breath checked while his mind turned. I had seen it before, and guessed he was preparing himself to divulge some secret.

'Of course, the curious thing is that we'd taken an interest in Dumont once before.'

'What? You knew he was a danger? And you left me to make him my interpreter, give him the run of my ship?'

Nevell sucked his lips together. 'Not at all. But we had suspicions. There were tell-tale signs, peculiarities, anomalies to which we are sensitive.'

'What *peculiarities?*' The whole government seemed united in securing my ignorance, distress and downfall, and I felt bitter anger that the one man I had esteemed my ally had now become a part of it.

'Be calm, Jerrold. There was no injury intended to you. They were merely the least signals, the stirring of leaves in the wind that might presage equally a storm or an evening breeze.'

'Spare me your poetry.'

'Very well – it was this.' Nevell leaned across his desk and extracted a slim book, bound in brown leather. I took it from his grasp, and turned to the title page.

'*Pharsalia de Lucan,*' I read. '*Traduit du Latin Original.* Is this the vital clue?'

118

'I told you it would appear insubstantial. As you can see, it is an edition of Lucan's history of the Roman civil wars translated into French. It was sent from France with a note from his mother, expressing her hope that it would ease his solitude.'

'But you stole it?'

'We borrowed it.' Nevell pressed forward on his elbows. 'Surely you see that a book sent to a Frenchman in England suggests only one thing.'

'That he has an interest in classical history?'

'That it is the key to a cipher, so that he may receive messages in code.'

Involuntarily, I dropped the book on the desk. With its elegant binding and marbled edges, it did not look like the primer of espionage.

'And have you used it to decipher any correspondence which would aid us?' It seemed that he should have said so if he had, but there was no accounting for the cards which Nevell refused to show.

'We have not. This came to us three weeks ago, and there has been nothing since.'

'Perhaps,' I reflected, 'its failure to arrive was noted, and they were alerted that you were aware of the stratagem.'

'Perhaps.' A hint of Nevell's usual vigour returned. 'But we took precautions. We forwarded Dumont one of . . . these.'

He pulled another book off the trolley and held it open for me to see. It was less professionally bound, and written by hand, but the ink was fresh and clear for me to read.

'*Vrai Histoire de Lucian*.' My voice betrayed my continuing puzzlement.

'Lucian,' said Nevell briskly. 'Instead of the Roman historian Lucan, we sent him the Greek satirist Lucian. Any message he received would have translated into gibberish, while we retained the proper key. And if he ever managed to query it with his masters in Paris – unlikely,

119

you'll agree – they could assume that an idle clerk who didn't know his Lucan from his Lucian had made the error.'

'But all this was in vain. No letters were sent.'

'No letters were sent *after* the book. But it remains entirely possible that they were sent beforehand. We cannot read the compassionate correspondence of every French prisoner in the hulks, much though we might like it, and any number of coded letters might have slipped through our net in advance of the cipher. Thus, even if we found the Lucan, we would not be able to use it.' He put the two classical works back in their position on the trolley. 'Did Dumont receive much correspondence, do you recall?'

I thought back to the bundle of papers I had examined in his cabin, berating myself for not having looked closer. 'He did. Some of his own, but many for the other men. As the translator, he had access to pen and ink: almost every letter on the ship must have passed through his hands.'

'Damn.' Nevell rapped a boot against the foot of his desk. 'Well, I have already asked the Admiralty to telegraph to Chatham and have Dumont's papers and effects sent here for examination. Perhaps that will turn something up.'

I did not care to admit that I had already examined Dumont's effects, for I knew it would provoke further questions which I would ill be able to answer. 'What might a coded letter look like?' I asked, feigning innocence.

Nevell looked at me crookedly. 'It could look like any other correspondence, from an invitation for dinner to a discourse on astronomy. But using a book as a key, you might expect something containing numbers, so as to indicate pages or words in lines.' He raised his eyebrows. 'Or not. If there were an accepted form for ciphers, Jerrold, it would hardly make for well-kept secrets.'

I barely heard his last words, for something he said had scratched at a dimly held memory. I thought back to the

cramped cabin aboard the *Prometheus*, to the confusion of
the day when Dumont escaped. I had searched his
belongings and found nothing. But there had been
his clothes, discarded under his cot when he dressed himself as Isobel. And between the unpicked threads of his
coat, I remembered, a packet which rustled.

'There *was* something,' I exclaimed. 'A letter from his
mother, sewn into the lining of his coat. A list of the letters
she had sent him. And some gibberish scrawled on the
back.'

'Gibberish?' Nevell almost bounced from his chair in
excitement. 'What manner of gibberish? And where is this
letter now?'

Such was the force of his voice that for a moment I was
quite frozen by its impact; his last question echoed around
the hollows of my mind. But gradually a warm sun of hope
began to dawn on me. I had been reading the letter aboard
Prometheus, I remembered, and had jammed it in my pocket
when Lebrett arrived. The maid had found it there in the
laundry, and returned it to me at breakfast.

I squirmed in my chair to free the opening of my pocket,
squeezed my hand in and felt the smooth crease of a folded
paper. I tugged it out, and handed it wordlessly across the
table.

Nevell held it out before him to catch the sun from the
skylight, and scanned its contents. He harrumphed under
his breath when he saw the meaningless phrases scribbled
on the underside, but otherwise said nothing as he picked
up two small books – the Roman Lucan and the Greek
Lucian – and disappeared into the room beyond. When he
returned, his hands were empty.

'I do not suppose you removed any other papers by
accident,' he said conversationally.

I glared at him. 'If you had been in my shoes, Nevell—'

'I would limp from the weight of those buckles.'

'You would count yourself lucky to remember your own

name.' I thought back on memories that had been all but driven out by subsequent events. 'The coat had been unstitched when I found it, yet that letter was still within. I wondered if perhaps there had been other documents he removed and took with him.'

Nevell frowned. 'It's an obvious hiding place. He might have hidden his money, or false certificates, or other papers he needed for his escape.'

'Or,' I countered, 'they could have been documents of great value to him.' I dug through my memories, turning them over to recall what the other prisoners had said. 'His fellow captives claimed he had spoken of having papers, secret papers that would help him escape . . . or some such boast. Papers he always kept on his person.'

'Where did they come from?'

'There was a woman, I think. A woman who visited him often. My informant implied she had given him the papers.'

Nevell sighed, blowing a haunting whistle through his lips. 'A messenger. A secret confidante. No wonder we never intercepted his letters. Did you learn her name?'

I shook my head. 'I believe the master kept a record of all visitors who called aboard the ship, lest the prisoners use them to upset the muster count, but I had no opportunity to check.' I paused, laying together my thoughts like dominoes. 'If he kept these documents so carefully hidden, and believed they would secure his freedom, then perhaps *they*, not he, are our true quarry. They may be . . .' I conjured my imagination. 'They may be secret plans, of vital importance to Buonaparte, stolen from the Admiralty or the Horse Guards. That would explain the First Lord's interest – and Major Lebrett's.' Every guess begged a hundred further questions, but I felt that with each thought I moved further through the labyrinth. 'What do we know of Dumont's past, anyway – was he captured at sea, or had he been at large in England before?'

I fell silent as I noticed that Nevell seemed to be paying me not the least heed; he had stood, and was staring up at the skylight rapt in concentration.

'Dumont had been aboard the *Prometheus* for several months,' he said absently. 'Surely the government would have stirred itself to action earlier if they had lost papers of such significance.'

'Then perhaps his lady visitor brought them to him.'

This time I did draw Nevell's attention, though it was hardly an admiring gaze. 'If you had succeeded in stealing these important plans which you surmise to have existed, plans clearly of immediate urgency, would you put them aboard an English prison ship for safe keeping?'

I had to confess I would not.

'It seems more probable to me,' Nevell continued, 'that these papers were brought to him to aid his escape – passports or money or suchlike. Or perhaps they were instructions for his own mission. Think of the number of accomplices involved, Jerrold: there was the woman who brought him the letters, the unnamed Frenchman whom you killed in the marshes, and who knows what others. The French would hardly have used so many valuable agents merely to bring a sailor home. They must have had – or have – some purpose with him, of which our government is aware and which it fears mightily. But what that purpose is . . .'

He trailed off into silence as a knock sounded at the door, and an elderly man shuffled in with books and papers in his knotted hands. The cuffs and elbows on his coat were worn down to their threads, and despite the fine summer weather his skin was sallow. He walked with a stoop, and would not meet my eye as he deposited his load on the desk, accepted Nevell's thanks and disappeared out of the room.

Nevell lifted one of the papers he had brought, cleaner and fresher than the others, and read it intently.

'The letter was in code,' he announced, with rather less ceremony than such a discovery was due. 'Obvious, really – almost clumsy. Half the dates it gave for the letters Dumont had purportedly been sent were months before he was even captured. I suppose you noticed that, Jerrold?'

I made a noncommittal noise. 'But what does it say?'

All Nevell's former urgency was gone, and he rested back in his chair as he held the decipherer's notes between his fingers. 'That depends. If you apply the code to Lucian, it says, *Of generous many kissed worry cities rivers seas. One had woman were carried loving. Many come carried come.*' He looked at me over the top of the paper. 'Hardly edifying – no wonder Dumont was perplexed. If, however, you use the Lucan we intercepted, it reads thus: *The emperor knows your predicament and will relieve you. Await the coming of our agent. You must trust him, for your mission must be victorious.*'

I pondered the message. There was an ineluctable thrill in finding coded references to the emperor, Buonaparte himself, and to missions of the first importance. But that excitement soon faded, leaving only a residue of anxiety.

'I do not see that this tells us much we did not know. It confirms that there were men sent to find Dumont, and that he does indeed have some nefarious purpose. It changes little: what doubt we lose is replaced by worry.'

'Yet it does not seem from this that Dumont's imprisonment was planned.' Nevell appeared to be thinking aloud, a most peculiar habit to observe in him. '*The emperor knows your predicament and will relieve you.* That evinces a plan gone awry to me. And if they can bring their agents into the country, why risk the dangers of adding an escaped convict to their number, with all the attendant chase and alarms?'

'Of course,' I pointed out, 'Dumont never knew this letter's true contents.'

'No. But if there were secret couriers, this woman whom you say visited him, then who can guess what he knew.' As he spoke, Nevell reached into another pile of documents and extracted an oilskin pouch, sliced open, from which he pulled another folded paper. 'Dumont was captured at sea in November. The ship had escaped after Trafalgar, but was brought to account soon after.' Nevell's eyes flicked over a page of tedious naval detail in silence. 'Dumont was brought ashore early this year and sent straight to the *Prometheus*, where he remained until this week.'

'If the French intended Dumont to perform some despicable service against the British nation, they could have done better than sending him into the charnel of Trafalgar.'

'I agree. So whatever their intent, they must have fixed on him after his capture. Once he was in the hulk.'

His logic was unimpeachable, and wholly unintelligible. 'What could they possibly hope for from a prisoner on a hulk? That he would dress up in the captain's lady's clothes and effect an escape?'

I could not see that we had progressed at all, but a thin smile had appeared on Nevell's lips, and his eyes were more settled than I had seen all afternoon. 'What indeed might they hope for from a prisoner on a hulk?' he repeated. 'A prisoner whose mission was of personal importance to Buonaparte himself, and of terrifying concern to our government. A prisoner who merited several agents to abet his escape. What indeed?'

'What indeed?'

'We shall see.' Nevell stood, and this time I sensed it was with finality rather than energy. 'I have some enquiries to make now, Jerrold. I will call at your boarding house tomorrow after breakfast. Perhaps by then we will have some better idea of Dumont's purpose – and even his whereabouts.'

'A final thought,' I said, stepping towards the door. 'Apart from the cipher key, you had no evidence against Dumont until this morning?'

Nevell hesitated uneasily. 'Nothing specific. But if you

feel we should have known more, you must recollect that we are a small office with an enormous task, and . . .'

I shook my head impatiently. 'I meant no slight. But three departments of government have been ordered to pursue Dumont with extraordinary despatch, and from the highest ranks. I have been directly instructed by the First Lord of the Admiralty, you by the Home Secretary, and Major Lebrett by whom we cannot guess.'

'Yes.'

'If you who watched Dumont's correspondence and I who was his gaoler harboured so few suspicions, how did the *cabinet* come to learn of the danger?'

It was an unsettling question to which Nevell gave no answer. And more unsettling still, I reflected, I did not think he had an answer to give.

10

Nevell insisted on seeing me out to the street – 'You might not be safe trying to leave by yourself,' he told me – and waved me away.

'Shall I find you here again if I have news?' I asked.

'You would probably find the door locked.'

'Then how . . . ?'

'If there is anything of note to report, I will find you.' I did not recall having given him the address of my lodgings, but that did not seem to trouble him. 'And if you discover anything' – he seemed to rate this a less likely proposition – 'you can ask the door clerk.'

'And until then? How do you recommend I proceed?'

Nevell shrugged. 'I recommend you use your initiative, seek out the enemy, all those wise maxims of your immortal leader.'

Which was easy for him to say – looking at the so-called immortality that those maxims had brought Nelson, I was in no hurry to follow them. And for the moment, my initiative was urging me to engage at close quarters with some hot food and a clean razor.

I turned to say goodbye to Nevell, but he was no longer there. He had vanished noiselessly, presumably back behind his blue door. No matter: if I felt downcast that he had provided fewer answers than I had hoped, the needs of my stomach and a rising tide of weariness distracted my disappointment. I strode off into the thick London traffic, glad that the satisfaction of my appetites at least should be an attainable end.

Not so attainable, though, that it did not lead me a merry chase. None of the shopkeepers would give me a ha'penny's credit, and I had to pay a testing visit to my prize agent to plead for an advance before I could satisfy my famished stomach and restore some discipline to my whiskers. By the time I emerged from the barber's, my cheeks stinging and raw, the sun had been eclipsed by high buildings, and much of the street was in shade. When I turned to make my way back west the great dome of St Paul's was cosseted in a copper haze, and the raucous noises about me sounded more muted, more distant, as though the world was beginning to relax its grip on the day. Even the choking heat seemed to have melted from the air by the time I climbed the stairs to Mrs McCaird's front door.

The landlady was awaiting me in the hallway. 'You've some visitors,' she informed me, doubt plain in her floury face. 'In the parlour.'

I was sure she had spoken of visitors in the plural, but when I opened the parlour door I saw only a single figure standing by the mantelpiece. He seemed to be toying with his hair in the mirror, but he snapped about the moment he heard me and drew himself up menacingly. Though alone, he manifested enough sneering malevolence for several men.

'Lieutenant Jerrold.' It was extraordinary how Lebrett managed to pronounce my title as an affront. 'I instructed you to remain here until I summoned you, yet when I arrived you were absent.' He flicked his hand as though removing a mote of dust from his uniform. 'Do not attempt to defend yourself. I have had my fill of your paltry excuses.'

128

'I was summoned to the Admiralty to receive vital orders. From my superiors,' I added, trying to regroup my strength for indignation. 'The men whom I am actually *obliged* to obey.'

Lebrett's chin inclined upwards as he drew a deep, hissing breath. 'While Dumont remains at large by your failings, I will oblige you to answer to *me* and none other. Your superiors are as complicit as you in this disaster, and it will ill behove you to trust to their protection.'

I flopped onto Mrs McCaird's divan. 'And what is it that you want of me?'

'Require of you.' Lebrett crossed to the window and stared out at the street. 'I require you to be at hand when we find the villain Dumont, so as to identify him with confidence. You will not emerge lightly if he is lost a second time by your derelict sense of duty.'

I was quite sure I would not, but I did not have so much faith in Lebrett that I expected him to haul in Dumont by his own coarse methods. Nor did I think I would meet much success while Lebrett hid his hand from me and refused to divulge the dark conspiracies of which Dumont was suspected. But I doubted he would enlighten me in his present humour.

'So where next?' I asked, trying to balance the anger and submission in my voice.

'Nowhere next,' barked Lebrett. 'Stay here until I call for you, damn you. All else – the Admiralty, your superiors and your own discredited notions – you may ignore.'

And with nothing more useful to impart, he turned on the heel of his gleaming boot and marched out of the house. In the hallway, I saw the landlady watching me through the open door.

'You spoke of visitors, Mrs McCaird,' I said, remembering her earlier words. 'I trust he was the only one.' I doubted I could face another after Lebrett's brief onslaught.

To my concern, the landlady shook her head. 'There's another waiting for you.'

My head toppled forward in a silent plea for mercy. 'Where is he?'

'She.'

'What?' Unlikely though it seemed, perhaps my prayers had been answered. 'A lady?'

'A *woman*.' Mrs McCaird pursed her lips so tight they almost vanished. 'She took a room next to your own.'

Though I could not think of any women who might seek me in London, the prospect of a mysterious lady awaiting me in the bedroom was too tantalizing to ignore. If it scandalized Mrs McCaird, so much more promising. Forbearing from trying her dignity with further questions, I bounded up the stairs with more energy than I had felt in days, blind to any consideration of who this visitor might be. It could hardly be Isobel, for I had written of my whereabouts only that morning, and I doubted even Nevell could contrive a return post to Chatham so quickly. But anyone desiring to see me for purposes other than abuse and insult was exceedingly welcome; if she also chanced to be a woman, and perhaps tolerably pretty, then I must absolutely demand to meet her.

The landing at the top of the steps frustrated me a moment: the landlady had said the woman was in the adjacent room, but there were two doors beside my own, one to each side. I did not like to disturb the innocence of other guests, for I feared my standing with Mrs McCaird was already unsteady, so I resolved to visit my own room first. A splash of water and a moment of repose would be a mercy after my long day in the grubby city; I opened the door and stepped inside.

Two thoughts struck me almost immediately. The first, and lesser, was that the maid had clearly inferred that having spurned one of her services, I spurned them all, for the bed was still unmade and the mud still prominent on the carpet. That was an irritant, but hardly surprising. What did confound me was that sitting on the unruly sheets, her knees pulled up to her chest and a book resting between them, was the unexpected visitor who had drawn the landlady's disapproval. Not a lady, but Isobel.

Such was my shock that I spoke the first sentence that reached my mouth. 'You could at least have made the bed.'

She looked up, her dark eyes narrow as a cat's. 'You could at least have told me you'd left Chatham and taken a holiday to London.'

Her words were a cruel rebuff, colliding with my joy at seeing her and forcing me into an involuntary defence. 'I wrote to you as soon as I knew, which was this morning. I was taken away from *Prometheus* yesterday, sent scrambling around the countryside, and finally hauled into a carriage for London.'

Isobel looked at me with scorn. 'Hauled into a carriage? You're a captain, Martin, not a tar to be picked up by the press gang.' She leaned closer. 'Were you drunk?'

'Of course not.' I hoped Nevell's brandy was quite gone from my breath. 'And besides, I no longer have my command; I am a lieutenant again.' If she had thought that my honorary rank could protect me from disaster, she had obviously forgotten the general pattern of my luck.

'A lieutenant?' Isobel closed her book and looked up at me in confusion. 'What did you do?'

'Nothing,' I insisted, with more force than I had intended. 'I did nothing at all. One of the prisoners escaped – Dumont, the translator – and the next I knew a lunatic Guards officer had come aboard, taken away my ship and forced me to hunt out the scoundrel. I was not even granted time to warn Samuel.' I looked around the room cautiously. 'Is he here with you?'

Isobel's pert face was a raft of barely contained emotions. 'He isn't – I left him in Chatham. He sat on the dock five hours waiting for you before he came to find me.'

Little idiot. 'And how did you find me?' Belatedly, the obvious questions began to assert themselves. 'I wrote to you this morning, but surely you cannot have had the letter already?'

'I went to the dockyard. The captain wouldn't tell me a thing, but one of the marines said he'd seen you, said you'd gone to London. So I went to the inn and bought a seat on the first coach.' She smiled coyly, for the first time since I had arrived. 'Coachman gave me a shilling back from the fare 'cos of my distress.'

I sat down on the bed beside her and patted her hand, all indignation and rancour gone. The poor girl, I thought: she must have been quite vexed with worry for what might have befallen me. 'Did you fear for my safety, my poppet?' I asked gently. 'I know I should have got word to you, but really it was so overwhelming . . .'

'I thought you'd run away with someone else.' Isobel's interruption was sharp and unforgiving. 'Thought you'd left me in Chatham to go playing with some jade you found on the waterfront.'

I gaped at her. 'But how could you think so?' I remembered my encounter with the maid that morning and moderated my indignation a little, but still the insinuation stung. 'Surely Samuel told you what happened?'

'Samuel was as confused as me. And when they told me you'd left the ship because of some girl who escaped in the carpenter's boat, what else was I to think?' She was up on her knees now, swaying slightly with the give of the mattress under her, and sounding close to tears. 'You took up with one girl you found in a tavern, Martin – what's to say you won't take up with another? Or with a red-headed hussy who waits about in your room and never sees to the bedclothes?'

It seemed the maid had returned offering a second chance of her favours. I could only imagine what Isobel must have thought of it, but I did not try to explain, for I

132

knew by experience my protestations would only lend her suspicions more weight.

'The woman in the carpenter's boat was Dumont,' I told her. Quickly, I described how he had stolen her clothes and escaped in disguise.

'And the maid?' Isobel demanded.

'Just a girl who . . . who misunderstood me. Without the least provocation,' I added. 'She probably sought a more generous tip. A tip for tup, so to speak.'

'I'll tip her right enough,' said Isobel darkly, ignoring my joke.

'Anyway, did you truly believe that I would abandon you so callously?' Now that Isobel's anger had subsided, I was beginning to feel aggrieved at the depth of her suspicions. 'After all our time together?' In fact it had been only a few months that I had known Isobel – in both the scriptural and literal senses – but the ordeals we had endured in Dover, and the lack of any chaperone in Chatham, made it seem far longer. And against the time that other women had suffered my company, it was no small duration.

My question lingered unanswered, and I did not press it. Through my fading indignation, I sensed there were perhaps further worries that bedevilled Isobel, but she kept them uncharacteristically quiet, and I felt no need to open new wounds. When she reached forward to squeeze my thigh, I shuffled closer so that I leaned against her legs.

'Besides, you're here now,' I said. 'God knows how. How did you manage to find one man in a city of a million?' It was a pertinent question, and I was curious to hear her answer.

She raised her head knowingly. 'I went straight to the Admiralty.'

I froze. 'You didn't ask for my uncle, did you?' Even without his current mood, I trembled to imagine how he would react to finding a dubious girl, little more than an urchin, passing herself off as my cousin. Or, by implication, as his daughter.

'Of course not.' Isobel laughed, her good spirits returning. 'I didn't know his name.' She paused, awaiting a helpful interjection which I refused to offer. 'I found a clerk and got to talking with him, and he was nice as bingo.'

Somehow the conduct Isobel expected of me and the behaviour she evinced herself seemed curiously at odds, but I did not press the point. 'So you came here, and scandalized the landlady, and took the room next door,' I concluded.

'I could hardly pretend I was your *wife*, could I, Martin?'

'Perhaps you should practise.' I reached my hand up to caress her neck, and let my fingers trickle down over her collarbone and into those places which must have beguiled the Admiralty clerk. Giggling, Isobel snapped her teeth at me, then gasped as I pulled her legs away and left her flat on her back. She had already kicked her shoes off, and I tickled her feet mercilessly while she writhed and squirmed, before sliding my hand up into the mysteries of her skirts.

'This is a proper establishment,' whispered Isobel, in passable mimicry of the landlady's prim tone. 'Such things are quite out of the question.'

'Well, if you're too proud for me, perhaps I shall take my suit elsewhere,' I told her. I felt her body tense, and shrink under me. 'I'm sure a kind word and a naughty wink would work wonders on Mrs McCaird.'

Isobel laughed; a low, wicked laugh that had come to betoken all manner of delights. 'I couldn't have you doing that to her. She'd be on her deathbed at the very thought of it.'

'Then for the grace of her soul, you had better submit.'

So submit she did, though there was little submissive

134

about it. And if she gave fuller voice to her exertions than was prudent with Mrs McCaird downstairs, we had at least learned one lesson. This time, all our clothes stayed on.

11

Whatever affront we might have given Mrs McCaird, she can have had few complaints of our custom. We had paid for two rooms yet needed only one, though I did give the covers and bolsters in the adjacent room a quick shuffle to suggest that we had derived some value from them.

Sadly, Isobel's haste had precluded baggage, so I was condemned to another day in my disreputable attire. She knelt beside me and tried to pull on the breeches, which remained obstinately shrunken after their half-washing, but collapsed into laughter when she saw my shoes.

'What are you wearing?' she asked, rolling on the floor in exaggerated mirth. 'Even the flashest smuggler in Dover, with his ship just come in, wouldn't have been seen in those.'

'The cobbler assured me they were the height of fashion. And my only boots were parted in the depths of a bog.'

'Well, you'll never catch your Frenchman in those. He'll see those buckles shining like lighthouses before you're within half a mile of him.'

'That,' I said sourly, 'supposes that I will one day be lucky enough to get within half a mile of him.'

We descended – at an interval of five minutes – to the parlour, where Mrs McCaird had arrayed the breakfast.

There were few other guests in her house: a gentleman up from the country for a trial; a governess awaiting a new position; a merchant recently returned from the Baltic who talked endlessly of marmalade – and as they were more punctual risers than we, we soon had the table to ourselves.

'So,' said Isobel, cramming a wide piece of toast into her mouth, 'what are you going to do today?'

My ignorant silence was broken by a sound at the door, two sharp knocks in quick succession. I heard Mrs McCaird shouting for her maid, but evidently the girl was less prompt in her duties than her pleasures, for at length the landlady herself came bustling out of the kitchen.

'That'll be the postman,' she said over her shoulder. She disappeared into the hall and I heard the sounds of the door being opened, followed by expressions of consternation. It seemed she had engaged in an urgent conversation with her postman, though I could hear only one side of it, and that more in the muffled pitch of her voice than any distinct words. Whatever was being said, it must have mollified her, for the initial tones of strident agitation soon gave way to a more reserved formality, and eventually a warm, almost respectful tenor. I even thought I heard a laugh, which I could hardly allow from her character.

She reappeared in the doorway, obscuring my view of the figure in the passage behind her.

'Mr Jerrold,' she said, fractionally less severe than was her habit. 'You have a visitor.'

With a winning smile at Mrs McCaird and a raised eyebrow to me, Nevell walked into the room. If he was surprised to see Isobel, he did not show it, but greeted her with rather more familiarity than was merited.

'Good morning, Miss Isobel.' He gave a small bow. 'I see you have found your cousin again.'

Isobel bobbed her head, pleasure colouring her milky cheeks. There was nothing she liked better than being courteously addressed, a legacy of her time in the

137

poorhouse, perhaps, and Nevell had a manner to make any woman feel a princess.

'Do you know Mr Jerrold's cousin, Mr Nevell?' Mrs McCaird seemed rather taken aback.

'Indeed yes,' said Nevell warmly. 'They have been quite inseparable since the poor creature was orphaned. Often she seems more akin to his sister than his cousin.'

And rather more like a mistress, though I did not say so. Nevell seemed to have achieved the improbable feat of convincing the landlady of both my respectability and Isobel's, and I would do nothing to disturb that precarious esteem.

There followed a brief pause, while Mrs McCaird hovered by Nevell's shoulder and he talked easily with Isobel about the sights of London, how she should on no account miss the amphitheatre, or the Vauxhall pleasure gardens, or the polygraphic exhibition which was held to be tremendously improving. I confess I felt a fork of jealousy pricking me as he did so, both at his easy mastery of London's ways and at the attentive rapture with which she listened. But at length, unable to linger any longer without appearing rude, Mrs McCaird excused herself into the kitchen, and Nevell was in an instant changed from tourist impresario to his usual businesslike self.

'Well, Miss Isobel,' he said, 'I fear we must take our leave, and allow you to see the sights of London for yourself.'

It was extraordinary: had I suggested such a thing, Isobel would have clawed and hissed like a wildcat to come along with me, but hearing it from Nevell she nodded demurely.

'When will you come back?'

'I hope to return by the dinner hour,' I said, assuming – a touch defensively – that she spoke to me. 'Unless by then I have found Dumont and am busy chasing him across the Thames.'

I did not think I would forgo my dinner that night.

* * *

'So where are we going?' I asked Nevell, as we left Mrs McCaird's house behind us and navigated our way through the eddying crowds. 'Have you a plan?'

Nevell nodded. 'Several.'

We walked on a few paces in silence. 'And will you divulge them to me?' I still felt a residue of chagrin at the way he had charmed Isobel, especially when my own manners seemed so often to provoke her, and I had little patience with his prevarications.

'Dumont's effects should be arrived from Chatham by noon,' said Nevell. 'In the meantime, I suggest we enquire in a few obvious places. Little may come of it, but I find it generally felicitous to keep the common ground well tilled.'

I rarely bothered to do even that much, but I had no better notion of my own. If Lebrett's visit the previous evening had achieved anything, it had emboldened my desire to find Dumont first, to seize the Guardsman's glory and lord it over him. Certainly, while Nevell was with me, Lebrett seemed far less terrifying.

'And where might these obvious places be?' In the search for Dumont, nothing seemed obvious to me, but there was a blithe confidence about Nevell that suggested he saw things rather more lucidly.

'Otto, of course.'

'Of course. Who?'

'Monsieur Otto. The only Frenchman at large in England. Legitimately,' Nevell added hurriedly, before I could point out the manifest inaccuracy of that description.

'A receiver of escaped prisoners?'

'An ambassador.'

I followed Nevell as he led me unhesitatingly through the busy streets, up to the market in Covent Garden where pretty girls offered fruits and flowers and other temptations. With thoughts of Isobel fresh in my mind I did no

139

more than admire the produce, though Nevell's pace would have allowed no dalliance anyway: we were soon clear of the piazza, and bucking through a succession of bewildering turns and changes. Here the faces were neither friendly nor wholesome, and it seemed these people had little to employ their days, for they sat on the steps of their ramshackle houses or stood together on the crooked street corners. Lascars and Negroes and Hindoos and gypsies became commonplace, their white eyes brimming with anger, while the shouts that the women called at us now seemed more taunting than enticing. Many of the bystanders looked down as we passed, and I wondered if perhaps we intimidated them as much as the reverse. Then I remembered the buckles emblazoned on my shoes, like beacons to those hungry stares, and felt my pace grow still less steady.

Nevell, though, was unworried. If I jumped when a trio of women began laying about one another like Furies, he passed serenely by; where I tensed to see a beggar lounging in my path, and did not breathe again until he was behind me, Nevell offered the unfortunate a smile and a greeting; with some of them, I even saw a coin or two drop into the outstretched hats. He seemed impervious to the surroundings and careless of danger, walking these ragged paths like a latter-day St Benedict. When at last the buildings and passers-by became more upright in their appearance, his manner did not change a whit, while I felt as though I had passed through the valley of the shadow and back into the sunny uplands.

We turned onto Oxford Street, a broad thoroughfare clearly in the throes of great change. Not long ago, Nevell told me, it had been on the extreme edge of the city, notable chiefly for witnessing the last journey of the condemned to Tyburn, and for the fine rustic views at the end of its side-streets. Now the speculators had moved in, and the only verdure to be seen was in the stiff patterns of regulated gardens, crisp centrepieces to the fashionable squares that hemmed the north side of the street. It was hard to believe that not five minutes earlier we had been in the depths of poverty and squalor.

We walked a considerable distance down Oxford Street, almost to its end, so that the turnpike gate and the park beyond were in plain sight before we turned right, finding ourselves almost immediately in another of the fragrant squares.

'*Et ici, la résidence de Monsieur Otto.*' Nevell, clearly transported by his subject, gestured to the far corner, where a large house stood in its own grounds, breaking the otherwise perfect line of the square.

'And what now? Shall we walk up to Mr Otto's front door and ask whether he has seen a renegade compatriot named Dumont, who happens to have half of Whitehall in a panic?'

'If you wish,' said Nevell politely.

'I don't speak French. It might hamper the conversation.'

'Then we'll have a word with Finch.'

I did not bother to ask who Finch might be, or whether he was English or French. Nevell, as was his habit, would reveal his purpose in his own inimitable way.

Which for once was almost immediately. As confident as if he owned one of the large town-houses himself, he sauntered into the garden within the square and began strolling down the gravel path. I followed him between high hedges, curving round in a long ellipse. My feet crunched in the stones, while birds chirruped from within the undergrowth and Nevell whistled a few bars of an unknown tune. The din of Oxford Street was almost blanketed out here, but from around the bend of the hedge I could hear the staccato clip of shears. Soon, as the path straightened, I saw a gardener before us, sucking on a pipe and pruning the shrubs with immaculate precision. He was older than I would have expected, his face leathered by the sun, and his bare arms were covered in a multitude of tiny scabs and scratches where he must have joined battle with a rosebush. His cap and jacket lay neatly folded at the side of the path, and what little hair he had was slicked back by the perspiration on his scalp.

'Good morning, Mr Finch,' said Nevell.

'Mornin', Mr Nevell.'

'How is the garden?'

'Thirsty, sir, with all this sun.'

'And how does Monsieur Otto fare?'

Finch laid down his shears and blew into the bowl of his pipe. 'Fair enough. Just the usual callers, mostly. 'Ave a look for yourself.'

He moved aside, allowing Nevell to step up to the hedge and press his eye close between the leaves. He squinted, and stared with rapt fascination, though what he might see besides twigs and caterpillars I could not imagine.

'Is botany another of your pursuits?' I asked.

Straightening himself, he tugged me forward. 'See what you make of it.'

I crouched to where his eye had been, marvelling at the absurdities to which he could incite me. The wiry hedge scratched at my cheek, and I jammed my eyes closed in alarm, but if I held my face still I found I could just keep it from harm.

I opened my eye carefully, and as I peered through the leaves I realized that Finch was no more a gardener than Nevell a deliverer of letters. Through some deft piece of inverted topiary, the inside of the hedge had been cut away to afford a view clean through to the other side, where the most slender covering of leaves disguised the aperture. And beyond that, across the square, I gazed straight onto the front of the ambassador's residence. I could see a doorman in blue livery standing very still by the gate, and a maid mopping the stairs; I even fancied I could discern an occasional movement behind the dark windows. As a hidden vantage it was impeccably chosen, and from the neatly tailored lines of the hedge I guessed Finch was assiduous in tending it.

I stood up. 'Do you believe that Dumont might seek refuge with the French embassy?' I looked to Finch. 'Have you seen a strange Frenchman, of middling height and delicate features, clean shaven, approach the house?'

'No, sir.' Finch was quietly adamant, and there was something in his eyes that implied he did not easily forget a face.

'Well, if you should see such a person, you know where to send word.' Nevell scraped his foot across the stones, like a horse pawing out its impatience. 'For now, we had best be about our enquiries.'

'Yes, sir.'

As Nevell turned to go, I bent down to have a final peek through the spyhole. If once you knew the spot it was easy to find, and I found myself admiring the gardener's handiwork again as the ambassador's residence leaped out from among the greenery. It seemed Finch would have to keep a steady eye on it, for even in the short time we had spoken the scene had changed: the maid and her mop had vanished, and the servant was now holding the door ajar. I peered closer, ignoring the scratching branches, and hoped my sight might penetrate the darkness within the house.

It could not, for against the brightness of the day the interior was too dim, but as I watched, a figure stepped out into the sunlight. I tensed, though I saw immediately he was too tall to be Dumont; his face was hidden for the moment, as he seemed to be speaking to another man in the shadow. Behind me I could hear Nevell muttering about wasting time, but I waved him silent and kept up my surveillance, intent on completing this little episode.

The man on the stair finished his farewell and turned his

back on the closing door, descended the steps and marched rapidly to the low iron gate. He paused to fiddle with the latch, allowing me a clear glimpse of his features, and in my mind I marked down his appearance as I imagined Finch must do every day. His long brown hair was loosely tied back with a green ribbon, the same hue as his coat, and he walked with a stride which I did not think would suffer delays even on the crowded streets of London. He looked to be about forty, though he did not wear the years lightly, and down his left cheek I could see a deep, crooked scar.

Recognition struck me like a cudgel, and in my excitement I almost overbalanced and toppled headlong into the bush. Fortunately Finch must have seen me wobble, for in an instant I felt his thick hand on my arm, drawing me back and steadying me.

'That man!' I exclaimed, more loudly than was wise. 'I know him.' I noticed the mystified looks on Nevell and Finch's faces, and remembered they could see nothing. 'A man just came out of Otto's house, a tall man with a scar on his cheek. A man I encountered two days ago, at an inn on the Canterbury road near Chatham.'

To Finch this was clearly gibberish, but Nevell had fastened on my meaning at once. He pushed me aside and stared out through the peephole. 'You saw him while you were hunting Dumont?'

'Yes. A surly fellow – an American. We heard reports of a foreigner at the inn and found him. Just before we saw the other Frenchman, the one we chased into the marshes.' As ever, my confidence began to ebb after the initial surge. 'Of course, it may be merely a coincidence.'

Nevell looked at me closely. 'The Post Office,' he informed me, 'does not believe in coincidences.'

'Then what shall we do?' I looked around wildly, fearful lest our delay give the American a chance of escape. 'Should we confront him?'

'We'll follow him.' There was no hesitation in Nevell's

voice. 'Or rather, I will follow him and you will follow me. Keep about fifty paces back, closer if I turn a corner, and watch for abrupt halts. And don't look at the American.'

'Very well.'

We left Finch to his pruning and ran back down the path to the opening in the hedge. I had no need to slow my pace, for by the time I reached the square I was already behind Nevell, while the American was gone from view. Nevell, though, must have seen his direction, for he was trotting briskly down a side-road back towards Oxford Street.

I rarely needed to worry about Nevell's injunction to keep behind him, for the American had a powerful gait and a wearying constancy in using it. We followed him across Oxford Street and south, with the green expanse of Hyde Park flickering in and out of sight down the roads to our right; through Mayfair, past the glorious homes of Piccadilly, and down St James's Street. I had to admire the man's taste, for it seemed we must have passed every fashionable house and mansion in London – at least the rascal had not led us into the depths of some rookery. He moved with apparent purpose, and I guessed Nevell must have some experience of such pursuits to stay with his quarry so long. For me, the American was the merest speck of green in the far distance, and that infrequently, while even Nevell's plum coat occasionally dipped out of sight.

Nor was the chase comfortable. I was unused to moving in such crowds, and with my eyes ranging far before me I could not heed the many feet, faces and elbows that jostled around me. In the service of the chase I was battered and abused, occasionally threatened with violence, and mumbled apologies were always on my lips. My new shoes, designed more for mincing between a carriage and a ball-room than for long miles of tramping, rubbed a pox of blisters into my feet, and when a pebble worked its way inside the leather there was nothing I could do but hobble on.

In the end, it was the shoes that undid me. The American's progress had slowed on Pall Mall, and I was at last having to take care to hang well back from Nevell. Thinking it would afford me a moment to remove the stone from under my foot, I knelt down in the road, hoping that some buck would not choose that instant to race his phaeton over me. The stone tipped out easily enough when I pulled off the shoe, but by the time I had managed to squeeze it over my tender foot again, Nevell was gone.

I cursed, and shaded my eyes with my hand as I searched the busy street for him. There was nothing, and in that crowd of dandies and beaus he would do little to stand out. I broke into a run, pushing my way through with rude desperation, heedless of the refined sensibilities I offended. It was impossible work, for I could not barge my way through the throng and scan for Nevell simultaneously. Risking a quick glance up, at the cost of an unseen elbow in my stomach, I saw that the road would soon end in a junction, and I would have to let luck and guesswork guide me. They had rarely served me well, and I pressed on with still greater haste and greater stir.

Given my haphazard, pell-mell progression, it was perhaps inevitable that I would eventually meet with a shoulder which refused to be brushed aside; outside Carlton House, amid the gaggle of sycophant spectators who had gathered at the royal residence, I did so. In my brief adventure, I had become expert at prising gaps in the crowd, and had perhaps started to apply greater force than was advisable. Thus there was a considerable collision when my leading shoulder met firm resistance, and it was all I could do to keep from tumbling to the ground. Any delay was frustration enough, but my hopes of catching Nevell receded still further as a firm hand grasped my collar and hauled me round to deliver a deserved rebuke.

'Why don't you take a damn closer look where you step,' growled an angry voice. It was an odd accent, touched with the burr of Devon but probably hailing from a good deal further west.

As the words of apology formed in my mouth, my contrite eyes raised themselves to meet his. They followed a green lapel, a hard chin, and eventually a weathered face with a wide scar down the left cheek.

Our eyes met, and his hand fell away as mine stretched out. He must have recognized me from the inn, or perhaps he had been watching me since, for his reflexes were astounding: my mouth had barely dropped open before he was away through the offended gentility, driving his way like the point of a sabre. I made to pursue him, but even as I stepped forward a plum-coated maniac sprinted past me, hopping over the scattered baskets and fallen limbs that littered the American's wake. I followed in his path, a progressive carnage which rounded Charing Cross and wreaked its way up the Strand, back towards my lodgings. Was that his goal? Did he plan to hold a knife at Isobel's throat to protect himself? But before I could contemplate that horror he had changed tack again, turning down a short alley which opened onto an enclosed market. Many of the stalls were bare by now, and the custom was light, but still we elicited angry shouts at our reckless progress, and an apple shied narrowly past my head.

Before me, the market ended and the street funnelled back into a narrow lane, beyond which I could see clear space. It was the river, brown and flat and laden with traffic. I felt a surge of triumph at the sight, for the lane ran right to the water's edge: the American had trapped himself in a dead end. Impending victory and a biting cramp slowed my pace, but the American had not surrendered all hope. He darted down a stone stair built into the river bank. Would he try to swim the Thames?

I reached the top of the stairs. Nevell was waiting a few steps down, while at the bottom the American stood on a wooden jetty that floated on the river. Green ooze and decaying ropes snaked across its timbers, while a dirty froth eddied against its side. The tide was high, reaching well up the river bank, and despite the lack of rain the current in midstream looked fierce. To our great fortune, and the American's ruin, there was no boatman.

He must have seen the futility of his position, but it did not blunt his fury. He swung around, careless of the slippery footing, and shouted at us in defiance. 'Come for my money, have you? I'd heard London was nothing but a den of thieves, but I never expected to be attacked so in public. You'd not ever see such a thing on the streets of New York or Boston, no, sir, but it seems in your country nothing is safe.'

'Come, sir,' said Nevell evenly. 'You exaggerate. London is no nursery, but those with little to hide have generally little to fear. Those who make strenuous efforts to avoid the attentions of the authorities, however . . .'

'The authorities?' The American's scar seemed to bulge out as his face swelled with anger. 'Is this another example of English liberty, that a man can be hunted through the street like a coyote for no cause? Who are you – the secret police?'

'Not at all.' For a man whose duties included spying on other people's houses, prying into their affairs and reading their correspondence, Nevell rebutted the charge with admirable indignation. 'Lieutenant Jerrold is in fact with the navy – I believe you encountered him near Chatham.'

The American turned his angry eyes upon me. 'Never seen him before in my life.'

Nevell left the denial unchallenged. 'But you were near Chatham a couple of days ago, were you not?'

'Where I go is my own business, damn you.' The American thrust both hands into the deep pockets of his coat, and stared belligerently. 'What of it? Is King George still in the way of condemning men without trials, of imprisoning them without justice?' One hand had emerged and was gesturing with animation, but the other, which drew my attention, stayed in the pocket and seemed to be grasping something. Something with a cylindrical snout that bulged against the fabric with menacing under-statement. I hoped Nevell had noticed it.

Perhaps he had, for his tone suddenly grew suspiciously soothing. 'I must apologize, then, if we have distressed you, Mr . . . ?'

'Brogarde.' His grip on the hidden item remained as resolute as ever, but some of the anger was cut from his voice. 'So if you aren't King George's secret police, and you aren't common thieves, who in hell are you?'

'Nevell. This, as I indicated, is Lieutenant Jerrold. And it seems we must beg your pardon, Mr Brogarde: we mis-took you for another man.'

Brogarde grunted. 'Then you had best beware, Mr Nevell. One mistake often sires another, and too often men get hurt.'

'We are seeking a man we suspect of aiding an escaped French prisoner of war.' Nevell talked on as if Brogarde had never spoken, but if he was testing the man's composure, he failed. Brogarde's face remained utterly unmoved.

'A French prisoner? Another man who failed to enjoy your famous hospitality, perhaps? I cannot say he would not draw my sympathy. But you'll excuse me, for I have pleasanter ways to waste my time than arguing with a tyrant's dupes.'

Nevell stood aside and let the man mount the stairs. He passed by me very close, far closer than was necessary, and let his shoulder jostle my own. Then he vanished into the marketplace.

'Why did you do that?' I exclaimed, as soon as he was gone from earshot. 'Surely you did not believe his denials?'

Nevell rolled his eyes. 'Of course not – he barely

149

bothered to deny anything, after all. But what else could we have done?'

'We could have hauled him off to Newgate and seen what a few days in chains did for him.'

'You surprise me, Jerrold,' Nevell tutted. 'Would you affirm his belief in the wicked tyranny of our country? If a man has not put himself beyond the pale of the law, or fallen into debt, you cannot simply cast him into prison. Besides, he had a gun.'

'I know.'

'And he discarded whatever he had of value.'

'What?' As ever, Nevell's conversation had swerved into enigma. 'What thing of value?'

Nevell shrugged. 'Something that he held as he inveighed against the King. Something which flew from his hand and sank into the river. Surely you noticed it?'

'I confess I did not. My attention was on the gun in his pocket.'

'A rather obvious distraction, did you not think?'

I did not. 'You say he threw something in the river?' I peered at the swirling water, its surface etched with the whorls and ripples of its currents. I did not think we would find anything lost in that murk.

'Yes. I could not see what. Perhaps later . . .' Nevell's voice trailed off as he climbed back up the stairs. 'For now, I must return to the Post Office. There are some details I must examine.'

'But what of Brogarde?' I persisted. 'How can you let him walk free after we had him cornered so? We may never see him again.'

Nevell had already begun to walk back towards the bustle of the Strand, but he paused a moment and turned to answer me. 'If Brogarde has truly been sent to retrieve Dumont, as seems entirely possible, then he is more useful at large than in chains. If he had found Dumont, or knew his whereabouts, they would not linger in London, so it

150

follows he must be seeking him as earnestly as we ourselves. While Brogarde is at liberty, we have two targets to chase – and I do not think he will vanish as easily as you suppose.' He laughed at my obvious misgivings. 'Set a fox to catch a hare, Jerrold, and the results may surprise you.'

I doubted that very much. The results, almost certainly, would be violent and bloody.

12

Isobel and I dined at Mrs McCaird's, taking great care to show due cousinly propriety, then escaped into the golden calm of the evening. The heat of the day which had so oppressed me was melting away, and a quiet breeze washed over my face under the deepening blue sky. We walked up the Strand arm in arm, indistinguishable from the scores of other couples of every rank, matched and mismatched, who promenaded in the evening light. The bright windows laden with their glittering wares delighted Isobel, and she was like a hound off its leash hanging back before some, darting forward to others, always wide-eyed and chattering away. I don't believe she had ever been to London – or even further from Dover than Chatham – yet she showed no sign of being overwhelmed by its vastness, instead glorying in its seductive variety. Several times she had to be prised away from inappropriate liaisons with shops offering patent cotton invisible petticoats, or pocket toasting forks, or cucumber slicers or other such frivolities. It was wearying work, and my legs were soon fatigued by the long minutes of uncertain hovering. The attendant physical hazards apart, I would rather chase Frenchmen and Americans any day.

'Perhaps we might visit the theatre, or the opera,' I

suggested. 'I am told it is very good. And most improving.'

Isobel peered at a handbill, one of several that had been nailed between two shops. 'Or this. *A grand panorama of Lord Nelson's triumph at Trafalgar, featuring not less than sixty ships rendered to the most perfect and exact detail on ten thousand square feet of canvas.*'

I scowled. 'Unless it shows some poltroon emptying his stomach in the *Temeraire*'s hold, I can hardly consider it exact. And seeing Trafalgar once ought to be enough for any man.'

'You never saw it,' Isobel teased me. 'You could find out what you missed.'

'I heard enough in the hold to know I missed nothing except offering my arse to Buonaparte's gunners.' My tone was more brusque than I intended, for though I was content that the fact of my survival redeemed the means which had secured it, I was suddenly loath to discuss it with Isobel.

'Then what about this?' Isobel moved lightly over my anger. ' "*The Fair Slave, or Moors and Africans*". *A splendid spectacle such as has never before been presented, featuring a procession of camels and* REAL HORSES.' Isobel bobbed up and down. 'That might be more to your taste, Martin?'

I could think of nothing more dangerous than a troupe of performing horses kicking their hooves near the audience's faces, but Isobel's eyes were alight with anticipation, and at least in the theatre I might rest my legs. Besides, I had never seen a camel.

We hurried down to Westminster, over the new bridge which resonated to the sound of revellers blaring horns from under the arches. The crowds were thick around the amphitheatre, and I need not have worried about the horses' hooves for the only seats we could get were high above the arena, more akin to the crosstrees of a man-of-war in the view they afforded. I had to crane so far forward I thought I might plummet into the entertainment, but it did not trouble Isobel, who laughed and clapped and cheered without compunction. The play demanded little concentration, for the meagre plot generally served only to afford successive pretexts for equestrian acrobatics, but we both emerged with merriment and laughter in our faces. Isobel skipped and pirouetted like Pegasus the flying horse, whom she declared she would one day own, while I screwed up my face and hunched my shoulders in imitation of the camels. Lingering queasiness from the high seats aside, it was the happiest I had been in days, and Dumont was exiled from my thoughts as we returned across the river and strolled around the canal in St James's Park. Isobel nestled against me, and had there not been so many other folk about enjoying the evening, I might have dragged her into the bushes without delay. Instead, I contented myself with thoughts of exertions to come, and tried to hasten the pace back towards Mrs McCaird's.

'What will happen when you catch him?' Isobel's question jolted me, most unhappily, back to the exigent concerns of the moment.

'I haven't the least idea,' I told her truthfully. 'Perhaps they will give me back the *Prometheus*. It rather depends how badly I fail them in between times.' Certainly my uncle would have little sympathy for my petition – if indeed he enjoyed any influence at all by then.

A man with a cow was selling mugs of freshly squeezed milk, warm from the udder, and I bought two, which we drank in silence. My thoughts had been fixed so narrowly on apprehending Dumont that I had not considered where success would take me, though the price of failure was clear enough. Nor could I guess what Isobel wanted, for though at first she had been happy lodging in Chatham and visiting me often, in recent weeks she had seemed dissatisfied, restless. From the enchantment in her eyes when they looked on London, I guessed that the attractions of a quiet life by the Medway were waning.

We were far along the path by now, with the spire of the Horse Guards barracks rising in front of us. It was not a sight for this carefree evening, and I steered Isobel to our left, to where the high wall of Carlton House rose above the trees.

'Maybe you'll catch a glimpse of the Prince of Wales,' I suggested.

I joined Isobel in peering towards the brightly lit windows, whose curtains the exhibitionist Prince had left undrawn. The sky was almost dark now, and the rooms within stood out like studs of amber, yet there was little to see beyond the occasional equerry scurrying past. Isobel, whose capacity for observation rivalled Nevell's, watched intently, but I had less patience: I was about to look away, when two figures in a bay window caught my eye. They stood a little way back in the room under a chandelier, and were perfectly illuminated in their conversation. One was a short, stout man, with a nervous face and grey hair; the other was taller, confident in his bearing, and dressed in the blue and red coat of the Horse Guards. I could scarcely credit what my eyes reported, but there was no denying the sharp nose, the large mouth, or the curt jerks of his head as he argued some point with his companion.

I tugged Isobel's hand. 'We should go. That man in there is Major Lebrett, and while I would give a good deal to know why he consorts with the Prince of Wales's household, I would give a good deal more to avoid any encounter with him.'

Isobel remained unmoved. 'Major Lebrett,' she repeated. 'The one who dragged you off from Chatham?'

'The same.' I was agitating to be away, both from fear of Lebrett and from concern at what Isobel might do. She could often seem careless of me, but her loyalties were deep and unpredictable. I would not think her incapable of marching into Carlton House to give Major Lebrett a brisk taste of her anger.

To the mercy of Lebrett's health and my career, she relented. With a final curious glance at the figures in the house, she allowed me to take her arm and steer her down the Mall and back to Charing Cross. The roads were emptying now, speeding our progress, though the number of women prowling at the mouths of dark alleys testified to the extent of the commerce still to be transacted. I watched them nervously, too afraid of robbery to feel excitement when they lifted the hems of their skirts, and when linkmen called out offers to light our way home, I refused with stiff silence. There were few men I would trust to lead me into the dark places of London, and they would certainly not be found holding guttering candles on crooked sticks in the shadows of the Strand. Besides, we did not have far to go, and my cowed spirits lifted as Mrs McCaird's front door approached. Seeing Lebrett had shaken me, but I could not be troubled to think on it now: far more appetizing was the prospect of taking Isobel upstairs and seeing just how she might look in a patent invisible petticoat.

So advanced were my thoughts of wickedness that I did not see the carriage drawn up across the street. I stood on the doorstep rapping on the knocker, trying to unlace Isobel's stays through her dress and ignoring her mock indignation. As so often, my lust proved stronger than my sense of preservation, and even when the driver jumped down from his box I did not turn to see him. Only when I felt a hand touch my elbow did I spin round with a yelp of terror.

'Lieutenant Jerrold, sir?'

I did not recognize him, but he made an unlikely villain, dressed as he was in an ill-fitting coat, and with his hat in his hands so his features were plain to see. He had the broad face and gruff voice of a labourer, and his master, whoever he might be, had not refined him so much that his eyes kept from darting to Isobel's bodice, which had slipped a good inch past propriety with my meddling.

'Who are you?' I demanded, fear swelling my voice.

'Williams, sir, the coachman.'

'And what the devil do you want?'

'I was told to fetch you, sir.'

'Fetch me? Fetch me where? Who sent you – was it Lebrett?' Had he seen me staring at him through the window? 'Or Nevell?'

The coachman shook his head. 'Mr Perceval, sir.'

'Who the devil is Mr Perceval?'

'If you comes with me, sir, you'll meet him.'

I was about to reply that I would do no such thing, that I would go to bed and see to Isobel and certainly not enter strange carriages at midnight, but the coachman had not yet finished speaking.

'It's about the Frenchman, sir. Mr Dumont. Mr Perceval says he might help you.'

It was a strange kind of help that could not wait for a decent hour and a proper invitation, but then nothing about the pursuit of Dumont was convenient or civil. Still I hesitated, held between hope and fear and a profound reluctance to leave Isobel.

'You'd best go,' said Isobel. She hardly sounded certain, but it made my decision inevitable. Promising to behave myself, I kissed her on the cheek and crossed to the carriage, just quick enough to avoid meeting a furious Mrs McCaird on the threshold. Though as the coach rumbled into the night and the boarding house disappeared around the corner, I had to reflect that even the wrath of a thousand landladies might be preferable to this unknown adventure.

13

It was a long, dark road that we drove, and I spent most of it seized with terror. I was alone in the carriage without any lamp, and even with the curtains drawn back I could see little of our journey. We rumbled over one of the bridges, and almost immediately the lights of the town faded into memory as we passed through unseen fields and meadows, an invisible wasteland stretching out on either side. Occasionally I could see an inn sign hanging still in the orb of a lantern, but otherwise I might have travelled over an open, moonless sea.

Some way past Southwark, panic set in. I felt a frantic urge to beat on the window and demand the driver stop, or to throw open the door and fling myself out – anything to be away from this remorseless journey – but terror kept me rooted to my seat, my fingers pressed into its leather as though I hung from a precipice. Memories of the dark, solitary moments of my life visited themselves upon me: the *Temeraire*'s hold, the gaol at Dover, the bilges where a cruel lieutenant had made shivering midshipmen hunt rats.

Somewhere in the darkness, though, my fear must finally have drowned my nerves, for I had little sense of the wheels grinding up a gravel driveway, or the carriage slow-ing, or even the door opening: it was a hand on my knee that tugged me back to wakefulness. Thankfully I was too drowsy to embarrass myself with fits of fainting or squeals of horror, and I was being led to the brightly lit front door of a large house before I properly recollected my situation. There was nothing on the house to identify it, and the grounds were so wrapped in tall trees that we could have been in Westminster and I would not have known it. But I did not think we were in Westminster: the midnight air was crisp, scrubbed of all the poisons and fumes of London, and when I looked up I could see a galaxy of stars spangled across the sky. A breeze brought the dry smell of pines to my addled senses.

The man I followed stood aside to let me pass through the door, and I saw with surprise that it was not the burly coachman but a scrawny man with a crooked face in footman's livery. Even in the lamplight I could see that his wig had lost much of its powder, taking on the mottled appearance of a cowhide, while his scarlet coat was crusted with wax and other marks. Whoever this Mr Perceval might be, he clearly did not take care to maintain his establishment. Nor was his house so grand as I had first thought, for though sumptuously decorated its rooms were scarcely larger, or more extensive, than my father's rectory.

I saw the servant eyeing my coat, and realized I had little authority to criticize slovenly dress.

'A navy man, are you, sir?' he asked with bald impertinence. 'You'd not be the first, you know. She's a taste for young sea captains. Likes to lick the salt off them, I don't wonder.'

I should have damned the rogue for his cheek, but I was so startled that I forgot. 'She? Who is *she*? I came here to see Mr Perceval.'

We were standing in a hallway, and as I spoke Mr Perceval's name a door at the far end opened and a round face peeped out. 'Is that you, Roberts?' he called. 'Is Lieutenant Jerrold come?'

'Come for his interview,' the footman answered. He did not bother to straighten his pose or stand to attention, but waved dismissively towards the open door. 'Mr Perceval's in the drawing room. And Her Highness.'

Not sure whether to expect the fiendish Mr Perceval who kidnapped men off the streets, a succubus intent on ripping away a sailor's uniform or a princess of the realm, I tottered forward into the drawing room.

At first I could not tell who greeted me, for the few candles there were had burned low, and the dark walls did little to reflect the light. The room seemed to be filled with moonlight, for every part of its fabric was blue: the two divans and armchairs, the open curtains, the paper on the walls and even the carpet were all differing hues of blue. A wood fire glowed in the grate, its occasional flames shooting me glimpses of the surrounds, while beyond the tall windows I could see the leaves and fronds of many plants, and the reflection of a glass roof over them. A noise on my left drew my attention to a dark doorway, and I thought I heard the sound of muslins or silks rustling up a stair, but I saw nothing.

'Please sit down, Lieutenant Jerrold. I must thank you for attending me here in this far-flung place, at this far-flung hour.'

It was the man who had called me in, sitting on one of the divans beside a pile of scattered papers. He was dressed from head to toe in black, which emphasized the very white skin of his soup-dish face. He was not a handsome man, for his lips seemed to intrude too far across his cheeks, and his thin hair was tied back untidily, but even seated there was a restless eagerness in him. Though he did not move, nor did he seem ever to be still, and there were sparks in his round eyes that would not admit to repose. Not only did I find my fears instantly in retreat, but also, curiously, my resentment.

'Where am I?' I asked, sinking into a blue armchair.

160

'Blackheath,' said my host. 'Near Greenwich.'

'The footman made reference to a princess, or some lady of royal blood. Is this a palace?'

My host looked uncomfortable. 'It is not a palace,' he said simply. 'And we are far from the orbit of Windsor here. But I forget my manners – I am Perceval. Spencer Perceval.' He looked at me hopefully, as if I might recognize the name, but though it had a faint resonance I could attach no meaning to it. 'I must apologize for approaching you so abruptly and spiriting you away.'

'Next time you might send a card with your servant.'

He laughed; a warm, genuine laugh that eroded my pique immediately. 'I will endeavour to do so. But time is essential, and my enemies keep many spies.'

He seemed remarkably cheerful for it. 'The French?'

'They too, no doubt. My immediate enemies are rather more ... immediate. I understand you have met Major Lebrett.'

I nodded. Though I was too unnerved to drop my guard, I found myself growing ever better disposed to the mysterious Mr Perceval. 'Major Lebrett has deprived me of my command and dragged me halfway round the south of England in search of the Frenchman Dumont.' I paused, finally remembering why I had been enticed to meet Mr Perceval. 'Your coachman said you could help me in my search for him.'

Perceval rocked back and forth a little on his seat. 'Lieutenant Jerrold, I will be candid with you. I have brought you here under something of a misapprehension. Though I would dearly love to have intelligence to impart, in truth it is *I* who must seek your help. I see you do not recognize my name, but I am in Parliament. I served in the last ministry under Pitt, and I now lend my strength to keeping those who revere his memory united in opposing the new government. A government which currently aspires to inflict the most infamous piece of judicial

161

assassination seen in this country since the Star Chamber. The Prince and his friends . . .' He must have seen the incomprehension writ across my face, for he paused. 'But perhaps I exceed the bounds of discretion.'

'You exceed the bounds of my understanding. In truth, sir, I do not follow the affairs of Parliament closely.'

'Of course.' Perceval's dizzying rocking eased a little. 'We who inhabit the sphere of Westminster forget how inconsequential our feuds and allegiances may seem to the world beyond. You are aware, of course, that after Pitt died a new ministry, composed principally of those who had been his foes, took office.'

'Yes.'

'And you are aware, perhaps, of their patron?' At that I shook my head. 'Mr Pitt and his adherents governed always with the full support and confidence of His Majesty the King. It was perhaps inevitable, therefore, that when the King's son wished to assert his independence of his father, as sons do, he associated himself with Pitt's opponents.'

'The Prince of Wales?' In whose house I had seen Lebrett only that evening. My head was beginning to ache as I tried to grasp all the threads which tangled around Dumont and the eminent men who sought him, but at last some were beginning to connect with each other.

'The Prince of Wales,' Perceval agreed. 'He patronizes Fox, Grenville and the rest of them, for while they administer the government he will find more favour than from the father he has so ably disappointed.'

The outcome of his logic at last presented itself to me. 'So if the government falls, the Prince's influence will wane.'

Perceval nodded vigorously. 'Precisely.'

'And Dumont poses a threat that the ministry fears may topple them.' I looked up suspiciously. 'But if you wish to see the ministry deposed and your own friends in Downing

Street, surely you have an interest in seeing Dumont succeed?' I suddenly felt a great isolation in this dark house in Blackheath.

Perceval showed no offence. 'Not at all. I know that we in the Commons are not always esteemed the most reputable of men, but there are bounds to our ambition. A latter-day Guy Fawkes might equally bring down the ministry, but that does not mean I would hand him the match. Rather, I would like to know why exactly Mr Dumont causes the ministry such discomfort, if by that knowledge I might gain an advantage.' He stared into my eyes, all playfulness now vanished. 'That is why I asked you here.'

There was a long, uncomfortable pause. The logs in the fire spat and crumbled into coals. I twisted the buttons on my coat and tried to lay hold of my churning thoughts, though really the only course open to me was honesty.

'I have not the least idea what Dumont's particular threat is. Indeed, I had hoped you might tell me. I was captain of the hulk in which he was imprisoned, and I never imagined that he was anything other than a forlorn Frenchman who wanted to see his home. I thought nothing of him until Major Lebrett appeared threatening every sort of violence and punishment, but by then it was too late.' I fell silent, remembering. 'I suppose Major Lebrett is connected with the Prince.'

'He is.' Perceval's eyes were still hard upon me, scanning my face for signs of deceit. For all his clownish looks and frivolous manner, he was never one to accept anything unchallenged.

'And the Princess?' I prompted. 'The lady whom the footman hinted at?' In the bawdiest terms, as I recalled.

'The Princess of Wales. This is her house.'

I could do nothing to mask the amazement that stretched my mouth wide open. To be brought to an unknown house at midnight was queer enough: that it should be the mansion of the Princess of Wales, and that she should be mere feet above my head, was inconceivable. How could she figure in this? And what might be her connection with Mr Perceval?

'It is strange that if the Prince is your enemies' patron, you should be found so late in his wife's company. I wonder, sir, if you have been truly candid with me.'

At that Perceval laughed, and the vigour returned to his cheeks. 'You are very shrewd, Lieutenant – more so than I had been led to expect.'

I allowed the insult to stand unchecked with the compliment.

'But you are ignorant of certain material facts. The Prince and his wife are estranged, and she is exiled from court. I tell you this in the greatest confidence, Jerrold, but with his allies in power the Prince now seeks an Act of Parliament to annul the marriage. Most irregular, but he has his reasons.'

'So the Princess has become a pawn in your party schemes. And you would make Dumont another.' I could not guess the measure of this man, who smiled so brightly and bore such a chivalrous name, yet who made my uncle seem a political ingénue. 'I want no part of it.'

'The Princess's affairs are none of your business.' Perceval was robust in his own defence, though never aggressive. 'But if you knew the gross slanders insinuated against her, in such a manner that she cannot defend her-self, you would perhaps feel more sympathy. It is alleged that she is an adulteress, which for the wife of the heir to the throne is high treason. Party advantage or no, who would not defend a gentle lady from such venomous malice?'

I sensed he might have continued in such a vein for some minutes, for he had the manner of a barrister making his plea, but his fine speech was rudely interrupted by a sudden chime from the mantelpiece. I had noticed a small

164

clock in the form of an oriental pagoda standing there, the firelight reflected in its jade casing, but as it struck the hour a door in the front sprang open and two porcelain figures rolled out. I stared in astonishment, for they seemed to be wearing nothing but their conical hats, and every detail of their bodies was depicted with scandalous accuracy. Driven by some unseen mechanism, they swivelled about like soldiers on parade, but there was nothing martial in the way the female figure bent at her hips while her partner moved up behind her and began thrusting forward with mechanical ardour in time with the striking of the hour. When the performance was complete, they straightened, and withdrew into the privacy of the clock.

Wide awake and seized with embarrassment, I turned to look at Spencer Perceval. Clearly the clock's antics did little to stir him, for there was nothing lascivious in his face – only a slightly pained frown.

'Her Highness,' he acknowledged, 'is not so meticulous as she might be in defence of her virtue. But if that is the hour, and if we have little more to impart to each other, we should return to town. You will accompany me in my coach?'

If the alternative was to be marooned here in this exile with an abandoned princess and her wanton timepieces, I would have driven the coach myself. I waited while Perceval gathered together his papers, then followed the sly footman back to the carriage. What must he have witnessed, I wondered, if even the Princess's toys were so brazen?

Perceval seated himself beside me in the coach and rapped on the panel. I watched the house recede into the night without regret.

'You may feel I have been less than frank, Lieutenant,' Perceval said as we clattered down a steep hill, 'but I have truthfully told you all I know, and more than strictly concerns you.' Certainly my imagination wanted for nothing. 'I hope that if you do discover this curious threat of Dumont's which terrorizes the government, you will inform me of it immediately.' He raised a hand to still my inevitable protest. 'Naturally your first duty is to your superiors, and a fallen minister must have little to commend confidence, but you will find I do have some small interest remaining – and justice, too, which must merit something.'

Precious little, I thought, when princes and governments were involved.

'You may write to me at my house in the Gray's Inn Road,' Perceval continued. 'Though you must be discreet, for I do not think all my letters go unopened.' I guessed I knew the man responsible. 'Now let us talk no more of this affair, for it would be a tedious journey back otherwise.'

It would have been a tedious journey back in any event, but Perceval made an unexpectedly engaging companion, and chattered away amusingly enough while the carriage rolled along the silent road back to London. He raked over the gossip of the moment that exercised society, and if it was insignificant next to what I had already learned, at least he told it with wit and humour. We discussed the First Lord's reforms, of which he naturally disapproved, and the recent impeachment of Lord Melville, whom he defended as a victim of faction. At some point I am sure he informed me that he had calculated the world would end in nineteen hundred and twenty-eight, but we were at the outskirts of London by then and I was hearing his words only in snatches. At length, amid the clamour of dustmen and night-soil collectors, I returned to Mrs McCaird's just as the first tip of the sun crept over the horizon.

14

*You look horrible.'

There is a curious tendency in the human race to draw
others' attention to the visible ravages of their distress, as if
it might somehow bring comfort, and in this habit Isobel
was no exception. I opened my eyes, feeling my mouth as
foul as a bilge, and looked at her through the thump of a
headache.

'What time is it?'

A clutch of church bells supplied the answer before
Isobel could speak, striking – in so far as I could hear one
from another – nine times. I shook my head, wondering
how long it might be before I could hear a clock and not
think of Chinese obscenities.

'I can't have had more than four hours' sleep.' I spoke as
much to myself as to Isobel. 'No wonder I feel horrible.'

'Was it worth it?'

I could think of few things that would warrant feeling as
I did, and in the absence of the Princess's favours, none I
had met the night before. 'No.'

'But what did he have to say, that Mr Perceval?'

Despite my obvious longing for my pillow, it seemed
Isobel was determined to make conversation. 'He wanted
to be the first to know when I captured Dumont.' I rubbed

my face against her nightdress. 'He and the First Lord and my uncle and Lebrett and Nevell alike. All they seem to share is their optimism that I may one day find the villain.'

As if to underscore the urgency of that task, there was a knock at the door.

'Your friend Mr Nevell is downstairs,' came Mrs McCaird's voice. 'Shall I bring him up?'

I groaned. 'I am just attending my toilet, Mrs McCaird. Would you entertain Mr Nevell until I am composed?'

From the enthusiasm of her response I guessed it would be no imposition on her, though Nevell might think otherwise. I dressed as hurriedly as I could, my aforementioned toilet reduced to little more than a splash of water across my face and a few swipes with a hairbrush.

'I cannot imagine when I will be back,' I told Isobel, lacing her into her stays. 'It rather depends on whether I am kidnapped by members of Parliament, thrown in the river by violent Americans, or run through by French desperadoes.'

'I thought I'd go to the polygraphic exhibition.' Isobel seemed untroubled by my prospective fates. 'They say it improves.'

'Against my day, anything would be an improvement.'

I rescued Nevell from Mrs McCaird's solicitous attentions and stepped into the street. Despite his encounter with the landlady, he was in ebullient spirits, though they did little to loosen his tongue. When I asked where we were bound, all he would say was 'Not far.' But if he was obscure, he was at least honest with it, for in a few short minutes we had crossed the Strand, passed through the market where we had chased the American the day before, and emerged on the river bank. The river was at low ebb, a comparative trickle in the cleft of the sloping mudbanks. The small craft that crowded it at the best of times were now squeezed almost solid in the stream, though many had been left behind to lie askance in the ooze until the next tide came to resurrect them. A thin scum of water still coated the reaches between, on which the sun shone like a burnished mirror, but if I shaded my eyes against the dazzle I could see an army of thin figures scuttling over the mud like crabs.

'Mudlarks and scuffle-hunters,' said Nevell. 'They poach a living by sifting through the rubbish and debris that falls overboard off the ships and barges. Not all of it accidentally, of course, but sometimes they turn up a gem.'

We reached the top of the stairs where we had cornered the American. At its foot, the wooden landing stage lay useless on the riverbed, while the green weed that crusted it dried and stank in the sun. Just beyond, with a pair of broad planks tied to his bare feet, one of the scuffle-hunters was probing the mud with a long pole. I tried to ignore him, for I have always felt disengagement to be the best protection against the criminal classes, but Nevell bounded down the putrid steps and hailed him loudly.

'What success, Perkin? Have you found anything?'

Despite my misgivings, I had followed Nevell, and so had a fine view of the scuffle-hunter as he turned and straightened to give his answer. He was an extraordinary fellow, seemingly returned to that primitive clay from which his maker first moulded him. The boards must have supported his weight, yet his feet were cased in mud so thick you could not see the toes; his shirt and trousers needed only a good firing in a kiln to become permanent; his face was smeared with dry mud like a savage Indian's, and his hair was moulded into strange tussocks by the grime that infused it. His back hunched him almost double, and his entire appearance was of an enormous snail crawled forth from the slime. Only his eyes, very white, betrayed the man within.

'Found a few odds, we 'as.' Even his words sounded like

earth, perhaps because he had so few teeth to form them. 'Rope fer pickin'. Coals fer cleanin'. Finest French silk fer the ladies.' As he named each item he drew it from a dirty sack tied to his waist, though I would have been pressed to recognize the sodden, misshaped lumps he presented. 'I got three blades, four bullseyes an' a pair o' Georges, nine blowers an' a sneezer.'

If Nevell was addled by this improbable list, he gave no sign. 'May I see the snuffbox?'

The scuffle-hunter shuffled to the landing stage, leaving his pole upright in the riverbed, and passed some small object to Nevell. I would have thought a man as fastidious as he would have trembled to come so close to this walking midden, but he acted as though he were taking a teacup from a servant. Crouching down, he rinsed the item in a shallow puddle by his feet, then held it close to his face as he prised open the lid.

'Ah ha. How much for this?'

The scuffle-hunter wheezed, like a door creaking open. 'Shillin'. An' another crown fer what's in it,' he added craftily, as Nevell reached for his purse.

'Have a pair for your trouble.' Nevell threw the man a couple of coins. If the planks on his feet or the stoop of his back impeded him at all, you would not have noticed it by the deft way he snatched the money from the air. He bit the coins with his tooth, tapped his hand to his forehead in salute, and ambled away to find some new piece of jetsam.

'I suppose you will eventually explain why you have just paid that vagabond ten shillings for a derelict snuffbox,' I said. 'You could have had a newer, cleaner specimen for less from the tobacconist.'

'But then I would have only a box.' Nevell tossed me the article in question, almost upending me as I flailed to catch it. It was a handsome piece, though a little rudimentary; the hand that had carved the ivory had not always been steady, but the designs etched into the lid were executed ably enough. A ring of stars surrounded a small ship, a sloop or perhaps a frigate, with its sails hung out to dry. An assortment of fishes, daggers and mermaids ringed its sides.

'I would say this was carved by a sailor.' I felt that for once I might have the advantage over Nevell, and was keen to demonstrate it. 'The men often carve them in the dog watches. You could find one for a fraction of what you paid in any dockside alehouse.'

'But I would say that this was not carved by an English sailor.' Nevell retrieved the box from my care. 'You see these stars inscribed in it – thirteen of them. What does that suggest to you?'

'That it was unlucky? Certainly unlucky for its owner if he dropped it in the river.'

Nevell stared at me with amusement. 'My dear Jerrold – you really can be the most extraordinary buffoon at times. Only yesterday you watched an American stand on this stair and fling some small item into the river, while today the scuffle-hunter drags out a snuffbox engraved with the emblem of the rebel American colonists. Can you truly see no connection?'

'It was the American's.' The protest against Nevell's insult that I had been preparing died stillborn as I saw how obtuse I had been.

'And why would the American cast away this trinket, which I surmise he carved himself, unless there was something in it he did not wish us to discover?'

With dainty precision, Nevell lifted a soggy scrap of paper out from within the box. Water must have seeped in, for the snuff was caked onto it like wet sand, but it trickled off as he unfolded the tight creases and delicately stretched them out. I was surprised it did not melt apart in his hands, but though a few tears appeared at the edges the whole remained intact. It was not even soaked entirely through: the middle portion was almost dry.

171

Nevell laid the paper out on one of the steps. Much of it must formerly have been covered in writing, but most of that was now reduced to illegible stripes smeared into the paper. In the lower half, though, where it had been most tightly folded, the letters had not smudged into each other, and in the brightness of the morning we had all the light we needed to examine them.

'*at Black* ... something ... *tavern, Holborn. Eleven o'clock.*' Nevell looked up at me. 'I believe we have a page from his diary here, or a note of an engagement. There is no date, alas, but as it was past eleven when we found him yesterday, I think we may presume that this refers to today at the earliest.'

Still stinging from having been called a buffoon, doubly so for having deserved it, I was quick to voice the obvious conclusion. 'We should make for Holborn, then, and find this tavern – the Black something. If the American has been sent to join with Dumont, this must refer to a meeting he has arranged. If we hurry, we may apprehend them together, and at last discover the truth of their nefarious scheme.' After which, I thought, I would have to decide which of my many suitors to inform first.

Nevell, who was carefully sliding the paper into an oilskin pouch, chuckled. 'I applaud your spirit,' he told me, in a manner that implied rather less approbation of my reason. 'But you should beware over-excitement. The American, Brogarde, may merely be meeting an old shipmate to swap scrimshaw and memories. Who is to say whether Dumont will be found there?'

I refused to be cowed by his moderation. 'We shall find what we find,' I said philosophically. 'But at least we can begin by finding this tavern.'

Inevitably, we could not. Half an hour later we were standing outside a draper's on Holborn, staring hopelessly at two rival hostelries: the Black Swan on one side of the street, and the Black Bull opposite. The creatures on their signs faced each other as if in preparation for some bizarre bestial contest, but neither suggested itself as the American's obvious destination.

'A true conundrum. No wonder he wrote it down.' Nevell was sanguine about this reverse. 'We had best split our energies. Do you prefer the Swan or the Bull?'

I glanced between them. The Swan seemed marginally the less inviting of the two. 'The Bull.'

Nevell nodded. 'I shall take the Swan. Try to find a seat by the window, and keep your eyes as much on the street as the door. If you see Dumont or the American enter the Swan, come across immediately. I shall do likewise if they make for the Bull.'

I disliked the plan, not least for the chances of having to face the steely American on my own, but I could see few alternatives. 'What if the American has not come to meet Dumont?' I objected. 'Or else, not only Dumont? What if he has a gang of desperate cut-throats with him? We shall be of little use against them.' One of us even less than the other.

'We shall have to hazard it.' Nevell checked his watch. 'It is past a quarter to eleven, and we have little time. I shall send a runner to the Post Office to bring help – we employ some stout men there who should be equal to the task. In the meanwhile, we shall have to stand the watch ourselves.'

There was little more to be said, and with the appointed hour fast approaching I crossed the street into the dark interior of the Black Bull. If I had deemed it a fraction more inviting than its neighbour, I found little inside to recommend it – certainly not the customers, who were a coarse and vulgar rabble. A mug of ale improved my spirits somewhat, and I took a second mug with me as I made my way to the tables by the window. Seating myself with a view towards the door, I sipped my drink and kept watch, wondering at the likelihood of Brogarde or Dumont appearing, and how I would fare if they did.

173

It was a nervous lookout that I maintained, and a mountain of doubts as to whether I could even expect my quarry did nothing to improve my humour. Several times I looked across to the Black Swan, but between the thick lead and the smeared panes I could see nothing of Nevell; I could only hope he was primed in his position. I tried to remain inconspicuous, but it was difficult when I had to gaze at every man who entered or left the tavern, and the number of suspicious, often hostile glares that I drew in return did nothing to calm me. This was a pathetic plan, I decided, and had I not known Nevell would berate me for leaving my post I would have given up and returned to Mrs McCaird's, to rest a head that wide-eyed staring and a quart of ale had pounded almost to breaking.

As so often in my career, my eyes were fixed far in the distance when danger appeared close at hand. I was scanning the street, wondering whether I had perhaps missed Brogarde entering the Black Swan, when a jolt to the table startled me. I was no longer alone: an unsavoury ruffian whom I had seen entering a few minutes earlier was now seated opposite me. He was neither Dumont nor the American, though by his olive skin and matted beard he did not look English either. He wore a ragged waistcoat over a shirt that seemed to be woven from grime, and he watched me as if expecting me to speak. I tried to ignore him.

'Do you look for someone?' he asked. He had a curious accent, and I struggled to understand his guttural words. Clearly I had not been as subtle as I had hoped, if even he had noticed my vigil. I deliberated whether to speak honestly or not – he might, after all, be one of Nevell's auxiliaries, though he did not look like an employee of the Post Office. After some pause, I chose compromise and a nondescript grunt.

'I look for a man who look for someone,' he informed me.

I squirmed in my seat. Was this a lascivious advance? We

had often been warned in the navy of the peculiar habits of foreigners, and though I had dismissed it then as understandable vilification, perhaps I had been wrong.

'I am looking for someone,' I informed him, 'but he is not you.'

I did not care to admit even that much, but I had hoped a staunch refusal would deter the man. Instead, it seemed to encourage him; his eyes widened, and he leaned forward in confidence. His breath smelled of fish and onions.

'Dumont? You look for Dumont?'

I was so astonished I could not deny it. Clearly he must be one of the Post Office men, perhaps in disguise. 'I am looking for Dumont,' I affirmed. 'Did Nevell's message find you?'

The man shook his head, his long hair swinging about his face. 'I hear from Monsieur Otto. He tell everyone your message. Dumont, he is with – *comment vous dîtes?* – the smith.'

The hopes I had leaned on crumbled to dust, and my understanding with it. Monsieur Otto was the French ambassador whose house we had watched from behind the hedge – obviously I had sent no message through him. And how could he know Dumont's whereabouts, unless . . . ?

The man opposite stood, extending his hand to me urgently. 'Come,' he said simply. 'Dumont wants very much to see you, Monsieur Brogarde.'

Alone and helpless, I could only follow him out of the tavern. The misconception was all too awfully clear: the trap we had set for the American had sprung back, and I was snared. If the ruffian had mistaken me for Brogarde, as it appeared, then he might well bring me to my quarry. But he might equally be leading me to quiet oblivion, to a blade across my throat in some forgotten alley. Even if I did meet Dumont, what would he do when he saw that his expected ally was in truth his former captain and gaoler? I had seen in the Chatham sawpit what he would do to those who stood in his way.

I looked back in misery, desperately hoping that Nevell would have seen my plight and followed. There was no sign of him.

'You are worried they follow us?' My guide had noticed my glance. I opened my mouth to deny it, but he was still speaking his rough, fractured syllables. 'Good. We have always to be careful. Otherwise . . .' He drew his finger across his neck.

It was an image that preyed ever stronger on my mind, and I could barely stomach seeing it mimed before me. My legs sagged, their strength lost; I had to pretend I had tripped on a paving stone to explain the convulsion which shuddered my stride. Where in Christ's name was Nevell? Surely if he had been watching customers entering the Black Bull, he would have noticed the strange manner of my leaving – he was rarely, after all, unobservant. Though it would be wholly in keeping with my luck if that had been the moment some serving girl caught his eye.

And if he had not followed swiftly, he would have little chance of finding me now. My French guide had led me off the main road and down a narrow lane. There were neither passers-by nor loiterers in this street, the one corner of London where that could be so, and even so close to noon the sun could not pry a way between the looming buildings above.

You must keep calm, I told myself, mouthing the words over and over again to compel belief. You must keep calm. If the Frenchman thinks you are Brogarde, he will hardly visit harm upon you. You are safe for the moment. You are safe . . .

I was not safe. Lost in my terror, I did not see the hand that reached for me until I was spun about and pushed violently against the side of a house. My knees gave way and I collapsed. A firm palm on the back of my head pressed my forehead into the crumbling stone wall, and even when I felt another hand reaching over my shoulder I could not move. But I did not feel the cool steel I had expected; instead, surprisingly soft cloth was being pulled over my head. Would he garrotte me, choke the life from my windpipe? No – the cloth was not coming down to my throat. It rested just on the bridge of my nose, covering my eyes so that even had I not screwed them shut I would have been blinded. The hand was off the crown of my head now, though I felt the pressure restored as something was knotted hard against it. I had been blindfolded – in preparation for murder? It seemed strangely redundant.

'You will excuse me.' Stranger still, there was no malice in the guide's words. 'We must have care. Perhaps you are not who you say.' He chuckled, to show what nonsense he thought such a possibility. 'Now I move you.'

I would have thought that little could oppress me more than being blindfolded by a French criminal and herded through unknown streets, but the euphoria that followed my reprieve from death proved an improbable tonic. My limbs relaxed, my heart eased, and I moved where the Frenchman indicated without complaint. Perhaps I exaggerate, for there was no comfort in being driven through the sorts of streets where a blindfolded man drew no comment, and even with my captor to guide me it was still a tripping, unsteady progress. By the surrounding sounds and smells I guessed we were deep in one of the mean parts of London, a rookery, perhaps; the voices that chattered about me were shrill and often angry. At first I tried to count the turns we made, but they were many and sudden, and soon I gave up. I sensed we walked on unmapped streets, and I did not think anything I did would help me find this place again. Nor perhaps escape it.

'*Attention!*'

The Frenchman's warning was just too late to keep me from catching my toe on a raised threshold, but he managed to grab hold of my coat before I sprawled on the ground. Even as I caught my breath I felt his hands loosening the scarf around my head, and in a second my eyes were open and unfettered, blinking at my new surrounds.

My first thought, even allowing for my recent blindness, was that the light was brighter than I'd expected after the dark passages and dim corners of the earlier slums. Then I saw the reason: the house I stood in had neither roof nor ceiling, but was open from the ground to the sky. Charred walls towered around me, while the floor was covered with ash and rubble and cracked beams lying askew. It must have been eviscerated by fire, a fire which had also brought down the wall that divided it from its neighbour; for though the adjoining building retained its roof and floors, one side was entirely exposed, like an architect's diagram or a doll's house. The place stank of smoke and piss, and from within the more intact house I could hear the sullen sound of voices.

'*Venez.*'

The Frenchman led me into the shadow of the ground floor of the surviving building. The doors and windows had been nailed over with planks, but I could see a few palliasses lying on the ground near the walls, and a crooked ladder rising through a hole in the centre of the ceiling. My guide waved me to mount it, though I was all too aware of how clear a target I would be to anyone watching from above. If Dumont was there, he would recognize me at once. But my guide was climbing up beneath me, chivvying me along, and I had no alternative but to continue.

Several pairs of eyes watched me haul myself through the hole, and mercifully none was Dumont's. Two heavy-set men sat under a window playing cards, while in the middle of the room a third figure, older and thinner, pored over something on a table. It was a crude piece of furniture, seemingly made from a dismembered door athwart two

178

trestles, and it sagged under the weight of a myriad jars and bottles. It was like something from a drunkard's paradise: brandy and wine and gin bottles of every shape and colour, glass and earthenware, arranged in loose rows before a man who looked altogether too sober for such a collection.

'I would not drink from those. I use them for my inks.'

The man at the table, who must have seen my gaze, spoke slowly and with great care. He sounded foreign, though more cultured than the brute who had fetched me, and from the calm authority in his tone I sensed he was the leader. He wore a butcher's apron over his clothes, and his shirt sleeves were pushed back above his elbows; on his nose, beneath a loose mop of white curls, a pair of very round spectacles watched me carefully.

'You are Monsieur Brogarde?' he asked.

I managed a noncommittal murmur.

'They call me the smith. *Le forgeron*. We were not sure to expect you. The message was . . . not clear.'

I grunted something which may have sounded like an apology.

'You are fortunate we found Dumont – or that he found us. For a man so important, his escape was not planned so well as you should.'

'The best laid plans . . .' I tailed off quickly, fearful of saying anything which would betray that I was not American. This man might live in a burned-out ruin, but there was an intelligence behind those spectacles that belied his circumstances.

'What do you do here?' I spoke again, trying to keep the desperation from my voice. As long as Dumont was absent I could continue this charade, and every minute that it lasted extended the slim but solitary hope that Nevell might find me.

The spectacles rose up the wrinkled forehead as he squinted at me. Had I revealed myself?

'Did they not tell you? I practise my craft.' He held up a

179

piece of paper before him. 'A five-pound note from the Bank of England. They say the truest flattery is imitation, and so I flatter the English. You see how I help the men who come to my house.'

He was a forger, I realized, and a damned able one so far as I could tell. Was he also a receiver of fleeing prisoners? How many, I wondered, had made good their escape with the passports and money he could conjure?

But as I pondered that, I lost the forger's attention. He looked over to the man who had led me there, and waved him to another ladder which stood in the corner of the room.

'*Allez chercher Dumont, Georges*. Georges came from the *Vigilant*, at Port's Mouth,' the forger explained.

Even before the man was halfway up the ladder a pair of feet had appeared, dangling through the opening. They found a purchase and began to climb down, rung by rung, while I watched in sickened impotence. The only exit was the hole in the floor by which I had come up, and though there was no wall on my right to impede me, I did not care to risk the leap onto the treacherous stones below. Even if it did not break my leg, I would not know where to run, and I doubted these Frenchmen would be slow in pursuit.

'*Voyez. L'américain est arrivé.*'

I turned back. The object of so much anguish and effort stood at the foot of the ladder, a few yards away, staring at me in utter confusion. So much had passed since last I saw him that I had almost forgotten his true appearance, recasting him in my mind as a hulking, iron-faced villain, but in fact his features were smooth, almost feminine, and his frame was slight. I could see how he had passed for Isobel in a bonnet, for his black curls hung low over his face. His skin was darker, though, and now graced with several days' beard. His eyes were wide with surprise and – unexpectedly – fear.

Not so much fear as to silence him. Though clearly

unable to comprehend how I came to be there, Dumont could see enough to know my danger. He shouted out a stream of panicked French, and before I could move an inch the two card-players had sprung forward and thrust me against the wall. The third man, Georges, stood by the table, and I saw that a knife had appeared in his hand.

'*Vous en voulez?*' He proffered the knife to Dumont. Again the sight of the savage rent in the carpenter's throat flashed into my thoughts, but Dumont proved un-expectedly squeamish: he shook his head, and looked away.

It was no reprieve. With an indifferent shrug, the ogre with the knife stepped forward, stretching his arm as if afraid of straining it by striking too soon. Pinned down by his companions, I could do nothing but watch the wicked blade approach, hovering in the air before me.

Perhaps because my mind had already surrendered to death, the shot surprised me least of all in that room. Shards of wood flew from the ceiling, and I saw the forger clutching his face where it bled from the splinters. The men holding me let go in surprise, and with the burning impulse of flight driving me I flung myself forward. From the corner of my eye I thought I saw Nevell's head rising through the hatch in the floor. Wreathed in smoke and dressed in his red coat, he appeared like some demonic jack-in-the-box. The nearest Frenchman lunged for him with a knife, but he had not reckoned on Nevell's thoroughness: a second gun was waiting no more than a foot from the man's face, and he fell back screaming.

Nevell vaulted off the top of the ladder and crouched low, sweeping his gun about the room in search of new danger. He did not have far to look, for there were still two of the French ruffians standing uncertainly by the far wall, while the forger was on his feet again with a smashed bottle in his hand. In the opposite corner, Dumont cowered under the ladder.

All eyes were on Nevell, and I saw my chance. While his opponents hesitated, I launched myself towards the forger; he had his back to me and came down easily under my charge. He was a wiry fighter, clawing and heaving to throw me off, but the extra girth I had gained aboard the *Prometheus* served me well, and he could not dislodge me. As I wrestled him, another shot exploded above my head. For a second I feared one of the Frenchmen had found a gun, for surely Nevell could not have reloaded so soon, but Nevell was standing and one of his enemies was not. The other saw the gun must now be empty and charged forward, flailing his arms like a prize fighter, but Nevell stood his ground undaunted, and when the man was almost upon him he raised the pistol and rammed it into the man's breast. There was no explosion, but unfathomably it halted the Frenchman, who stared down at the blood seeping across his chest with mortal incomprehension.

I had no time to admire the victory, for Nevell's shots had filled the room with smoke and I had lost sight of Dumont. Letting go my grip on the forger, I plunged forward to the corner where I had last seen him. I could discern little, but before I was halfway across the room I heard the sound of a movement to my right. Heedless of danger or peril, I threw myself towards it: I could not countenance Dumont escaping this trap. My aim was true, and there came a sharp cry of anguish as my shoulder dug into something hard.

'Take that!' I roared, pummelling him with merciless abandon. All the days of fear and frustration were channelled into my arm, and though I did not always strike my target I felt a savage power surging through me. 'You've led me a hellish dance, you murdering villain, but you'll not escape our chains this time.'

'Jerrold?' Through the rain of blows, my prisoner found his voice. 'Jerrold, you oaf, what the devil are you doing?'

The smoke parted, and my fists fell to my side. Though

battle had blackened his face and dishevelled his coat, even in my fury I could not mistake the voice.

'Nevell?'

He glared at me, blood oozing from a cut below his eye. 'Indeed.'

'I thought you were Dumont. I . . .'

The rumble of sliding rocks behind me forestalled my apologies. With Nevell beside me I ran to the open edge of the room and looked out over the devastated shell of the adjacent house. A figure in a torn shirt and yellow trousers disappeared into the street beyond.

'*No!*' The error of my brawl with Nevell had done nothing to curb the desperate frenzy that ruled me, and thinking only of Dumont, of the absolute imperative of allowing him no escape, I jumped from the edge of the house onto the rubble below. It was not a high leap, and Dumont must have made it before me, but the landing was treacherous and I felt a wrench as my ankle twisted in the broken stones. Still my mind refused to allow defeat. With spasms of pain shooting through my foot, I hobbled to the open doorway and peered into the street.

There was no sign of Dumont.

I slumped against the blackened wall as quick footsteps came up behind me. Wiser than I, Nevell must have taken the ladder, but it had served him no better. One look at the street confirmed the hideous, impossible truth.

Dumont had escaped. Again.

15

'Stay here,' Nevell told me.

'Where are you going?'

'For help, of course.' Nevell rubbed his cheek, where a large bruise was beginning to flourish. 'To call out the runners, the Horse Patrol, the River Police, the Charleys, the dragoons and anyone else who can catch the villain before he escapes. You should wait here.'

The prospect of waiting in that derelict building in the heart of a rookery, crippled as I was and with a quartet of Frenchmen who might not yet be dead, was unappealing. 'I am hardly—'

'Take this.' Nevell threw me the pistol he still held. 'And these.' A small ammunition pouch followed it through the air and fell at my feet. 'If any of them are still alive, try to keep them so.'

Before I could object, he slipped out through the broken doorway and disappeared.

With a sigh, I lowered myself onto a block of rubble. The uneven edges dug into my backside, but it was a relief to take the weight off my injured foot. After all the uproar of the battle, my surroundings seemed unnaturally still: even the street outside remained hushed. Clearly the tenor of the neighbourhood was such that a few gunshots on a Thursday afternoon drew scant attention.

Wondering what I would do if a curious neighbour should emerge, I looked at the pistol I held, the weapon with which Nevell had somehow accounted for three Frenchmen. It was a remarkable device, with two muzzles mounted one above the other and a short bayonet on a sprung hinge set beneath. The blade was still extended, wet with blood. No wonder Nevell had been able to fire without reloading, and then, with his shots exhausted, turn the gun into a rapier.

Holding it gingerly to avoid cutting my wrist, I took some powder and shot from Nevell's box and prodded them down the barrels. I could not see how it worked, for there appeared to be only a single trigger, flint and frizzen, but the mere weight of the gun in my hands was reassuring. More than reassuring, for after a few moments sitting there I felt sufficiently emboldened to return to the house and investigate. As long as the Frenchmen within remained dead, it would be more satisfying than having my buttocks dented waiting for Nevell.

It was hard work mounting the ladder with my hobbled foot – the same poor foot, I noticed, as had lost its boot in the Medway swamp – but I managed to haul myself up the rungs. As I came through the trapdoor I jerked my gun about in awkward defence, but none of the Frenchmen moved. Two lay by the wall where Nevell had felled them, while the third, who had run onto the spike of his gun, was immediately behind me. Of the forger whom I had wrestled to the ground, there was no sign.

Careless of giving offence to the dead, I swore aloud. Another French blackguard escaped, another link with our quarry lost. He must have scurried away while Nevell and I were distracted by Dumont, and I had little doubt that he would be as far away as his compatriot by now. But there was still the second ladder leading into the attic, whence Dumont had come, and I did not discount the possibility that the forger might have hidden himself there. Clutching Nevell's pistol tighter, I endured a fresh bout of pain and worry as I climbed again, my approach utterly betrayed by my constant wincing and wheezing.

Thankfully, there was no-one to hear me. When the side of the house had collapsed it had taken a fair portion of the roof with it, and it was easy to see that under the skeleton of beams and rafters that survived, the room was uninhabited. I scrambled through the opening and crawled across the rough floor, protecting my head as much as my foot, to a small bundle in one corner where the roof still stood. There was a straw mattress with a blanket, and balled up at its head a blue dress with a white collar. I unfolded it, patting the fabric for any hidden papers and thinking how much more pleasant had been the last time I felt it. I did not intend to take it back to Isobel after all the wickedness Dumont had concocted in it.

There was nothing in the dress, nor in the blanket either. I tried poking Nevell's bayonet into the mattress, but struck nothing save the floorboards beneath. Leaving Dumont's few possessions where they were, I slid back down the ladder to the main room and crossed to the forger's desk. It was scattered with papers, mostly Bank of England notes, drawn in perfect facsimile and with the ink still fresh on them, but a few looked to be reproductions of forms or passports. One in particular, weighted under a bottle of green ink, caught my eye, for it seemed curiously familiar.

The Commissioners for the Transport Service and for the care and custody of prisoners of war having concluded an exchange with the government of France, the bearer, as described and detailed on the reverse, is to be immediately afforded safe conduct and speedy passage aboard the ships of the Cartel, as may next be convenient upon his arrival in Plymouth. Given on this twenty-seventh day of July, 1806.

I blinked. No wonder it had appeared familiar: it was a passport for exchanged prisoners, their ticket back to France. As *Prometheus'* captain I had signed several in the previous months. Clearly the forger had somehow obtained one; and copied it liberally, for there were half a dozen or so more under the ink bottle. Even the seals on them were perfect replicas.

The sound of sliding rubble outside interrupted my thoughts. Nevell had returned. I crossed to the edge of the room and looked down.

'Did you find him?' I called. The words died away quickly, dragged down by the dust in the air.

He shook his head. 'I've arranged for runners to patrol the streets, and riders at all the bridges and toll gates out of the city. Whether he runs or stays, he can't elude us for ever.'

'He's managed it well so far.' I waved the paper I still held in my hand. 'But I think I know where he'll make for.'

'Where?'

'Plymouth. I found a supply of forged passports for the Cartel ship.'

It was flimsy enough evidence for going gallivanting across the country, and I fully expected Nevell to reject it immediately. To my surprise, he gave the impression of considering the suggestion, before raising his head. 'Plymouth,' he repeated. 'That would reckon. But he'd need to be quick to reach it before the alarm was raised.'

I had little idea why Nevell should think it so likely, but I was gratified he had not dismissed my notion out of hand. 'If we wasted a day or two searching London, he might have all the time he needed,' I suggested.

Again, Nevell was in unexpected agreement. 'He might well.' He fell silent for a moment, then twitched his head and stared directly up at me. 'You'd best fetch your belongings from your landlady's, Jerrold; I shall meet you there in an hour.'

'And then?'

Nevell smiled. 'We go to Plymouth.'

I had not thought it would be as easy as that, but I had reckoned without Nevell's extraordinary sway over the Post Office machinery. Somehow he contrived to find me a chair to take me back to Mrs McCaird's, and I had been there barely a quarter of an hour when his coach drew up outside her door.

'Have you made your farewells to Isobel?' he asked, meeting me on the doorstep.

'I've left her a note.' Isobel had been out, doubtless improving herself, and if I felt sadness that I would not get a kiss to speed me on my way, it was tempered with relief that I would be spared the task of explaining why I hastened away from her again.

The coachman appeared by Nevell's side. He wore two pistols at his belt, I noticed, and had the build of a pugilist. 'Take your box, sir?'

'I have none.' It seemed a poor prospect to be undertaking a five-day journey without so much as a clean shirt, but until Dumont stopped dragging me inexorably across the country, I feared I was fated never to patronize a tailor.

I stepped up through the door, and settled myself on the bench facing the driver. Even without the motion of the road it was an uncomfortable perch; after three hundred miles of it, I doubted I would ever want to sit again.

Nevell seated himself opposite me and rapped on the roof.

'Gratified as I am by your trust in my opinion' – I broke off as the coach jolted forward – 'I do feel that a forged pass in a ruined house is rather slim evidence to send us away to the ends of the country. Do you not agree?'

'Not at all.' Nevell's shoulders swayed easily with the rhythm of the carriage.

'But why so much haste?' I pressed, irritated as ever by

his niggardly answers. 'Dumont cannot have left London in the last hour and a half – he must still be somewhere in the city, even if he does purpose to make for Plymouth. And with the hue and cry up, he can hardly book himself on the next coach from the Golden Cross. If he reaches Plymouth in a week he'll count himself damned lucky.'

'You underestimate him. As have we all. You saw those banknotes on the forger's table. If Dumont managed to snatch but a handful of them, he'll find a private coach and fresh horses in every town. He knows that time is our ally, and speed his only hope. He's desperate, Jerrold, and desperate men do not dally.'

'Perhaps not. But a forged piece of paper does not mean he is hurrying to Plymouth. Why not Dover, or Sandwich, or any hamlet on the coast where a fisherman can be persuaded to cross the Channel on a dark night? Why risk the longest possible journey to our most fortified harbour, in the slim hope that a Cartel ship will sail before the inevitable pursuit catches up with him?' A hole in the road stopped my little rant as my head was bounced against the roof.

Nevell watched me calmly. 'Perhaps because he does not appreciate the distance involved, or because he believes the search will be strongest nearer London. But the true reason we are travelling so precipitately to Plymouth is that it makes perfect sense.'

'To your eye, perhaps.'

'Listen to me.' There was the merest hint of impatience in Nevell's voice. 'I am as ignorant as you as to why an unremarkable French sailor should cause such panic at the highest levels of government. But I may exercise a guess. I told you at the Secret Office that we had taken an interest in Dumont for some time, ever since we suspected he might be receiving messages from France in cipher. Our fear was that he might figure in a scheme to incite a concerted mutiny among all the French prisoners in England.'

'Did you have any evidence for this?' As ever, on the rare occasions when Nevell chose to be frank with me, I found his theories utterly incredible.

'Nothing specific,' Nevell admitted. 'But there have been rumours of such a plot swirling about for months now.'

'Rumours,' I snorted. 'Nevell, I was gaoler to eight hundred of these prisoners, and if I had a guinea for every time some such dastardly piece of villainy was rumoured, I'd have retired from the navy inside a month. Half the time they were trying to stir up mischief and put some fear into us; the other half were pathetic attempts to earn rewards by men who'd lost all else in gambling.'

'Of course there are always rumours,' said Nevell coolly. 'As there are always rumours that the Corsican ogre is about to appear on our shores with a hundred thousand men. As you know, their frequency does not mean they can all be dismissed.'

'No,' I allowed. 'But of all the dangers that concerned me aboard *Prometheus*, I did not lose a single minute of sleep worrying that a concerted league of Frenchmen might rise up across the country.'

'Nor, I suppose, did you worry that your interpreter would abscond dressed as your mistress, and bring down your entire command in ruin.' Nevell sounded almost waspish now. 'It is my job to treat seriously with rumours, and when I see them increase markedly, as they have in the past months, I treat them more seriously still. Prisoners are escaping in ever greater numbers, and those we find are turning up in the most unlikely, far-flung places. Look at this.' He reached into the leather bag which sat on the seat beside him and withdrew a map. 'Across southern England, from the Medway to the Dart, there are a dozen prisons and eighteen parole towns, most of them on the turnpike roads and all stuffed with French sailors and officers. Then there are the hulks, concentrated at Chatham, Portsmouth and Plymouth, in dangerous

190

proximity to our most vital naval yards and anchorages. Imagine, Jerrold, if they all rose up together. They could paralyse the country, block our harbours, wreck our fleet and tie up tens of thousands of troops trying to quell the rebellion. If Buonaparte managed to reinforce them from Brest or Cherbourg, they could hold out for months, perhaps even act as a bridgehead for a full-blown invasion.'

Aware that he had lost his habitual serenity, Nevell paused and leaned back. 'Of course, that last possibility is remote, but the damage a revolt could do remains fearsome. Whatever the outcome, it would certainly topple the government of the day.'

He fell silent again as the carriage began to slow. Looking out of the window, I could see the wooden gate of the Hyde Park turnpike, where dozens of hawkers milled about offering various comestibles, cushions, diversions and almanacs to those making the journey west.

Ignoring the press of men, Nevell unlatched the door and pushed it open. Almost immediately, a young pedlar had hopped up onto the step and thrust his cheery face into our compartment.

'Beggin' your pardons, sirs, but if you've a penny or two spare after payin' the toll, you'd not do better'n investin' in a little information.' He pursed his lips together, and nodded soberly. 'Forewarned is forearmed, they says, an' it's the road you don't know as is most dangerous.'

'Get out,' I snapped. If there was one thing I would happily leave behind in London, it was the constant and unflagging attentions of commerce, which made the whores of Portsmouth seem shy as nuns. Nevell, though, did not damn the man his brazen impudence.

'What do you have for me, Higgins?' he asked crisply.

A stack of pocket-size books was thrust before us. 'Starck's Compendium. Reverend Lawrence's Tour to the West of England. Paterson's New and Accurate Description of the

Roads. 'E ain't been seen 'ere, Mr Nevell, nor on the New Road neither.'

These final words flowed on so effortlessly from his patter that I almost failed to notice them – as, I belatedly realized, must have been the intention.

'How much for the Lawrence?' Nevell asked.

'Eight shillins, sir.' Balancing the pile of books in one hand, the pedlar deftly slid a volume out and passed it to Nevell.

'Thank you.' Nevell dropped the coins into the man's palm. 'Keep up your vigil, and send word to the Post Office immediately you see him.'

Touching a knuckle to his forehead, the pedlar swayed backwards and vanished into the crowd. Nevell pulled the door shut as the coach's wheels began to grind forward again.

'I take it you knew him,' I said, lacking any more intelligent comment.

'I know many people,' said Nevell cheerfully. 'If you were a hunted fugitive, would you approach a gate watched by a squadron of dragoons, or one served by a ragged man selling travel literature?' He tossed the book into my lap. 'Even if he had nothing to report, at least you now have something to pass the hours.'

Something with which I was intimately acquainted before we had even reached Staines. Nevell could often be an amiable companion, but on that journey he kept to himself, lost in private and unspeakable thoughts: on the few occasions when I attempted conversation, an uninterested reply and a reproving stare were my only reward. The jittering motion of the coach was unrelenting, bruising my back and thighs, and leaving every muscle sore with tension. Our pace demanded frequent stops to change the horses, but despite my plaintive looks there was never the least delay at the inns. The time it took to get a new quartet of unfortunate nags into the traces, and a few words with the ostlers to ascertain whether Dumont had passed, was all Nevell allowed us. The sun began to dip into the horizon ahead of us, but if the coachman found himself blinded he did not let it slow him. The air inside the cabin was stifling, but when once I opened the window a great plume of dust came pouring in, coating my clothes and the seats and sending me into a profound fit of coughing. After that I suffered the heat in silence.

Evening wore on, and somehow, between the creaking of the springs, the rumble of the wheels, the snap of the driver's lash and the hammering of hooves, I fell into a sort of trance, staring at the passing landscape without comprehension. It had been a day of bewildering turns, of near victory and nearer disaster, and at its end I was happy simply to be alone with my thoughts.

Somewhere past Frogmore, pausing for yet another change of horses, I noticed the coachman lighting the lamps on the side of the carriage.

'Will we continue all night?' I asked. Weariness and worry inflected my voice: my aching body craved the softness of a bed, and feared for the brigands we might meet on the road after dark. Already the sun had sunk behind a small copse, and the blue of the sky was deepening quickly.

'Not all night,' said Nevell, trying to stretch some kink out of his neck. The long hours of constant noise and motion seemed at last to have drained his energy, and his face was drawn. 'Even a man as determined as Dumont would struggle to match our pace, I'd say. We'll press on to Basingstoke and pass the night there.'

'Why not wait here?' I asked. 'As you say, he's unlikely to be ahead of us. Rather than racing him to Plymouth, let him run straight into us.'

Nevell shook his head. 'Assuming he will travel by road – which he may not – he has a choice of routes as far as Exeter. He may have taken the Bristol road, and plan to drop south later. We would look a fine pair of fools if we were still sitting here when word came from Plymouth that he'd sailed away on the Cartel ship. Besides, I agreed with Major Lebrett that we would meet him in Salisbury tomorrow noon.'

'*What?*' The fragile peace I had imposed on my thoughts was shattered at the sound of that dreaded name. 'Lebrett? Why the devil did you send for him?'

'Because whatever his motives, he yields to none in his desire to see Dumont apprehended. With the situation so grave, your personal animosity must be ruled by necessity.'

Even if all England was to be consumed in fire and rout, it would be a long time before I could greet Lebrett with anything other than horror. I sat through the last stage of the day in miserable silence, gobbled down a few lumps of beef at the inn at Basingstoke, and retired to my room. Though a slab of rock would have seemed like a feather bed after the bucking carriage, I found no solace in the mattress: the prospect of long hours on the road and a rendezvous with Lebrett allowed for scant comfort. It was well past midnight when I at last forced myself to sleep.

16

Nevell had us away at dawn, which in high summer was dismally early. The only mercy was that the first stage of our road was in reasonable repair, and by careful adjustment of the pillow I had purloined from the inn I was able to snatch a few miles of sleep. At last the seemingly endless sequence of late nights and hard days overtook me, and it needed a sharp tug at my arm from Nevell to wake me as, two hours later, we rolled into Andover.

'Is it breakfast time?' I asked, with faint hope. I feared Nevell's itinerary made little allowance for sustenance.

To my surprise, he acquiesced. 'See what you can forage for us. I must go and see the parole agent.'

'Why the parole agent?'

'Because among his charges here he numbers one Captain Troufflet, Dumont's erstwhile commander. If there is a conspiracy afoot, it stands to reason that Dumont might seek him out.'

I did not ask how Nevell came by his intelligence, but allowed him to hurry away, while I ambled down the high street. The air was fresh, for the dusty road had not yet been stirred, and there were few passers-by. Most of the shops remained closed until a more fashionable hour, but I found a baker who sold me two loaves of bread. I tore into the warm dough like a foxhound, and had eaten half a loaf in front of two astonished maids before I recollected myself and headed back for the privacy of the coach. For the number of hours I had spent seated or in bed, I had worked up a prodigious appetite.

Nevell was waiting for me by the coach, stroking the horse's nose as he fed it a carrot.

'I don't think the agent expected to be roused at this hour, but he directed me to Captain Troufflet. I assumed you would want to accompany me.' He took the bread I offered, and tore off a hunk.

'I had thought to repair to the inn and see if I might find a mug of beer to wash down my breakfast. Do you expect the captain to have any useful intelligence?'

Nevell shrugged. 'If I only sought answers where I expected to find them, I would find far less than I expected.'

As a rule, I found far less than expected wherever I looked. But I forsook my beer – it would only have occasioned further delay down the road – and instead followed Nevell down the high street to a bright red front door.

'They're upstairs, the officers,' the landlady informed us. She was a pinched woman, with suspicious eyes and an ungainly nose, and I felt her gaze watching us all the way up the cracked staircase. From behind a door I heard the most incongruous sounds of revelry: the clatter of glasses, the chatter of voices, and the laughter of women.

'How long did I sleep?' I wondered aloud. 'Is it evening already?'

'Half-past seven in the morning.'

Nevell rapped sharply on the door. The noises within ceased abruptly, succeeded by a few mutterings and the sound of unsteady footsteps approaching. With a grunt and a creak, the door edged open.

'*Oui?*'

If ever there was a man to prove the full worth of a commission, it was the officer who now stood before us in the doorway. While the men in the hulks had been reduced to pitiful wretches of skin and bone, he was ravaged only by vice. The fruits of captivity had expanded his belly to such girth that three of the buttons on his breeches had to remain undone; his shirt was untucked, and open well down his chest. His face had taken the colour of burgundy, and his dark hair was tousled and uncombed. Even his moustache had wilted. His words, when he spoke, were laced with brandy and tobacco.

'You have interrupted a meeting of the Philosophical Society,' he informed me, leaning his vast bulk against the frame.

From the room within, I heard a young lady's voice start to talk, and then break off in a fit of hushing and giggling. Philosophically speaking, I guessed we had much in common.

'Are you Captain Troufflet?' Nevell asked.

'*Non*. He has gone out.'

'Where?'

The Frenchman blew air into his florid cheeks, so that they puffed out like bladders. '*Je ne sais pas*. Perhaps the road.' He belched. 'He has enjoyed very much philosophy last night.'

'Thank you.' Disdain was evident in Nevell's voice. 'Tell me, *monsieur*, has anyone called for him in the last day or so?'

'I called for 'im,' a girl's voice piped up from inside. A brief, lewd rendition of precisely how she had called him followed. 'But 'e wouldn't stay with me. Must've lost 'is 'eart to the Yankee.'

No sooner had she spoken than I heard a commotion within, a tussling followed by a thud and a brief scream. Nevell kicked open the door, slipped past the French officer and burst in on his companions. It was dark inside, for the curtains were still drawn across the window and the fire in the grate had burned out, but there was no mistaking the stale debauchery which passed for the transactions of the Philosophical Society. Two French officers were sitting on a bed leaning against a wall, while on the floor another of their number was straddling a young woman, his hand pressed over her mouth. Three more girls stood gaping in a corner, crooking their arms over their chests in half-hearted attempts at belated modesty. Empty bottles and clothes and scattered cards and ash were strewn about the room.

'Let her go,' Nevell shouted. 'Let her go or I'll see every man here sent to the hulks at Portsmouth.'

Breathing hard, the Frenchman got off his knees and sat heavily on the bed. 'The English girls,' he muttered. 'They should save their tongues for—'

'Silence!' Nevell held out a hand and pulled the girl to her feet. So surprised was she by the kindness, she did not even pull her dress up from about her waist.

'You said an American called for Captain Troufflet.'

'Cap'n Truffle.' The girl looked at the floor, volunteering nothing further.

'Did you see him, this American?'

'Yep.'

'What did he look like?'

'Better'n these pigs,' said the girl, jerking her thumb at the men on the bed. 'Taller, thinner. 'Stinguished, I s'pose. But dangerous. There was a terrible scar.' She dragged a grubby fingernail down over her cheek.

'Was there another man with him?'

'No.'

'And when was he here?' Nevell's hand, I saw, had gone to the holster sewn inside his coat.

The girl shrugged her plump shoulders. 'I weren't checkin' the clock. Hour ago?'

At that, even Nevell could not contain his impatience.

We tore down the stairs three at a time, almost crushing the curious landlady who had been listening from their foot, and flung open the door.

'Captain Troufflet,' gasped Nevell on the threshold. 'Did you see which way he went?'

'Didn't see 'im leave,' said the landlady haughtily. 'Where 'e goes's 'is own business, so long as it's in the town. But 'e usually goes south – says it takes 'im nearer 'ome.'

We sprinted back to the coach and clambered onto the driver's box. There was barely room for three of us up there, and with our frantic, lurching progress I several times found myself sliding precipitously towards the edge of the seat. The growling of the wheel beneath sounded terrifyingly loud, and one leg of my breeches was covered in the grime it threw up before we had gone a quarter of a mile. But I clung on, and prayed there would be no sudden ruts or holes to bounce me into oblivion.

In our haste we had forgotten to take a description of Captain Troufflet, but we had little trouble identifying him. He was standing on the roadside by a wooden post, about a mile out of Andover, the only traveller at that hour who was not clearly destined for labouring in the fields. To the frustration of my hopes, he was alone.

'Don't move another step,' I shouted, leaping down from the carriage in relief.

Any satisfaction I gained from the fact that he did not move was tempered by the small, unworried smile that played across his face.

'I could not move another step even if I wanted it. If I leave this road, or pass this post, I break my parole.' He waved an arm across the surrounding fields, where a dozen heads could be seen protruding from the waves of corn. 'They will be happy to report it if I do so.'

'What can you tell us of a man named Dumont?'

Captain Troufflet leaned back against the post. 'Nothing. The name is nothing to me.'

'He was a carpenter's mate aboard your ship.'

'There were six hundred and thirty men aboard my ship. I did not know all of them.'

'You met a man an hour ago,' Nevell interrupted, changing tack. 'An American named Brogarde. What did he want?'

'And where is he now?' I added.

Troufflet's smile disappeared. 'First you ask about Dumont, then Monsieur Brogarde. I think you know very well what the American asks me.'

'I would like to hear you tell it.'

'I tell you what I have told him. Dumont was on my ship, yes, but I did not know him. I have never thought of him until today. Now in one hour I am asked two times about him.' A hint of the smile returned, as of a man resigned to standing at the fringe of events he did not understand. 'I wonder why Dumont is so important, but I tell you the same. I have not seen him.'

Nevell looked at Troufflet disbelievingly. 'Is that all the American asked you?'

'It is all.'

'He did not try to interest you in breaking your parole?'

Troufflet spread his arms wide in innocence. 'I am still here.'

I could see that Nevell found the answer utterly inadequate, but I had little time for his dark theories and suppositions. 'How long since the American left you?'

'An hour. He went south,' Troufflet added, anticipating our final question. I thought I sensed a tinge of envy in his tone. 'I hope you do not find him.'

'Perhaps the American is not spreading sedition and mutiny.' I had to shout in Nevell's ear, for we were on the roof of the carriage and the wind was billowing and snapping about us.

Nevell scowled. 'Perhaps there were things which Captain

200

Troufflet did not admit. He told us nothing he could not see we knew.'

I looked away, scanning the horizon to our left for any sign of a horseman. Brogarde must have ridden all through the night to have overtaken us, for he could not have left London before we did. How had he known? Was it pre-arranged, or had the escaped forger found him and confided all? It scarcely mattered. Now we knew we were in a race to catch Dumont, and the coachman gave his fresh horses no quarter as he scourged them forward.

'Seven miles to Salisbury,' said Nevell. Already I could see the famous spire of its cathedral rising before us, but still no horsemen broke cover. It would be a test of endurance and nerve, this chase, for we could not use our beasts so cruelly for long. If Brogarde managed to maintain his lead for another hour, we could pursue him all the way to Plymouth and never see him.

A toll gate beside a whitewashed cottage slowed us, though a blast of the post-horn would have seen us through.

'Has a horseman passed recently?' Nevell asked. 'A tall man with a scar on his cheek, an American?'

The hunched gatekeeper spat out his tobacco and looked up. 'No, sir,' he said huskily. 'There's an ox-cart back a times. None other. Quiet mornin'. Though fair,' he added, glancing at the sky.

'Absolutely.'

'Rain comin' though, I'd say. Felt it in the knees.'

Nevell looked at the cloudless sky but made no comment. For my part, I did not need an old man's bones to predict glum weather. It would be in perfect harmony with the other frustrations of the day.

A busier road and flagging horses slowed our progress as we drew near to Salisbury, but it made little odds. The American must have slipped off the road, and there was nothing we could do save follow it fruitlessly. The town was busy that Friday morning – the market was on, and every inhabitant seemed to have emerged to mingle, shop and gossip in the sun. Nowhere, however, were the crowds so thick as before the inn, where a troop of Guards were drawn up in immaculate array. The townsfolk thronged about them, the girls staring up at the sleek horses, the boys at the long horse-pistols, the women at the proud chins and stiff breeches, and the men at their womenfolk. I looked at their commander, pristine in his blue coat and gold lace, and groaned. His hat covered his eyes, but the hawkish nose and hungry mouth were unmistakable.

'Mr Nevell,' he said coolly. 'You are fifteen minutes early.' His tone implied it to be a failing.

'We were in pursuit of an accomplice of Dumont.' Nevell jumped down from the coach and approached Lebrett's horse. Reluctantly, I followed.

'He escaped, I take it.' Lebrett looked over Nevell's head to our empty carriage. 'Or have you already reposited him in the gaol?'

'He escaped, but he cannot be far. He was little more than an hour ahead of us at Andover, and we have made good time since. If you sent out your men in cordon, they might yet find him.'

Lebrett snorted. 'Have you spent so much time with Lieutenant Jerrold, Mr Nevell, that you forget the object of our charge? Our task is to apprehend Dumont. Even if Buonaparte himself were skulking about in a hedgerow, I would care not a jot until Dumont was dead or in my custody. Do I make myself plain?'

'Quite.' Nevell turned his back on Lebrett and walked back to the carriage. 'Jerrold!'

Feeling Lebrett's scornful gaze following me, I crossed to the coach. The driver had disappeared, doubtless to wash the dust from his mouth in the tavern, and Nevell was pulling out his trunk.

'What are you doing?' I asked.

'I am leaving you for a short time.'

'Leaving me? With Lebrett?' In my inglorious career I had shared wardrooms with incompetents, drunkards and vainglorious heroes: rarely had I worked with such a wilful contrarian. 'The American Brogarde is nearby, and Dumont likely with him, yet Lebrett will not chase him and now you will not even stay in the vicinity.' I was used to Nevell's irregular comings and goings, but this seemed nonsensical. And, in as much as it marooned me with Lebrett, unconscionably cruel.

'There are reasons, Jerrold,' said Nevell darkly.

'Good reasons, I hope.'

'If Dumont's aim is to spread rebellion, then it is unlikely that he and Brogarde will take the same road. I shall ride north to Devizes, and see if Dumont has been seen there. I shall also call at Bristol, for that would be the fulcrum of any great uprising.'

'And I?' I asked bitterly. 'What shall I do?'

'Keep to your course. I will leave you the carriage, and attempt to make a rendezvous at Plymouth. Doubtless Major Lebrett will escort you – see what intelligence you can pry from him. I suspect he has information which he has not imparted.'

It seemed every man I met knew facts about Dumont that he kept to himself, and Lebrett was the last from whom I would expect to prise anything. But Nevell was set on his plan, and no amount of pleading would swerve him.

'Have you concluded your gossiping?'

I turned round, to see a black stallion with a white blaze on its forehead standing over me. From high on its back, Lebrett was glaring down.

'We have made our arrangements,' Nevell told him. 'You are to accompany Lieutenant Jerrold to Plymouth, while I—'

'I am *going* to Plymouth,' Lebrett interrupted him.

'Lieutenant Jerrold will accompany me, lest I need the use of him. Whither you go, Mr Nevell, I confess I do not care. Scampering after Americans, perhaps.'

'I will meet you in Plymouth,' said Nevell. 'We will see there who has achieved the more.'

I doubted that honour would go to me.

17

There has always seemed to me something of hubris in travel – if the Almighty had meant us to go so far, he would doubtless have supplied more comfortable means than tossing ships and bouncing carriages – but the next two days were dismal even by those standards. I suppose it was not the worst it could have been, for Lebrett chose to ride with his men rather than sit with me in the coach, but otherwise I journeyed without physical or spiritual comfort. The coachman spoke hardly at all to me, and Lebrett never a civil word; the only intercourse I had was with turnpike keepers and ostlers when we stopped to change horses, always asking for news of Brogarde or Dumont, and always meeting blank faces. For the rest of the time, I read the book that Nevell had given me, the *Tour to the West of England*, until I must have known the particular histories of every town, hamlet, port and castle from Dorset to Land's End. It did nothing to cheer me.

Nor did I even see much of the countryside we passed through, for the gatekeeper's knees had proved remarkably prescient. Whether Lebrett's malevolence infected even the climate, or whether my tormenting angel wished to heap further calamities upon me, I do not know, but the golden summer ended a little past Shaftesbury, when the clouds opened with two months' pent-up ferocity. The road became a sticky, sucking mire, slowing our pace and spraying thick mud over the windows. One of the horses went lame halfway through a stage, and I, as the only member of the party who travelled in shelter, grew even more unpopular. Between the mud on the outside of the glass and the damp fog within, I could see little of the landscape we crossed: I could but gain an impression of the gentle, green hills of Dorset giving way to a sharper, spikier landscape of rock and furze and twisted trees, a wild and unforgiving place whose atmosphere was soured still further by the low clouds and sheeting rain.

On the third afternoon we reached Exeter. The rain had slowed during the morning but was now as hard as ever, and I was looking forward to escaping my dank carriage for a warm fire and cheerful company at the inn. As I emerged from the coach, I saw to my surprise that Lebrett was still mounted, and arguing with the coachman over the wind.

'We've no business goin' further now,' the coachman was protesting. 'We'll never make Plymouth tonight, an' there's nothing but moor twixt 'ere an' there. We'd not see a blind thing on them moors, an' if we lost a wheel or took a tumble, we'd be stuck out there 'til dawn.'

As a rule, I avoided Lebrett's conversation as much as possible, but this sounded like reckless lunacy. 'Surely you cannot intend to carry on,' I called, stepping gingerly through the muddy yard. 'Not with the weather blowing up a storm, and the light almost gone.' A gust of wind spat raindrops against my cheek, underlining my words.

'Keep your idle mouth shut on matters which do not concern you.' In a black riding cloak that covered him almost to his knees, Lebrett looked like some macabre bat. Thick with water, it gleamed evilly in the dim light.

'It concerns me mightily if you aim to drive us to our ruin.' The boredom and discomfort of the last few days, as much as fear for my life if we crossed the moors in darkness, put rare steel in my words.

Lebrett, though, could parry any man's steel with his own. 'You will be snug enough cosseted in your carriage. As for the road, your driver should manage to follow it.' Behind him, I saw the grooms leading out a team of reluctant horses. They skittered and shied as they were made fast in their harnesses, and seemed no more eager than I to prolong the day's journey.

'It's not right,' the coachman muttered, his words barely audible over the mounting storm. 'It's a fearsome mistake you're makin', sir.'

'We will hardly help our search by wrecking the carriage,' I added.

Lebrett's stallion, perhaps unsettled by the nervous coach horses, reared under him. 'We will continue until I call a halt, damn you. Now get back on that coach before I take the lash to you and the horses.'

It was the worst stage of our journey, and I hated Lebrett for every inch of it. From Exeter the road rose steeply through a forested escarpment, cutting back and forth across the hillside at impossible angles, but that was positively benign compared with the descent we then had to navigate. The carriage's wheels slipped and skidded as we careered round corner after corner, and I was astonished that the horses did not buckle under the strain and let their burden roll over a precipice. The leather springs were stiff with all the moisture they had absorbed, and with the constant changes of direction I found myself flung about as violently as ever I had experienced at sea. Once I swear the coach must have slid over the lip of the crag, for its right side dropped hard and only the driver's desperate use of his lash pulled us back onto the road in time. Nor was there ever the least respite, for as soon as we had reached the bottom of the hill we had barely time to cross a narrow stone bridge before making another ascent, this one almost steeper than the last. I thought of the woman whose coach the marines had pushed out of the ditch near Chatham: if we fell off the road here, we would tumble all the way back to the valley floor, and there would be little anyone could do to right us.

At last the road seemed to straighten, its gradient to ease. That was our undoing. How the horses found strength to keep hauling us along I do not know, for I had expected them to fall down dead in the traces, but with a straight path and a gentle incline they must have discovered some deep reserve of strength. Though the day was all but gone, and the way almost invisible in darkness, our speed increased. Even the coachman seemed infused with a new confidence, and I heard him hollering the horses ever forward.

'This seems a little reckless,' I muttered to myself. 'I wonder that he can see where he travels.'

I have ever had a facility for ill-timed speculation, as if my thoughts alone could spur divine correction. Hardly had the words left my lips when I heard a terrible, grating rumble; screams from the horses and shouts from the coachman. The front corner of the carriage plunged away beneath me, and I slid to the floor as the rest of the vehicle followed it. For a second there was a relative silence, then a great blow struck us and I was pitched into the air to the accompaniment of the tearing and ripping of wood. Still, I sensed, the carriage was moving, but instantly fate belied me again, for with a crushing thud its motion stopped, catapulting me to the fore of the cabin. The calm which followed was broken by two distinct cracks: the leather springs that had endured so much broke free, and suddenly I was lying against one door of the carriage while the other pointed to the sky. Somewhere through the ringing in my bruised ears I heard the sound of a solitary wheel spinning in emptiness.

I lay there for some minutes, too battered and numb to move, hoping that help would come, that Lebrett and his troopers would have seen our calamity and rushed to aid us. No-one came.

'Lebrett!' I called, my voice weak yet strangely loud in the upturned cabin.

There was no answer.

Through my pain, I became aware that there was a chill damp seeping into me. Was it blood? It was too cold for that. I reached a hand under me and felt about. It came away wet, and as I licked my finger I realized it was water. Fresh, crisp water, trickling in through the shattered window that had become the floor. Dragging myself to my knees, I splashed some over my face, which stung from the mask of cuts and grazes I had sustained in the accident. We must have tumbled off the road, down a bank and into a stream.

Still no help came. Had Lebrett outstripped us so far that he had not noticed our disaster? Or had he indeed witnessed it, and deliberately left us to our fate? It was a monstrous thing to think of any man, but if I could think any capable of it, it would be Lebrett. And where was the coachman?

As the minutes flowed by, and the pool of water at the bottom of the carriage rose, I began to feel the terrible loneliness of my predicament. What had become of my companions I did not know, but if they were here they would surely have rescued me by now. I must be alone – in the godforsaken wilderness of Dartmoor, on a stormy night, with little hope of aid or shelter.

But whatever my surroundings, staying in the upturned, waterlogged carriage would avail me nothing. I looked about the cabin, but I had only my little leather book, lodged in the corner of the seat. I took it and thrust it in my pocket, for if I were to find myself lost in the moors, at least its maps might serve some use. Then I pushed open the door above my head, fastened my hands on what had once been the step, and hauled myself out.

The carriage swayed precipitously as I emerged onto its side, and I hastily leaped off it onto the ground, wincing as a spasm of pain shot through the foot I had injured in London. It remained tender as I clambered over the uneven ground to the front of the coach, to see what had become of the driver.

If my situation was bad, his was worse. He had been thrown a short distance from his box and lay sprawled on the embankment, limp and unmoving, though his left hand remained clasped tight around the reins. A broad trail of blood ran down the centre of his face. He was dead, and though I had said barely a dozen words to him in the past three days, I felt a welling anger that Dumont's chase and Lebrett's brutal insistence on continuing the journey had claimed an innocent life. I stumbled across to him, and somehow summoned the nerve to press two fingers to his pale throat. There was no pulse.

My thoughts were more inclined to rage than mourning, but a looming fear for my own life drove out both. I doubted there was much traffic on this road at any hour: now, I was sure, there would be none until morning. A glance at the horses confirmed that they would not help. The lead pair, their harness broken, had vanished; their less fortunate companions both lay on their sides, crushed under the falling carriage. One did not move; the other whinnied plaintively, and pawed at the ground with desperate jerks of a fractured leg.

Moving round, I managed to unlatch the box where the driver had sat. The door flopped open, revealing the black bag in which he had carried his few effects, and – wrapped in canvas – a pair of long pistols with a powder horn. I took them both. My hands shivered from shock and cold as I tried to load them, and thrice the ramrod slipped and hit my ribs, but eventually I managed to get the balls down the barrels and some powder in the frizzen. I wound some canvas around one and laid it on a rock; the other I took in my hand as I climbed a little way up the slope until I was above the wounded horse. Trembling, I extended the barrel towards a spot between the sad, round eyes.

The rain had ceased and the wind dropped, leaving the explosion ample space to echo across the moor. I did not look at the result, for the blood which flecked my face and shirt revealed enough; instead, I took the second pistol and scrambled up the embankment, following the ruts which the carriage had torn out of the earth.

I reached the road and paused. What now? It would be two hours or more to retrace the route to the last village we had passed: the next might be five minutes or five hours. How long would my feeble foot sustain me? And what if I encountered bands of ruffians on the road – highwaymen or smugglers or their ilk? A single, damp pistol would be little protection then. But I could hardly pass the night in that forsaken place.

I resolved to turn back. Some men trust to luck; experience has taught me to think better of it. However hard the effort, at least I could know that it would be of finite duration, and that succour would await at the end. In the opposite direction, uncertainty would drag on my foot-steps like irons.

Yet even so, I was reluctant to commit myself to so long a journey. I took a final glance to the west. The last traces of blue had vanished from the sky, and there was no moon: I could not even see shadows. The vast, wild emptiness of the place stretched unbounded in my imagination, and I felt the perfection of my fearful solitude. It seemed impossible that any path would bring me home.

But in that instant of despair, a yellow light flared on the horizon. In a second it was gone, leaving me to wonder what illusions my troubled mind devised, but in another moment it reappeared, definitely in the same place as before.

I rubbed my eyes. Was this some sort of beacon, a gang of villains signalling to each other? If so, would it be wise to approach it?

A rustling above my head drew my eyes upwards, and I saw the boughs of a great willow swaying under a gust of wind. Its leaves were the shutter that had hidden the light; when I stepped past the tree, I could see the yellow glow constant and unblinking across the moors, a mile or two distant on my right. Surely it must be a house. The road veered to the left, but that did not dissuade me: the prospect of warmth, nourishment and comfort was all. I hurried back down into the gully, past the broken carriage, and struck out across the moor.

I had never been to Dartmoor before or perhaps I would have thought better of it, but by the time I had acquainted myself with the uniquely inhospitable topography I was too far advanced and could not countenance turning back. The ground seemed to come in three varieties: sharp and rocky, where every step risked further damage to my ankle; scrubby and spiky, where gorse and brambles tore at my legs; or – most common – damp and boggy. The contours of the land were shrivelled, full of dips and hillocks and little valleys, and in every one of them I found an icy stream to splash across. Half the time at least the light was invisible, and then I would have to quell my natural panic until I crested the next ridge, and could reorient myself. For a long time it seemed I grew no nearer, until I began to wonder if it were not some faery or sprite, tempting me into the clutches of a lethal mire. Between the tumble in the carriage and the vicious attentions of the moor, there was not a bone or sinew in my body that did not groan with every step. Only a simmering fury at Lebrett gave me the strength to persist.

At last, as even that impetus was beginning to fade, I met a low, stone wall. I quite literally ran into it, for I was staggering like a drunkard now and could barely see two paces before me, but between the uneven stones which capped it, across a neat garden, I found the source of the light I had chased. It was not a malevolent will-o'-the-wisp: it was a house, and every one of its windows radiated a warm, beckoning glow. My weariness forgotten, I heaved myself over the wall, slithered down in a shower of pebbles and mortar and stumbled forward to the door. I thumped it with all the power I could summon, then subsided against the coarse stone of the house.

The door opened, and I almost fell to my knees.

'I thought it would be you,' said Lebrett contemptuously. 'You took your damn time.'

I lifted a fist to strike him, but had not the strength to wield it. My arm flopped impotent by my side.

18

'What the devil have you been doing?'

If even Lebrett, who habitually regarded me with cold indifference, was shocked by my appearance, I quailed to think how awful I must look.

'Our carriage went off the road into a ditch.' My voice was weak with fatigue and emotion. 'The coachman and the horses were killed.'

'Oaf.' Lebrett's eyes betrayed no hint of sympathy. 'He should have watched where he drove.'

'He should not have been on that road in the first place.' Somehow, Lebrett's inhumanity kindled a last spark of energy in me, and my words grew hotter. 'We should have stopped in Exeter, as I told you. It was madness to continue in the dark, and the coachman has paid the price of your arrogance. It is your fault he is dead.'

Lebrett's eyebrow twitched. 'Have a care, Jerrold. His job was to drive his coach; mine – and yours – is to apprehend Dumont. Pray you are better suited to your task than he was to his.'

'Damn you, Lebrett. How can you stand there, so smug? How many other men will die in this ridiculous hunt of yours? You and Nevell can mutter dark hints about the danger Dumont poses, but to me it is you who seems the real threat.' Almost unthinkingly, I pulled away the canvas that covered my gun and began to raise it.

'You had best put that down.'

'You had best convince me that there is good reason for this fatal pursuit.' The words emerged from my mouth almost unwilled. Part of me – a detached, rational part – screamed obloquy that I should act with such abandon, but another, deeper part thrilled to the savage clarity of the moment.

'Who is this, Lebrett? Is he your colleague?'

The interruption achieved what my reason and Lebrett's menace could not. I lowered the pistol, and looked over Lebrett's shoulder to where a short, stout man in a Chinese dressing-gown stood under the chandelier. His hair was grey and uneven; his face, though full, seemed inexplicably nervous. Perhaps it was because a blood- and mud-soaked man with a gun stood at his front door.

'Good heavens!' he exclaimed. 'Who is this blackguard?' He began to move to a carved chest by the wall.

'This blackguard is the colleague I spoke of. You see I did not exaggerate.'

Two porcine eyes swooped over me, taking in my bedraggled state. 'Indeed not. Tell me, sir, have you been bathing in the mire?'

'Major Lebrett's insistence on pressing forward proved fatal for my coachman. Our carriage left the road; he and his horses were killed. I saw your light and made my way here across the moor. It was the only house I saw. I did not guess it was where you had come, Lebrett.'

Our host's lips puckered out a little, though whether in sympathy or disapproval I could not tell. There was something familiar in the man, though circumstance had driven out all memory. 'That was rash,' he reproved me. 'The country around here is a veritable archipelago of bogs and swamps. Ponies vanish in them all the time; a man would be as nothing to them. You should have followed the road, which passes not fifty yards from here.'

'Next time I will know.'

'But dear Lebrett forgets his manners. Permit me the honour: Thomas Tyrwhitt.'

'Jerrold. Lieutenant Jerrold.'

He clapped his hands together. 'Capital, Lieutenant, capital. Then I am your superior, for I am Vice-Admiral of the counties of Devon and Cornwall.'

'And where do you moor your fleet?' I asked, incredulous that this hellish night had now resulted in my swapping witticisms on a squire's doorstep.

He laughed more loudly than was sincere. 'Very droll, Lieutenant. You neglected to mention how amusing the gentleman is, Lebrett.'

'Lieutenant Jerrold is adept at concealing his virtues.'

'You will forgive me, sir, if I do not indulge myself in company,' I said. 'It has been a hard day. If I might beg a bed of you, I will excuse myself. Unless, Lebrett, you intend to drive on further tonight.'

'We will continue in the morning.'

Tyrwhitt's butler showed me to a spare room. Like the rest of the house, it seemed to have aspirations beyond its origins: the heavy farmhouse walls had been covered in delicate paper, and hung with fashionable views of Brighton. The rain, which had started again, pelted at the windows, and I had the servant lay a fire in the hearth before he left. Though in the rest of the country it was almost August, here it seemed the depths of February.

Beside the gusting of the wind outside, and the crackle of the logs in the grate, the house was still. I pulled off my mud-soaked coat, which had begun to resemble a vagrant's, and began unbuttoning my shirt. From somewhere below I heard an old clock striking midnight, and the shadows on the walls seemed to grow darker. I laid the pistol on the table beside the bed, for if I was to sleep under the same roof as Lebrett, in the home of his friend, I would want it close by.

But I could not rest yet. Now that my other comforts were supplied, an aching hunger kicked up in my stomach. My dinner had been brief, and somewhere back in Somerset; breakfast was so far away I could not remember it. If I tried to sleep before eating I would do nothing but listen to the complaints of my belly. Tyrwhitt's figure gave grounds to hope that his kitchen would be well supplied, and as I did not wish to court unpopularity with the servants I took a candle and slipped out of the door.

The dim wick revealed little of the unfamiliar house, and I was forced to move with care to be sure I would not trip at the head of the stairs and meet the same fate as the poor coachman. I descended slowly, keeping close to the banister lest a creaking board draw attention. After the inauspicious manner of my arrival, I did not want to bring further suspicion on myself – least of all from Lebrett. I doubted he would have forgotten the gun I had pointed at him, nor that he would eventually seek revenge for the affront.

I reached the tiled floor of the hallway and looked about, wondering where the kitchen lay. The chill air was tinged with smoke, wood and tobacco commingled, while the gap beneath the facing door emitted both a blade of light and the muffled sound of voices. With unthinking curiosity, I stepped closer.

'Our esteemed patron is most distressed that this matter has yet to be resolved. He communicated his displeasure this morning.' It was Tyrwhitt. Even from our brief acquaintance, I recognized his fussy voice.

'We'll catch the bastard,' Lebrett answered.

'Most probably. But will it be before he can work the mischief we fear? And what will you do when you have him? Return him to the hulks? Hang him at Portsmouth as a seditious French agent?'

I heard the ring of iron on stone, and the crackle of sparks, as someone stoked the fire. 'I'll kill him as soon as I have sight of him. It's the only way we can be certain.'

I did not hear Tyrwhitt's response, for my mind was trembling at the brutality, so frankly expressed, of Lebrett's intentions. That Dumont was an outlaw and a murderer I knew; that he posed some remarkable danger to the nation I could not doubt. But that he should be condemned to immediate execution without quarter seemed unforgivable. I had accompanied Lebrett – in as much as I had had any choice – to see Dumont brought to justice, not shot down in cold blood. If he were dead, how could I embarrass Lebrett with his secrets?

'And what of the handsome lieutenant you've brought to my house?'

That stopped my thoughts. I inclined my ear closer to the door.

'What of the poltroon?'

'Do you trust him?' Lebrett must have made some answer with his face, for Tyrwhitt continued. 'Do you believe he is in league with our enemies?'

I almost lost my balance and crashed into the door. In their time, any number of superiors had suggested that my incompetence made me more use to France than to England, but this was the first time anyone had seriously considered it might be deliberate. I leaned nearer still to hear Lebrett's reply.

'If I thought for one second that Jerrold had betrayed us, or even guessed at Dumont's true significance, he would not be lying in comfort in his bed upstairs.' I shrank back. 'I fear his incompetence is no disguise, but merely his true, woeful character.'

'A shame,' murmured Tyrwhitt. 'He seemed so charming.'

'He is a worm, beneath even your interest.'

'You will admit it is most peculiar that Dumont should

have escaped so ably, and so soon after we became aware that he possessed the papers. It smacks of conspiracy.'

'If our opponents had the least notion of Dumont's value, you can be sure word of it would have reached the newspapers. I have seen not a breath of it.'

'Nor I,' Tyrwhitt acknowledged. 'Yet you say Lieutenant Jerrold met with them in London – twice. Is that not significant?'

'One was his fat fool of an uncle. He knows nothing and cares nothing, save for his position. The other, Perceval, is wilier, but he has caused enough stir at Carlton House already with his Princess Caroline nonsense. If he knew, he would have revealed it.'

Their next words were lost to me under the clatter of the poker. When at last I could hear again, Tyrwhitt was speaking.

'You ought to visit Lulworth before you leave this part of the country. I am told it was through intermediaries there that he made contact. You should establish with certainty that they are equally ignorant. We cannot afford to leave any loose threads in a matter of this delicacy.'

'There will be no loose threads,' said Lebrett, his voice coarse with menace. 'You may rely on it that I will see to that. Now where is your butler? This bottle is empty, and I have not yet had my fill.'

I froze as I heard the scrape of a chair, and then footsteps approaching the door. I could not run, for he would be out in a second and would surely see me on the steps; but nor did there seem to be any shadows nearby deep enough to hide me. What could I do? I had made little sense of their conversation, but Lebrett's hard words left no doubt what would befall me if I were found eavesdropping. Yet still I stayed rooted to the ground.

The tinkle of a bell in some far corner of the house struck me like a lance, so little did I expect it. On the other side of the door I heard the footsteps retreating again, and the sounds of someone settling back into a seat. He must have been summoning a servant. My heart galloping, I fled upstairs and threw myself under the covers. All thoughts of supper were forgotten, but I heard the grandfather clock strike one before I finally drifted into sleep. Before I did so, my last conscious action was to reach out to the side table, to reassure myself that the pistol was in safe reach.

19

I slept as uneasily as any man who has just heard dire threats against his person, and woke early. The fire was nothing more than grey ash, and there was a sharp chill in the air which kept me under my blanket long after I heard the house stirring. My mind still spun, thinking on the inexplicable conversation of the night before. They had talked of enemies, but their belittling references suggested it was my uncle and Mr Perceval whom they apprehended to be dangerous, rather than the French. They had spoken also of their patron, the Prince of Wales. At last I could place Tyrwhitt's hazy familiarity: it was he I had seen with Lebrett in London, through the windows of Carlton House. Clearly even then they must have had eyes on me, if they had witnessed my midnight excursion to the house in Blackheath with its obscene clock. And they had mentioned papers, papers which Dumont had and which they wanted – or needed. Were they the same papers, I wondered, that Dumont had sewn into the lining of his coat, that he had boasted were the keys to unlock his bondage? It suddenly seemed overridingly urgent that I should know.

I huddled further into my bed at that thought, for though I could not recall Lebrett's exact words, I could remember their sense. If I even guessed at the truth of Dumont's position, I would enjoy no repose. Thinking how Lebrett had let the coachman die so casually in the cause of his obsession, I trembled to wonder what evil he would work on me.

I was still lying there, trying to recollect Mr Perceval's lecture on the factions of government, when a footman summoned me.

'Mr Tyrwhitt sends respects, sir. He and the major are waiting.'

'Damn them both to hell and inform them I will not leave my bed' was what I wished to say, but my words came out as indistinct acquiescence. My rebellion was limited to a protracted shave, and a futile five minutes trying to scrub the dead horse's blood from my shirt. Unable to defer my appearance any longer, and reluctant to provoke Lebrett to rage, I emerged.

Lebrett and Tyrwhitt were already in the saddle, their horses pawing at the driveway in impatience. Against the drab moorland, Tyrwhitt was resplendent in a violet pelisse and feathered hat; Lebrett, in his immaculate uniform, merely looked ominous. Though little sun escaped the high clouds, his spurs seemed to gleam with wicked intent.

'At last Lieutenant Jerrold rises,' said Tyrwhitt merrily. 'I trust you slept well, sir.'

'Your bed was most comfortable.' I looked about. A third horse, a bay hunter, was being held by a groom, bridled and ready to ride. I assumed it was for me. Of the other Guards in Lebrett's troop, I could see nothing.

'Marvellous.' Tyrwhitt beckoned the groom forward. 'As you have so unfortunately lost your coach, I will give you the pick of my stables to take you to Plymouth.'

I lifted my foot into the stirrup and swung myself onto the horse, cutting an ungainly figure as I did so. It was as well my uncle was not a general of dragoons, for I have never been comfortable with any beast larger than a spaniel, and my equestrian achievements have rarely surpassed staying on the mount of the moment.

The reference to my carriage reminded me of its poor driver, presumably still splayed out in the gully. 'We must ride back and recover the coachman's body,' I announced, 'before foxes and crows attack it.'

'He can rot where his incompetence left him,' snapped Lebrett. 'Your indolence has delayed us enough already. I have had to send my troop ahead to ensure Dumont is not in Paris before we reach Plymouth.'

'I will send one of my tenants to retrieve the corpse.' Tyrwhitt spoke with the smooth manner of a natural diplomat. 'It would be best if you informed his family, for doubtless they will wish to bury him.'

'Enough!' Lebrett touched his mount with his spurs and started forward. 'If we reach Plymouth to see Dumont waving at us from the stern of the Cartel ship, we will regret this frivolity.'

I had little love for Mr Tyrwhitt – quite apart from his being a friend and ally of Lebrett's, I did not care for his sly glances and bluff façade – but I had to appreciate the bulwark he supplied against Lebrett's vicious temper. While the major rode ahead, Tyrwhitt trotted contentedly beside me and expounded the unlikely merits of the landscape.

'I have had this land some twenty years already. I intend to make it the capital of the moor.'

'You'll be busy.' All about me I could see nothing but harsh valleys and yellow hillsides, fractured by the strange, vertical rock formations which they called tors. It seemed that primordial giants must have laid great slabs of stone atop each other to serve as tables or stools, for surely nature could not have raised such queer tumours.

'I *have* been busy.' Tyrwhitt's breast swelled with pride as he gazed out over the wilderness. 'Modern, patented methods will make this land a garden, succulent with fruit and rich with promise.'

Perhaps, in time, they would, but for the moment that promise remained hopelessly distant. I could not even see evidence of the agricultural miraculists who were to effect this transformation: a solitary farmhouse was the sole signifier of habitation, and even that seemed derelict, its roof stove in and its grounds overgrown.

'Have you managed to grow more than moss and heather?' I enquired.

'Indeed yes. The Bath Agricultural Society, no less, have awarded a medal for the flax produced from my estate.'

'Are these decorated flax plantations nearby?'

'They lie fallow at the moment,' Tyrwhitt admitted. 'The soil . . .' He waved his arms, almost toppling himself from his horse. 'The soil requires improving.'

'The climate, too.' The high cloud that dulled the landscape had not burned away, but appeared to be descending.

'Nothing can withstand the ultimate triumph of progress. Private genius and industry will drain swamps, break rocks and tame the moors. All I require for the moment is a kernel, a single seedling whose offshoots will fertilize the ground and attract others. Where men go, commerce follows, and there is no barrier of nature to withstand the sway of commerce. And, by the grace and wisdom of the navy, I now have just the seed I need.'

He gestured ahead, and I peered forward through the mist that had come down as he spoke. Before us, at the roadside, I could see scores of men, dark shadows against the grey of the fog. The hammering crack and chime of iron on stone reached my ears, a staccato clank beneath shouted orders and groaning beasts. The air rang with the blows of chisels and picks, while the labourers stretched as far as the veiling mist would let me see.

'Is it a mine?' I asked. I knew from the Reverend

Lawrence that tin and copper were to be found in these parts.

'Not at all. We do not burrow – we build. What you see, Lieutenant, are the foundations of the edifice that will bring life to the moors and prosperity to the town. An edifice in which you, of all men, should take a peculiar interest. This is to be a gaol for prisoners of war, five thousand of them, and it will be the making of Dartmoor.'

I gaped at him. 'You are building a prisoner-of-war depot? In this godforsaken place?'

Tyrwhitt scowled. 'It may appear unpromising at present, but we are building the future. Your hulks will be broken up for firewood, for they will not be needed: here the prisoners will enjoy solid quarters in a wholesome atmosphere, and all at a fraction of the cost of the prison ships.'

I wiped away the layer of damp that the wholesome atmosphere had left on my saddle. If this was high summer, I pitied the wretches who would be confined here in winter. 'Who chose to build it here?'

'A commission entrusted with the task. They were gracious enough to accept my humble proposals, and to agree with my assessment of the incontrovertible merits of this place.'

Lebrett twisted round in his saddle to look back. 'How fortunate that they should listen to their chairman.'

'The needs of five thousand men and their captors will naturally stimulate trade and commerce in the village,' Tyrwhitt continued, undaunted by Lebrett's mockery. 'Princetown will flourish to the glory and enrichment of its patron, the Prince of Wales.'

'The Prince of Wales?' I echoed. 'I'd heard his debts were severe, but I did not guess he'd become contractor to the navy. Or gaoler in chief.'

'His Highness has graciously leased me the land for the prison. Almost everything you see is his.'

At last I understood the truth of this desolate scheme. The Prince's friends in government had appointed his chief tenant to a commission which had recommended that the new prison be sited in the midst of his estates, so that he might profit both by the contract and by the concomitant surge in commerce. It was a deft piece of political chicanery. Nor did I have to guess whose quarries were excavated to supply the forbidding stones that I could see being heaved across the road to be shaped by the masons.

'When will it receive its first Frenchmen?' I asked.

Tyrwhitt shifted uncomfortably in his saddle. 'The surveyor assures me that the major part will be completed by the end of this year.'

I peered closer. I could see the first storey of a long blockhouse, and the foundations of another, but the only structure that seemed entirely finished was the gateway. It stood in proud, useless solitude, for the surrounding wall was not yet built; its angled corners gave it the semblance of something fashioned by a distant and ancient race. Carved across the top of it was the inscription PARCERE SUBJECTIS.

'Virgil,' I said, feeling a rare benefit of my education. '*Pity the vanquished.*'

'It encapsulates our hope that this will be a most humane institution,' Tyrwhitt explained. 'Far removed from your foetid hulks.'

I could not share his optimism.

We did not linger by the prison, or at the Prince's Arms, the one useful achievement Tyrwhitt had brought to Princetown. Beyond the village the moors opened out again, and we rode in silence while I tried to shuffle my thoughts into some sort of order. Tyrwhitt and the Prince of Wales were closely joined in their business interests; the Prince acted as sponsor to the government, and the government wanted me to find Dumont. Did that mean

226

that the Prince himself wanted me to find Dumont? That seemed outlandish – though no more so than much that had already passed. Despite the fact that the Prince was about to become owner of the largest prisoner-of-war depot in the country, I did not imagine he was so concerned with the specifics of escaped Frenchmen. What of Lebrett? He was a servant of the ministry and a friend of Tyrwhitt, who had referred to a mutual patron they enjoyed. That must be the Prince – I had, after all, seen them together in Carlton House. And then there was the matter of the papers I had overheard them speaking of, apparently the true cause of Dumont's importance. What were they? And how had he contrived to come by them aboard my ship?

All the time that I pondered this, the road had been climbing to a low summit. We had reached it now, and as we wound our way past an outcropping of rock I could look down into the next little vale. A shallow river meandered through its base, the water black and hard, and just before the bridge a coach was halted. There seemed something unnatural about it, though I could not quite see what; more urgently, I could see no reason why it should have stopped there unless accident or villainy had waylaid it. I kicked my horse's flanks, and clung on to its mane as it trotted down the hill.

As the slope levelled, I managed to drag my eyes up from the ground beneath. The coach seemed undamaged – all its wheels were on, and neither axle appeared broken – and I could see no highwaymen or desperadoes lurking nearby. The reason for its stillness, though, was embarrassingly evident: what had struck me as odd from the ridge, I realized, was the fact that the traces lay empty on the ground, the harnesses discarded beside them. Of the horses that had presumably pulled it this far across the moor there was no sign.

'Thank the Lord Christ you're 'ere.' The coachman, an elderly man in a brown coat, emerged from the lee of the carriage. 'They's made away with the 'orses. If you's fast, yous could catch 'em yet.'

'Certainly not,' snapped Lebrett. 'We have more urgent business than saving you from horse-stealers, with whom you yourself are as likely as not in league. We may, when we reach Tavistock, inform the ostler of your plight.'

'Who has made away with the horses?' I asked, ignoring Lebrett's bile.

'Twain the passengers.' The coachman glared angrily at Lebrett. From the window behind him, I saw four anxious faces peering out. 'Joined at Exeter, they did. Should've knowed they'd be trouble on account they was foreign.'

'Foreign?'

'Yankee, one of 'em. 'Is scar should've known me to be careful.'

'An American, with a scar? And his companion – a shorter man, of slight build and dark, ringed hair?'

The coachman's eyes broadened. 'Aye – just so. You knows 'em?'

'All too well. They took your horses—'

'Called a stop, an' took 'em straight out the 'arness. They's armed.'

'Which way did they ride?'

The coachman pointed down the valley, to where the river disappeared out of sight. 'Southerly. T'wards the coast.'

Even Lebrett reacted to that. 'Tyrwhitt! Ride towards Plymouth as fast as you can and find my troop of Guards. Bring them back here and follow our tracks.' He turned to me. 'Are you armed, Jerrold?'

I held up the long pistol I had taken from the wreckage of the coach.

'Then follow me.'

It was a nightmare of a ride. Only the superb quality of the horse saved me, and he must have grown heartily sick of the maladroit handling of his terrified rider. Riding

228

across ground that was alternately bog and boulders would have tested me at a walk; at full gallop, trying to keep pace with a cavalry officer, it was nigh on impossible. Lebrett, whatever his human deficits, was a ferociously able horseman. I almost strangled my poor mount, so tight did I clutch his neck, and could look at nothing save the ground that rushed under the racing hooves. Had I been alone, I might have ridden clear past Dumont and never seen him.

Their tracks, though, were easy to follow: the earth was black beneath the spiny grass, and with each bound the horses left dark welts in the soil. Sometimes water or stones obscured it, but Lebrett had a huntsman's eye and could ever see it emerge further down the course. Always we had the bubbling river to our right, expanding ever wider across the valley as the myriad streams we splashed across fed into it.

At length, though, the trail turned away from the river and up a steep incline. The ancients had erected a diminutive monolith at its crest, and Lebrett paused for a moment beside it to survey the land before us. Breathing hard, and trembling with the panic of the ride, I reined in my horse beside him.

The clouds, which had been lifting ever since we left Princetown, were now so high they had begun to drift apart, letting veins of blue between them. It brightened the air, though our surroundings still seemed drab, and opened a window through which, in the far distance, we could see the furrowed slate of the sea.

'They're not making for the Cartel ship,' I said, my throat rasping from sharp breathing. 'They must have found some smuggler to embark them from a deserted beach.' I peered forward, but it was as yet too far and hazy to see if a ship was waiting in the distance.

'And there they go.' Lebrett made no gesture, but spurred his horse onward down the hill.

I delayed a moment, trying to see where he had spotted

them, but his sight was keener than mine. I kicked my mount in the ribs, and plunged after Lebrett.

We rode for miles, though I was too busy trying to keep my backside in the saddle to count them. Once we entirely lost their trail in a marsh, but Lebrett never deviated from the line he swore they followed. Our horses began to tire; my back and legs ached from squatting in the stirrups so long, while a nasty sore began to blossom on my thighs. If I ever saw Isobel again, she would think I had contracted a peculiarly exotic species of pox. Still I saw no sign of our quarry, though occasional shouts from Lebrett, far ahead, suggested he glimpsed something.

Gradually, it seemed that the heights grew lower, and the dips more shallow. The tawny grass of the moor grew greener, and at length turned to pasture; now we traversed meadows and fields, chasing sheep and cows from our path. I could see farmhouses scattered across the countryside, and to my left the steeple of a church, while before us the sea loomed ever closer.

'There.' Lebrett had his sabre drawn, and was pointing it towards a cliff top barely two hundred yards distant. Two white horses were nosing at a patch of grass, their flanks still heaving from their efforts. Of their riders, there was no sign.

'There seems to be a way down over here,' I called, edging my mount forward towards the lip. I had no desire to plummet over the edge, or to have it collapse beneath our weight, but there was a break in the rim where a cascade of pebbles formed a natural ramp down to the sandy bay below.

'I'd not want to navigate that on a horse,' I said.

'Doubtless you would not. As likewise Brogarde and Dumont feared to attempt it, I surmise.' Lebrett swung himself out of his saddle and led his horse to a stunted sapling that grew from the cliff. He looped the bridle about the trunk, then drew a carbine from its holster. It reminded me of his vow the night before: to kill Dumont as soon as he had sight of him. Dismounting with rather less grace, I made fast my own animal, took my pistol, and moved towards the top of the slope.

'Where is your ammunition pouch?' Lebrett, who had taken his own from his saddlebag, was staring at me as he primed the carbine. 'Is your aim so true that a single bullet will suffice?'

The way my arm was shivering, I would be lucky to hit the sea from the surf. But Lebrett's point was alarmingly true: I had only one solitary shot allowed me – less, if the ball had fallen out during the ride. I took the powder horn and poured a little into the pan, wondering at the immense misfortune of my predicament. How had I contrived to be in this lonely place, with desperate foreigners before me and a malevolent Guards officer my sole companion, with only one ball to account for them all?

Lebrett jerked his gun towards the beach. 'Lead the way. If they see you as you emerge, draw their fire so I may shoot them down.'

I disliked the plan, for I feared I could play my part all too well. 'If you go first and fire, then I will be able to cover you while you reload.'

'Get down that incline now!' As if for effect, a roll of thunder chose that moment to peal across the sky. Seabirds rose squawking from the cliffs, and I felt a fat raindrop land on my nose. 'If you dally any longer, our guns will serve as little more than clubs.'

He had one hand on the hilt of his sword, and the way his blue eyes stared at me left no doubt he would run me through if I did not obey him. Cursing inwardly, but too achingly aware of his sabre to damn him to his face, I turned and began to pick my way down the slope, slipping and stumbling as the loose scree tumbled away in tiny cascades beneath my feet. Every clattering stone sent sparks through my spine, for I feared Dumont and Brogarde might hear me, feared they might be sitting on the beach with a gun trained where I would emerge. Yet still it was nothing against the terror instilled by Lebrett.

As the slope eased, the beach began to come into view. It was not a wide cove, but the sea had chewed a deep bite out of the shore, and the twin promontories that framed its mouth thrust far out. I could see no other way down, save for a sheep track which meandered up the eastern cliff at the far end. If Brogarde and Dumont were here, they would have little effort guarding the approaches.

I glanced back to ensure that Lebrett had followed me. I half expected that he would abandon me, would leave me to take Dumont's bullet alone, but the prospect of finishing the Frenchman had drawn him close behind me. He gripped his carbine in his right hand, steadying his balance with the other, and flicked the barrel impatiently when he saw my delay. Mercifully, circumstance kept his well-honed tongue in check.

I crouched low, trying to keep myself as small a target as possible, and pushed my pistol out before me. The wind was rising, blowing gloomy notes through the gaps in the stones, and the rain that drummed on my hands was beginning to fall with greater conviction. Squatting like a duck, I struggled forward, jerking my gun about in awkward convulsions as I scanned the beach for any sign of Dumont.

And suddenly, he was there. One moment he was blocked by the rising cliff on my left; the next I could see him standing on the shore about halfway along the beach, staring out over the water towards France while the breeze ruffled his unruly hair. I inched closer, all the while aware that the American remained at large and out of sight.

I turned back to warn Lebrett, but he must have seen Dumont already. He was kneeling on the broken stones, his carbine at his shoulder, his eye squinting down the barrel with intent concentration.

'What are you doing?' I called, as loudly as I dared. 'We should wait until we have a clear shot at the American. With him despatched, we can capture Dumont at our ease and . . .'

But Lebrett ignored me. The hammer on his gun was already cocked back as he made minute adjustments to his aim, steadying it against the wind. I had only seconds to move, and no time to think, but my anger at him – coupled with an abhorrence of seeing Dumont executed without warning – drove me. I ran forward, heedless of danger and the slimy footing, and cannoned into Lebrett. He must have seen my approach from the corner of his eye, but he did not turn from his target. He pulled the trigger of his carbine just as I met him, so that our collision seemed to be not flesh with bone but flint with steel: sparks flew, and gritty smoke exploded into both our faces. My eyes wept with the stinging and my cheeks burned, but I had enough presence of mind to spring back to avoid Lebrett's furious, swinging punch. The momentum dragged him forward a few steps; then he halted, straightened, and pulled his sword from its scabbard.

'You damned, treacherous blackguard,' he snarled. Black powder and red blood gave his features a diabolical hue, even without the contorted rage writ across them. 'I was warned you might be in league with our enemies; I should have rid myself of your miserable, scheming company days ago. You—'

His long sword trembled in the air as he spoke, yet it remained impotent while I stood there with a loaded pistol. In the fury of the moment, I might have shot him dead in an instant, but my revenge was pre-empted by an explosion from the beach. A shower of stony splinters erupted from the rock beside me, and I dived to the ground in terror. Intent on Lebrett, I had lost all thought of other enemies, who were now fully warned to our presence. Darting my eyes around, I saw a cloud of smoke rising from some rocks at the western corner of the cove, where Brogarde must have been keeping watch. Indeed, as the wind whipped away the fog, I could see the shoulder of his green coat protruding from behind a boulder, and the flashing movement of metal as he rammed home a second bullet.

Before I could look for Dumont, the noise of tumbling stone on the slope above snatched my gaze away. My enemies were all about me, and I could not think of one but another would take his chance. I had taken my eye off Lebrett, and I flung my eyes upward, expecting to see his sabre lunging towards me. Yet he had been as surprised as I by Brogarde's shot, and had failed to take advantage; now he was running away from the beach and away from me, scrambling up the incline to safety. It was a cunning choice, for there the American would be unable to see him, and though I still had my pistol, I would not shoot him in the back.

Brogarde had no such scruples. Even as I watched Lebrett's legs vanish over the lip of the slope, another shot slammed into the cliff face just to the right of my head. A hail of rock fragments stung my cheek, though they felt little different from the raindrops that were now rattling down on me. Thunder rumbled across the mouth of the cove, and I cupped a hand over the frizzen of my pistol. With only a single ball, I could not afford a misfire.

But nor could I wait while Brogarde peppered me with musketry – nor did the top of the cliff offer any refuge while Lebrett was there. Counting off the seconds since the last shot under my breath, praying that Brogarde would not have reloaded already, I staggered across the skidding rocks and onto the damp sand of the beach. The bay curved further in to my left before emerging at the far end, and if I could put the bend of the cliff between me and Brogarde I would have a far more favourable position.

'Stop there!'

Long years of abuse from my uncle and superiors had

accustomed me to obeying orders: like a puppet, I halted and spun about to see who had spoken. It was Brogarde, and the sight of him sprinting through the streaming rain stilled my limbs a second longer in shock.

'Run!' he shouted, contradicting his previous command. He was coming on at me fast, a cutlass in his hand but – to my enormous relief – no gun. 'Run!'

As he repeated his cry I realized that he did not address me. He was calling over my shoulder to Dumont, and as he charged towards me I saw his intention was to delay me long enough for the Frenchman to make his escape. My mind, perplexed and bewildered by the onslaught of my enemies, at last began to move. I lifted my pistol, pulled back the hammer and squeezed the trigger.

Somehow, through all the rain and my tumbling about, my powder had stayed dry and the ball in the barrel. My arm went numb from the rebounding explosion and I rocked backward, but Brogarde, barely ten paces away, collapsed onto the beach. I did not spare him a moment's thought, but turned on my heels and started running for the far edge of the cove, following the deep footprints Dumont had dug into the sand. Rain poured down about me: earnest, fat-bellied drops that burst on my hands in plumes of spray or were driven into my face by the rising wind. It must have been some time before noon, but the sky was black, and even as I drew nearer the cliff it continued to recede from my sight. I just snatched a glimpse of a dark figure clinging to the sheep path halfway up before he vanished in the clouds of rain.

At the foot of the cliff I paused. Trusting my life to a crumbling track up a sheer slope would have seemed a forlorn idea on the best of days: with a storm deluging over me, it seemed the depths of madness. Yet having pursued Dumont so far, could I abandon the chase when he was only a few yards ahead of me? And the beach was not necessarily a refuge, for if Brogarde had survived my bullet he would be after me in seconds. Nor could Lebrett be far away.

Damning myself for a fool, I climbed onto the narrow path. It was as precarious as I had feared, for in the rain it had become a natural stream-bed for the water trickling down the cliff. My silver-buckled shoes grew limp and distended as I splashed up the uneven track, skidding on the loose stone and accumulated sand. I twisted my body around and pressed it against the cliff face, but even with my splayed arms grasping the rock I never felt more than a few inches from oblivion.

Gasping with exhaustion, my clothes leaden with water and smeared with mud, I hauled myself over the last parapet and ran forward before the onrushing wind could blow me back down. My eyes and ears stung from the onslaught of the storm; so intent was I on trying to gaze ahead, I almost did not see the movement on my left. Only when the figure had raised himself from his knees did I notice him, standing on a hummock some twenty feet away, on the extreme edge of my sight.

'Dumont!' I shouted, unable to check my astonished cry. 'Dumont!'

He looked towards me, and our eyes met. Where I had expected to see defiance, or anger, or desperation, there was only exhausted misery.

'Dumont,' I said, a third time. 'Come here.'

He ran.

For an instant, a listless despair kept me rooted to the ground, for I could scarcely believe I had come so close again and not caught him. Then resignation struck, and I set off after him. It was a dim hope in that blind haze of rain, but I had taken leave of my senses, surrendering to whichever malevolent fate demanded I should chase Dumont to destruction. On treacherous rocks, and then sliding grass, I ran with long, floundering strides, my head lowered and my arms flung out for precarious balance.

Once I thought I saw him, but it might as easily have been a bush or a tree: I was past caring. I splashed through a high stream and up its muddy bank; I tore my breeches on brambles and jarred my knee on upturned rocks. I ran like a lunatic, like Orestes before the Furies, for though I was the pursuer I felt that I myself was hunted. In my frenzied mind, I almost imagined I heard a rumbling behind me, the pounding of some infernal hound snapping at my heels. But hounds do not have hooves, and these were not imagined: I was not so lost that I did not recognize the sounds of a horse – or horses – closing in on me.

Never slowing my pace, I looked back. Out of the fog I heard a harness jangling and a raging voice shouting abuse. A dark spot appeared in the rain, dancing above the ground. Swiftly, it melded into the bounding nose of a black horse; then I could see its eyes, its pricked-back ears, its flying mane and its thundering forelegs. It was directly behind me, surging on as if to crush me under its hooves, yet all I could do was keep running away as fast as my dying legs would bear me.

The beast and its rider leaped into view. Ever running, I saw over my shoulder the gleaming black boots, the sodden blue coat, the sharp jaw and the blade reaching forward. He must have recognized me, but he did not touch his reins. Instead, I fancied I saw his spurs prick a little harder into the heaving flanks. He lifted his sword with a howl of triumph, and I saw there would be no escape for me.

With a blow like a felled oak, I struck the ground, burying my face in mud. The last thing I saw was flailing hooves flying over me.

20

By some concoction of fatigue and pain, I lay for hours where I had fallen, sometimes asleep and dreaming; sometimes awake and believing I slept. Only when the late afternoon sun touched my eyes did I open them long enough to discover that I was awake and – more importantly – alive. Although I did not have high expectations for my place in the eternal kingdom, I hoped it would not include the racking pains in my shin, my knee, my chest and my chin. I felt as though a cannon had been dropped on me, and it seemed a small miracle I had power enough to raise myself on my elbow and survey my battered body.

It was not a comfortable sight. I had been called worm often enough by my uncle: now I looked the part, as though I had crawled through a tunnel of mud. My clothes were plated with a layer of grime that was now drying in the sun, and if I were not careful, I would end up an effigy of myself.

I looked about. It was no surprise I was in such condition, for I had lain all afternoon in a ditch. To judge by the impression I had left, I must have struck it with great force.

I rubbed my shin, which smarted like an anvil. On the bank of the ditch behind me, a gnarled tree root arched out of the ground: it must have caught my leg and pitched me forward on my face, into the hollow. I remembered Lebrett charging out of the fog on his beast, lifting his sword to strike, and wondered if that root had saved my skull. If so, a bruised shin was a price I could happily pay.

The thought of Lebrett seemed to chill the warmth of the day. I had threatened to shoot him; then he had tried to kill me. I feared he would deem it an unfinished business rather than fair exchange. I pulled myself up the embankment and surveyed the ground about. The sky above was blue and clean, but the earth still bore the marks of the storm. I could clearly see the heavy hoofprints of Lebrett's horse churned into the black soil. They led away across the field, dark scars in the shimmering grass.

I looked back, whence I had come. I had no idea how long I had sustained my demented sprint through the mist, but I had travelled far enough to leave the cove out of sight. I shivered, remembering the battle there. Should I return, to see if Brogarde still lived? That did not recommend itself, for Lebrett would have seen him fall too, and I assumed he or his men would return eventually to find the body. I did not wish to encounter any of them.

Looking at my attire, however, I could see that few men would want to encounter me either: the meanest vagabond begging his living in the gutter would seem a prince next to me. Down the sloping meadow, a quarter of a mile distant, a stream twinkled in the sunlight, and I resolved that a clean suit of clothes would improve my situation admirably. I limped through the soaking grass, aching with every step, until at last I was on the grey, moss-grown stones of the chattering brook.

The water was running pure and clear, though I winced when I touched it for it was icy cold. But the sun was still strong, and I needed little incentive to peel the sticky clothes away from my skin. Peeking about to see that I was not observed by a passing shepherd or cowherd, I sat on a warm stone by a pool, naked as Adam, and admired the magnificent collection of scrapes, scratches and bruises I had collected across my body. First I scrubbed my shirt, then my breeches, and then my stockings, letting the water fret at them until they were recognizable for their original colouring. I laid out each in turn to dry in the sun, coming at last to my coat. It had borne the brunt of my suffering: a long tear was ripped into the left-hand sleeve, the hem was ragged, and there was barely an inch of cloth to be claimed as blue.

I patted the pockets, wondering whether I had left anything of use in them. In one I found a torn cartridge-paper, a penknife and my meagre purse; in the other, something far bulkier. A book. I pulled it out from between the muddy folds of the coat, trying to keep its cover clean. I could not imagine why I should have carried a book so far, through violence and pursuit and battle: how could I have forgotten it?

A glance at the spine and all became clear. It had been so constant a companion in the last few days that I had ceased to feel its weight at my side. Alone in the coach, I had not found it stimulating reading, but now I hugged it like a willing virgin. There are men I know – more than you would think – who carry a Bible with them always, adamant it is the key to salvation: I was saved by the Reverend Lawrence's *Tour to the West of England*. All the author's failings – his priggish style, his dull anecdotes, his tedious obsession with the Saxons – I forgave, for here I had a map and a description of the roads. I threw my coat into the pool, watching the water eddy around it, then threw myself in for good measure. My mother had often lectured me that polished shoes and a spotless shirt would carry a young gentleman far; with a map and directions, I could at last escape this miserable corner of the kingdom, and find some more sympathetic company. Then I could think about how to settle my account with Lebrett.

*　*　*

240

If the Reverend Lawrence was to be trusted, I decided that I must be somewhere between Plymouth and Dartmouth. I hesitated to choose between them, for there was every chance that Nevell might be in the former, but it was equally likely that Lebrett or his cohorts would be there too. Dartmouth seemed a less obvious choice, and would not necessitate passing by the cove again. From there, I could perhaps find a boat to take me up the coast – to Portsmouth, or even to Rye. If I could only reach London, I must surely find allies against Lebrett and his party.

I sat in that frigid pool until my aches were numbed and every last speck of mud and blood was washed from my prickled skin, then allowed the sun and soft breeze to dry me on a rock. There was something pure about lying there loose and naked: with the stiffness in my bones, I would have been tempted to stay until dusk. I had had little repose since Dumont slipped away in Isobel's dress, but this seemed a poor time to indulge myself. If Lebrett caught Dumont, it would not be long before he turned his attentions on me. If Dumont were still at large, then finding him myself would be an immeasurable advantage.

Perhaps the stream had frozen my brain, or the sun softened it, but for a brief moment I almost felt optimistic. I pulled on my clothes, startled by how white my breeches had become, and set out, keeping the declining sun behind my left shoulder. For a time, my thoughts were happy to keep pace with my progress, concentrating on the terrain and my immediate surroundings. Soon, though, they began to scurry ahead, worrying at how I would proceed when I reached London. I had stood twenty feet away from Dumont and failed to catch him: how, in all England, could I find him now that our paths were split and his trail lost? Should I even squander precious time going to London, when he must remain somewhere in this vicinity? If he could evade Lebrett's hunt for a few days, he might well

241

happen upon a willing fisherman to ferry him across the Channel. But I was in no position to wander the Devonshire coast, keeping watch for every least ketch that might aid him. Most likely, I would succeed only in finding Lebrett's scouts.

And still I worked in utter ignorance of Dumont's mysterious significance, the reason the Emperor of France and the King of England were engaged in such an almighty tussle over him. It was a problem I had returned to time and again in the past days, yet never with the least progress: all I could do was scavenge my memories of him, and of the dark words, dangerous threats and fragmented hints I had heard from Lebrett. I tried to think back on the conversation I had overheard in the night at Tyrwhitt's house, for then Lebrett had been at his most unguarded. He had said he would kill Dumont on sight, a boast he had so nearly made good at the cove. He had spoken of papers, I remembered, papers whose ownership had sparked his interest in Dumont. And there had been something else, something to do with loose threads and intermediaries. Somewhere Tyrwhitt had advised Lebrett to go.

So far ahead had my thoughts run that I walked straight into a solitary apple tree, aggravating the injuries to my legs and yelping with surprise. It proved the dangers of my surroundings were not all Frenchmen and Horse Guards – inattention could be an equal hazard. Yet in that moment of pain and shock, a name burst into my agitated mind. *Lulworth*. That was where Tyrwhitt had told Lebrett to trim his loose ends, where intermediaries lived through whom Dumont had communicated. And there was more, for I had seen the name elsewhere in the past week.

Shivering with hope, I pulled the book from my pocket. The thin pages were matted together where rain had seeped into them, but the text remained clear. I turned through them, prising some apart with my thumbnail, until I found the paragraph I sought:

LULWORTH. Deemed by some the most magnificent seat in the nation, this remarkable estate, some sixteen miles by road from Weymouth, enjoys all those pleasures which one may venture are the preserve of the English country. Seat of the Weld family, acquired by them in the reign of the first Charles, the castle is constructed in the form of a perfect cube, which some have attributed to Inigo Jones, though this is disputed. In Saxon times . . .

I snapped the book shut. Whether the knock with the tree had shaken my thoughts together or merely unleashed my fancy, I could not tell, but I was certain I had met the name of Weld before since leaving the *Prometheus*. I thought of a dusty road and a file of marines, and an elegant coach stuck in a ditch. She had said her name was Mrs Weld, I was almost sure of it: I remembered her voice and perfume floating out of the dark cabin. And Dumont's fellow prisoners had spoken of a woman who visited him, who filled him with hope and talk of escape. A woman who brought him secret papers.

With every turn of this chase, I felt my understanding recede, yet my spirits rose and my stride lengthened as I continued through the fields. Even if I did not find Dumont at Lulworth, even if Mrs Weld had absented herself, I held on to the belief that I might grasp one of Lebrett's loose threads. And by that, I hoped, I might at last start to unravel the impenetrable web that surrounded Dumont.

21

For a place that had suddenly assumed such tremendous significance, Lulworth was surprisingly easy to reach. A day's walking brought me to Dartmouth – a pleasant town, at the mouth of a deep gorge – where I found a passage to Weymouth for the next day, and some news. A troop of cavalry had ridden through that afternoon, I heard, asking all about if anyone had seen a desperate Frenchman on the run from the hulks. That cheered me, for I was now in a race with Lebrett to catch Dumont, and as long as he hunted, I had hope. His news had caused quite a stir in the town, and they talked of little else at the inn that evening – one local elder even called for an ancient chain to be stretched across the river, to cork it up lest the French spy bring the whole of Napoleon's fleet to sack their homes.

While I was there, I wrote a letter to Nevell explaining my suspicions, and another to Isobel assuring her I still lived. Then, next morning, I found the master who had agreed to take me across Lyme Bay on his barque, and sailed on the tide. It was a peaceful crossing: perhaps on Dartmoor the rain and storms still flogged the land, but here the sun beamed benevolence on our progress, while a west wind speeded us up the Channel. Though the sea and I have rarely been allies, the novelty of being alone

244

and free of haranguing superiors was wonderful, and I almost regretted it when at last I disembarked onto the quay at Weymouth.

Weymouth was a busy town, filled with chirruping ladies who had hit upon the notion that the sea was an efficacious restorative. It seemed never to strike them that if salt water were a cure, naval officers would be perfect Methuselahs, not the sickly and feeble sorts familiar to me. Worse were their mincing husbands, who promenaded along the esplanade in earnest demonstration of their sophistication and gentility, much of it consisting of sneers at my attire and witticisms against my appearance. I escaped them as swiftly as I could, and found a carter who would take me, with a dozen casks of smoked haddock, as far as the village of Wool, from where I could see high turrets rising behind a screen of trees.

Whatever nefarious schemes I might uncover within Lulworth Castle, I had to admire its aesthetic perfection without. It had neither the sprawling disorder of a truly ancient castle, with the additions of centuries scribbled one upon another, nor a modern attempt to anticipate the ruin of history. It was a castle as a child might have drawn it: perfectly square, with stout round towers at the four corners and a neat row of crenellations edging the roof. A captive princess and a moat would have completed the effect; instead, bizarrely, its owners had added a domed mausoleum directly adjacent to it, nestled among wild trees and almost as high as the castle itself. It seemed too big for a folly, and bespoke a morbid taste on the part of the occupants which unsettled me. More benignly, a broad terrace ran around the lower reaches of the building, and on the wall facing me a double stair rose to a classically framed door.

Unsure how to proceed, or how perilous this castle might prove, I hesitated at the foot of the stairs. I did not want to find myself numbered among the denizens of the mausoleum, or racked in the dungeon by Dumont's conspirators. The brushing leaves in the surrounding trees seemed suddenly sinister, and I could almost believe that the chattering birds might be piping a warning to me.

A scream tore through the air, and I almost leaped off the path. But it was not a scream of gruesome torture – instead, it seemed more the scream of a child revelling in some high-spirited game. It sounded again, accompanied by high shouts, and in a moment I saw three girls in white dresses come sprinting round the corner of the tower, waving their arms as they chased each other with abandon. They skidded to a standstill as they saw me: the tallest pulled herself up to her fullest height, while her sisters squatted beside her and peered at me shyly.

'What do you want?' asked the eldest, who could not have been more than ten years old.

I lifted a hand to raise my hat, and remembered it had been lost somewhere on Dartmoor. 'I beg your pardon, my ladies, but is Mrs Weld at home?'

The girl frowned, while one of her sisters sucked on her thumb and the other pulled gargoyle faces at me. 'Mama is in the castle,' she said seriously. 'Are you one of the friars?'

I have been mistaken for many things in my life, but never a monk. 'I am merely a visitor,' I told her. 'I need to speak to your mama.'

'Do you know the password?'

I balked. I had anticipated every variety of obstacle and hindrance in meeting with Mrs Weld, but I had not expected to swap secret words with a winsome sprite.

'Oak,' I hazarded, settling on the first object I caught sight of.

My interrogator knelt down, spreading her dress about her, and conferred in whispers with her sisters.

'That isn't the right word,' she announced.

'Oh.'

'But you can come in if you want.'

'Thank you.'

Utterly disarmed by her pug-faced innocence, I forgot my apprehensions and mounted the stairs. The girls ran to the door, scrambling over each other to reach it first, and squeezed through. They disappeared into the dim hall beyond.

Caution reasserted itself as I stepped through the doorway into the entrance hall. Through a door on my left I could see the classical forms of an airy dining room, while above me I heard scampering feet rushing up the stair that wound its way about the walls. After a pause, and some excited murmuring, a more measured tread started to descend. But I paid it no heed, for my eyes were fixed on the wall which faced me. A triple portrait hung there, heavy in its gilded frame, and so tall that the figures were almost as large as life. It showed a man flanked by two women, though there was something in their proportions which was not quite right, as though one figure had stood nearer the artist than the others. The man had a broad, pale forehead divided by a sharp widow's peak; to judge from his dress, he had been painted some decades earlier. His dark eyes stared out over my shoulder, not with arrogance or hauteur but with simple, contented superiority. The woman on his right stood by him with calm poise, her attentive eyes staring at her husband; she had a kindly face, but was otherwise unremarkable. To his left, however, was where my eyes fastened, and my heart tightened. The second woman seemed somehow nearer than the other two, though her arm rested on the gentleman's. Her round face was very pale under a halo of puffed-out curls, yet there was nothing frail or passive in it. She could not have been more than twenty at the sitting, and though in reality some of that youthful life must have rubbed away in the course of years, there in the picture it remained as coy and vivacious as when the paint was damp.

I suppose I had come expecting it, yet I was surprised by how suddenly I was transported back to a dark carriage on the road from Chatham, and the pervasive scent of rose-water. And how my heart thumped to know I had arrived in the right place.

'You have called to see me, sir?'

I looked up. A lady was standing on the third stair, leaning forward on the banister, while a child hid itself behind the skirts of her dress. Her honey-brown hair was curled up in an elegant pineapple over her dainty face, which gazed down on me with the mildest hint of quizzical disapproval.

I could see immediately that she was neither the woman in the painting nor the one in the carriage. 'I beg your pardon, madam. I called to see Mrs Weld.'

She did not move from her perch on the stair. 'I am she.'

'Oh.' My mind flapped for a response. 'I thought perhaps – though clearly erroneously – the lady in that portrait might be Mrs Weld.'

The Mrs Weld before me gave a delicate grimace. 'She bore the name once, some thirty years ago.'

My hopes plunged. 'She is dead?'

The present Mrs Weld looked at me as though I were moonstruck. 'Her husband, Mr Edward Weld, died tragically. The estate and title passed to his brother, my husband. His widow had to move elsewhere.' Her fine nostrils twitched. 'Mercifully, she remarried before she gained her current notoriety.'

'Notoriety?' I had thought I sought a woman of the utmost mystery, who travelled in darkness and hid in a castle on the Dorset coast. 'What notoriety is this? Do you know where to find her? What name did she assume?'

Mrs Weld laughed, though there was no amusement in her eyes. 'Of course you jest, sir. I fear to count the times her sorry past has been examined in the press, and in the tongues of gossip. Even among the farthest Chinamen, I

248

doubt there are many ignorant of what befell Mrs Edward Weld.'

I lifted my hands. 'I confess – and you must believe me – I am entirely ignorant.'

A rash of colour rose on her high cheekbones. 'Ignorant indeed, sir. I had thought there were none in the world unacquainted with her story.' At last she must have seen the mystification writ across my face, for her manner became more direct. 'After the death of her husband, Mrs Edward Weld married Thomas Fitzherbert, and though he did not long survive the union, she kept his name in her infamy.' A pointed stare failed to pierce my incomprehension. 'I dare say you will find Mrs Fitzherbert, as she is now named, in Brighton.'

In the whirl of confusion that her final words provoked, I could at least understand why she had insisted I must know of the former Mrs Weld. Of course I did – even I, who heard so little of the fashionable chatter and heeded less, did not need to be lectured on her notoriety. Mrs Weld might be the obscure widow of an unremarkable scion of the Dorset gentry; Mrs Fitzherbert's name was famed across the kingdom. But knowing her identity did little to resolve the mystery: indeed, it merely demanded a hundred further questions, each wilder than the last. Most pertinently, what connection could Dumont possibly have with the principal mistress of the Prince of Wales?

I was about to excuse myself when I remembered one final detail outstanding.

'Has there been any communication for Mrs Fitzherbert of late? I know,' I added hastily, 'that she has been absent thirty years, but I have had reports that a correspondent may have sought her here.'

'When her whereabouts are so widely reported, it would be a curious fool who looked here.'

'Indeed.' Unless she were a perfect liar, Mrs Weld clearly

had neither dealings with nor interest in the woman I sought. Yet I had overheard Tyrwhitt saying that Dumont had sent letters through intermediaries at Lulworth.

'I wonder whether any servants survive from your predecessor's household?' I tried.

Mrs Weld eyed me with the deepest suspicion. 'What do you want of my servants?'

'Madam, your predecessor is implicated in acts of the grossest ignominy.' I realized that if gossip was accurate, this was hardly out of the ordinary. 'A French spy is at large in this country, and I believe that he made contact with her through friends in this house. If you know nothing, then I can only infer that some member of your establishment was complicit.'

I had lifted myself to my full height and tried to invest my voice with gravity. It did not seem to impress Mrs Weld.

'I dare say there must be many on the estate who survive from that time, though most would have been but children then. Within the household there is only one. Sir Edward's widow took her maids with her when she left, and the rest of her servants have either been dismissed or found other employment over the years.'

'But one remains,' I prompted. 'Where might I find her?'

Mrs Weld fluttered a thin wrist to her right. 'Cleaning the chapel. Her name is Lucy.'

'I am most grateful. You may have served your nation an invaluable turn.' I bowed a little and left, ignoring the disbelief plain in her face.

I emerged onto the terrace and descended the stairs, too fuddled to enjoy the dusty warmth of the summer day. Mrs Weld had indicated that the chapel was to her right, but disconcertingly the only structure I could see – indeed, could hardly avoid – was the huge mausoleum. It seemed curiously practical for a house of the dead: there were plentiful windows to illuminate the eternal darkness, and two chimneys to warm the chill of the grave. A stiff pair of columns guarded the door, which looked to be in regular use.

Wary of incurring Mrs Weld's anger by despoiling the graves of her ancestors yet unable to see where else to go, I walked towards it over the lawn. My misgivings deepened as I approached, for I could swear I heard a mysterious, high-pitched wailing within. Had some banshee risen from the dead to haunt the estate? If she had, she kept the lock well oiled, for the handle gave easily to my touch. I did not believe much in ghosts, holy or unholy, but deep superstition still almost brought me to cross myself before I passed the threshold.

'Poltroon,' I muttered. The room I had entered was more a saloon than a grim house of death: white-panelled doors picked out with gold led off from its curved walls, and clear sunshine streamed through the high windows. At one end, on a marble plinth, a gilded altar dominated the room with far more garish ornament than my father would ever have allowed in his church. There was no phantom, unless the old woman who knelt before the altar, polishing it with a toothbrush, was an apparition. The wailing I had heard before, I realized, was in fact nothing more than her song.

'This seems a remarkably cheery tomb,' I said, uncertain of my ground.

I had not intended to frighten her by it, but at the sound of my voice the maid dropped her brush in fright. Perhaps she too thought the building haunted.

'Mercy, sir, there's nothin' cheery in frightin' me half to the arms of Death.'

She stumbled to her feet, wincing as she unbent her joints. It was hard to tell how old she might be, for long service had worn lines on her face and a stoop in her back. The grey hair that fell from under her cap was thin and ragged, and the indistinct sagging of her words was explained by the utter absence of teeth in her gums.

Clearly she had not been so assiduous with the brush in her mouth as on the altar.

'Are you Lucy?' I asked. Once again, it was hard to believe this withered crone could be an agent of the enemy.

She bobbed. 'Yes, sir. Or aye-aye, as you might say, bein' a naval gentleman.'

I was gratified that she recognized the cut of my coat, despite the layers of misfortunes stained into it. 'Do you know many sailors?'

From under the years of toil and labour, a twinkle appeared in her dull eyes. 'Knowed a few, here and there, now and then, over the years. You gets 'em passin' through, up from Weymouth or Poole and there.' She cocked her head across her shoulder with an alarming leer. 'Been a while, though.'

'Surely not.' I tried to tread the fine line between gallantry and slander. 'Did you ever know a French sailor?'

Even if I had spared her dignity with my previous comment, these words brought indignation to her face. 'Course not, sir. I'm an honest Englishwoman, me. Wouldn't take up with no foreigners.'

'Of course not. You have served here for some time, I believe.'

'Thirty-three years,' she confirmed.

'You must have attended many masters and mistresses in that time.'

'Two lords, three ladies.'

'So you will have seen Mr Edward Weld's wife.'

'Both of 'em. Mrs Juliana and Mrs Mary. Of course, she got drove off when Mr Edward died. Went to London, they say, and took up with—'

'I know.' I glanced around, lest anyone hear us. 'Tell me, Lucy, have you had any word from Mrs Mary recently? A letter, perhaps?'

The woman seemed to shrink back towards the altar. 'She told me I wasn't to speak of it,' she protested. 'Not to the new mistress, not to no-one. She said I'd burn in the flames of hell if they ever found out.'

I looked at her severely. 'Lucy, your former mistress is in a great deal of trouble. She may be in danger of her life.' Not least from me, if I ever found her.

'No,' the maid insisted, wiping her hands on her apron. 'No, sir. I'm not to tell of it.'

I gazed at her in teeming frustration. Even my vague morals generally precluded threatening elderly maids, but now I could not help it. 'If I tell Mrs Weld that you have had dealings with your former mistress, what do you think she will do?'

The maid stared up at me, terror and hatred balanced in her eyes. 'You wouldn't peach me to 'er. She'd turn me out on my end. She's a fearful temper when it suits 'er, and she 'ates Mrs Mary like the Dark One 'imself. What's a woman like me to do then? They'd not even take me in at the poor'ouse.'

I believe if she had kept up her plaintive pleas for another minute, I would have collapsed in shame and guilt. As it was, I just managed to stand silent and glare at her across the chequered tiles.

'There's little to say anyhow,' she mumbled. 'Twenty years ago she came 'ere – ten years almost exact since she left – and told me she had a fearsome secret.'

'What was that?'

'Didn't tell me, did she.' The maid paused, struggling to continue, and I berated myself for having interrupted her. 'Said she needed my 'elp. "Course," says I. "Lucy," she says, "if ever you gets a letter addressed to Mary Smith" – that bein' 'er family name – "I wants you to send it straight on to me at this address I give you, and not to tell a soul." That was all, sir, and I plum forgot it until six weeks ago, when I heard the new mistress wonderin' why she'd 'ad a letter for Mary Smith.'

'So you stole the letter . . .'

'It weren't meant for 'er!' The maid stamped a foot with unchecked anger. 'I got it from the 'ouse and sent it on. Cost me ten pennies, too.'

'And where did you send it?'

My heart heaved like a bilge-pump as she gave the brief answer. It made perfect sense, and I would probably have happened on it myself had I thought long enough. I reached into my pocket to give the woman something for her help, to refund the postage she had paid out of her wages at least, but I had only a single guinea and I would need all that for my journey. I told myself she would not have taken it anyway.

Feeling about as tall as the miniature saints on the wall above the altar, and not a fraction as holy, I slunk out of that tomb-like chapel. I had not enjoyed threatening a poor maid who had served her mistress so faithfully, but I had discovered what I needed to know and that was almost justification. How wise I was to be tracing Dumont's plot backwards, when he was doubtless moving ever on, I did not know, but I had little alternative.

At the inn in the village, I left letters to be sent to London, and worked through a bottle of claret while I waited for a wagon to start me on the next stage of my journey. Dumont's whereabouts might be a mystery, but I was confident that if I could find the many-aliased Mrs Weld I would be a great deal closer to knowing. With luck, I might even draw nearer the man himself.

22

❦

It took me three days to reach Brighton, and if I did not use the hours to develop any useful plan or strategy I at least found ample time to discuss my destination with those who shared my journey on the mail-coach roofs. There was not a stage I endured or an inn where I paused where some bore did not, on hearing of my object, launch into a rapture on the restorative power of sea-bathing, the magnificence of the improvements wrought on the town, and the best vantages for viewing the Prince of Wales strut about. By the end of it, the company of Reverend Lawrence would have been a welcome tonic, had I not sold the book to a west-bound gentleman to buy a bottle one night. It dulled the tedium of inane chatter a little.

I reached Brighton, a one-time fishing village now much in the clutches of progress, on the evening of the third day. Through my companions' enthusiasms, I had ascertained that the place to stay would be the Castle Tavern, a grand building, more castle than tavern, near the fashionable meadow where the *ton* gathered to preen themselves. Next door, the cause of this celebrity was evident in the wide mansion that overlooked it. I could hardly imagine a more bizarre architectural beast: it had the solid, square wings of a rustic farmhouse, but between them rose the body of a miniature Pantheon, circled with columns and capped with a spired dome. Behind it, the vast skeleton of some new, unfinished monstrosity towered against the sky. If this was the aesthetic of our esteemed Prince of Wales, whose famous house it was, it seemed his tastes were as promiscuous as his morals.

'You may have a room with a view of the sea for eight shillings, or of the pavilion for twelve,' the tavern-keeper informed me. He was a young man, younger than me and far better kempt. His hair was grown out, and curled so prettily it must have been the work of a hot iron, while his face bore the wounds of an attempt to shave close to the bone. He stank of perfume, yet his hands, when he took my money, were calloused. A hundred scrubbings and doses of lavender water could not completely efface the taint of fish, and I guessed he would keep a nervous eye over his shoulder when the press gang visited town.

'Is the Prince at home?' I asked, as he led me upstairs.

'He arrived last week.' My host's voice was as primped as his appearance. 'You may see him from your window, if he takes a turn about the Steine.'

'Where?'

'The Steine. The meadow before the marine pavilion.'

'For twelve shillings, I trust I will be afforded that pleasure.'

I did not linger long in the room. I preferred not to dwell on the mean accommodation my twelve shillings had bought me, and as the Prince was apparently shying away from the public, I would see little from my exorbitant perch. I descended to the street, more interested in finding the woman who had brought me here than in ogling a debauched prince.

The address the maid at Lulworth had given me was on Castle Street, which I hoped would be close to the eponymous tavern. I sought out the tavern-keeper to confirm it.

'They knocked it down to clear room for the stables,' he told me.

Boor though he might be, I did not think the Prince kept his mistress with his horses. 'Was the house demolished recently?' I asked. 'An acquaintance of mine sent a letter there only a few weeks ago. She would be most distressed if it had gone astray.' As would I, if it emerged that my quarry no longer kept a house here.

'They built a new one, just down the road,' the tavern-keeper lectured me. 'End of North Street. You know who lives there, does you?'

I noticed that his polished accent had tarnished in his eagerness to impart gossip. 'I do.'

'I seen her myself,' he said slyly. 'Most days, in fact. She comes to the assemblies in our ballroom Monday nights.'

'Have you seen her receive visitors?'

'Lots. And all hours, too. Very sociable lady, she is,' he said with a giggle.

'Is she there now?'

He shrugged. 'See for yourself.'

The house, barely three hundred yards up the road, seemed the product of the same eclectic imagination as had produced the Prince's pavilion. A colonnade on six pillars fronted it, with a verandah in the Indian style flanking it, while the walls were painted a shade of green that reminded me of being sick at sea. The balcony projecting from the first floor was masked with iron screens, whose leaf-like scrolls obscured anyone within. Was she standing there, I wondered, watching for Dumont? Watching me?

I climbed the stairs that rose to the front door and pulled the bell cord. The waning sunlight shone off the handle, reflecting golden beams over my face, and I had to squint to protect my eyes. Although the house did not have the fame of its near neighbour, I still noticed a few people in the streets behind me pausing to examine my errand. What new scandals would they be attaching to my name?

A stern-faced maid, some years past her prime, answered my call.

'My compliments.' I forewent my winning smile: her expression announced it would avail little. 'Is your mistress at home?'

'My mistress is at the races in Lewes. I do not know that she is expected to return soon.' She spoke with the polished boredom of someone who parried numerous enquiries. 'Would you care to leave your card?'

'Thank you, no. But I should be grateful if you could inform your mistress . . .' I paused as a notion struck me. 'Inform her that Monsieur Dumont called for her. She may find me at the Castle Tavern.'

The maid looked briefly curious that a manifest Englishman should be styling himself as a Frenchman, but did not question me. I had spoken on the spur of the moment, and doubted my wisdom even as I said it. Mystery clung to those who surrounded Dumont; I hoped that by spreading a little enigma of my own, I might somehow disturb them into revealing themselves – though not in such a manner, I belatedly prayed, as would bring them to my door with cudgels and cutlasses.

With little else to do until the lady returned, I began an aimless exploration of the town. Until recent years, I understood, it had been no more than a fishing village, before the discovery of sea-bathing and the attentions of the Prince of Wales drew hordes of visitors seeking health and celebrity in equal measure. Now the town rushed to escape its simple past, and the labours of progress were everywhere. The shoreline had been embanked and was lined with shops: taverns, inns, bookshops and – for those too delicate for the sea – vapour baths. The beach, which must once have thronged with fishermen's boats, now hosted a fleet of high-wheeled wagons, which pointed towards the water like the supply train of Canute's army. I had seen similar vehicles in Weymouth, for they were the mechanical innovation that had made sea-bathing possible for gentlewomen of refinement. At this hour, with the tide still only half in, they were deserted.

Although numerous placards and bills proclaimed the benefits of bathing – it was a particularly excellent treatment, it seemed, for the debilitation of nervous energy and languid circulation – I chose to forgo that tonic and instead turned inland. All of the extensions to the town seemed to have been concentrated along the waterfront and there was little depth behind it, but I managed to find the Post Office to see whether Nevell had answered my letter from Lulworth. There was nothing for me, and I felt a keen pang of isolation as I realized I would have to continue this madcap quest unaided a while longer. The melancholy of the thought demanded solace, and after a few minutes' more desultory wanderings, I began to make my way back to the Castle Tavern for a restorative glass or two.

The street was still busy, filled with braying fops and powdered ladies milling about to little productive purpose. Some declared their arrogant boredom in loud, crowing tones; others, whose dinner invitations were perhaps still in doubt, looked nervous and harassed. As ever, I stood about two inches taller and several rungs lower than my neighbours.

It was as well, though, that I was not one of those oafs captivated by the quality, for otherwise I would never have seen him. As it was, I allowed my eyes to range over the crowd in search of genuine amusement, and so saw the distinctive plume of a white feather on a black bicorn hat pushing through the crowds. Its wearer's eyes were hidden under the short brim, but the pronounced nose which seemed ever to be sniffing the air was singular enough to be unmistakable.

I stopped short, ignoring the shout of damnation as a dandy cannoned into me from behind. How had Lebrett come to be here? I had assumed he would stay near

Dartmoor for at least a week, trying to roust Dumont from whichever foxhole he had vanished in. Had he captured the Frenchman, and arrived in Brighton to finish the affair by snaring his accomplices? Or had he followed me here? I remembered his horse crashing over me in the fog and the furious threats he had made at the cove. I had seen enough of his obsession to be sure Dumont would remain his first priority – but after Dumont, I had a clenching fear I would be next.

I struggled through the crowd and pressed myself into a doorway in the hope that Lebrett would not see me. He was not alone, I saw, as I let my rapt eyes follow him: two broad-shouldered Guardsmen trailed him, and by the crown of a hat I could see another, shorter man beside him. I crouched nearer the ground, lowering myself behind the wall of humanity.

But Lebrett did not pass. Just before he came level with me he turned away to his left and barged across the current of traffic to the door of a tavern. Rather ominously, his two Guards took up positions as sentries on the door; his third companion, still obscured by the intervening crowd, followed him in.

I did not think he had seen me, else he would surely have lunged straight for me, but he clearly wanted no disturbance while he spoke in the tavern. Whatever his conversation held, it must be important. If that were so, then whatever its subject I would want to hear it, either to catch Dumont or to fox Lebrett. Either seemed a worthy aim.

I moved away from the doorstep and, with a conspicuous attempt at stealth, let the eddies of traffic carry me across the street towards a narrow lane beside the tavern. I had intended to find a back door but saw immediately that I could do better. A dray-cart was drawn up before me, almost entirely blocking my way, and a team of porters and barrelmen were manhandling huge casks into the open doors of a cellar. The sight of so much ale spurred a keen thirst, but I quashed that thought and approached the man whom I guessed to be the foreman.

'Your pardon,' I said grandly. 'I have need of an inconspicuous entrance.' I tapped a knuckle against my nose. 'It would be superfluous to mention the reason.'

The foreman looked at me as though I had a bay tree growing out of my head. 'You wants to go in the 'atch?'

'Precisely.' I wondered if even the grossest tourist from the *bon ton* ever spoke in the cream-thick voice I had put on. 'Nothing less.'

'An' why'd that be, sir?' The foreman clearly could not choose between bemusement and hostility; his tone veered from one to the other.

'Were I to venture in by the front door, I fear it would cause something of a commotion,' I expounded. That much was alarmingly true. 'You see, there is a lady within.'

The foreman's shoulders relaxed. 'An' a jealous 'usband watchin' the door?'

I clapped him on the arm. 'You understand my predicament. May I pass?'

He stroked his forefinger along his chin. 'I'd consider it.'

Now it was my turn to take his meaning. 'For a consideration, perhaps.' I fished in my pocket and felt the cool silver of a shilling. It was my last: I would have to forgo refreshment in the tavern. How I would settle the account for my room, I could ponder later.

The foreman took my coin, squinted at it, then waved me forward. 'Luck to yer. Just don't be corkin' 'er bung'ole in my cellar.'

'I wouldn't dream of it.'

'An' mind yer 'ead,' he called, a split second before I felt my brow crunch into an oak beam.

A fraught passage through the fumes and hazards of the dim cellar brought me to a ladder, which in turn raised me to the tavern larder. I looked hungrily at the cheeses and hanging joints that crowded the shelves, mindful of how meagre my dinner would be without money, but a residual honesty – and my father's successfully instilled fear of constant supervision – stayed my stomach. Before I could be caught, I slipped out of the door and down a passage towards the noise of revelry and celebration.

After so many days of misery, at last my luck turned right. Doubtless seeking privacy, Lebrett had taken a table in the corner farthest from the front door, and as I drew near the heavy curtain that masked the end of the corridor I heard his sharp tones clearly drifting under its tassels. His words were broken by the hubbub in the room, shouts and the clinking of glass and china, but he must have been directly on the other side of the curtain and there was little natural discretion in his voice. Polonius-like, I pressed my ear to a slit in the fabric and listened.

'He'll come back here, I promise you,' Lebrett was saying, 'if he has not arrived already.'

I froze. Did he refer to me?

'Without the American to hold his hand, he has no choice but to throw himself on that damned woman's mercy.'

'Have you a spy on her house?'

'Two. They have seen nothing yet – save the persistent Lieutenant Jerrold.'

Even as I clutched the curtain in shock, I heard an irritated tutting. 'He has proved a remarkable nuisance, Lebrett, despite his fine figure. You assured me he would be a pliant tool ignorant of his ignorance.'

'So his superiors told me – and so he seemed to me. Perhaps our enemies have co-opted him. Certainly he could hardly have done worse if they had dictated his every move.'

'Yet still you allow him his liberty.' It was Tyrwhitt who spoke, I realized. And clearly they thought Dumont to be in Brighton as well. It seemed all my foes were flocking together like crows.

'My watchers failed to recognize him. It was only when they described him to me that I knew him. They will not let him escape again.'

There was a pause, and a scraping of cutlery: perhaps they took some mouthfuls of food, while I was gnawed by terror.

'And what if Dumont finds a way into the pavilion?' Tyrwhitt asked eventually. 'What if he reaches the Prince before we can stop him? Perhaps he has not come for help from that woman, but to exact some violence on the Prince.'

'The Prince has guards,' answered Lebrett, unworried. 'Far more dangerous is the damage he may wreak if we do not retrieve those papers. Once we have them, we may all breathe freer. And turn our attention to the lamentable Mr Jerrold.'

'Nonetheless, the Prince will expect to hear our progress, slight though it is.' I heard the scrape of chairs. 'We had best repair to the pavilion before he settles into the evening's entertainment.'

It was evident that they had left, but I allowed a full five minutes before I dared surrender my hiding place and squeeze my way out onto the street. Lebrett's Guards were gone, having doubtless accompanied him to the Prince's pavilion, but that was little solace. I began to regret taking a room at an inn so close to Lebrett and his agents, though in truth Brighton was hardly the place for a man seeking anonymity. With barely a dozen streets, there were precious few places to hide from the host of enemies who abounded here.

I stood there a moment deliberating my course, feeling my heart beat each second I stayed exposed. Fear cramped my thoughts, but there was little choice. I had no friends in Brighton, and knew no refuges. I would have to return to the Castle Tavern and sit out the adventure in my room there. Perhaps, I comforted myself, an inn so much at the centre of things would be the last place my pursuers looked.

I hurried back, scurrying across the open square before the inn and almost hurling myself through the door. The hallway was mercifully empty, so I did not have to fear Lebrett's spies; I ran up the stairs, bounding like a squirrel, and paused breathless at my door. Though I knew it was unlikely, I still listened for any pursuit coming up behind me.

Without my touching it, the door swung open. I was looking over my shoulder, down the stairs, and did not see it; I sensed a movement, and perhaps heard the squeak of a hinge, but it was only the sound of words very near my ear that spun me about.

'If you're trying to be secret, you could do better than crashing about like a cart-horse.'

I looked down at the diminutive, barefoot figure standing cross-armed in the doorway. Her dark hair was uncovered, and the neck of her dress low over her bosom: had I not made the mistake once before, I might have taken her for a practised temptress.

'Hallo, Martin,' she said.

'Hallo, Isobel.'

23

‘What are you doing here?’ I asked, a vigorous half-hour later. We lay side by side on the bed, hot and damp from our exertions, while I trailed my hand through her unlaced bodice.

‘I got your letter and took the first coach. I’ve been here a day already watching out for you.’

It seemed there were more eyes peeled for me than for Dumont in this town. I gave her a squeeze. ‘I’m glad you’re here. And glad it was you who found me.’

‘Who else was looking?’ she asked, lifting my hand away. ‘Not another of your fancies, was it?’

I sighed, and planted my hand back where it belonged. ‘If you think I have had time to seek out such pleasures in the last fortnight, you clearly have little idea what I’ve endured.’

‘It’s hard to tell when I’m always waiting for you in empty beds at strange inns.’ Isobel sat up. ‘Makes me feel like someone who does it for a living.’

‘Well, it would be a better living than the one I have at present,’ I snapped. ‘If you want to go out and be shot at by lunatic cavalry officers and desperate Frenchmen, I will happily sit here and wait to pleasure you.’

Taking a stern tone with Isobel rarely cowed her. More

commonly, it was like a rag to a bull. 'Is that all you want me for? To wait around to tup you?'

'All I meant . . .' I began, tailing off as I realized I did not know what I meant. 'I'm glad you're here, not just for your physical delights – though obviously, ah, they're delightful – but because I am in a barrel of trouble at the moment.'

I had hoped to play on Isobel's sympathy. I fear I did not stir it, but at least I touched her curiosity.

'You're always in a barrel of trouble,' she said severely. 'Since I've known you.'

'There were three months of blessed peace aboard the hulk,' I reminded her.

'Storing it up for now.' Isobel shuffled down the bed, making herself comfortable. 'Why don't you tell me where you've been, to start? The last I knew was you left a letter saying you were gone to Plymouth. Did you find your prisoner there? What are you doing in Brighton?'

Trying to avoid a lascivious impression, I reached an arm around Isobel's thin shoulders and tucked her in against me. She did not wriggle away. As so often, I had begun things clumsily and in the wrong order entirely, but now I told my story from where I had left her: the journey to Devon; Tyrwhitt's house; the chase across the moor and the battle in the cove; Lebrett's attempts to murder Dumont, and then to ride me down; my expedition to Lulworth and the extraordinary intelligence I had found there which had brought me to Brighton.

'Dumont had written to the woman, who styled herself Mrs Weld, by care of a servant at the castle. She passed the letters on to Brighton. The so-called Mrs Weld then went to Chatham, several times, and visited Dumont aboard *Prometheus*. She gave him certain vital papers, I think, which Lebrett is desperate to retrieve; she also helped him plan his escape. When I met her on the road the next day, she must have been seeking Dumont herself, to take him to safety. When they failed to rendezvous, Dumont fled to London and she returned to Brighton.'

'And now you think Dumont's come back here to find her?'

'Lebrett thinks so. He wouldn't have travelled so far if he didn't believe it.'

Isobel wrinkled her nose, as she always did when she was in thought. 'So if you find Mrs Weld, you can find Dumont.'

'It isn't so simple,' I said wearily. 'I know where Mrs Weld is. She lives in a green house down the road.' I pointed out of the window.

'I don't understand. You can watch her front door until Dumont comes up, then snatch the pair of them.'

I sighed. 'Matters are rather more complicated. You see, Mrs Weld is not really Mrs Weld. She held the title once, but no more. She is now known, and indeed infamous, as Mrs Fitzherbert.' I saw that Isobel, whose gossip touched on less rarefied circles, did not know the name. 'The Prince of Wales's mistress.'

Any satisfaction I felt at having surprised Isobel with this twist was dissipated by my own profound ignorance of its meaning. Since the maid at Lulworth had told me the name I had wrestled, chivvied, harangued and abused it, but still I could not conceive why the Prince of Wales's very public mistress, a woman whose notoriety even I knew, should be aiding an escaped French prisoner of war. I could make not the least sense of it, but I feared it bore heavily on the reason the Prince's allies in government, and his partisans Lebrett and Tyrwhitt, were so eager to apprehend Dumont.

'The Prince is hardly unknown for philandering,' I mused, trying to keep hypocritic judgement from my voice. 'He cheats on his wife with his mistress, and on his mistress with any number of other women who take his fancy.' I remembered the house in Blackheath where his wife lived, with its erotic clock, and decided they were probably well matched. 'Perhaps Mrs Fitzherbert has decided to revenge herself on him by aiding an enemy of his government.'

'No more than he deserves,' said Isobel. For a girl who had leaped into bed with me at the drop of a drink, she had since discovered a curiously prim morality. I did not know that I approved.

'Perhaps she has stolen these secret papers from him, and given them to Dumont to take to France. No wonder the Admiralty and the Horse Guards were so quick to lumber in: imagine the scandal if it were discovered that their patron's mistress had passed sensitive intelligence to our enemies.' I paused, thinking of the mounting tally of dead Frenchmen our chase had left strewn across the country. 'And imagine the lengths to which Buonaparte would go to get his hands on the documents.' Suddenly the interests involved in the affair seemed infinitely more serious, and wholly terrifying. Even in that stuffy room, I shivered, with sufficient feeling that Isobel burrowed her arm behind my back and pulled me towards her.

'We'll survive this all right,' she told me.

Her reassurance was kind, but it did not stop me having awful dreams that night.

The air was warm and close when I awoke next morning. A thin plane of sunlight had worked its way through the crack in the curtains, catching the drifting dust like fish in a net. Extricating myself from Isobel's hot embrace, I crossed to the window and pushed it open, letting the cooler air flow over my face. It must be early, for as I looked down I could see only tradesmen and delivery boys scuttling across the square below on their errands. An extraordinary number seemed to make for the side gate to the Prince's marine pavilion, doubtless to supply the wants of the famous royal appetite.

But what of Lebrett's spies? He had said he had men

watching Mrs Fitzherbert's house, men who had seen me make my first enquiry. I had announced I was staying at the Castle Tavern: would they have followed me here, be loitering outside even now? How would I get past them? I craned my head forward, wondering if they would be obvious. I could hardly expect they would be mounted on chargers and clad in gold-braided topcoats.

As befitted spies, they were inconspicuous – so much so that I could not see them. A fashionable carriage was driving past, and a gang of workmen were ambling down towards the seafront, but there were no masked ruffians with telescopes screwed to their eyes. I leaned further out, hanging on to the window frame, but apart from a pair of milkmaids gossiping I could see nothing more. One of the workmen shouted something to a milkmaid as he passed, and she answered with a coy giggle. The noise must have startled a dog that had been sleeping under a bush, for it bounded out and disappeared round the corner.

A small hand grasped my collar and hauled me back into the room.

'It isn't that bad,' Isobel reproved me. 'Just 'cos I've turned up, doesn't mean you have to end it.'

'I was looking for Lebrett's spies. I can hardly venture about while they may see me.'

Isobel pushed past me and ducked her head outside. 'It's probably those two.'

'Which two?'

'The two gentlemen sitting on the bench. The one who's reading a newspaper, and the other who's trying to light his pipe.'

I peered out cautiously. The bright sunshine made the shadows all the deeper, but in the shade of a willow tree, opposite the tavern and a little further down, I could see the bench Isobel described and its two occupants.

'Why them?' I asked, a little aggrieved. It was such an obvious place for a lookout I was amazed I had not noticed it.

' 'Cos it's an obvious place.' Isobel seemed insensitive to my feelings. 'And 'cos I saw them there last night as well.'

'You saw them last night?' How had she noticed them when I had not?

'A woman on her own gets to looking out for strange men doing nothing very much.' She gave me a dark look. 'That's how I spotted you the first time.'

I did not care to be numbered among such company, though I suppose I had little grounds for outrage. More important was the question of how we would evade them.

'I'll distract them while you slip past,' Isobel announced.

'But they're dangerous men.' I did not like Isobel to be consorting too closely with them, and I certainly did not like the thought of having nothing but her charms to shield me.

'I'm a dangerous woman.' Isobel shuffled her arms through the opening in her stays and turned her back to me. 'Best lace me tight though, just to be safe.'

A quarter of an hour later, I stood in the door of the Castle Tavern and watched Isobel stroll across the square. She turned into the street, and as she drew level with the bench a handkerchief fluttered from her hand and fell to the ground. Rather than crouching to retrieve it, she bent from the waist so that the specially loosened neck of her dress sagged dramatically. She appeared to have some difficulty getting hold of the handkerchief, and maintained her revealing position for some moments. Her face was flushed when she straightened, and it seemed the most natural thing in the world that as her eyes alighted on the bench, she should repair to it for a rest. Without hesitation, she squeezed herself between its two occupants and sat back, mopping her cheek and playing her fingers over her bodice.

From my vantage, I could not see how the men reacted, but I had to hope they would find Isobel's charms as irresistible as I did. At least, almost as irresistible. I began to edge my way around the fringe of the square, keeping in the lee of an iron fence. It masked me for a little way, but all too soon I was at its corner and forced to step out into the road, into the clear sight of the men on the bench.

I peered round the corner. Isobel was chattering away loudly, leaning forward and gesticulating with an arm. Her other hand, I saw with pained jealousy, rested on the knee of the man with the pipe. I could barely keep from staring, but they were rapt in Isobel's charms and did not look at me. Trusting to the strength of Isobel's attraction, and praying that Lebrett did not choose that moment to visit his agents, I stepped forward. My gait was clumsy and awkward, cramped by the fear of observation and the need to be relaxed, but there were no shouts and no heavy hands on my shoulder. I began to quicken my pace; I was halfway across the road now, halfway to safety yet in ever greater peril as well. If they glanced away from Isobel now, I would be ruined.

Something tugged at my sleeve, and I squeaked like a mouse. I cursed myself for coming unarmed, and was wondering how mighty a punch my feeble arm could muster, when I saw my assailant was not either of the men from the bench but a young boy of about twelve. He was barefoot, dressed in short trousers that were almost the full length on his slight frame, and a voluminous shirt. Had I noticed the tar smudged on his cheek and hands, I might have surmised he was apprenticed to the sea; as it was, I was too busy staring desperately at Isobel and her watchers to see if they had spied me.

''Ere for the bathin', is you, sir?' asked the boy.

'Not really.' I was desperate to be off the street. Brighton held enough dangers for me without the hindrance of a puppish hawker trying to prey on a tourist.

'It 'tenuates the blood,' he informed me, in words he must surely have learned from his master.

'I don't care.'

'An' strengthens the solids.'

'My solids are perfectly well ordered, thank you.'

'Your circulation's not so well, though. You're pale as a gutted herring, if you don't mind my saying . . .'

'I do mind it, actually. And I mind it even more that you persist in harassing me when I have urgent business to attend to.' I peeked over my shoulder. Even Isobel's charms must eventually prove finite.

'You could learn something,' the boy announced, much to my surprise. 'S'posin' I was to say . . .' He paused, furrowing his brow and concentrating so hard he went almost cross-eyed. 'Prothemeus.'

'*Prometheus?*'

He nodded proudly. ' 'S it.'

I leaned closer, my fear of being caught overtaken by confusion that this urchin should know my business. 'Who told you to say that?'

'Gent.'

'And what else did he tell you?'

'That you should go sea-bathin'. Mirac'lous for the constitution, it is.'

Enigmatic messages from unknown gentlemen were not my preferred route to follow, but those who wished me ill would probably have sent a prizefighter with a cudgel instead of this sprat of a sea-bathing evangelist.

'Very well. But quickly – and not past that bench.' I had lingered far too long in the watchers' field of view; I did not now want to parade past them.

The boy clapped a fist against his forehead. 'Follow me.'

Nowhere was far to go in Brighton, and my reluctant trailing after the boy did not last long. Walking away from the watchers, we turned left almost immediately and were quickly on the seafront. This had been embanked above the beach, and surmounted with new buildings offering every facility that a lady of refinement might require for modest and private bathing preparations.

'In there,' said the boy, pointing to a white door. 'Straight through.'

Blushing a little to be seen entering a ladies' facility, however discreet, I pushed the door open and hurried in. To my regret, there were no gentlewomen *en déshabillé* in the cramped room, though even if there had been they would not have excited much arousal. Propriety demanded small, high windows, as inaccessible to light as to prying eyes, and I could barely make out the door which I guessed the boy had meant me to take.

The boy had said that sea-bathing would improve my circulation, and there was now an unintended truth in those words as my heart began to beat with ever more urgency. I had supposed my enemies would not hesitate to seek me out with violence; how much more convenient to lure me to a dark, deserted room. But there did not seem to be anyone in there, friend or foe. My feet tingling with every step, I edged forward to the far opening, pushing through a curtain into an even darker passage. It was built of wood, for I could see splinters of daylight breaking through the uneven joins of the planks, and my footfalls thudded on the floor. I seemed to be on some walkway built out over the beach.

Without warning, the passage shuddered, as though I were in the belly of some enormous beast and had woken it. The motion tumbled me onto my knees, and as I tried to find my feet I heard a grinding rumble stirring beneath me. I rushed back the way I had come and pulled away the curtain. There was a steep wall, its lower portion crusted with barnacles and green weed, and a door set a good six feet off the ground. It was receding behind me; an expanse of murky beach was spreading between us, and I could see two parallel tracks gouged into the shingle. I was in a bathing machine, I realized, listening to the squeak of the axles and the complaining growl of the wheels. Was I being dragged out to sea so that my body could be sunk without witnesses?

I looked down. The tide must be quite high, for we were already past the edge of the shore and progressing into ever deeper water. The waves sparkled in the summer sun; doubtless a poet or a painter could have made a pretty enough picture with them, but to me they appeared more like bobbing knife-blades waiting to flay me alive. That was better than whatever fate awaited me in the coffin of the bathing machine, though. I pinched my nose, and prepared to leap into the sea.

'In the name of decency, Jerrold, you should wait until the driver lowers the canopy,' said a voice behind me. 'Otherwise you'll scandalize the fine sensibilities of Brighton.'

I spun about, and almost fell backwards into the sea in my surprise. With the curtain held back, I could see further into the depths of the bathing machine – little more than a glorified cart, really, from whose tail a canvas screen allowed the modest to enter the water. There, seated on a bench against the back wall, his head cocked to one side, was Nevell.

It would take more than sea-water to strengthen my solids after that fright. 'I thought you'd brought me out here to be chopped into pieces and spread over the waves as fish food,' I said, my voice a quavering mixture of anger and relief. 'Next time, you could call on me in my room at the inn.'

'There are too many eyes watching Brighton, and we are both among their objects. Now drop that curtain down before we become a public spectacle.'

Reluctant though I was to drown myself in darkness again, I let the curtain fall over the back of the cart. 'Does this mean you have intelligence to impart?' I asked. 'Or did you just hope to improve my constitution?'

Nevell laughed. 'If half the rumours I have heard are

274

true, your constitution needs little improvement. I came as soon as I got your letter from Wool. It's an extraordinary connection you have dredged up between the good Mrs Fitzherbert and our renegade prisoner – and not one which will please a great many people.'

'Had you any notion of it yourself?' Half of me longed for information which might enlighten the murk that surrounded this affair; the other half rather hoped I had trumped Nevell to this particular insight.

'There were signs, of course, but nothing to suggest the entire truth. For instance, the extraordinary lengths the Prince's allies in government went to to find Dumont. The fact that their parliamentary opponents scented partisan blood.' Nevell raised his shoulders in a rare gesture of defeat. 'We never suspected that the Prince's mistress had helped effect Dumont's escape.'

'And given him crucial papers. That seemed almost more important to Tyrwhitt and Lebrett.'

Nevell made a face as if he had just bitten into a foetid cheese. 'Lebrett. There is a rumour in London that he has sworn to see you dead – hanged, shot or cut down, he does not care.'

'He's already tried to pulverize me under his horse.' Although I trembled to hear Lebrett's intentions spoken so baldly, there was a certain relief in having things in the open. If I ever again found myself facing him with a loaded pistol, I would suffer little compunction in pulling the trigger.

'He is now in Brighton.'

'I know.' I recounted the conversation I had heard the night before. 'They think Dumont is here too.'

Nevell sighed. 'Tyrwhitt, Lebrett, Dumont, you and I, and the Prince and his mistress too – all gathered together. I wonder which of us will find our quarry first.'

For my part, I was glad Nevell had found me. I would have loved to be rid of the entire problem, to flee to the safety of Chatham or my parents' house in Hampshire or even out to sea, so legion did my problems appear. But as it seemed I would not see the end of this until Dumont was captured, or dead, and his papers retrieved, it would be good to have help.

'Do you have any hint as to what these papers might contain?' I asked.

'None. Every office of government denies anything is missing.'

'Naturally they would say so.'

'That is not official news. It comes from rather more open sources.'

'Their post?'

Nevell bowed his head in mock penitence. '*The eyes of the Almighty range throughout the land*. Our motto.'

'But you cannot see into Dumont's pocket.' I paused, thinking. 'If the ministers of government do not refer to these documents in their own private correspondence, then they must be of the highest importance.'

'Or else . . .'

'Or else what?' Having been entirely candid with Nevell, I would have little patience if he started to play at riddles again.

Nevell gave an opaque smile. 'Or else they have nothing to do with the government.'

I scowled. 'I hardly think that the First Lord would have intervened in this affair himself if it did not concern the government.' Nevell moved in mysterious ways, but on occasion he could knot himself up in foolery.

'Certainly the best way to find out will be to ask the man himself.' Nevell looked at his watch. 'If Dumont has come to Brighton, it can only be to see one of two people. We are neither.'

'Mrs Fitzherbert, the Prince's mistress,' I hazarded. 'To ask for more help in escaping, or possibly to collect another of these vital documents. Who is the other?'

'The Prince, of course.' Nevell rapped on the front partition of the bathing machine. 'We had best get back to shore. Unless, of course, you wish to take the sea-water.'

24

'Why the prince?' We were walking to the Post Office, which, by happy chance, offered clear views over the Prince's pavilion. Though I was immeasurably emboldened by having Nevell beside me, I still checked anxiously over my shoulder every few seconds.

'Because clearly he is embroiled in this somehow. His mistress has helped Dumont escape, and passed him these papers — it follows that the papers belong either to the Prince's government, or to his own household. It is from the latter that his mistress would be more likely to have obtained them, and which, if she wished to be revenged on her faithless lover, would afford more spite.'

'And if the Prince were humiliated, his friends in government would be damaged by association.'

'Precisely. This is a delicate moment for their alliance, as he tries to use their power to divorce his wife, the Princess Caroline, in a rather unsavoury fashion. Further scandal could ruin them all.'

'But what could those papers contain which would so embarrass the Prince?' I wondered aloud.

Nevell snorted. 'What could not embarrass him? You know his reputation.'

'If he's half so shameless as Martin, he won't care a

farthing,' broke in a new voice. 'He'd leave an honest girl to the mercy of two unspeakable villains and never come back for her.'

'Miss Dawson.' Nevell raised his hat. 'Has this cad forsaken you?'

'You'll be the first to know when he does,' said Isobel, curtsying like a countess. 'One day he'll run away and I'll forget all about him.'

I did not care for being discussed thus like a dog. 'I was called away by one of Nevell's little tricks,' I explained. 'As for Lebrett's spies, I feared more for them than for you. What did you do with them?'

'I slit their throats and dragged them under the bushes.' Isobel laughed at the shock on my face – I could never be sure what she might do. 'No, I prattled on a bit, until you were gone, and then I told them they could find me in the Ship if they wanted. They haven't moved since,' she added, evidently aggrieved.

'Happily for them,' I said. 'Otherwise I might have had to cut their throats and dump them in the bushes.'

We reached the Post Office. At a few words from Nevell, the clerk took us through a private door and up some stairs to a broad room on the first floor. It was furnished as an office, though there were no papers on the desk and no quills in the inkstand. In the far wall, a high window looked out across the Prince's lawns.

'This should do.' Nevell dragged a chair across the carpet and set it beside the window, facing towards the front portico of the pavilion. 'If you sit opposite, Jerrold, you should have a view of the grounds.'

'I'll sit between,' Isobel announced. 'To see what you miss.'

I sank happily into the upholstered chair, and for two minutes gazed seriously out across the gardens. To my disappointment, no-one approached. To my irritation, Nevell seemed to address his purpose with no little frivolity. He played with the buttons on his waistcoat, drummed his fingers on the tabletop, scratched the back of his neck and seemed not to pay anything the least attention.

'If you would like a rest, I'm sure Isobel could take your place for half an hour,' I said eventually. In negligence of duty I yield to no man, but in a town infested with my enemies I could see the value of vigilance. It irked me that Nevell, so quick to command me, should treat his task so lightly.

'It passes the time,' he replied.

'So would a bottle of hock – a good deal faster.'

'That would be irresponsible,' he reproved me. 'It might dull our faculties.'

It would at least dull my lingering terrors. 'Your own faculties seem a trifle distracted.'

Nevell sighed. 'I've told you before, Jerrold: the surest way to miss something is to look too closely for it.'

'Tell me about this woman,' Isobel interrupted. 'Mrs Fitzherbert. Who was she that the Prince of Wales took up with her? I thought princes only sauced around with ladies.'

'This prince would help himself to a Deptford fishwife if she were to hand,' Nevell answered. 'Mrs Fitzherbert, however, is cut from a finer cloth. She was married once to Mr Weld of Dorset—'

'Where I discovered her significance,' I interrupted.

'And again to Mr Fitzherbert of Staffordshire. Widowed both times in a matter of months.'

'Poor woman,' murmured Isobel.

'Was there anything untoward in the deaths of the husbands?' If she had inflicted so much misery on me, who knew what other mischief she might have worked.

'One died of a fever, the other of consumption. By the age of twenty-five she was twice widowed, and possessed of a substantial inheritance.'

'How fortunate.' I winced as Isobel slapped my hand.

'Then, at some point in the eighties, the Prince

met her in London and insisted she become his mistress.'

'No doubt she was only too happy to leap into the future monarch's bed.'

'Not according to my reports.' Nevell broke off in mid-speech and jerked his head towards the window, like a cat noticing a bird from the edge of its eye. For a few moments he kept his gaze unbroken; then, as abruptly, he turned back to us. 'Obviously I was barely ten years old at the time, and far removed from London, but the gossip was that the virtuous Mrs Fitzherbert, from devout Catholic stock, rebuffed him.'

'Not for long, clearly.'

'Not for long. Apparently the Prince threatened suicide if she did not succumb.'

'What a passion it must have been,' said Isobel. For all the toughness of her forthright exterior, she could prove unexpectedly susceptible to tales of romance. 'You've never said you'd die for me, Martin.'

'I've no need to raise my hand against myself, my dear. There are always those about who would be happy to perform the service.'

'It was a great scandal at the time,' Nevell continued. 'The Prince taking so public a mistress before he had married. After he married Princess Caroline, everything calmed down. Now he and Mrs Fitzherbert summer together in Brighton as quite the most intimate of friends.'

'Still?' I asked. 'There has been no recent split?'

'Not at all. They were seen together yesterday at the races.'

'It seems unthinkable that they should remain so close while she is trying to embarrass him and his friends in government by passing papers to a French agent. Unless her treachery is unknown to him?'

'The government are well enough aware of it.' Again, Nevell's head twitched as something outside the window caught his eye. 'They must have informed the Prince.'

He lapsed into silence. As ever, all our speculation would bring us nothing until we had the fugitive and his papers in our hands.

We passed a long day in those chairs, until my knees grew stiff and my back ached. A servant brought us dinner from the inn down the road, and Nevell permitted me a welcome, if insufficient, glass of claret as we reminisced about our days in Dover. Isobel provided unceasing commentary on the fashions that paraded before us, approving some and damning others, which was one way at least of staying alert to the passers-by. I would usually have played a similar game by judging the ladies without their dresses, but in Isobel's company it seemed impolitic. All the while, except when a particularly gaudy spencer or feathered hat drew Isobel's ire, I kept my eyes fixed on the grounds of the Prince's house. I grew so sick of it that in my mind I had eventually razed the entire edifice with broadsides of cannon fire, ideally as Lebrett and Dumont mounted the steps. The sun circled the sky in its lazy summer course, while constellations of the *bon ton*, hardly less dazzling, inscribed their own orbits in the grounds of the marine pavilion. I could not find it in me to be confident of even noticing our quarry, for there was an endless queue of visitors; Dumont might have sauntered past in an admiral's uniform and I would never have seen him.

As evening drew near, the sun began to set its face to the pavilion, throwing long shadows across the lawns and gardens. It did little to cool the air, which was choked with the heat and sweat of the day, but it did seem to herald the withdrawal of the promenaders for dinner. Amber light shone off the front windows, and I wondered what genteel deceits passed behind the mirrored façade.

'What's that?'

I looked up. 'Where?'

'Over there, by the elms.'

'I see nothing.' Though they were in such deep shade that I could hardly be sure.

'I thought I saw movement.'

I peered closer through the window, fogging it with my breath in my hurry. I rubbed the moisture away. 'I see three gardeners who have been there all day, two footmen at the door, and a groom leading away some horses.'

'Hmm.' For two minutes Nevell moved nothing but his eyes, skimming them across the sumptuous gardens with ferocious purpose. 'Perhaps it was nothing.'

The sun continued its regression, and I began to wonder how we would fare once it had vanished. I feared it was more than likely that Dumont would wait for the blanket of darkness before approaching, when we would be blind to his movements.

'Are you armed, Jerrold?' Nevell asked suddenly.

'No.' I wondered what had prompted the thought.

Nevell pulled a slim pistol from the inside of his coat and slid it across the table. The craftsmanship of its decoration looked perfect, and I guessed at least as much effort again had gone into its workings. Probably more than my erratic skill merited.

'I shan't weigh you down with extra shot. I'd much prefer to catch Dumont alive, so use it only in the last extremity. I imagine that will be at close enough quarters that a second bullet would be redundant.'

'If Lebrett and Dumont come at me together, I'll have difficulty deciding where to aim.'

'I could not presume to govern you.' Nevell's voice remained light, but his face was drawn. Even *his* patience must have been tried by the futility of the long day's watch. He stared out across the lawns, playing with the buttons on his waistcoat again, while I tucked the pistol into my belt and wondered if it would see any use that night.

'Christ.' The shock in Nevell's tone jolted me back to the present. 'Do you see that, Jerrold? By the portico?'

Valiantly though my eyes battled the twilight, it availed nothing. 'I see nothing.'

Nevell slammed his hand on the table. 'Precisely – nothing. Where are the footmen?'

Though it was hard to be sure, he seemed to be right. The two footmen who had stood under the columns of the portico were gone, and light spilled out of the open door behind.

'They've probably gone for their supper,' I suggested. 'Or to swap duties with another pair. Or . . .'

But Nevell had no desire for innocent hypothecation. Leaping to his feet, his chair tumbling unheeded behind him, he placed his hands under the frame of the sash window and heaved it open. The table trembled as he stepped up on it; then he had ducked through the window, dropped to the ground and started running across the Prince's garden.

'You'd best follow him,' said Isobel. 'He can't storm that house on his own.'

I did not think I would tilt the odds so much in his favour, but Isobel was already pushing me after him.

'I'll find a constable,' she called. 'You might need help. Or have some explaining to do.'

I had no time to consider it, for I was already bundling myself over the window ledge and falling down onto the soft flower bed below. It was not the first time I had left a house by such a route, but never before had it been to pursue a mad postman towards a royal residence. The gardeners gave me baffled looks, and angry shouts when my progress took me through their more delicate creations, but I ignored them all as I sped after Nevell. The naked timbers of the unfinished building rose away to my left, while before me the four columns that supported the pediment over the front door seemed to bar my way like a portcullis. Nevell was standing under them, his twin-barrelled pistol in his hand.

'It seems the footmen did not retire to powder their wigs.' He pointed to a thin trail of blood scuffed across the marble floor.

I already had my gun out, having pulled it from my belt when I started running, but now I tightened my grip. Whatever Dumont had done with the footmen, they were nowhere to be seen, but the memory of the carpenter's apprentice in the sawpit at Chatham gave me all the clues I needed to surmise their fate.

Beyond the portico, a wide door gave on to a bright room. Without pausing for discussion, Nevell pushed through it; I had little choice but to stick my pistol out before me and follow.

I stepped into the hall, and almost blasted off my solitary bullet as I came face to face with two hunched figures dressed like monks in dark, flowing cassocks. They were at least as large as life, but raised on plinths so that they frowned down on me, while bright lanterns hung on the poles that jutted from their hands.

'No need for introductions,' muttered Nevell, hurrying past them. They were statues, of course, though with their cloth robes and shaded faces it took me a second to be sure. Above them, a narrow gallery soared beneath the ceiling, and I squinted to check that no assassin perched atop it.

Another door led further in to an anteroom. I hurried into it behind Nevell, too afraid to wonder that I actually trod inside a prince's mansion, yet amazed by the exotic extravagance of it. The new room we entered had a deep red floor and was hung with broad paintings of scenes from the orient: coolies labouring in rice fields; wizened old men sucking on opium pipes; mandarins in bright robes standing under strange, fluted roofs. There was a flat, unnatural simplicity to the images, yet they groaned with the weight of their gilded frames, which were wrought into the shapes of dragons and willows. On either side, long corridors stretched away.

'Do you know where the Prince's quarters are?' I asked Nevell. The fantastic surrounds seemed to hush my words.

Nevell shook his head. 'I'll go left; you right. Call if you find him.'

'You may hear my shot first. Or the sounds of my capture.' Our unsubtle entrance must have provoked an alarm outside, for I could already hear shouts in the garden. It made an even more unsettling contrast with the empty passages within.

'Take care. Lebrett may not be far off either.'

With that cruel thought, Nevell turned away. With the utmost reluctance, I set my back to him and began to move down the dim corridor. Chinese lamps hung on heavy black chains from the ceiling, their circles of light like islands on the dark floor. I tried to keep to the shadows between, certain that this eerie silence would soon be broken by my pursuers yet too much in the grip of fear to move faster. What would my uncle say, I wondered, when he heard I had been found running around the Prince's house waving a pistol?

It seemed I had travelled miles down that corridor when I found the door, though when I glanced over my shoulder I saw I had come barely ten yards. I almost did not see it, for it was set back into the wall and in complete darkness. No light slipped out from under it, and I would have dismissed it as a cupboard had I not seen the brass dragonhead handle protruding. I put my trembling hand to its snout and twisted, grateful that the household was sufficiently well maintained that the hinges did not squeak.

Glad for any chance to be out of that corridor, I slipped inside. No lamps or candles burned within, but the far wall was lined with windows which admitted the last lees of daylight from the bruise-blue sky. It must be the saloon, for I could see the lumpen outlines of chairs and divans and low tables.

Well aware that I had little time to linger in empty rooms,

I returned to the door. Marshalling my courage to brave the exposed hall again, I was about to leave when a curious scent caught my attention. Two scents, in fact, mingled together, and I reckoned the reduction of my vision must have empowered my nose, for they were quite clear. One was a charred odour, as of a candle recently extinguished, which seemed odd at an hour when the lights were being lit. The other was a gentler smell, more delicate, yet in the instant I recognized it it froze me like the stink of death.

I turned back. Silhouetted full against the windows, a woman wearing rosewater perfume stood in the middle of the room.

'Lieutenant Jerrold.' Her voice was elegant and brittle as porcelain. 'Have you come for my son?'

25

If she was surprised to find me armed with a pistol in her paramour's saloon, she hid it well. I could find not even the veneer of composure. My right hand slumped to my side, and it needed three babbling attempts before I could voice a single one of the myriad questions storming my mind.

'Your son?'

'Frederick. Or Monsieur Dumont, as his current notoriety has him.'

This was too much. I did not know the niceties of form in the presence of a prince's mistress, but at that moment I did not care. Without seeking permission, I groped for the nearest chair and let my incredulous limbs sink into it. It seemed the only way to steady myself.

'Dumont is your son?' What remained of my sanity almost precluded the speaking of the words, but I forced them out. 'And you are Mrs Fitzherbert, mistress to the Prince of Wales?'

'I am Mrs Fitzherbert.' Annoyance touched her speech; perhaps she did not care to be reminded of her position. 'Dumont is my son.'

'Whom you helped escape from my ship.'

She tossed her head, the wide halo of powdered curls trembling about her face. 'I tried to help him. In the end, he was resourceful enough to manage it on his own account.'

'Then what were you doing the next morning in your coach? Visiting relatives in Rochester?'

'I was looking for him.' With a rustle of skirts she swept forward and poised herself on the edge of a sofa. The exposed skin around the collar of her dress was white in the gloom. 'But he did not know I was there, and so he sought his compatriots in London. After that, he tried Plymouth – Buonaparte had sent agents to find him, and they thought to smuggle him out from the Devon coast, but again you thwarted it.' She sighed. 'Finally, helpless and alone, he came back to me, his mother. Though I suppose you know all this.'

In a way, it was astonishing to hear my own journeys mirrored back on me from my quarry's perspective, but there remained too many questions unanswered. 'You say he is your son, yet how did he turn out a Frenchman? Was there a third marriage?'

She gave a laugh heavy with sadness. 'There was, though not to a Frenchman. When Frederick – Dumont – was born, I had recently travelled to France. I wanted him raised in the Roman church, and a family I had met in Calais agreed to adopt him to avoid scandal. It may seem hard for a man your age to believe, but France was not our enemy twenty years ago.'

'So your son grew up a Frenchman. Did he know the truth of his birth?'

'Never. And I could hardly correspond with him, for fear it would reveal my secret to our enemies. The mails are not safe.'

'Indeed not. But you knew he had joined the navy.'

'Not until three months ago. His foster parents knew that if he was ever in distress, they could write to me by care of an old servant at Lulworth. When I discovered he had been captured, and was chained up in that hellish prison ship . . .' Her voice trailed off. 'What would a mother not do for her son?'

'What did you do?'

'I begged his father to intercede on his behalf, but he would hear none of it. He disowned the boy long ago, and he had his own troubles pressing him. When that failed, I confess I acted with abandon: I gave Frederick tokens by which I thought he could negotiate his release.'

'Tokens?'

'Papers. But he did not use them as I had expected, to bargain with the authorities.' Mrs Fitzherbert dabbed a handkerchief to her chest. 'He was embittered by his father's rebuff; he wrote to France, to the government of Buonaparte, offering them the papers if they could conspire to free him.'

I whistled between my teeth. 'You put papers of such import into the hands of a Frenchman? Were you mad?'

She twisted her fingers together. 'I was demented with worry, and furious with my husband. And the papers were nothing more than the boy's birthright.'

'What—'

All the time she spoke she had managed to keep a smooth formality to her words; now it began to crack. 'They sent agents, spies to prise him from your captivity and take him back to Paris in triumph. Frederick mistrusted them – they do not care for his freedom, or for his comfort. To them, and to their wicked emperor, he is nothing more than a trophy, a stick with which to beat the King and work mischief.' A tear found its way down her cheek. 'All that matters to them is his father.'

'And who is his father?'

Mrs Fitzherbert took a ragged, sobbing breath. 'His father, Lieutenant, is the Prince of Wales.'

For a moment I was dumbstruck, before reflexive scepticism took command. 'That's ridiculous. You said his father was your third husband.'

It was an unwise tone to take with a lady of sensitive condition: she rose from her bench and flew at me. Her arms were surprisingly strong for one so frail, and I cowered beneath her blows like a kitten.

'My husband is the Prince of Wales,' she hissed. 'Married before God and sanctified by the Pope himself, long before the Prince made bigamist of himself with that Brunswick harridan. My son, should he choose to claim it, is rightful heir to the crown of England.'

She laughed, a terrible laugh of hatred and contempt. 'The papers I gave him are the proof of his claim, certificates of my wedding and his patrimony signed by the Prince before witnesses. That is why Napoleon will give no quarter in trying to bring back my son, and why Tyrwhitt and Lebrett and all my husband's sycophants in the government tremble that he might succeed.'

Her rage subsided, and she retreated sobbing to her sofa. It was as well, for in the impotence of my shock I could not have raised a handkerchief to stop her.

'Your son ... the Prince ... Buonaparte ...' Each word seemed to choke my tongue in its impossibility. 'But where is he now? In Brighton?'

Mrs Fitzherbert slumped down. 'He was here with me. He told me everything. He is just a boy whose world has been upended many times over in a matter of weeks. He came to me because there was none other he could trust.'

'And now? Is he in this house?'

She shook her head. 'He was taken from me minutes before you arrived. A tall American with a scar came on us unwarned and announced he had a ship to speed Frederick to France. Neither of us could resist him.' Her shoulders rocked back against the cushions. 'Please, Lieutenant, you must stop them, or my son will be torn apart by the powers which wrestle for him across the Channel. There will be no peace for Frederick in Paris, only an endless circus of exploitation. You must bring him back.'

'Which way did they leave?'

Mrs Fitzherbert twisted about and pointed behind her. 'Out through the windows, across the Steine. I saw them make east along the Newhaven road.'

She fell silent as a furious uproar erupted in the corridor outside. I could hear running footsteps, and many voices shouting at once. Had they found Nevell?

'One of my companions is about in this house,' I told her. 'Can you ensure he is not arrested as a common burglar? Nevell is his name. Send him after me. Quickly,' I added with fervour. I did not want to come upon Brogarde and Dumont alone.

'God speed, Lieutenant.'

In truth, I would rather His protection than His despatch, but I did not say so. I crossed to the window, which I saw still stood ajar, and ran out across the Steine. The lamps along its far edge sent rippling waves of orange light across the grass, and lengthened the shadows of the gentlemen and -women who still drove their phaetons and curricles about the drive, or walked along it arm in arm. There would be rich takings for pilferers and pick-pockets here, I thought, and surely they would not go unguarded. Sure enough, amid all the respectable swagger, I saw a lantern lifted high on a pole hobbling through the crowd. I made towards it.

He was not a figure to instil fear into the hearts of thieves. His back was bent, as if from a life of bearing too many burdens, and his wide-brimmed hat was pulled so low over his gnarled face that the notorious highwayman Macleane could have walked past and suffered no rebuke.

'Are you the watchman?' I demanded.

He craned his head back a little. 'Aye.'

There was little purpose in asking him to accompany me. At his pace, Dumont would be in Paris before I was out of Brighton. 'A dangerous French prisoner is at large, and making his escape even as we speak. There is a thousand pounds' reward on his head, and the larger part of it will be yours if you can roust out some constables, or preferably a squadron of dragoons. Can you do that?'

The man's hat flapped in consternation. 'A thousan' pounds? Bless you, sir, for a thousan' pounds I'd go to Windsor an' bring out the King 'isself.'

'The local fencibles will suffice. This man, and his companion, are making for the coast, along the Newhaven road. Doubtless they have a boat waiting in some cove. You must hurry, man, or your reward will sail to France before our very eyes.'

The watchman stiffened to attention, knocking his lamp-stick against the side of his head. 'Coun' on me, sir, coun' on me.'

I would not have done so by choice, but I had none. Praying he would find help quickly, I ran on, pushing through the assembled throng and down the dark road that led east. Clearly it had caught the speculators' eyes, for the entire landward side was covered in the rubble and dust of emerging mansions. Some were almost complete and towered into the night; others were little more than heaps of expectant bricks, the new fabric of a town unfurling itself.

After a few hundred yards the houses dwindled to a clutch of crooked fishing shacks, then to nothing. I had not taken the watchman's lantern, for I feared to reveal myself so obviously, but the moon was past the half and high in the sky. Trees and grass and hedgerows appeared black and grey before me, while to my right I could see the wide sea, hear it whispering on the shore. The moon hung above it, throwing a silver path across the water as if opening the road home for Dumont.

The sun was long gone, but the air was still warm; after a quarter of a mile I was soused with sweat. I would dearly have loved to throw down my coat by the roadside, but though my shirt had suffered many indignities in the past weeks, it was still white enough to herald my coming to any who watched. I had to button it up and struggle on. I still had Nevell's pistol in my pocket, but I preferred not to come so close to Brogarde that I could be sure of hitting him with my single bullet.

It was an unnatural journey. Every second minute I craned my head over my shoulder, hoping for the hoofbeats of reinforcements, yet when once I thought I did hear a noise I half leaped into a bush at the side of the road, for fear it might be a smuggler or highwayman. No-one came. The road was easy to follow, but I was constantly stumbling and tripping in my attempt to keep an eye on the coast, looking out for the telltale signs of lights or figures on the beach.

It was as I came to the low crest of a rise in the road that I saw it. The bright avenue that the moon cast on the water seemed to be swinging after me like a pendulum, so that it always drew a straight line between us; there, as I stood on the rise, it was broken by the unmistakable shape of a vessel at anchor. In the gaze of the moon she was clear to see: a single-masted cutter, quite small, lying a few cables out from the shore. She was still and peaceful as a stone carving, but the sight of her gripped my heart with untrammelled panic. She could easily be a revenue cutter, of course, in which case her aid would be invaluable; but it seemed more likely that her purpose there was entirely malign. Still that was not proof of her being Dumont's transport, for no doubt any number of illegitimate craft were sneaking their cargoes ashore that night, but I could hardly ignore her. A path led away from the main road between two forked trees; bunching my coat yet more tightly about me, and drawing my pistol from its pocket, I turned towards the beach and began to creep my way down.

The rocky soil under my feet quickly gave way to sand as I descended, deadening my footsteps and allowing faster progress than I might otherwise have dared. It was still slow going. The uneven landscape was full of sound and shadow, and though it must have masked my own approach, it masked any enemy's equally. Once I almost put my foot in a rabbit burrow; another time, my rustling against a branch drew a fluster of angry wings. I had to keep my eyes tight on the path, and it was only when I noticed that the incline had eased, and that the lapping of water was now close at hand, that I realized I had come to the beach.

I had stopped not a moment too soon. Peering out from behind a low bush, I saw a scene all too familiar from my days hunting smugglers in Dover. A small boat rested in the surf, so tentative on the land that it rose and fell with each wave. Grouped before it were four men: three in variously disreputable combinations of loose trousers, striped smocks and squat hats; the fourth, in clothes which were at once better cut and worse worn, was Dumont. All four shuffled their feet and glanced about, as if waiting for something, though I was amazed they could stand there in silence when escape was so nearly assured.

'How long to Dieppe?' Dumont asked in his accented English. He sounded nervous, awkward, as if trying to force conversation with unfamiliar company.

'Day, more or less. Pends on the wind. An' more, if 'e don't bloody 'urry.'

Again they lapsed into silence, while my thoughts battled each other in my head. I had one pistol and one bullet and one hand shaking so much I would as likely put the shot straight into the sand before me. Even if by some miracle I hit Dumont, it would still leave me facing his three companions – and had I wanted him murdered on a beach, I could have let Lebrett take his shot at the cove in Devon. I glanced back up the path, praying for help charging down the coast road, but the only sounds were the calling of a barn owl and a small stream trickling through the undergrowth.

In mounting desperation, I stared back at the beach. If I dallied any longer, Dumont and his accomplices would surely be gone, bound for the triumph of France and away from all hope of capture. I had chased him from the bogs of Chatham to the desolation of Dartmoor and halfway back again: now, it seemed, I had caught him at the final step only to see him fly away.

So bound by these thoughts was I, and so gently did the steel nuzzle up behind me, that I did not feel it until it was pressed quite firmly against the nape of my neck. Even then, I had barely registered its presence before the voice spoke.

'Mr Jerrold. Come to wave us goodbye, have you, after all our adventures together?'

Thankfully, my fear came as a vice rather than a spur: had I moved, I suspect he would have blasted my head clear off my shoulders. Nor did I need to look round to see who he was, for the biting American drawl was clear enough. In between spasms of terror, I cursed myself for forgetting him, for failing to notice his absence on the beach. I doubted I would have long to regret my error.

'' Oo's 'at?' hissed one of the men by the boat. With no apparent movement, a cutlass had appeared in his hand.

The gun-barrel pressed harder against my neck, and I stumbled out onto the beach.

'An old enemy,' said Brogarde from behind me. 'Been behind us all the way since Chatham, but now's got a spot ahead of himself. Put a ball in my arm in Devon, God damn him – not many men do that and live to brag of it, Lieutenant.'

'Well, don't shoot 'im, for the love o' Jesus.' Thank God at least one of them was on my side. 'You'll bring every constable in Brighton down on us. Better t' slit 'is throat quiet like.'

'You know what 'appened with the last cackler we done,'

spoke up his companion. 'Couldn't move for a fortnight for all the 'goons champin' about.'

'If Mr Brogarde keeps to 'is bargain, we'll not move for a fortnight anyhow. Not till every cask of 'ollands an' ale in Dieppe's been drunk dry.'

'*Non.*'

The two men who had been speaking, whom I presumed to be smugglers, looked about as Dumont spoke. There was a deep unhappiness on his youthful face, and his fingers were twisted into the pocket of his jacket, but he stepped forward.

'Brogarde, you cannot murder Captain Jerrold.' He faltered under the incredulous stares which fixed on him, but found the courage to resume. 'He has been much good to me. If not for him, I might have died before I escaped.'

'If you're that grateful, I'm sure we can fix it that you go back aboard the *Prometheus*,' said Brogarde irritably. 'I'm paid to get you to Paris and to brook no delays – and I owe Mr Jerrold a particular debt in lead.'

'You cannot kill him.'

'Well, we damn well can't leave the bugger on the beach,' broke in the first smuggler. ' 'E's 'eard where we're bound, an' 'e'll 'ave every ship from Dungeness to Plymouth down on us if 'e gets loose.'

I heard a frustrated sigh from behind me as Brogarde considered this unlikely plea. I could barely understand Dumont's apparent kindness myself, for apart from making him my translator I had shown him not the least favour aboard *Prometheus*. Whatever I had done, I fervently prayed it would prove sufficient to stay Brogarde's vengeance.

The muzzle against my neck pulled away and I tensed, feverishly wondering if Brogarde had tired of Dumont's obstinacy and was clearing a path for his knife. My legs began to shake, my stomach to rebel; I wanted to snap my head about to see what fate awaited me, yet the grip of terror kept my eyes fixed forwards. Then something exploded against the back of my skull in a blinding flash of pain, and my fears ebbed away with my consciousness into a pool of darkness.

26

I was awoken – if indeed I had been asleep – by the smell
of brandy. It was that which persuaded me to open my eyes,
for I reasoned that while I could smell spirits I could not be
completely lost. Neither, though, was I in rude health: my
surroundings seemed to roll and sway before me, and when
I lifted my head to look about a shaft of pain skewered it. I
was in a small room with wooden walls and a low wooden
ceiling through which thin bars of light pressed in. A small
door was opposite me, but when I tried to reach for the
handle I found my hands were bound together behind my
back, entirely numb from where I had lain on them. The
odour of brandy, which had so revived me, was everywhere,
yet I could see not a drop of it to drink, nor even a hopeful
cask.

As I lay there, the pugilists who had taken residence in
my head subsided, and a few tentative thoughts began to
venture forth. Disconcertingly, no amount of thinking
could stop the room heaving so much I feared it would
upset the delicate peace in my stomach. It was only after a
few moments' painful concentration that I drew the
obvious conclusion: I was on a boat, at sea. The creaking
and groaning I had taken to be the sinews of my mind
were the ropes and lines above me, while the movement

I could see was nothing more than a gentle Channel swell.

A wave of nausea that had nothing to do with the motion crashed over me. I was in the smugglers' cutter, dragged aboard by Brogarde and bound for France. Dumont must relish the irony: not only would he find his freedom, but he would bring his former gaoler back in bonds, unless I was poisoned by the fumes in the air first. No doubt on the return journey this room would be packed with casks of contraband spirits. With little else to hope for, I wondered whether they kept any aboard for the crew.

A noise at the door drew my head up faster than it could comfortably endure, and I groaned in unison with the rusted hinges as they swung open. A shadowy figure ducked under the frame and moved tentatively forward, crouching like a miner under the treacherous ceiling.

'Captain Jerrold,' he said. 'I have brought you some water.'

'Brandy would be better.'

'Soon you will have plenty. In Verdun, or wherever they will send you.' Dumont squatted before me and held a tin cup to my lips. The water was stale and warm, but my mouth welcomed it. A small trickle drizzled down my chin.

'What a perfect revenge,' I said. 'The captor captured.'

Dumont scowled. 'If I wanted revenge, I could have let the American kill you on the beach. Do you prefer that?'

'No,' I conceded. Being tied up on a ship full of smugglers was an unenviable condition, but if Dumont could bring me safe to the authorities in France, I could offer my parole and enjoy a life of circumscribed freedoms in some provincial town far from the sea. In time, I might even bring Isobel over. Certainly it would be a safer way to see out the war.

I remembered Brogarde's gun against me. 'Why did you stop him?'

Dumont was silent as he sought the words. 'I . . . have owed you a favour. You were kind to me on your ship – and

300

on the beach, near the Dartmoor, Brogarde has seen you stop the soldier from shooting me. I am not so ungrateful.'

'You weren't so kind to that poor carpenter's boy whose throat you slit in the dockyard, after he helped you escape.'

A tremor passed across Dumont's soft features. 'Do not talk of him. He was an evil man. He dragged me into the pit because he thought I was a girl. When he found I was not, it changed nothing. I had to kill him for my own life.' He stared down at me, pleading in his face. 'There has not been a night since that I have not dreamed of him. Three times Brogarde has told me my screams will have us catched.'

He pressed a hand to the timbers above to steady himself. 'All I have wanted is to go home. Now, I do not think I know where it is.'

His face was very pale, though whether from the fumes, the pitching deck or the vivid memories I could not guess. Unsteady on his feet, he turned and left the cabin.

I slumped back, and yelped as I crushed my tied hands against the wall. Struggling forward, I managed to rock onto my knees: it was barely more comfortable, but it did transfer the pain away from my wrists. Even on an incomprehensible day in an incomprehensible fortnight, it had been strange to face Dumont at last, to hear his self-pitying view of events. Stranger still, I reflected, if his mother had told the truth and he was indeed the son of a prince, the heir, of sorts, to the throne of England.

I shook my head, wondering if so much confusion and mystery could resolve into a semblance of order. All I earned was a fresh crack of pain through my skull – compounded a second later by the bang of the door flying open.

'Come on deck,' said a recognizably American voice. 'Dumont's ridiculous mercy may yet serve us a turn.'

He hooked an arm under my shoulder and pulled me to my feet, narrowly keeping me from colliding with the ceiling. I struggled to form a question, to wonder what new evil he planned for me, but he led me without a word through the door and towards a narrow companionway. Even with his hands on my ribs to steady me, I had a deuce of a job climbing it with my arms fastened behind my back: each time the boat caught a wave one of my shoulders was jarred against the side of the hatchway. By the time I staggered to the deck, I needed no bonds to cramp my arms.

As Brogarde mounted the ladder behind me, I stared about at the boat. She was a cutter, similar to the *Orestes* I had sailed on in Dover though slightly smaller, and with no armament save a swivel gun on each bulwark. I counted about two dozen men on deck, none of them busy, for her huge gaff sail and boom were swung out almost square to the keel as she ran before the northerly wind. Whatever Brogarde had done to me on the beach – and I guessed by the rising lump on my neck that he had tapped me with the butt of his pistol – I must have been unconscious for some hours, for the boat and all the sea about were clear in the new light of dawn. Across every hazy horizon I could see no sign of land.

'Welcome aboard the *Lucky*,' spoke a man from the tiller, whom I recognized as one of the ruffians on the beach. He who had been concerned with giving me a quiet death, if I recalled rightly.

'What do you want of me?' I asked, trying to summon dignity.

He gazed at me carefully. 'You're Mr Jerrold, ain't you?'

'I am.'

'The one what did for young Drake up in Dover a few months back?'

I swallowed, then nodded. 'A friend of yours?' I asked tentatively.

He spat over the rail. 'Competitor. Reckon you did us a favour, clearin' 'im out.'

'Oh. Er . . . Good.'

'Never mind your reminiscences.' Brogarde was on deck now and crossing to the starboard rail. 'Someone hold a glass to his eye. Tell me what you make of that, Mr Jerrold.'

One of the smugglers lifted a telescope before me. I leaned towards it, and cried out as the motion of the deck stove it into my eyeball.

'For God's sake, Brogarde – you'll blind me if you do that. Untie one of my hands at least, if you don't want this stuck through my skull.' My eye stung horribly, and I could not even rub it to ease the pain.

'Cut those cords,' snapped Brogarde. 'But keep two guns on him.'

A coarse hand seized my wrists, and I felt the flat of the blade sawing between them. In a moment, my hands were free and I was desperately trying to rub some blood back into them.

'The telescope, Mr Jerrold. What do you see?'

It felt awkward trying to use the spyglass with my left eye, and it took me a few seconds to get my magnified bearings. Nonetheless, hours and months of practice soon steadied my hand as I swept the lens along the horizon.

'A ship!' In my surprise, I let my gaze falter, and I had to wave the instrument about several times before I retrieved the image. 'Near enough dead astern, following our course.'

'What sort of ship is she?'

I squinted through my open eye. 'Two masts, fore and main. Ship-rigged. A brig, I'd say. Can't see her colours.'

'How many men aboard her?'

I shrugged. 'Seventy-five. Maybe as many as a hundred.'

'And guns?' Brogarde's voice was taut as the halyards.

'Fourteen,' I guessed.

'All like I told you,' said the smuggler beside me. 'What'd you need 'is lordship's word for?'

'Two pairs of eyes are better than one, Captain,' said Brogarde coolly. 'Will she overhaul us, Lieutenant?'

I glanced at the set of the sails. 'Probably.'

'Sure as flounder's fish,' corrected the captain. 'Savin' the wind takes it into 'is 'ead to go back where 'e come from. I seen 'er crawlin' up on us since daybreak.'

I looked back through the telescope. Even in the few minutes we had been discussing her, she seemed to have grown larger in the glass.

'How far to France?' asked Brogarde.

'Too far an' more.' I saw the captain's hand drift towards the knife at his belt, and guessed Brogarde had noticed it too. 'I've runned ten score cargoes 'cross this sea, an' carried more free tradin' bacca an' 'ollands 'n you could smoke or drink in two lifetimes. I'll not see me ship or me fortune taken now when all I've aboard is a single, stinking Froggy an' 'is friend.'

If Brogarde was alarmed at the prospect of being abandoned in the Channel by faithless friends, he hid it well. 'You'll lose neither your ship nor your fortune, nor indeed your life,' he told the captain. For the hopeless tenacity of his optimism, at least, I had to admire him. 'If all goes well, you may even have a brig at your disposal to expand your enterprise.'

The captain leered at him with a disbelief I wholly shared. 'An' if it goes bad?'

'Then I hope your insurers will care for your widow.'

An hour later I stood beneath the naked scaffold of spars, watching the brig sweep down behind us and trying to give a semblance of authority. It had been hard enough on ships where I held the King's commission: on this smuggler, with twenty surly ruffians on deck and Brogarde's pistol aimed straight at my belly, it was nigh on impossible. I was grateful for the support of the stern rail, which alone offered any strength, but it could not allay the fact that my legs, and most of my innards, seemed turned to water.

'Ready for your role, *Captain* Jerrold?' asked Brogarde. He was sitting against the starboard bulwark, his gun out of sight between his knees, switching his gaze from me to the brig and back again every few moments.

'I'm ready to be cut down as a pirate or hanged as a traitor,' I said honestly.

'At least they won't shoot you for a spy. Not in uniform.'

His assurance did nothing to soothe my worries. I did not think that the thin ribbon of white paint around my lapels, still sticky to the touch, would convince the authorities. And though the hat jammed over my head seemed genuine enough, I had not enquired how the smuggler who'd lent it to me had come to own it.

'A little to starboard, if you please,' I told the helmsman, feeling I should give some semblance of command. All I got for reply was a suggestion as to where I could steer myself.

'Here, Monsieur Brogarde.'

Dumont had emerged from the hatch and come aft with a candle and wine bottle in his hands. I watched the bottle greedily as he passed it to the American, who uncorked it and sniffed.

'I've a taste for some of that,' I said, with more eagerness than was respectable. 'Calms me before battle.'

'If you do as you're told, there'll be no battle,' snapped Brogarde. 'But you may drink if you wish.'

He handed the bottle to Dumont, who gave it to me. My shivering arms seemed to draw strength merely from holding it, and I tipped it eagerly to my lips.

'Ugh!' A mouthful of red wine sprayed across the deck, drawing angry looks from all the crew who were in spitting distance. Some of it fell in the damp paint on my coat, turning the makeshift piping pink.

'Not to your taste, Lieutenant?' enquired the captain.

'I should have thought a smuggler would have the pick of his wares.' I wiped my mouth on my sleeve. 'Or do you use it for scouring your guns?'

The captain looked unconcerned. 'Always seein' to the customers, never to ourselves.'

'If the contents aren't to your taste, pour them away,' interrupted Brogarde. 'I need the bottle.'

With a prayer for any passing fish, I upended the bottle and watched its fluid drain into the sea. When even the dregs were gone, Brogarde took it back.

'Now, Dumont, your papers.'

Dumont looked unhappy at this, and seemed about to argue, but there was something in Brogarde's scarred face which did not brook dispute. Divorced from their exchange, I stood still by the rail, all fears forgotten as I waited to see the papers that had dragged me through so much toil and danger.

Dumont reached inside his coat. For a moment, all the sounds of rope and waves and hull and gulls faded to nothing, and I heard only the scratching of fingers on oil-cloth. Then the hand emerged clasping a wrinkled brown packet. Trembling, a look of anguish on his face, Dumont passed it to the American.

'You've suffered much for these,' said Brogarde gently. 'We don't want to see them harmed now.'

He took out a penknife and cut through the rough fabric of the pouch, extracting two small pieces of yellowed paper. I was amazed that he could sit there on the deck and hold them so easily, these papers that could ruin a dynasty and shatter the state: each time the breeze snapped at them, my heart seemed to shrink.

'Have you read these, Mr Jerrold?' Brogarde enquired. He might have been talking of a newspaper or a recent novel.

'I've been told what they contain.'

Brogarde lifted them close to his face. '*We, the undersigned, do witness that George Augustus Frederick, Prince of Wales, was married unto Maria Fitzherbert, this 15th of December 1785. George P, Maria Fitzherbert, Henry Errington, John Smythe.* Straightforward enough.'

'It leaves little doubt.' Each word plucked at me like a

musket ball: it seemed incredible that I was standing on the deck of a smuggler, with an English brig drawing ever closer to us, while an American mercenary read a prince's secret wedding certificate.

'I prefer the other.' Brogarde shuffled the papers. '*I, the undersigned, do witness and swear that the child Frederick Walter, born this 29th of September 1786, is the right offspring and legitimate heir of mine lawful marriage unto Maria Fitzherbert. George P.*'

He looked up. 'I'd venture it's not since the Intolerable Acts that one of your royal family has signed himself into such trouble. You'll keep a room for me in Windsor Castle when Boney enthrones you, won't you, Dumont?'

Dumont mumbled something indistinct, his cheeks reddening.

'But for now, you'll agree, we've suffered too much to hazard these papers in anything so crude as a sea-battle, especially if the enemy can outman, outsail and outgun us. It would be a shame if these went to the bottom of the ocean.' Clenching his pistol between his knees, Brogarde rolled the two pieces of paper tightly together and pushed them through the neck of the bottle. He jammed the cork in after it, thumping it with his fist until it was almost flush, then took the candle and tilted it so that drops of hot wax sealed it closed. At last, he stowed it in his pocket.

'At least if I go down, these will survive. A last gamble, Mr Jerrold: to trust the fate of nations to tides and currents.'

'I'd choose to think you 'ad more faith in your plan,' the captain broke in. ''Cos if you're goin' down, you'll likely drag us all in with you, an' the ship too. I wouldn't want that.'

'Plan for the worst and no worse will befall you,' said Brogarde blithely. 'Now, Captain, what signal would you expect to receive of a navy ship intercepting you?'

'Heave to and prepare to be boarded.' The smuggler captain and I spoke as one.

307

'How do they make the signal?'

'A shot across the bows is 'ow they most often says it.'

'They might construe that amiss. Do you have signal flags?'

'Reckon so. Got enough canvas in the locker to sail an Indiaman.'

'Do you know the signal, Mr Jerrold?'

I started, not expecting this question. 'Ah . . .' I was reluctant to announce that I usually relied on an eager midshipman and a signal book for such purposes. 'Er . . .'

'I knows it,' said the captain. 'Seen it often enough.' He kicked open a weathered chest and rummaged inside. 'It's these as you want.'

'Then run them up the mast.'

I watched as two of the smugglers tied the flags to a halyard and hauled them to the masthead. The pursuing brig was less than half a league back now, and closing quickly; I could see her topmen racing along the yards to reef sail so that she did not overhaul us completely. She had no quarterdeck, but from aft I could see the gleam of a telescope trained on us.

Almost as soon as our signal was up, she answered with one of her own. I glanced between our mastheads: the flags were identical, and they must have had it all set to hoist when we showed ours. I fancied there was a petulance in the way her flags cracked in the breeze, as though our smaller vessel had no right making demands.

'Do you have an ensign?' I asked the captain.

'Red, white or blue? Or you could 'ave Portuguesey colours – Spanish, Frog, Yankee, Dutch, Danish. I likes the Barbary jack meself.'

'The red ensign will be fine.'

Again, the brig answered almost immediately with a red ensign of her own. We were both sailing under topsails alone now, drawing little more than steerage way: she was coming up on our starboard quarter, and soon we would be broadside to broadside. Except, I remembered, that the *Lucky* had no broadside.

'Get below, Dumont,' Brogarde ordered. 'Are you ready to help the cause, Mr Jerrold?'

In the cause of saving my skin, there was little I would not do. I nodded, and grasped the rail tighter.

'Your men ready, Captain?'

'Aye.' The *Lucky*'s captain looked down the length of his ship. From the deck of the oncoming brig, it would doubtless seem that his crew were busying themselves with routine shipboard tasks; less obvious would be the arms heaped in the lee of the gunwales. Cutlasses, axes, daggers, pikes, pistols, muskets and blunderbusses: a motley selection of desperate weapons. I prayed to my maker that there would be no cause to use them.

'*Lucky* ahoy!' The brig was sliding up on our beam now: I could see the knot of officers at her stern, the men crouching beside the guns that faced us. One of the officers had a speaking trumpet in front of his face, adding a tremolo buzz to his voice.

'Brig ahoy,' I shouted back, unaided. 'What is your business?'

'*Lucky* ahoy,' repeated the man from the brig. I feared my quavering words had not reached him. 'Who are you, and what is your business?'

'Captain Jerrold,' I yelled. 'Hunting a French fugitive I believe . . .'

'*Lucky*, we cannot hear you. Starboard your helm.'

I glanced at Brogarde, trying to pretend I did not. 'Shall we close with her?'

Brogarde nodded. The tiller edged over, and after a few seconds our bow began to swing towards the brig. We were running beam to beam now, like a pair of horses in the traces, though the adjustment to our course was edging us ever closer together. Unbidden, some of the men hauled on the braces to bring our topsail round.

'*Lucky*, what is your business?' There were now scarcely thirty yards of water between us: any closer, and I think our yardarms would have grazed each other.

'Captain Jerrold,' I called again. 'We are hunting—'

For a second time, my words were cut short by an interruption from the brig's deck. This time, though, it was not for fault of hearing: my words must have been all too plain. Another blue-coated figure snatched the speaking trumpet from the officer who had hailed me and pressed his mouth against it.

'Jerrold? Jerrold, you blackguard! What the devil are you doing here? Trying to escape to France with your friend Dumont, are you, you damned traitor? Your treasonous meddling is finished, Jerrold!'

He swung round to the officer beside him, revealing his hawkish nose and lupine jaw in silhouette.

'Fire!'

27

Despite our signals and ensigns, they must have had their suspicions of us, for the guns went off almost immediately. Mercifully, it seemed they had loaded when they still expected a running battle, for instead of a faceful of grapeshot that would have cut us down to a man, we were met with half a dozen cannonballs screaming across the meagre space between us. It was so quick that I did not even register the wall of flame, nor the roar of the explosions; only the ripping and crashing as their iron tore through our spars and rigging. So close were we that their burning wadding rained down over us amid the canvas and cordage: through the carnage, I saw one of the smugglers pull open his trousers and try to piss one out. Lumps of timber the size of a man's leg thumped into the deck, while the mainsail lay draped above us like a shroud.

'Damn you, Lebrett,' I shouted. 'We surrender! We surrender!'

'In hell we will.' Brogarde's forehead had been gashed open, but it had not drained the mettle in his voice. 'Our only hope now is to close with them.'

As if he could guide the boat by thought alone, his words were drowned by a new noise from above. An almighty thud shook the ship to her keel, followed swiftly by a volley of snapping stays and splintering spars. Despite the onslaught of the broadside, we had kept our headway and drifted right up against the brig. Now her rigging was tumbling down over her, sliced apart as our fallen mast drove a path through. The brig's timbers were pressed hard against our own, and from where I stood I could see the knees of her company scrambling to her rail.

'Take 'em,' bawled the smuggler captain. 'Take 'em without quarter, for by God they'll give you none.'

'By God, sir, we will not.' One of the brig's officers – her commander, I supposed – leaped down onto our deck, pistol in one hand and sword in the other. The pistol exploded into the face of the nearest smuggler and was thrown away before the victim had crumpled to the deck; the sword flew between his hands, and instantly was parrying a mighty axe-blow. Before the smuggler could recover his balance, a second figure had arrived beside the officer. A moment later, his straight heavy-cavalry sword had transfixed the man's neck.

'Lebrett,' I hissed, watching in horrified awe as the blade came clear in time to skewer a second smuggler. The man stopped short as blood bubbled from his chest, and could do nothing as Lebrett set his boot against his midriff and yanked his sword out.

More boarders were pouring over the side now, cascading down in a welter of flashing steel and guns. One of the smugglers managed to get a match to the larboard swivel, cutting a bloody hole into the line of boarders, but within moments the gap was plugged with new arrivals and the fighting became yet more desperate. Most of the smugglers had clustered together for'ard, where the spreading tide of invaders pressed them hard against the prow, while a small group of men remained knotted around the captain and me. Amidships, we held hardly any ground at all. And Brogarde was nowhere to be seen.

'Have that, Froggy!' I jumped back in terror as a cutlass

swiped through the air, even before I had registered the meaning of the shout. In the incomprehensible surge of battle I had forgotten that I had no ally in it: I was enemy to sailor and smuggler alike. Again the cutlass lunged at me, and again I cowered back. Instinct had lifted my arm to parry it when I realized I was not even armed. A bloodied tomahawk lay abandoned on the deck; I ducked to retrieve it, and managed to swing the unfamiliar weight into the path of the next blow.

'Not me, you fool!' I shouted as our faces pressed close together. 'The enemy!'

My blue coat with its makeshift piping would never have got me inside the front gate of the Admiralty, but in the whirl of battle it gave enough of an impression that my assailant stopped his attack and blinked an apology, before turning to hack at some less fortunate foe. I stumbled away, desperate to find a corner where the battle raged less fiercely, but on that tiny deck there was nowhere to turn.

I cursed, and might have sobbed had my emotions not been overwhelmed with terror. In every fight I had fought, I had wished to have no part in it: now I saw that the one fate worse than taking part in battle was being in battle with no party. Whoever won, I would lose. Not that the victory would be contended much longer, for the out-numbered crew of the *Lucky* were reduced to so few that they could barely carry the fight.

I was still backing away when my heel caught on some piece of debris behind it. I tottered, then fell backwards onto the deck, sprawling over the obstacle that had tripped me. It was the leg of a corpse, I saw with fresh horror, blood spreading across its shirt and dribbling from the slack corner of its mouth. For a second its blue coat and brass buttons spurred the hope that it might be Lebrett, but he had the devil's luck and would not go so tamely: this must be the lieutenant who had commanded the brig. An unfired pistol was tucked into his belt.

I lay there a moment longer, glad to be below the altitude of bullets and swords, yet aware that a zealous stroke might slice into me still. Reaching across the corpse beneath, I tugged the pistol free and checked its priming. The new protection did nothing to release the clenching dread in my stomach, but it gave me the power to right myself and regain my feet.

I need not have risked it. No sooner was I upright than an enormous explosion burst out from for'ard: a gout of flame and steam rose in the crack between the two prows, and a shudder rippled through the spine of the ship. Several of her planks broke free of their nails and sprang loose, while a torrent of grey smoke rolled back along the deck. Together with those around me I was thrown to the floor, as cries of shock and disbelief echoed from all quarters.

Beneath my outsplayed arms, I felt the deck begin to list to starboard and to tilt forward. There was a rumble, and I watched a brass spyglass roll past me into the scuppers.

'She's shipping water,' a frantic voice called from somewhere before the mast. 'They've blowed her guts out.'

'Get back!' yelled another voice. A broad-shouldered boatswain, pike in hand, ran to the rail and hauled himself up the side of the brig. 'Cut her clear before she goes down.'

I could scarce comprehend this sudden turn, but the brig's crew were now scurrying away, clambering up the hull of their ship and vaulting onto the safety of her deck. Swords and muskets were left forgotten in the rout: the only blades which swung now were on the side of the brig as her men attacked the web of fallen rigging that tangled our ships together. Nor did the *Lucky*'s crew press their newfound advantage, for the few that survived were running to the rail and leaping overboard, doubtless to find the flotsam which littered the sea.

'What the devil . . . ?' I wondered aloud, raising myself on my arms.

'The race is not always to the swift, nor the battle to the strong.' Brogarde came hobbling out of the smoke that had consumed the forward half of the vessel. Dumont was behind him. 'Help me with this damned boat.'

He did not speak to me – indeed, he had not noticed me, for he walked straight past to the davits at the *Lucky*'s stern. One of the pair had been shattered in the battle and hung limp like a broken arm, but the other survived to dangle the jollyboat just out of sight. Brogarde began hacking at the rope with a cutlass, while Dumont looked on mute.

A deathly calm had come over the *Lucky*. To starboard, there was still the noise and confusion of the brig's crew desperately trying to wrest the ships apart, but that was well above our deck and growing ever more distant. For'ard, our hull seemed to be consumed in a frenzy of hissing and popping, and ever thicker clouds of smoke had seized the air about me. Even Brogarde and Dumont, mere feet away from me, were little more than shadows in the fog.

Rather later than every other man, and surprisingly late for someone with so keen a sense of self-preservation, I realized *Lucky* was sinking. Brogarde must have tried to blow open both ships' hulls with a keg of powder between them, hoping perhaps to escape in the confusion. The brig had limped away but would survive; there would be no salvation for the *Lucky*. The pitch of her deck became steeper as the sea flooded her bilge, and I could hear her timbers groaning under the shifting strain. With the brig's side lost from sight, I had not realized how low we had sunk, but now water was slipping over the gunwale and in a matter of minutes she would founder. I pressed my palms to the heeling deck and tried to lift myself up.

But before I could stand, the unnatural hush was broken by heavy footfalls approaching like the thump of a drum. Knowing that I had no friends aboard this drowning ship, I pressed myself back against the deck.

'Dumont! Where are you, you royal bastard? You may be going to a watery grave, but it's I who shall send you there, damn you.'

Lebrett strode through the fog, a pistol in one hand and a sword in the other. The blade was bloodied to its hilt and his blue coat was cut open in two places, yet even on the sloping deck he moved with unflinching purpose.

The click of a gun being cocked rang out across the deck.

'If you come one step closer, Major, I will blast your head from your shoulders.' Brogarde's voice was unyielding. 'Dumont and I are expected in France.'

'You and Dumont are awaited in hell. I will send you there myself.'

I crawled forward, the dead lieutenant's gun tight in my hand. Through the drifting smoke I saw Brogarde standing by the larboard rail, now very high in the air, his pistol aimed dead at Lebrett's chest a few feet away. Lebrett's gun was trained back at the American, but his gaze kept jerking to his left, where Dumont stood shivering in the water that surged about his ankles.

'If you shoot me, you'll have no bullet for Dumont,' said Brogarde.

'If I shoot you, I'll rip the bastard apart with my bare hands.'

'And who shall I shoot?' Trembling, I wedged my foot against the counter frame and lifted my pistol.

Three desperate pairs of eyes fixed on me.

'You will shoot Dumont, if you wish to redeem the shreds of your miserable life,' hissed Lebrett.

'You'll keep your finger off that trigger if you want to save yourself,' Brogarde advised. 'This is our quarrel.'

'Shoot Dumont,' insisted Lebrett, who would doubtless have done so himself if he could have changed his aim without drawing immediate fire from the American.

We stood frozen in silence, four men and three guns,

while beneath our feet the deck buckled and heaved. Unearthly moans shook the air as if the sheeted dead had left their graves, the sinews of the ship twisting themselves apart. I looked between Lebrett and Brogarde, each of whom had tried to kill me, each of whom desired Dumont for his own ends, each of whose pistol was locked onto the other. I did not know which I would rather see dead.

With a final, mortifying shriek, the deck lurched downwards. Two pistols exploded against each other, and as I floundered for the rail I saw Lebrett and Brogarde both collapsing into the flooding water. Blood welled from the American's chest, and from Lebrett's shoulder, yet you would hardly have known it, for no sooner did it rise than the sea washed it away.

'Kill him,' gurgled Lebrett. 'Kill that bastard.'

I looked down at my unused pistol, still chaste in my hand. The sea was rushing up, yet my mind was strangely absent: the smoke in my lungs and the shots ringing in my ears and the taste of blood in my mouth seemed to lift me above the churning waves. Then I saw Dumont, almost up to his neck in water yet still clinging to the submerged rail, and the desperation in his eyes drew me back to the raging turmoil about me.

Without thinking, I threw aside my gun and dived forward for a hatch-cover that had sprung loose and was floating on the sea. Wrapping one hand through the lattice, I reached out the other for the Frenchman. A salty wave slapped into my face, stinging my eyes; when I reopened them, Dumont was still where he had been, still clutching the ship even as it pulled him down.

'Dumont!' I called, shipping a mouthful of water for my trouble. 'Take my hand, damn you.' I stretched further, feeling my fingers slipping on the slick grating. 'Try, damn it! For your mother's sake, if nothing else.'

As though he were letting go a piece of his soul, Dumont let himself drift free of the ship. He popped up like a buoy, yet immediately sank back in a fountain of splashing limbs and plaintive cries.

He can't swim, I thought. I was gripping my flotsam as though we were forged together, but even I would not let a man drown before my eyes. I kicked out with all the force I could muster against the swirling current; my legs hammered at the sea while my free arm stretched for the Frenchman. For long moments my splayed fingers brushed through empty water; then something solid butted my fingertips, but at once my momentum pushed it back. Summoning every curse and imprecation I knew, I made a final lunge. Again my hand struck something solid, but again it drifted just beyond my grasp. I flailed in the water, scything my arms about in such fury that I could have knocked Dumont unconscious and barely noticed.

Once more I made contact, and this time I managed to fasten my fingers on to something. Not knowing whether I had found Dumont, a rising piece of the ship broken free or even a corpse, I clenched it in my fist and heaved. The effort almost overturned my makeshift raft, but the bite of my grip must have given new life to the drowning man. His body shook as he kicked out, and then he was rising towards me, breaching the sea and sprawling out, half dead, on the floating hatch.

I made sure his arm was lodged securely into the grating so that he would not slide into the depths, and lay back on the sodden platform. Tiny waves pricked at me between the open timbers, but I did not care.

'God damn you, Dumont,' I spluttered, choking down all the water I had inhaled. 'I've caught you at last.'

About ten feet away, a corked bottle bobbed gently past.

28

The board room at the Admiralty was still. Above the First Lord's head, the brass wind-gauge still confidently proclaimed that the wind was southerly, but nothing disturbed the quiet of the room save the occasional discreet slurp of tea from a cup, and the chime as it was replaced on its saucer. As the First Lord made to speak, two pairs of eyes swivelled dutifully towards him.

'And after this, the brig rescued you from your raft and returned you both to Brighton, three days ago.'

I nodded.

The First Lord swayed a little in his chair, then turned to his right. 'What has become of the prisoner now?'

'He is secure,' said my uncle shortly. His face was crimson with heat and anger; he kept tugging at his collar, as if it was slowly throttling him.

'We may wish to examine him at a future time,' the First Lord announced. 'Tell me, Lieutenant Jerrold: did you ever discover the reason for all this commotion?'

Even I could see that such an admission would invite untold trouble. 'I, um, believe he had some papers.'

'Ah yes, the papers.' The First Lord straightened a little in his seat. 'What became of them?'

I had expected this question, and dreaded it. 'They were

319

destroyed when the smugglers' boat sank. They fell into the sea and dissolved to pulp.' It was a lie, and might well return to curse me, but there was little else I could say.

'You are certain? You saw this yourself?'

'Before my very eyes.'

'Hmm.' The First Lord sipped at his tea, a crease disfiguring his smooth features. 'Well, Lieutenant, after your earlier lapse you appear to have acquitted yourself with some distinction. Stowing away on that smuggler so that Dumont would not escape was a bold act indeed. Were it not of paramount secrecy, I dare say the *Gazette* might make something of it.'

'Thank you, sir.' I tried to avoid my uncle's incredulous gaze. After all I had suffered, I reasoned I might as well draw some merit from the affair.

The First Lord tapped a long index finger on his desk, where half a dozen papers lay scattered before him. 'There was a cavalry officer with you. Major Lebrett.'

Despite the stuffy air and the warmth of my seat, I felt as though a cold breeze had drifted over the table. 'Yes, sir.'

'He was present at the action with the smuggler?'

'Yes, sir.'

'I have had a communication from his superiors in the War Office. They wish to ascertain the facts of his fate. The reports of the brig's crew state that he went missing in the battle, that they could not find him when they were forced to cut free from the sinking ship.'

I did not recall any of them searching particularly hard. Perhaps I was not the only one to embellish my tale. 'Major Lebrett died, sir. A glorious death in the service of his country. I saw him cut down in a throng of smugglers as he battled to reach Dumont.' It was another lie, of course, but I did not wish to leave any dissatisfaction with his death that might result in later enquiries.

The First Lord scrawled a brief note in the margin of his paper. 'Very good.' He looked up at me, perplexity still souring his face. 'You are sure he did not reveal to you the true nature of Dumont's importance?'

Did he suspect something? I shrank back in my chair, wondering if I would be spared no rest until I had admitted my dangerous knowledge and been suitably silenced. I had not asked to know it, I pleaded mutely – I had not even asked to be part of this sordid enterprise. It was Lebrett who had forced me into accompanying him, Lebrett who had harried and harangued me until I had no choice. Would he now reach out from his wet grave to draw me in with him?

In desperation, I looked into the First Lord's eyes. They were smug, lazy eyes, as of a cat surveying a bowl of cream. Yet as I sought some hint of compassion in them, I saw they were not quite so rigid as I had assumed. He was not toying with me to my destruction, but watching me with . . . *curiosity*.

A balm of relief seeped into my soul. The First Lord was as ignorant as I had been, I realized. In spite of his exalted station, the Prince had confided nothing to him. His persistence was not from the belief that he had caught me in a lie, but because – as a gossip and a politician – he was desperate to understand what had passed.

I felt a great smile pulling my lips apart, and rapidly quashed it. It would not do to be seen gloating over the First Lord.

'Lebrett told me nothing,' I said truthfully. 'His secrets accompanied him to his death.'

The First Lord huffed through his nose, and stirred his tea vigorously. 'Very well, Lieutenant, it seems our business is concluded for the present. You may return to your ship at Chatham. She will require a new commander, after your subordinate's accident.'

'Accident, sir?'

The First Lord fished out another paper from his sheaf. 'It seems Mr Mallow fell down the companionway five nights ago while inspecting the ship after dark. Almost broke his neck. He has been sent to the Greenwich hospital, where I fear he will be some time convalescing. Careless fool – we have no room for men like that in the navy.'

This time, there was nothing I could do to hide my smile.

'You may think,' the First Lord continued, 'that your service in this business deserves better reward. I may be minded to agree with you. The hulks are no place for a man of action, I dare say.'

'No, sir.' If he thought me a man of action, then my lies had sunk me in more trouble than I'd guessed. But the prospect of returning to the *Prometheus*, to that horde of gaunt and hopeless faces waiting each day for the war to end, left a foul lump in my gullet. I would be glad of an excuse to escape it.

'I shall see what can be found for you. Doubtless your uncle will have some views.'

'You may be certain of that, sir,' my uncle confirmed.

'Very good.' A servant who had been lingering invisible by the door pulled it open, and I realized the interview was closed. 'I shall send despatches to your lodgings.'

'Thank you, sir.'

I stood, and flinched as my uncle made to follow. He would have his own questions to ask of me, I guessed, and I feared they would be more trenchant than his superior's.

'No, no, Admiral.' The First Lord waved him down. 'We have business to discuss, you and I.'

'Of course, sir.' My uncle thumped back into his chair. 'I shall find you later,' he threatened.

'I shall await you with pleasure,' I lied.

The crowds of London were busy as ever when I came out onto Whitehall, but I barely noticed them. I drifted through, swaying in the pressing and shoving which surrounded me, so oblivious that I did not notice the man who followed me from the Admiralty gate until he caught my arm at the spire of Charing Cross.

'Lieutenant Jerrold! A word, if I may.'

I looked back to see the pale, clownish face of Spencer Perceval grinning up at me. As before, he was dressed entirely in black, and as before there was a puckish mischief in his eyes.

'You're not going to force me into a coach and take me to a man-eating princess's house again, are you?' I asked warily.

He chuckled. 'I regret not.'

'A pity.'

'May I walk with you a little way?'

'I'm only going a little way, but you may accompany me as far as I go.' It was hard to hold a conversation amid the bustle of the street – but harder, I guessed, to overhear one, which was probably his purpose.

'How is your maligned Princess?' I asked. 'Has the wicked Prince divorced her yet?'

Perceval shook his head. 'His case is built on lies and insinuations. A court of monkeys would dismiss it in a second. Even this government, I feel, will not countenance it for long – though I shall make life perfectly miserable for them until they give it up. But how is your cause?'

'The man is captured, and the papers gone,' I told him.

He frowned. 'Not in the hands of the Prince of Wales?'

'No.'

'And did you discover why—'

'Even if I did, it would not be something I could divulge.' I had long been kept ignorant with similar excuses, but now that my role was reversed I drew no pleasure from the power of my knowledge. Merely knowing the secret made my existence precarious enough; publicizing the fact would cheapen my life still more dramatically.

'I doubt it was anything you could have used to embarrass the government,' I comforted him. 'Simply a personal matter.'

'In my occupation, the personal is inextricably political,' Perceval told me. 'And the more scurrilous or reprehensible it may be, the more political it becomes.'

'On this occasion, you will have to find another stone to cast at the ministry.'

Perceval laughed. 'Fear not, Jerrold – I shall do precisely that. A gaggle of mediocrities with the arch-libertine as their patron should afford opportunity enough.'

We had reached Mrs McCaird's lodging house, and I turned to mount her steps.

'Farewell, Mr Perceval. Remember me when you are First Lord of the Admiralty. Or, indeed, the Treasury.'

'I will, Lieutenant. I shall follow your exploits with interest.'

'I doubt the *Chronicle* will report them.'

He disappeared round the corner into the Strand, as I waited for an answer to my knock. When the door swung open, though, it was neither the landlady nor her maid.

'Ah, Jerrold. I feared your uncle might have taken your exploits amiss and transported you to Botany Bay.'

'I see you've found new employment as Mrs McCaird's doorkeeper, Nevell. Are the rewards better than at the Post Office?'

'The pay is worse, but the benefits are considerable. I believe she is in the kitchen baking scones even as we speak.' He ushered me through the hall into the drawing room, where Isobel sat reading a novel. 'How was your interview?'

'Satisfactory. I survived as best I could, not knowing what had become of Dumont or of his infernal papers.'

Nevell looked affronted. 'Dumont is in the care of the Post Office, as you well know.'

'You didn't tell me what you'd done with him.'

'Sent him away.' Nevell brushed a speck of dust from

his crimson coat. He seemed rather pleased with himself.

'Where have you sent him? Is *he* on the boat to Botany Bay?'

'By the heartfelt plea of his mother, and a quick intervention from the Post Office, he is currently taking ship for Quebec. He will be able to establish a new life there, freed from the burdens of his unwanted history.'

'And you trust him to cause no more mischief?' Though I had rescued him, I felt aggrieved that after so much tribulation and effort he had been allowed to go free.

'If Dumont stayed in England, whether returned to the hulks or in his mother's house, he would be dead within a week,' said Nevell flatly. 'He has too many enemies. And if he chooses to reveal the truth of his birth once in Quebec, it will avail him nothing. Without his certificates, he would merely be another rascal trying to blackmail the Prince for an annuity.'

That sparked an unwelcome thought. 'The certificates,' I prompted. 'What became of them? I assured the Admiralty that they were lost at sea.'

'Then I presume they must have been lost at sea,' said Nevell, unhelpfully.

'You know full well that they were not. We opened the bottle together when I returned to Brighton.'

'So we did.'

'I left them in my room at the tavern. When I came back, they were gone.' I did not recount the horror, anger and misery the loss had provoked in me, the way it had shadowed my every thought for the past three days. 'As you had just taken the coach to London, I assumed you must have made off with them.'

Nevell spread his arms in innocence. 'I never touched them.'

'Then . . .?'

Isobel dog-eared the page of her novel and looked up. 'I took them.'

'What?' Rage would doubtless be swift to follow, but for the moment my incredulity allowed no space. 'You took them? From my room?'

'Our room.'

'And in all the time since, when I was in despair because I thought they had been stolen, you did not think to mention it?'

'I had to wait until we'd left Brighton. I thought you wouldn't tell your uncle you'd lost the papers, and once you'd told him they were destroyed you couldn't go back on it.'

'*You . . . You . . .*' My fury strangled all attempt to find invective suitable for Isobel, sitting calmly on her chair looking up at me. 'And what did you do with them?'

'Gave them back to their rightful owner.'

'Dumont? Are you mad? Did you not hear what Nevell just said? In Canada, with those papers, he could—'

'Not Dumont. His mother, Mrs Fitzherbert.'

'But she's the woman who—'

'They belong to her,' said Isobel firmly. 'She's lost her son twice over 'cos of her terrible husband, and he's treated her worse than mud. Those certificates are all she's got to show the justice of what she is. Without them, she's a whore and her son's a bastard.'

'That's exactly—'

'It may not matter to you, Martin, but it's the world for her. After what she's suffered . . .' Isobel trembled slightly. 'And if she ever wants to give the Prince his comeuppance, she's more right than anyone to it.'

I collapsed into an upholstered chair. I could not believe that after so much struggle, I had been betrayed by my own mistress. If those papers ever became public, I would be condemned for a liar and a traitor. For years, perhaps decades, a single slight or indiscretion by the Prince might be enough to provoke his long-suffering, long-hidden wife into publishing his bigamy. How could I persevere with any

326

career while that danger hung over me? It would ruin my life – if indeed I lived.

And yet, as I considered it, I found I could not maintain my anger. I knew little of Mrs Fitzherbert's plight, but if she had lived twenty years as the secret wife of that bigamist, self-indulgent pig, in contravention of all the laws of succession, and subject to the malicious whispers of court gossip, she must have endured more than I ever had. She had lost two husbands to early deaths, a third to his own narcissism, and a son to the implacable force of circumstance. If she could find comfort in those papers, which as Isobel said were hers by right, who was I to deny her? Besides, I thought with gleeful malice, what torments would the Prince and his conceited sycophants suffer if she could hold such a scandal over them?

I reached across and squeezed Isobel's hand. 'It was a kind thing to do. I hope she was grateful.'

'She'll see they're held safely. And she'll try to keep the Prince's friends off us.'

'Good. While men like Tyrwhitt know, or suspect, what I have discovered, I shall keep a stout lock on my door. I fear I have made some powerful enemies in this affair, and I doubt even Mrs Fitzherbert's good attentions will deflect them for ever. I may yet have to take a commission in the farthest ocean to escape their snares.'

There was a pause, then Nevell cleared his throat. 'Actually, Jerrold, I had been contemplating much the same problem.' I looked at him in surprise. 'Perhaps it would be best if you found employment abroad for a few months.'

He reached into his pocket and withdrew a thin slip of paper. 'I believe I have just the errand for you.'

THE END

Author's Note

Many of the characters in this novel are drawn from history, and much of the basis of the story is factual. Naturally, I have taken liberties, but generally only on the hazy borders of historical fact.

The treatment of prisoners of war has always been a difficult question for wartime governments trying to balance the competing demands of security, economy and humanity. Nonetheless, there is little doubt that the prison hulks of the early nineteenth century were a particularly miserable solution for all involved. Commanding officers ranged from the uninterested to the sadistic; crooked contractors made fortunes exploiting a literally captive market; and the ships that were used often had no business remaining afloat. The succession of British victories at sea produced a constant influx of French prisoners, and Napoleon consistently refused to arrange their release by swapping like numbers of British prisoners. As France's population outnumbered Britain's, he calculated that he would gain more by depriving his enemy of manpower than by augmenting his own forces; the cost to the British Treasury of keeping the prisoners also served his war aims. Unwanted by either side, many prisoners spent years in the hulks with escape or death their only hope of relief. For a comprehensive history of the subject, Francis Abell's 1914 book *Prisoners of War in Britain* (now out of print) remains unique.

Within the limitations of a first-person novel, I have also tried to convey the political climate in Britain at the time – not easy in an era when there were no parties as such (the names Whig and Tory are later labels retrospectively applied), no recognized offices of Prime Minister or Leader of the Opposition, and when factions coalesced around personalities rather than formal organizations. In brief, after the death of Pitt the Younger in January 1806, his government collapsed and a new ministry under his arch-enemies Charles Fox and Lord Grenville was appointed. They faced little serious opposition, as the factions that had supported Pitt would not now unite behind a single spokesman, but one of their most consistent and ultimately successful critics was Spencer Perceval. As part of his strategy for harassing the government on all fronts, he took up the cause of Princess Caroline against her estranged husband the Prince of Wales, who had attempted to mould a mix of rumours, lies and slanders into legitimate grounds for the divorce he craved. Eventually, Perceval's help saved the hapless (though by no means innocent) Princess, and served to embarrass the Prince's accomplices in government.

Much of the novel revolves around the character of Dumont and his secret papers. Although contentious, there is plenty of circumstantial evidence and speculation that such a person existed: one of the more widespread theories suggests that he grew up in Catholic Spain and later joined the American navy. At least one of the papers that Dumont carries in the book is quoted verbatim, and is now in the Royal Archives at Windsor.

Much help and many efforts produced this book. On the research front, my debts include those to Chris Nowakowski for firearms training, Siân Jenkins for equestrian advice, and Mike and Jane Jecks for their kind hospitality on Dartmoor. The staff and resources of the British Library, the Caird Library at the National Maritime Museum and the National Archives at Kew were tremendously helpful, while visits to Lulworth Castle, the Chatham Historic Dockyard, the Household Cavalry Museum in Windsor and the Brighton Pavilion proved essential.

As ever, I'm immensely grateful to everyone at and around Transworld who worked on this novel, particularly Simon Thorogood and Selina Walker for their thoughtful editing, and Nik Keevil and Philip Hood for their excellent artwork. Throughout the process, my agent Jane Conway-Gordon kept me well supplied with shrewd advice and chocolate cake. Ongoing encouragement from family and friends, particularly those who read and commented on both this and *The Blighted Cliffs*, made the writing far more enjoyable than it would otherwise have been. Without the constant support of my wife Emma I would probably still be staring at the title page.

THE BLIGHTED CLIFFS
By Edwin Thomas

Book One of the reluctant adventures of Lieutenant Martin Jerrold

Not many men emerged from Trafalgar without an ounce of credit, but Lieutenant Martin Jerrold R.N. managed it. In February 1806, he is given one last chance to redeem his reputation and dispatched to Dover.

Things don't augur well when, walking off the effects of a night in the tavern, he stumbles across a corpse lying on the beach. And they take a distinct turn for the worse when he is suspected of murder. With the local magistrate determined to see him hang, Jerrold knows clearing his name will require an improbable reversal of his miserable fortunes. Somewhere in Dover's twisted streets, someone must know something. But he soon discovers that nothing is as it seems in a town where smuggling is a way of life . . .

Distrusted by his superiors, set upon by suspiciously well-informed thugs, attacked by the French at sea but finding sympathy in the less-than-respectable arms of Isobel, Martin Jerrold has two weeks to save his skin – or perish in the attempt.

The Blighted Cliffs marks the beginning of a rich, swashbuckling adventure series, featuring a reluctant hero for whom life rarely turns out as he intends.

'At last, the nautical Flashman! Martin Jerrold looks set to become one of the great British anti-heroes, boozing and lusting his way through Regency England' Andrew Roberts

'Will fill the gaping hole stoved in the timbers of the sea-saga genre by the sad death of Patrick O'Brian . . . Jerrold swashes his buckles and splices his mainbraces to good effect' *Scotland on Sunday*

'Rip-roaring . . . a rollicking yarn with razor-sharp dialogue, introducing a hilarious protagonist' *Good Book Guide*

0 553 81514 8

BANTAM BOOKS

TREASON'S RIVER
By Edwin Thomas

Book Three of the reluctant adventures of Lieutenant Martin Jerrold

August, 1806. When you have just offended the most powerful men in England, you can stand firm, or you can run. Which is why Martin Jerrold finds himself sailing away as fast as the wind can carry him, in the employ of the Secret Office.

There are rumours of a conspiracy in America and Jerrold's mission is simple: infiltrate the conspirators and stop them at all costs. His journey will take him across pirate-infested seas, through the American wilderness and down the mighty Mississippi river. Enemies are ranged against him – agents of Spain and America are trying to kill him, and the plotters are growing suspicious of his intentions. Then there is the lovely Miss Lyell, who seems to have her own plans for Lieutenant Jerrold.

His instructions ring in his ears: *find out what the conspirators intend and stop it.* But as each bumbling step takes Jerrold further into danger, he slowly realizes that his very presence within the conspiracy could be the spark that ignites a disastrous war between England and America.

The stakes are high – the entire future of Britain's war against Napoleon rests in his not-so-capable hands. One wrong move and the consequences would be catastrophic, even by Jerrold's own lamentable standards.

0 593 05066 5

COMING IN APRIL 2006 FROM BANTAM PRESS

BANTAM PRESS

As the war against Bonaparte rages to its bloody end upon the field of Waterloo, a young officer goes about his duty in the ranks of Wellington's army. He is Cornet Matthew Hervey of the 6th Light Dragoons – a soldier, gentleman and man of honour who suddenly finds himself allotted a hero's role . . .

'Captain Matthew Hervey is as splendid a hero as ever sprang from an author's pen . . . What a hero! What an author! What a book! A joy for the lover of adventure and the military buff alike' *The Times*

'Mallinson writes with style, verve and the lucidity one would expect from a talented officer . . . his breadth of knowledge is deeply impressive even if it is modestly entwined in the fabric of this epic narrative. Kick on, Captain Hervey, we cannot wait for more' *Country Life*

Follow the adventures of Allan Mallinson's hero, Matthew Hervey, in:

A CLOSE RUN THING
0 553 50713 3

THE NIZAM'S DAUGHTERS
0 553 50714 1

A REGIMENTAL AFFAIR
0 553 50715 X

A CALL TO ARMS
0 553 81350 1

THE SABRE'S EDGE
0 553 81351 X

RUMOURS OF WAR
0 553 81352 8

BANTAM BOOKS

A SELECTED LIST OF NOVELS AVAILABLE FROM BANTAM AND CORGI BOOKS

81416 8	THE CRUSADER	*Michael Eisner*	£6.99
81534 2	HOUND	*George Green*	£6.99
50714 1	THE NIZAM'S DAUGHTERS	*Allan Mallinson*	£6.99
50713 3	A CLOSE RUN THING	*Allan Mallinson*	£6.99
50715 X	A REGIMENTAL AFFAIR	*Allan Mallinson*	£6.99
81350 1	A CALL TO ARMS	*Allan Mallinson*	£6.99
81351 X	THE SABRE'S EDGE	*Allan Mallinson*	£6.99
81352 8	RUMOURS OF WAR	*Allan Mallinson*	£6.99
14838 5	THE GUARDSHIP	*James Nelson*	£6.99
14842 3	THE BLACKBIRDER	*James Nelson*	£6.99
14843 1	THE PIRATE ROUND	*James Nelson*	£6.99
14960 8	BY FORCE OF ARMS	*James Nelson*	£6.99
14961 6	THE MADDEST IDEA	*James Nelson*	£6.99
14962 4	THE CONTINENTAL RISQUE	*James Nelson*	£6.99
14963 2	LORDS OF THE OCEAN	*James Nelson*	£6.99
14964 0	ALL THE BRAVE FELLOWS	*James Nelson*	£6.99
81216 5	GATES OF FIRE	*Steven Pressfield*	£6.99
81332 3	TIDES OF WAR	*Steven Pressfield*	£6.99
81386 2	LAST OF THE AMAZONS	*Steven Pressfield*	£6.99
81307 2	THE LEGEND OF BAGGER VANCE	*Steven Pressfield*	£6.99
81514 8	THE BLIGHTED CLIFFS	*Edwin Thomas*	£6.99
05066 5	TREASON'S RIVER (Hardback)	*Edwin Thomas*	£16.99
14795 8	SHADOW OF THE OSPREY	*Peter Watt*	£6.99
14796 6	FLIGHT OF THE EAGLE	*Peter Watt*	£6.99